SOFT TALES FROM A
REFUGEE CAMP

Soft Tales from a Refugee Camp

Gabriel Watermiller

This is a work of fiction. Names, characters, places and incidents either are the product of the author's imagination or are used fictitiously, and any resemblance to any actual persons, living or dead, events, or locales is entirely coincidental.

This book was printed in the United States of America.

Cover photos: Gavril-Iuliu Morariu, F.R.P.S.

To order additional copies of this book, contact:
Xlibris Corporation
1-888-795-4274
www.Xlibris.com
Orders@Xlibris.com
84730

CONTENTS

*To my brothers and sisters, political refugees
from the communist countries, who in
their search for an elusive freedom,
sacrificed everything.*

*To the memory of my parents who died just
before all that socio-political madness ended.*

PROLOGUE

Unde este prea multă deșteptăciune este și multă prostie.
Where there is too much cleverness, there is also a lot of
stupidity.

—Romanian adage

It was late evening on October 9, 1944, at the Kremlin. In the spacious smoke-filled room, seven men gathered around an antique table richly adorned with intricate carvings. Five of them sat at the beautifully finished table, a pair facing the other three. Another two, of much lesser importance, respectfully stood at a small distance behind them.

On a baroque guéridon between two heavily curtained bay windows, a Chinese vase from the Ming period containing huge white chrysanthemums enlivened the otherwise austere surroundings. A large painting, signed "Shishkin" in Cyrillic, hung on the opposite wall. Ilya Shishkin was a nineteenth-century Muscovite artist who understood better than anyone else the melancholic poetry of the Russian countryside, which he rendered with unrivalled authenticity in his landscapes. The table was made of precious wood in Italy in 1880 for Czar Alexander II. It now belonged, as everything in the Kremlin, to the people of the Soviet Union, who enjoyed such valuable possessions through their self-styled representatives only.

The Moscow Kremlin was initially a fortified wooden enclosure masterfully rebuilt by Italian architects in brick and stone sometime in the fourteenth century. Within its anachronistic walls provided with ramparts, towers and battlements, this venerable structure contained an old imperial palace and other more modern official buildings of a variety of architectural styles, each reflecting some past era of Russian history. At the end of their successful struggle for power and after obliterating the ruling czars, victorious Bolsheviks made the Kremlin their headquarters. In the 1930s, its name became synonymous with communist imperialistic policies, which during World War II were willingly forgotten by Allied politicians eager to see the Kremlin exclusively as a symbol of resistance against Hitlerism.

The two principal characters at the meeting were both short of build, stocky, and smoked heavily. The one who was cleanly shaven preferred Havana cigars and the other, a stern looking man with a graying moustache, favored a briar pipe. Carefully dressed for the occasion, the former in a dinner jacket and the latter in a simple but fine military uniform without any particular sign of rank or medals, they sat relaxed at the table under the glittering crystal chandelier, conversing amiably through their interpreters, Major Birse and Comrade Pavlov. Their origins, background, and behavior were worlds apart.

The civilian was Winston Churchill, Great Britain's prime minister, scion of one of the oldest British noble families, related to many kings, several long dead but some still alive. Trained as a cavalry officer, he had studied in the best schools, painted acceptable watercolors as a hobby, and wrote history when he wasn't involved in politics. His position at the table was largely due to the will of his people expressed in democratic elections.

The soldier, Joseph Dzhugashvily, was a defrocked priest of humble origins and an ex-bloodthirsty bandit known worldwide as Stalin, the dictator of the Soviet Union. He had ascended to his current position by ruthlessly killing friends and foes alike, having a hand in the extermination of almost an entire Russian imperial family, and was solely responsible for the assassination of millions of his countrymen. He survived by bullying his colleagues into submission and by terrorizing, torturing, and brainwashing his people.

The two leaders had only a few things in common, one being that—for the moment—both were invested with extraordinary powers and commanded huge armies deployed on vast expanses of land and sea. Each separately controlled the life and death of approximately a fifth of the earth's population. They also liked the good life and strong drink and—because they had eaten a fine dinner just before the meeting—were satisfied and friendly, like two big cats basking in the sun after a filling meal.

The topic of discussion was Poland, the country whose invasion by Germany had caused the war they were currently winning. As always, this was a delicate issue. To make things more complicated, each of the two leaders had a different government for Poland. The legitimate one was in London, where its members had taken refuge after their country's occupation. It organized armed resistance behind German lines and recruited troops formed from Polish émigrés, who died gallantly by the thousands, side by side with the British, on several fronts around the world. The other was in Lublin, a small industrial city in eastern Poland, where it had been staged only days before by Stalin's henchmen. This puppet government had already accepted the Soviet annexation of almost half their country's ancestral territory. They would later be rewarded with an equivalent span of land taken from the vanquished Germans. For the moment, however, the Muscovite bosses needed time to consolidate their position. The proposal to bring representatives of both Polish governments to Moscow for mediation was therefore accepted with relief by the two leaders.

While Churchill naively hoped for free elections in Poland at the end of the war, as Stalin shrewdly let him believe would happen, the Soviet dictator knew better. His armies had already seized the entire Polish territory and had unchallenged control over the so-called Lublin provisional government, in which several members were Russian subjects, one of them being a field marshal of the Soviet Union. Indeed, after that fateful evening, Poland didn't enjoy free elections or any real political freedom for almost half a century.

During a short pause, Sir Archibald Kerr, the British ambassador who was seated beside the prime minister, opened his attaché case and produced a picture in a silver frame. It was Churchill's autographed photograph, which he offered Stalin as a sign of appreciation.

So far, the evening's discussions had gone smoothly. Years later, in his memoirs, Churchill would confess his lasting impression of the special treatment given him during that fated meeting. Coming from war-weary Britain, where not only food but also the simplest amenities of civilized life, such as hot water, were sometimes missing or rationed, the extravagant luxury of Russian hospitality overwhelmed him. He had been smitten with delighted enchantment by Stalin's friendly manners and was in a concessionary mood. Churchill's joviality further increased when the door opened and a blonde maid dressed in austere black and wearing a starched white apron rolled in a table of drinks. Four tall good-looking butlers followed, also dressed in black and carrying big trays of food. All five were colonels in the KGB, the Soviet secret police, trained as high-class waiters. On the trays were fine china bowls filled to the brim with black and red caviar, flat gold-rimmed plates loaded with smoked sturgeon and shrimp puffs, lobster on barquettes, and piles of smoked salmon canapés. The group came to a stop, accompanied by a faint clink as the bottles of brandy, vodka, and a fine selection of wines jingled together.

Outside that room, it was bitterly cold, and Russia was hungry. After the Bolshevik revolution and throughout the war, the lack of food was endemic. At that precise moment in many parts of the Soviet realm, people were dying of starvation and hypothermia. In the Kremlin, however, there was no shortage of any kind. The waiters immediately started to serve.

"The Balkans!" Anthony Eden, the British secretary of state for foreign affairs, whispered into the ear of the prime minister, who was just enjoying a sip of vodka. It was an appropriate reminder. The Soviets had already swamped Romania and Bulgaria with several divisions, fast advancing west and south. There were numerous disoriented Allied agents and British partisans in those countries, especially in Romania. If not stopped, the Red Army could also easily occupy Greece, where that prospect had caused a strong communist upheaval. A fratricidal civil war seemed imminent in that country, jeopardizing Britain's major interests in the Mediterranean, the Middle East, and India. There were too many dangers lurking behind the scenes for comfort. Churchill put down the glass with a sigh. He really liked that vodka, but the time had come for serious business.

Comrade Pavlov took some time to translate the prime minister's introductory remarks and proposals. In the meantime, Churchill scribbled country names and figures on a piece of scrap paper, which he then pushed across the table to Stalin. As an overture, he offered Romania and Bulgaria to the Soviets in exchange for Greece, with shared control of Yugoslavia thrown in as a bonus.

Stalin considered the proposal with a poker face. There was a sense of mounting tension in the air. Everything in the room was silent except for the antique grandfather clock, the work of the eighteenth-century Swedish clock maker Gustav Nylander, which diligently tick-tocked the seconds away. As all watched, Stalin made a large tick on the paper with his blue pencil, showed it for a moment to Molotov, his foreign minister, and passed the note back to the British. "Khorosho. Very well," he said.

In less than a minute, the fate of over a hundred million people was sealed. The Iron Curtain had fallen, and a long night of horrors descended over a significant portion of Europe as other countries were included in the deal during the next few days. The British prime minister knew his deed was unethical and regretted it for the rest of his life until he died at the age of ninety-one in 1965. Stalin died in 1953 at the age of seventy-four, but he never regretted a thing.

The tension dissipated. Churchill took the glass and raised it toward the Russians. "God bless you," he toasted, to the surprise of his company. It was a blunder, for everyone knew Stalin and his comrade Molotov were inveterate atheists and hated anything religious. Nevertheless, they all smiled, drank the finest Russian vodka, and were merry.

* * *

While the conviviality went on in the Kremlin, on a beeline two thousand kilometers southwest across the Russian steppes, right in the middle of the Romanian plains in Bucharest, the Popescu family celebrated Stefan's eleventh birthday.

No big party could have been organized for that year's anniversary. Six weeks earlier, the Russians had invaded their country; and since then, food had become scarcer by the day. People were also reluctant to go out at night, with so many unruly Soviet soldiers roaming the streets raping and robbing the passersby.

Food scarcity notwithstanding, Paula, Stefan's mother, had tried her best and prepared—from whatever she could find through relatives—a special diner, which was, in fact, the only enjoyable part of the evening. The four previous years of war and now the foreign occupation as well as the heavy fighting with the Germans were on everyone's mind. Bleak expectation was the prevailing mood in Romania during that fall, filled with uncertainty, and the small gathering at the Popescu was no exception. Among those present were Dan and Mircea, Stefan's schoolmates living next door; his cousin George; his uncle Alexandru, his mother's youngest brother; and Maria, his father's sister, with her husband Dumitru, the parents of cousin George.

Stefan's family lived in a rented apartment with a tiny dining room. His father, Andrei Popescu, was a public high school teacher, a category of employees that was always poorly paid by succeeding Romanian governments. He was a scholarly and honest man who would never have accepted presents from his pupils in exchange for better marks as some of his colleagues did in order to improve their standard of living. He neither involved himself in politics nor in the black market, which were rewarding pastimes for many of his countrymen, especially during the war. Andrei's record was rather unusual in a society prone to survive through the use of shady deals inherited from the Byzantine. Admired but poor, his family's modest lifestyle reflected Andrei's moral and ethical standards.

Guests and family stood about or sat around the dining room table, extended and festively decorated for the occasion. Apart from being crowded into a small room, the party had so far been a culinary success. Paula was an accomplished cook and, knowing her guests well, had prepared a beloved dish for each of them.

The grown-ups talked quietly, their voices subdued to almost a whisper. Dumitru, a surgeon at the Central Emergency Hospital, had just broken the news about the spread of exanthematous typhus brought by the lice-ridden Russian troops, which raged not only across the countryside but also in the big cities. The hospitals were overcrowded, and several terminal cases were recorded every day, lately even in the capital. A vaccination campaign had started, but so far, the epidemic hadn't shown any sign of slowing down.

"This is the seventh time in our history that the Russians have invaded us, and they have always brought with them long-lasting occupation, famine, death, and diseases. The last time it was cholera. Before, the plague. Now typhus fever. What else is new?" Andrei said.

"And this is only the beginning," Dumitru murmured, shaking his head. "I hear the communists are ready to take over the government and install a regime of terror."

"The communists? No way! They don't have more than a hundred members in the whole country. Who will follow them?" Andrei asked.

"There are already more than that, compliments of the Red Army," Dumitru said.

"A bunch of foreign agitators. Nobody in his right mind will listen to them," said Andrei, who—as a youth—had had to fight hard for his rights. Brought up in the northern part of Romania, which prior to the First World War had been under Austro-Hungarian rule, he was a patriot and couldn't believe someone would consciously give up freedom.

"You haven't heard about Poland, have you?" Maria, his sister, asked. "Dumitru's friend, who works for the British embassy, told us how a few days ago, the Soviets imposed their own government in defiance of the legal one. He also heard rumors about thousands of unwarranted arrests, torture cases, and assassinations. What do you have to say about that?"

"Rumors," Stefan's father deprecatingly said. "I don't believe in rumors."

"These are not rumors. And by the way, do you remember Katyn? Have you forgotten those Poles buried in common graves, all shot in the back of their heads by Stalin's butchers?" Maria's voice trembled.

Katyn is a wooded area in eastern Russia where Polish prisoners were shot and buried in common graves when the Soviet Union, in complicity with Nazi Germany, invaded Poland in September 1939.

"That was Nazi propaganda. Apparently, the Germans killed those Poles, not the Russians. Didn't they, Alexandru?" Andrei looked inquiringly at his brother-in-law, waiting for confirmation.

"How can you say that?" Dumitru cried without giving Alexandru a chance to answer. "A Red Cross international commission of experts from neutral countries clearly implicated the Russians. Even General Sikorsky, the Polish leader in exile, agreed with their conclusion. Were they lying?"

"They were all misled into believing that the Russians did it," Alexandru said. "Poland was still under German occupation when the commission started its inquiries. Surely, it was easy for the Nazis to feed them false information. The British government and Churchill himself vigorously defended Russia's innocence in this matter." He spoke with the assurance of someone in the know.

Alexandru was a handsome man in his early thirties. Intelligent and well educated, he had been a brilliant student at the Sorbonne. After continuing at the University of Gottingen in Germany for a masters in physics, his further studies had earned him a doctorate degree in mathematics from Oxford. Immediately after graduation, he was invited to give a series of lectures at Harvard. His professors predicted a great future for Alexandru. Unfortunately, the war had changed everything. Conscripted into the Romanian army at the beginning of hostilities, he was compelled to cancel the engagement with Harvard, and his scientific career came to a dead end. Alexandru wasn't sent into the battlefield, however. His background and fluency in several languages recommended him for a different kind of warfare. He was drafted into the military intelligence and soon became a much-sought-after code breaker. Recently, he had been temporarily transferred from the army's High

Command headquarters to the Ministry of Foreign Affairs, where a polyglot decipherer like him was much needed. Because of his new job, he was supposed to be well-informed about what was going on internationally.

"Maybe it was some Nazi propaganda. Maybe, maybe. But those British could have been misled too by the Soviets. How could they be so sure? I don't ever trust the Russians," Dumitru said.

Stefan's father looked at Alexandru, and both smiled conspiratorially. They had known Dumitru's idiosyncrasies for many years. Paula and Maria didn't smile, paralyzed by that inward killer of joy and happiness: the stab of visceral fear for their families and for their children's future. But they kept their worries to themselves, hoping against hope. In the coming decades when things got worse, this would become a predominant feature of Romanian behavior.

The boys paid no attention to their elders. They noisily amused themselves at one end of the table while nibbling from plates that Paula kept refilling. Stefan was seated between Dan and Mircea, who were teasing him. Suddenly, Dan snatched the book Stefan held with crossed hands close to his chest and passed it to Mircea. The boys struggled for possession of the book, pushing the table, which shook dangerously. Stefan's cousin George, who was thirteen and considered himself much older and more mature, stood up and looked indulgently over their shoulders.

The brawl drew Alexandru's attention. After a couple of drinks, he was in a cheerful mood. "What are you guys doing here?" he asked the boys, who abruptly ended their scuffle and looked at him sheepishly. Dan laid the book on the table; the other two pulled on their clothes to put on a decent appearance.

"Nothing, nothing!" Stefan hurriedly answered.

"Then why all the excitement?" his uncle insisted.

"It was a storm in a teacup," George said.

"I was showing them my present, the Admiral Peary's book you gave me, the one about his last polar expedition. And . . ." Stefan explained.

"He was bragging senselessly, that's why," George interrupted him.

"I was not." Stefan looked hurt.

"Yes, you were, silly," Dan said. "You were lying and bragging."

"Liar, liar," Mircea chanted.

"You are the liar, not I," Stefan shouted and jumped at Mircea's throat. With a swift movement, Alexandru caught hold of his nephew, preventing him from hurting his schoolmate.

"Now, now. Stop it! No need to fight." Alexandru grabbed a chair and sat down, still holding Stefan with one hand. "Let us see what the offending matter was."

"He said he would become a famous engineer and explorer like Peary," Dan said.

"So what's wrong with that?" Alexandru asked.

"More famous than Peary, he said," Mircea added.

"He bragged he will be the first to climb the Everest. But we know he is a sissy. He is afraid of the dark," George said and looked down at his cousin. He already imagined himself as a true, courageous man.

"I will! I will be the first on Everest, and I will become a professional engineer. Just you wait," Stefan shouted in a vindictive tone of voice, struggling to escape from his uncle's grip, "till I will grow up. Then I will show you."

The boys just laughed at him.

"Yeah, yeah. What do you know about climbing? You have never been on a mountain," George said.

"Uncle Alexandru will take me with him and teach me climbing. You promised, right, Uncle?" Stefan asked, ready to cry from frustration, his face reddened from emotion.

"I don't believe a word," Dan said.

"It is true. Next summer, I will take him for a couple of hikes in the Carpathians," Alexandru, who was one of Romania's leading mountaineers, confirmed.

"Hikes? That is not real climbing, is it?" Mircea asked.

"It is a long way from hiking in the Carpathians to conquering Everest," George said acidly. He knew geography, had read about expeditions to faraway lands, and dreamed of becoming a rock climber himself.

—

"So it is. Yet this will be a start for him. He will learn, if that is what he wants. Everybody can do the same with adequate training." Alexandru stroked Stefan's hair. "He is a good boy. He will become a great climber."

"Maybe," George hesitantly agreed.

"What do you mean by maybe? When I lecture at Harvard, we will go together to climb in the Rocky Mountains. I need a partner. Afterward, we can try our hands in the Himalayas."

"I would also like to come with you to the Rockies. Would you take me, Uncle?" George asked.

"Of course, if you are ready."

"When will that happen?" George's father asked, smiling indulgently. He came near their group and put a hand upon his son's shoulder.

"Pretty soon. The Germans will be finished by next spring. The war will end, and we will be free to travel again," Alexandru answered.

"Are you sure the Russians will let you go?" Dumitru was serious now.

"The Russians? They will be back in their country by the end of next summer. The Allies won't let them hang around after the war is finished." Alexandru spoke with confidence. "We will be free as we were before all that madness started. Take my word for it. You will see." He stood up.

"Oh, don't be childish, Alexandru. There are millions of Soviet soldiers under arms. By the time Germany capitulates, they will be all over Europe like hungry locusts. What about the communist puppets they bring with them? They will set up under the protection of the Red Army's bayonets collaborationist governments, which in return will let them stay forever. Nobody can stop them. Nobody will be able to order them back. The French don't count, and the British and the Americans are far away, while the Russians are here to stay," Dumitru said, frowning impatiently.

"I can't say too much, but we have guarantees. Our friends won't let us down. Churchill always loved Romania. He is a cousin of our late Queen Mary, a distant uncle to our young King Michael, don't you know? He is a great man who knows history, our history. He will protect us. If nobody else, then the British will restore our freedom. I am absolutely certain."

Winston Churchill was his hero, and Alexandru never lost his trust in the British.

Four years later, when he was dying a violent death, he was still hoping the Anglo-Americans would soon liberate his country. But at the time of his nephew's birthday party in that troubled autumn of 1944, none of those present could have imagined, even in their wildest nightmares, the atrociousness of Alexandru's last days.

Paula came in with the cake. Happy exclamations welcomed her as nobody expected such prodigality. The boys, who had forgotten their dispute, surrounded Paula with cries of delight, watching her light the little candles. They pushed Stefan close to the table, where he concentrated on blowing out all eleven flames. A burst of applause followed, and everybody joined in to sing the traditional birthday song, "Multi ani trăiască! May he live many years!" Then slices of cake were passed around on small plates, and more drinks were poured into glasses.

Demanding attention, Alexandru raised his glass. "May God grant Stefan many happy years. May he become a famous professional engineer and the first man on Everest," he toasted with a broad smile on his handsome well-tanned face.

Everybody present clapped their hands and cheered noisily. Paula gave her son a motherly kiss. She was unable to have more children and loved him more than anything on earth. The others also hugged and kissed him.

Stefan blushed, pleased to be the center of attention. One day, he would become a great man like Peary, he believed. Hadn't his uncle said so? Alexandru, although young, had the reputation of being a sage; and Stefan, like everyone else who knew him, trusted his uncle's judgement.

Expatriation for a Start

Stefan never climbed Everest, for the Soviet satraps of Romania didn't tolerate such bourgeois levity. As one of the hundred million humans relegated to the largest slavery-based system in history, he was supposed to exist for work only, toiling day and night to build the future paradise of workers on earth. Until that goal was attained, however, they had to dwell in a hell, which was much more easily achieved.

Stefan became a professional engineer and even acquired a certain notoriety in his profession, which, given the circumstances, wasn't really wise. He was intelligent and had an independent, creative mind, a dangerous personal liability in a totalitarian tyranny. In his maturing years, although he didn't die unnaturally or commit suicide as some of his colleagues did, Stefan had numerous occasions to regret being alive.

Then in his mid-forties, when he lost any hope of political change, he decided to flee the country. Opportunities for defection were scarce because even having a passport at home was illegal. Romanians were not permitted to travel outside the communist world. They could do so only on government business or exceptionally, with all sorts of restrictions, to visit first-degree relatives such as parents and siblings. Stefan had none of those assets. However, like any other Romanian citizen, he could apply every second year for a temporary passport to holiday in one of the sister communist countries—a request that was seldom granted. At times, Stefan's self-assigned task seemed to take him nowhere. Nonetheless, he persevered; and almost thirty-nine years after Churchill's deal with Stalin, he eventually managed to bring his family to the sunny side of the Iron Curtain, at the Greek border.

It was late summer and awfully hot. The border officer allowed the Romanians to rest for a little while in a tiny parking lot between the customs office and the army barracks. They didn't have entry visas for Greece, and the officer made an exception because the parking lot was located in the no-man's-land.

The winding road on which they had driven from Bitola among silvery olive trees and tall dark poplars made a wide bend at that point to avoid climbing the foothills of the Albanian mountains and ended up in front of a small group of unimpressive buildings. Blocking further access, a mobile barrier painted in lively blue and white had been lowered across the road, marking the official entrance into Greece.

On the Yugoslav side of the border, the craggy alpine silhouettes enshrouded in an iridescent purplish haze looked menacingly toward the sun-drenched plains below. From the parking lot, they could barely see down to the distant little town they had recently left. With its minarets and belfries spread at the mouth of the valley and dwarfed by perspective, it appeared almost unreal, like a delusive mirage.

At the guardhouse, the Greek flag hung lifeless along its metallic mast in the windless afternoon. Somewhere, a loudspeaker blared out enticing *sirtakis*. For the moment, there was no traffic and everything stood still, even the flashy evzone mounted guard outside his sentry box. The motionless sentinel—smartly dressed in a distinctive white uniform with red sash, stiff fustanella, and pomponed shoes—could easily have been mistaken for a statue. He didn't seem to pay any attention to them, pretending to be an inanimate ornament.

Their car was small, ugly, and shabby. Stefan used to say that it was the shame of the global automotive industry. The body was mostly pressed cardboard and cheap plastic, and it was equipped with a feeble two-stroke engine that burned spark plugs almost faster than it consumed gas. East Germany supplied the entire communist bloc with those sham vehicles, and Stefan had been on the waiting list for more than seven years before getting his. He wasn't a member of the ruling party, and every time his turn came, he was repeatedly demoted to make way for the brother-in-law or nephew-by-marriage of an influential member of the Party's nomenklatura who took the next available car. That went on for a number of years, until the government was forced through international trade agreements to import some Fiat cars from Italy; and then for a while at least, nobody from the leading circles was interested in anything else. So it happened that Stefan finally got his long-awaited vehicle. Shabbiness notwithstanding, it was quite an efficient mode of transportation as it had already been able to carry them that far from home.

Five passengers were crammed into the parked car: Stefan, his wife Lia, two teenage children—a boy and a girl—and their dog. The English cocker spaniel's pedigree was select, for the creature descended from renowned English and German purebreds. She was the only noble person in the family, Stefan used to say to his friends, the others being proletarians.

As soon as Stefan switched the engine off, they threw the doors wide open; but even so, it was devilishly hot. When the doors opened, the spaniel dashed out to the surrounding sun-scorched fields, followed by the girl, who tried to stop her but to no avail.

"Carina, Carina, come here! Come on, come back, you brat!" the girl shouted and ran after the dog.

"Leave her alone, Ana!" Stefan called in his daughter's wake. "Don't worry. She will come when she's ready."

The girl returned to the car, dragging her feet, looking tired and unhappy. None of them had rested well since leaving home, and after forty-eight hours, all were sweaty and exhausted. They had spent the first night in the car, at the side of the road somewhere near Sofia. Most of the second night, after their escape over the Bulgarian border, they had traveled through Yugoslavia on busy roads and slept only three hours, also in the car, cramped in their seats. Stefan's intention was to drive south as deep into Yugoslavia as possible before some overzealous policeman stopped them. It would have been a catastrophe to be sent back home under military escort. Now at last, that possibility was no longer of concern. Or perhaps, was it?

After finishing her routine in the dry brown grass, the cocker spaniel returned in a hurry, jumped on the backseat, and began scratching in earnest.

"The dog has collected some hungry fleas, I suppose," Stefan remarked.

"Speaking of hunger, let's have something to eat," Lia said.

"Yeah," Stefan halfheartedly agreed. "I am not very hungry." He was deadly tired and felt absolutely dejected, a combination that usually quenched his appetite. In his exhausted mind, he searched for solutions. *We've come this far and risked so much, only to be told by the Greeks that they won't let us in without a lousy entry visa,* he thought. To go back was similarly bad because they had neither money nor a proper visa for Yugoslavia. Defection was another possibility, yet he wasn't prepared to take that step right there at the border. For some reason, he felt the place was unsafe.

"I am terribly hungry," Val, their son, said. He was nineteen, tall and strong and always ready for a meal.

"So am I, Mama," Ana said. She was now stretching her shapely arms and legs in the bright sun. The girl was tall—all of them were—and good-looking.

The dog, who knew they were talking about food, stopped scratching and looked expectantly at Lia with glittering eyes, tongue hanging out.

Stefan absentmindedly watched his wife searching the trunk for the food. She moved with infinite grace even when tired. He had an impulse to show her some sign of tenderness, but this was no time for that. That was perhaps something for Stefan the dreamer. Now it was his duty to solve the immediate problem. His downcast eyes focused on more immediate objectives, missing the grandiose sight of Albania's rugged peaks unfolding in the background like stage props for a dramatic movie set.

The afternoon air was stifling. A suntanned young man casually dressed in white briefs and matching T-shirt came out of the guardhouse and sat in the shade of the building. He leaned against the wall and lit a cigarette, eyeing the girl. Making a fine show, the sentry began pacing with slow, elaborate steps between his box and the guardhouse. His relaxed movements had precision and elegance, like those of a ballet dancer. In his routine, he came near the resting man, paused, and exchanged a few words with him. Once or twice, he even looked furtively at the girl. That was when they shared a smoke, laughed, and then the soldier turned around and paced back with exaggerated seriousness. At the sentry box, he paused again and, with the ease that only lengthy training can give, performed a complex exercise with his rifle. The absence of a large audience didn't seem to deter him in any way, and the spectacle went on for quite a long time.

The music died, and it was quiet for a moment, the silence punctuated by the sound of the sentinel's shoes rhythmically thumping the concrete walkway. Then, without warning, the enticing accords of Zorba's *sirtaki* erupted into the empty area between the buildings, rushed across the parking like a sweeping wind, reverberating from wall to wall, and filling the space with irresistible energy. The afternoon didn't feel that hot anymore.

Lia handed him a sandwich wrapped in white writing paper, but Stefan didn't want to take it. "Eat," she insisted, forcing him to take the small greasy package. "You will feel much better if you eat."

Willy-nilly, Stefan took one bite and a second and suddenly realized how hungry he was. "This is still tasty," he said. "You were right. Makes me feel good."

"It is not bad. The butter melted a bit, but it is acceptable," his wife agreed. The sandwiches were already three days old.

Lia also fed the spaniel in a tiny plastic bowl placed on the ground near the car.

"May I have one more?" Val asked, watching with an envious eye as his mother helped the dog to a sandwich.

"You already ate four, dear. Wait to see what the others are doing," Lia answered. "You are not alone here."

"But I am hungry, really hungry. Give me one more, please."

"All right, all right! Here is one more, the very last one. Nobody had so many yet." Lia looked reproachfully at him. She loved her son dearly, although she knew how selfish he could be.

"No, thanks. I am finished," Ana answered when Lia offered her another sandwich. "I would prefer a drink."

Her mother produced a thermos and poured the liquid into four plastic glasses and into the spaniel's bowl. All drank lukewarm water. When the spaniel finished drinking, she climbed into the car, coiled on the backseat, and didn't want to come out anymore. Carina undoubtedly was a patriot. The Romanian rulers could have been proud of her: she obviously didn't want to live on foreign soil.

On the road, cars were coming and going again with deafening noises; and at the barrier, the officers were busy directing the traffic and checking documents.

Stefan stood up, took a few steps around the car, and yawned. He felt awfully tired and stiff. His lower back pain had returned during the night and now bothered him. "We must do something," he said. "We can't stay here forever."

"Let's go, let's go!" Ana cried.

"Go where? Are we finished with the meal?" Val asked. He was still hoping to get more food.

"I don't know. Anywhere. Dad will take us to some marvelous place as he usually does. Right, Dad?"

"Where do you think we should go? Have you made up your mind, Stefan?" Lia asked, looking at him inquiringly.

"Well, not really. We don't have too many choices, do we? Our status in Yugoslavia is unclear, and it wouldn't be smart to find out what it is. Here, they won't let us enter Greece without visas, and we don't have enough money to go to Belgrade to get them." Stefan paused and gave them a worried look.

"Let's go to Belgrade. I want to see Greece." Ana's voice was plaintive.

"We don't have Yugoslav dinars even for gas," Stefan said.

"Then let's go home and forget about everything." Ana pouted. She was a history buff, and visiting the Acropolis was one of her cherished dreams.

"This is always a possibility. If we can make it unhindered to the Bulgarian border, of course. It will also be hard to explain our presence on this side of the border to the Bulgarians . . ." Stefan left the sentence unfinished.

"Why do we have to go back?" Val asked.

"He is right," Lia agreed. "Why go back?"

"You mean not to go home at all?"

"Yes," his wife and the boy answered in unison.

"Perhaps you two are right," Stefan said. "We never discussed this until now, but from the beginning of the trip, defection to the West was constantly in my mind."

"Yes, yes. I want to go to America. I don't want to go back!" Ana shouted, pirouetting. "Dad will buy me a big ranch, and I will ride wild horses all day long."

"Cool down, dear," Lia reproved her.

"I don't want to return home either," Val said.

"This is not so simple. For a start, if we all agree, we must ask for political asylum here at the border. I would have preferred to apply for it in Athens because that was how acquaintances of mine did it. It would have been safer, and I would have known what to expect."

"But now we can't do it their way, can we?" his wife asked.

"Of course not."

"Then what will happen will happen. Surely, they won't send us back if we ask for refugee status."

"But what about the boy?"

"What about me?" Val asked.

"You are due for compulsory military service in three weeks. The failure to show up at your regiment will make you a deserter. This could mean up to five years of military prison if you ever go back."

"I would never go back."

"Ciao, ciao, communist serfdom," the girl crooned, paraphrasing Modugno's well-known Italian hit. She approached her father and affectionately put one arm around his shoulders. "You will buy me a ranch, won't you, Dad?"

"Now this is a serious matter." He gently pushed the girl aside. "Before we go any further, I want all of you to consider your answer carefully. If we ask for political asylum, we won't be able to go back for many years. Do you really want to do that? Instead, we can expect months, perhaps years, of waiting in a refugee camp. Also we would have to struggle for many years even after that because we will be poor and we don't have any relatives or friends wherever we are going. Think about it."

"I want to go to Canada, and I don't care how difficult it would be," Val said. "If you don't go, I will run away all by myself. That's what I'll do."

"I'll run with him. I am tired of lies and slogans and being watched and being afraid to say what I think. Also I want a horse and my freedom." Ana spoke so excitedly that she almost lost her breath.

"What do you think, Lia?" Stefan asked.

"You know, dear, that I will follow you to the ends of the earth," his wife jokingly answered. "I will go everywhere with you and the children," she said on a more serious tone, her eyes becoming suddenly wet.

"So you all agree. Then we should go and talk to the border people, and may God help us." In spite of his determination and courage, Stefan experienced a sudden pang of fear he couldn't immediately repel. It felt like jumping from an incommensurable height in the unfathomed sea below.

They cracked two windows open to make sure the dog had fresh air, locked the car, and walked across the hot pavement under the dusty young trees where the shade was almost nonexistent. A narrow walkway took them into the area between the buildings, right in the middle of a messy congregation of vehicles and people. From two big anachronistic Soviet Intourist buses, a continuous flow of noisy passengers disembarked under the watchful eyes of their chaperoning guides; and amid shouts and laughter, the Greek border police officers herded them into the main building.

Several Russians stealthily pointed their cameras all around, shooting fast groups of fellow tourists, the border facilities, and more. Instinctively, Stefan tried to hide himself behind other people to avoid appearing in those pictures. He was sure that some of the photographs would end up in the KGB's dossiers, and he didn't want to become part of their records. The presence of those well-fed individuals—with their smell of Russian leather, strong tobacco, vodka, and sandalwood—and the sound of their language, so familiar and much despised, had a curious, stirring effect on Stefan's mood. Mainly it was pure, blinding hatred that he was keenly aware of. Deep inside, he knew that this wasn't a Christian thing, and he felt sorry and contrite. Nevertheless, he couldn't prevent the resurgence of that ugly, overwhelming feeling, damaging, as always, to his peace of mind. Even now, late in his adulthood, Stefan was still very much haunted by atrocious childhood memories of little girls raped by the Russian soldiers, of teenage colleagues tortured to death, and by the ever-painful souvenir of his beloved uncle's final demise.

Although Stefan would never acknowledge it, he also felt a lot of psychological stress born from the visceral fear instilled in him by over thirty years of harsh occupation and associated terror. The Russians were his foes and always would be. In his view, the Intourist travelers—spoiled profiteers of the Soviet regime, so merrily gathered at the Greek border—represented the epitome of oppression itself. Brezhnev's son hunting with old nobility in France was another similar example that often came to his mind. Benefiting from the hard work of millions of people like himself, a chosen few would travel the world and enjoy life on proceeds gained by extortion, fear, mass murder, and sheer exploitation. He was inclined to blame them for all the ills he and his people had suffered since the end of the war: the lack of freedom, the cultural rape, the killing of the best, the unending shortages of all kinds—forgetting that many of those were perpetuated by Romanian themselves. At least, by some of the Romanians: the servile cowards, the backstabbers, and the opportunists. Here, for the first time in his adult life, he felt free to decide his future. This gave him an exhilarating feeling. He wouldn't let "them" take that freedom from him. In that particular instant, Stefan resolved that never, never again would he go back into slavery, no matter how dearly he paid.

It was crowded and excruciatingly hot inside the building, the room jammed with tourists waiting in long queues or elbowing their way around. Some sat at tables, diligently filling in various official printed forms, smoking, and chatting. Stefan and his family spent a long time standing in line before getting to the counter. When his turn came, he found himself in front of a tired-looking young brunette.

"We are asking for political asylum," he said and handed her all four passports together.

The clerk gave him an absent look and began leafing through the passports with a bored expression on her face.

"No," she pushed the passports back. "Go to Belgrade, to the Greek embassy, for visas. Do you understand?"

"You don't understand," he said without taking the passports. "We are asking for political asylum. *Asile politique*," he repeated in French. "Nous vous demandons l'asile politique." Stefan pronounced the words slowly and very clearly. The woman looked incredulously at him. Her sallow face expressed a mixture of confusion, puzzlement, and clerkish haughtiness. She didn't understand or perhaps didn't want to, although her indecision over what to do was obvious from her behavior.

A tall blonde, looking anything but Greek, seated at a desk behind the counter clerks, realized something was wrong and came over. With her hair neatly lacquered, her face carefully made up, and wearing an elegant blouse, she exuded professional self-confidence. The clerk, excited but respectful, said something in rapid Greek. The blonde watched Stefan severely.

"You don't have a visa. You must get one from Belgrade," she told Stefan when the girl finished.

"It is exactly what I advised the gentleman to do," the upset brunette said, looking resentful. She felt perhaps unduly diminished by the presence of this showy woman who was her supervisor.

"I know we don't have visas," Stefan answered.

"Then what's the problem?" the blonde snapped.

Carefully choosing his words, Stefan explained again what they wanted. In the end, he repeated the magic words several times, both in English and French: political asylum, *asile politique*. Finally, there was a spark in the woman's eyes, and an expression of understanding spread on her carefully made-up face.

"Oh, God!" she said and murmured something to the girl, who suddenly jumped up, alarmed. The blonde pushed her to sit down. "How many you are?" she asked Stefan, grabbing the passports.

"Four," he answered and pointed over the shoulder in the direction of his family waiting close behind him. "Myself and the three others."

"Come over here." She opened a door at the end of the counter and let them in. "Follow me."

They went along a narrow corridor with closed doors on both sides and then into a small room where there was an empty table and only two chairs. The acrid smell of cigarette smoke filled the room. The woman left without a word but returned shortly with two bottles of Coke and four glasses. "I thought you must be thirsty," she explained. "Please help yourselves." The blonde looked at Lia, who stood undecided, "Madam, sit down please. More chairs are coming soon."

A young man entered noisily, carrying four chairs, followed closely by a girl who came in with four cups of coffee, sugar, and milk and some cookies piled on a shiny copper tray. The girl returned twice, bringing more Coke and a jug of iced water. She was all smiles and said something in Greek before leaving the room.

When the fuss subsided and everyone had sat down, the blonde woman closed the door. She still had the passports in her hand. "Please drink your coffee and help yourselves to cookies. You have to wait until someone, a specialist, comes from Florina. We don't deal too often with cases like yours," she explained. "I have to leave you alone for a while."

"Would you be so kind as to tell me what is Florina, please?" Stefan asked.

"Oh, I am sorry," the woman said, "Florina is the nearby town, about fifteen kilometers from here. I hope you won't have to wait too long."

After she left, the Romanians drank coffee and ate cookies. The room was stuffy, but the coffee was excellent and the water refreshingly cold. They also tried the Coke. Now that they had taken the irreversible step, all four had a great deal of expectation. There was still incertitude in the air, and nobody was quite sure in which direction things would go. The adults talked sparsely, mostly about drinks and cookies, instinctively trying to avoid anything in connection with the last events or speculation about consequences. The teens, recalling the scenes they had just witnessed, chatted excitedly with the carelessness of youth, despite Lia's attempts to hush them.

Stefan didn't take part in their gabble. He was wondering if somewhere a hidden video camera stealthily watched them—and suddenly, he felt very, very old. It wasn't only the result of his exhaustion, although tiredness was a part of it. In fact, he had known all the time that he was too old for such an adventure. His yearning for freedom was, however, much stronger than the instinct for self-preservation. For the children, it would be completely different—he hoped. They were young, at the beginning of their lives, and deserved to be free at any cost to him. Their future lay in front of them and his sacrifice—if that became necessary—would be worthwhile. But the responsibility, the security of that uncertain future,—everything rested on his shoulders. It felt like a heavy load crushing him. *On the other hand, imagine what liberty can give you. Imagine that blessed freedom as intended by God,* he thought. *The freedom to speak and to think without fear of consequences. From now on you will be free to go unimpeded wherever your heart desires.* Oppressed for so many years, he hadn't yet learned that freedom depends not only on a declaration of rights but on money and several other things as well. It was too early for him to know the price of that wisdom. He would eventually find out.

Someone knocked at the door, and the blonde came in with two men. The youngest, tall and handsome, was wearing a uniform, which—they learned later—belonged to the tourist police. The second was a civilian, probably the same age as Stefan. They shook hands with everyone.

"These two gentlemen will take good care of you," the blonde said. She put the passports, some pens, and a stack of printed forms in the middle of the table and left the room.

It appeared that the civilian spoke Romanian. He was an interpreter, he explained, and his duty was to help the officer, who was a major, to deal with their case. His Romanian was flawless.

The major delivered a long monologue, interrupted once in a while to give the interpreter the opportunity to make his translation. He also paused when another round of coffee and soft drinks arrived, brought in by the same obliging smiling girl. In essence, after a very elaborate and polite welcome, he asked them if it was true that they asked for political asylum in Greece and then wanted to know their reasons. After the officer was satisfied with the answers, he invited them to fill in and sign some of the forms.

Everything was now happening very fast. They felt powerless to do anything but go along, as if being drawn into an irresistible whirlwind and propelled by an invisible overpowering force. The fear of an uncertain future, mixed with the exhilarating promise of freedom looming in the air, gave them an intoxicating lightheadedness.

Stefan and his family were much too involved in the events to realize what all this was about, yet it was really then and there that the most extraordinary adventure of their lives had just begun.

ON THE ROAD

The same senior police officer, which had interviewed them the evening before on their arrival in the city of Thessaloniki two days after their defection, came into the cell at 4:30 in the morning. The sun hadn't yet risen, but the gray light of the nascent day was already filtering shyly through barred windows set high near the smoky ceiling. The freshly shaven officer, dressed in plain clothes looked like a dapper no-nonsense businessman. The two uniformed young policemen he brought with him remained outside the unlocked grilled gate, submachine guns at the ready.

"Good morning, Mr. Stefan," the officer said in a soft, wheedling voice. "I am sorry to wake you so early, but you must leave. This is a prison, not a hotel."

Stefan pushed aside his sleeping bag and sat up on the narrow wooden bench, shivering slightly from exhaustion combined with the chill of the early morning. The bench was too hard a bed for someone so bony and slim and with a history of lower back problems. He hadn't slept at all and could painfully feel each of his bones. "I understand. We are ready. Where should we go?"

"Athens."

"Athens? It is a long way to Athens." Stefan unsuccessfully struggled to repress a yawn. "Unfortunately, we have neither enough gas nor money. How would we be able to travel in these circumstances?"

"The police bus."

"What would happen with my car?" Stefan asked.

"Leave it here. Come later," the officer answered brusquely.

"Do you have any place where I can park it?"

"*Ohi.* No. This is a prison, I told you, not a garage." He impatiently gestured toward the door. "You must go. Bus is waiting."

"All right. Let's go then. I wish we could know more about our fate," Stefan muttered.

"If you want to live in Greece, better learn Greek, sir," the senior officer said. "I am sorry, my English no good. You learn Greek, and I'll explain to you."

"I will, but that would be too late," Stefan answered with a shrug while gently poking at the sleeping bag in which his son was bundled up. "Wake up, Val," he whispered. "Wake up, my boy."

Val awaked with a jolt. "Ce se întîmplă? What is happening?" he asked.

"Trebuie să plecăm. We must go," his father answered. "We must hurry."

A little hobo had shared the cell with them during the night and now intently watched what was happening with round bleary eyes. He had lain directly on the wooden bench without a blanket or a sleeping bag. The boy had many small coins, which he spent most of the night counting in a muffled voice. Often, the odd coin would drop noisily on the concrete floor, followed by some more. The dreadful racket the urchin made counting and searching in the half-lighted cell as well as his personal worries had kept Stefan awake the entire night.

When the Romanians finished packing their sleeping bags and were ready to go, the hobo stuck by them. The officer stopped him unceremoniously. "*Ohi, ohi.* No, no," he barked. They spoke for a minute or so in Greek, and then the officer motioned Stefan and Val to leave the cell.

Lia and Ana came out of their cell smiling, happy to see the men of the family. They all gathered in the big ground-floor open area where three guards armed with submachine guns continuously kept a vigilant watch. Their belongings were also there, neatly piled up in a corner.

The whole building was brightly lit by numerous floodlights hanging at the level of the fourth floor. Wide metal stairs led to various floors built upon an array of intricate steel structures, where rows of barred cells lined tiered balconies protected by pipe railings and metal netting. Although some cells were occupied, many appeared to be empty. Everything was painted dull gray and smelled of oil paint and stale tobacco smoke. The Romanians had never seen such a prison before, except in American movies.

"Take baggage and go," the officer said, rushing them. On his orders, the two young policemen who accompanied him slung the submachine guns on their backs, nonchalantly grabbed some bags and suitcases, and unhurriedly carried them to the gate. One elbowed the other and smilingly said something, ogling Ana. Their superior, who saw the move, scowled at him menacingly. Then he unlocked a small, almost invisible door engineered in the tall and heavy steel gate and let the whole group out.

The street was empty and silent, and the morning was still young. In the east, only a diaphanous rosy cloud, silhouetted against the dark gray sky, marked the place where the sun lay still hidden behind the horizon. A huge army lorry completely clad in sheet metal and painted in dark camouflage khaki was waiting around the corner under two venerable plane trees, just behind Stefan's Trabant. No openings were visible in the metal body except the driver's door and the windshield. Stefan realized with a shock that the police bus was a prison van, one of the so-called Black Marias.

"Is that our bus? I don't like it," Ana said, her voice veiled with a tinge of anxiety.

"We have no choice, dear. Be patient. Everything will be different in Athens," Lia tried to soothe her.

"I don't want to travel in a police bus," Ana protested. "This is ugly, and it gives me the jitters. Why is Dad not driving our car?"

"I don't think we can do anything about this. It would be better if we could keep quiet and wait. So far, there is nothing wrong, my dear," her father said, trying to sound reassuring.

In spite of his apparent coolness, Stefan was apprehensive about their immediate future. So far, things hadn't evolved in the way he had imagined they would. The police "hospitality" didn't make him feel either free or safe. He would have preferred to ask for political asylum in Athens and deal with civilians and political authorities rather than at the border as had happened. It was too late now, and be that as it may, he resolved to mobilize all his optimism and strength in order to boost the family's spirits and courage. Having made up his mind, Stefan put on a confident face and, despite thirty years of atheistic indoctrination, relied ultimately—as he always did—on divine providence.

The officer knocked on the driver's door and a sleepy-eyed moustached face crowned by curly black hair appeared behind the windshield. When the man recognized his superior, he immediately opened a metal blind and lowered the side window. While they talked, another sallow face peered over the driver's shoulder. Soon after, some static noises and orders were heard. Eventually, a narrow door popped open with loud squeaks at the back end of the van, and a burly gray-haired policeman got off, the submachine gun dangling across his wide chest. The policeman placidly chewed a toothpick, which he didn't part with even when talking to his superior.

The men conversed for several minutes, and in the end, the young policemen were ordered to load Stefan family's things into the van, which they did, laughing and joking all the time. When they finished, the officer sent them away, shook hands with the older policeman, and said to Stefan in a commanding tone, "Now you go with sergeant in the bus."

"We must take the dog," Stefan said, undeterred by the commanding tone. The previous evening as their luggage had been moved inside the prison, the officer, when asked what would happen with Carina, was utterly scandalized. "Prison is for people, not dogs," he had said. Thus the spaniel, unlike her masters, slept comfortably in their car on her own blanket.

Stefan found Carina awake, standing on the front seat as if she knew he was coming. He put her on leash, but she didn't budge. It took persuasion to make her leave the car, and she agreed to follow him only when she saw the others waiting on the sidewalk.

"You ready? You go in bus now," the officer ordered.

"Just a moment, sir. I don't want to leave my car like that," Stefan said. "This is not an abandoned vehicle. This is my car, my property, which I intend to keep."

"Sorry, you cannot take it. Not now, maybe later . . ."

"I understand that, but at least give me a place to park it safely. Please, sir. Allow me to park it near your building."

"*Ohi*. No, there no place. This is prison. Cars forbidden in front of prison. Understand?"

"Yes, I understand, but there is some room beside your building."

"*Ohi, ohi!* No, no. No room. Absolute not."

"There is, sir. I can show it to you. Please, sir, allow me to show it to you."

The exasperated officer rolled his eyes in despair and, after letting out a resigned sigh, halfheartedly agreed, "Okay. Show."

Stefan left the dog with Lia and led the officer behind the building, to the big metal gate through which they had come out earlier. There was a wide paved driveway connecting that gate with the street, probably designed to permit the access of police vans directly into the prison's main hall. At the end of it and on the other side of the building, the pavement extended with a spacious concrete platform partially surrounded by a high fence covered in climbing yellow roses currently in full blossom. The fence separated the next door neighbor's private flower garden from that concrete platform.

"There," Stefan pointed at the empty platform. "Plenty of room there."

"Impossible, impossible," the scandalized officer cried. "This for colonel, for general. Not for you. Impossible."

"Sir, my car is small. There is enough space there for several vehicles. This car is my only property. I left everything behind in Romania. I don't have any other property—no money, no house, no land, no jewelry, nothing. I don't want to lose my Trabant. I have a big family. I need a car. Please, sir, please help me," he implored.

The officer considered the Romanian without answering for what seemed like a long time. The silence lasted so long that it began getting on Stefan's nerves and he was almost ready to give up. It would have been a mistake as in the end, the man turned his eyes from Stefan to the platform and back, and then a faint smile lighted his face. "Okay," he said, "bring car. You," he pointed his index finger first at Stefan's chest and then at his own, "and me in big trouble." He pointed his finger at his chest again, "I lose job, you lose car. Understand?"

"Thank you. Thank you very much. I hope your superiors will understand. Thank you," Stefan said, deeply moved by the man's sudden change of mood.

"Okay, bring car. Quick. Hurry." The senior officer made a dismissive gesture, giving him a gentle push on the shoulder.

Stefan ran to the Trabant, clinking the keys. "I am allowed to park next to the building," he happily shouted to his people, who stood undecidedly on the sidewalk in the burly policeman's company. He tried the contact at once, and the motor reluctantly came alive, belching a cloud of black smoke. He warmed up the engine before awkwardly turning the Trabant in the middle of the street, incommoded by the police van stationed too closely. Then he drove to the back of the prison where the officer was waiting, pacing impatiently.

After Stefan had parked at the far end of the platform and locked his car, the two walked together to the front of the building where the officer shook hands with him. "Good luck, Mr. Stefan. God bless you," he said, "and please learn Greek language."

Stefan tried to thank him again. "No, no. Go now. Very late," the man stopped short his effusions and left in a hurry, almost running.

The police van was empty and poorly lit. Inside, it was divided in two compartments separated by a metal wall. From the first, a tiny boxlike cubicle at the tail end where the burly policeman presided on a folding stool beside a radiotelephone hanging on the wall, one entered the next compartment. This was much bigger, and a solid steel door fitted with a sophisticated lock isolated it from the warden's cubicle. The main enclosure was furnished with several wooden benches, lavishly inscribed with graffiti in both Greek and Latin characters. Other illegible hermetic signs, ephemeral mementos celebrating obscure existences of immortality-starved convicts, were scratched all over any accessible surface. The benches formed two equal rows, leaving a rather narrow passage in between. There were also four barred glassless windows, two on each side, covered in sheet metal blinds with a mere slit left open at their bottoms. The available daylight and fresh air came in only sparingly through those slits.

As soon as the Romanians stepped in, the policeman locked the door from the outside in a deafening concert of squeaks, creaks, and bangs. Nothing moved afterward, and no signs of takeoff preparations could be heard.

"We should sit at the rear. In any event, it would be better for us to be close to the door," Stefan said.

"Couldn't we try to escape somehow," Ana excitedly asked, looking at her father with shining eyes, "like in the movies?"

"We are not interested in escaping, dear," Stefan said. "We don't want to antagonize our hosts. This is not a movie. You should understand that."

They stored their luggage behind the last bench on the right side row, on which Lia and Ana had decided to sit, and placed the smaller bags under their seats. No more than two people could sit side by side on each bench, so Stefan and Val seated themselves on the one in front of the girls. Carina climbed beside Ana, curled in the corner between the girl and the wall, and closed her eyes as dogs usually do when sick or stressed.

The family had barely finished these arrangements when, accompanied by a huge commotion, the door flung open and three men stormed in. Two of them—an older peasant type who badly needed a shave and a rough-looking beardless boy with his face devastated by acne—were together. They were dressed in coarse woolen trousers and matching black vests, their heads covered with identical cloth caps. Without looking around, they went straight to the opposite end of the compartment, taking over the front bench. They had no luggage.

The third—a scared-looking barefooted teenager—was blond, almost albino, with his face and other exposed skin markedly sunburned. He wore dirty shorts, a coarse linen jumper that must have once been white, and carried an unpacked sleeping bag. The youth came in shivering uncontrollably, and after collapsing on a seat, he withdrew into his mummy-bag, only to fall asleep immediately. For a long time, he was periodically shaken by convulsion-like shivers, which didn't seem to trouble his sleep.

Soon afterward, the engine came alive noisily, sending vibrations through the entire van. Several backfires shook the vehicle mightily before it settled into steady motion. The foul stench of exhaust gases that initially infiltrated the compartment, making the passengers cough, gradually dissipated and finally they were off.

Stefan, seated by the window, found a hole in the blind big enough to allow him to see outside. There were actually several such small peepholes, probably made during the long years of the van's service by its industrious involuntary passengers. From his precarious vantage point, he watched with interest the vehicle's slow progress through unknown and empty streets, informing his family as the landscape changed. Not for long though, because shortly after their departure, the van pulled in beside an official building with a big Greek flag hanging above the main entrance. The place was silent at that hour and appeared to be deserted.

The driver blew the horn repeatedly until, from a narrow courtyard shaded by a row of branchy mulberry trees, a smart-looking young soldier dressed in a new uniform came carrying a khaki duffel bag. The soldier lazily walked to the van and talked to the driver, smoking a cigarette. The burly policeman, still carrying his inseparable submachine gun and chewing the toothpick, opened the outside door at the back end of the van and joined the party. They chatted in a friendly manner, having fun like old acquaintances seeing each other after a long absence. The soldier produced a handful of printed papers with stamps and signatures, which they passed around, reading aloud and commenting merrily about the contents. Their socializing went on for some time until, at the policeman's instigation, the soldier grabbed his duffel bag and got on. The soldier was still smiling when he martially marched in and greeted everyone with a sonorous "*Kali mera*. Good day." After disposing of his bag on the bench, he took the empty seat in front of Stefan's.

At the next stop, still inside the city boundaries, on a quiet street bordered by magnificent linden trees, they picked up an attractive young woman who was waiting outside a modern, opulent villa. The newcomer, dressed in a well-cut tailor-made suit, seemed to be a professional of the managerial type. She came in with haughty airs, gracefully walking on a pair of high-heeled shoes exquisitely matched by her big designer leather bag. After a disparaging, cursory glance at her fellow passengers and carefully sweeping the bench with a perfumed handkerchief, she seated herself decorously on the bench by Lia's side. The woman never talked to anyone.

After that stop, the van was driven much faster, and Stefan could tell they were out in the country, on a four-lane highway. It was breakfast time, and Lia distributed among her family some peaches and a handful of biscuits. The fruits were bigger than any peach they had ever had in the past, each the size of a small cantaloupe, sweet and juicy. Those were the last four of a dozen or so presented to them by the friendly police chief before leaving Florina. The spaniel refused to eat, looking at them with sick eyes.

For the next several hours, the van didn't stop at all, and the monotonous rattling of the engine made everyone sleepy. The inside temperature gradually increased as the sun climbed higher in the cloudless sky, pleasantly warming the uninsulated sheet metal body. Nobody showed any inclination for conversation, and the passengers, except for the woman who remained composed and alert, had fallen asleep. Stefan, bored with watching the mostly brownish arid slice of the roadside continuously unwinding in front of the peephole, went into a sort of hypnotic trance. He wasn't dozing, or at least he didn't want to. Neither was he dreaming. He was having a sort of vision, as if he was watching a slow-motion picture composed of faint images of the road interwoven with fleeting memories of the last three days erratically coming and vanishing, kaleidoscoped into oblivion. He succumbed to the gentle but irresistible lethargy, which slowly took over his mind until he completely lost the notion of time.

Stefan couldn't say how long this state of prostration had lasted when he came to his senses, awakened by a succession of bumps and jolts. The van had left the highway and was painstakingly negotiating a dirt road crossing sun-scorched fields overgrown with low scrub.

Through his peephole, he could see a chain of lofty, craggy mountains in the distance, enshrouded in a dusty haze that covered the horizon like a heavy curtain, their foothills covered in the dark green foliage of indistinct woods. Then the road dwindled into a mere track winding through a grove of ancient olive trees, their silvery leaves shining brightly in the sun. As the van progressed, the trees became older, fantastically contorted, and widely spaced; and Stefan saw the uncertain contours of massive buildings appearing beyond them.

When the bus drew nearer and stopped and the dust settled, he could see that they were in front of a high-walled compound. Heavy machinegun barrels menacingly protruded from the embrasures of tall watchtowers strategically placed in the corners and connected by sturdy walls topped with several rows of barbed wire. Bunches of powerful reflectors were installed on metallic frames erected on the edge of the walls, some turned inside and some directed outside. The only opening in the solid square structure of concrete and stone was closed by a heavy steel gate. High on top of the gate, from a narrow balcony protected with sandbags, two guards in full battle gear watched the vehicle through their binoculars. The entire setup suggested a fortress expecting a long siege or perhaps a high-security prison.

"This cannot be a refugee camp," Stefan whispered to his wife. "This is not our final destination, I hope." The scene completely disconcerted him; it wasn't what he expected to see.

The gates automatically opened without delay to let the van pass through. During a short pause, immediately behind the gate, the driver spoke to the duty officer, an elderly warden who didn't leave the comfortable chair on which he sat by the doorframe of a small office. Then they drove along a clean paved avenue between two rows of giant cypress trees before stopping again in the shade behind a modern three-story building with wide windows. Many other similar buildings could be seen scattered among leafy chestnut trees and Aleppo pines, separated by well-tended flowerbeds. Several guards in uniform, armed with submachine guns, patrolled the deserted alleys in pairs.

As soon as the bus stopped, the professional-looking woman resolutely stood up and impatiently pounded on the door. When the burly policeman grumblingly unlocked it, she left the compartment without a word. From the nearby building, a middle-aged policewoman came out to welcome her and, after checking some papers the newcomer presented, led her along an adjacent alley. They chatted amicably, walking side by side and moving lasciviously—especially the ex-passenger—as though their hips were on swivel joints, until they disappeared from Stefan's sight.

"What is that good-looking lady here for?" Stefan asked the guard who, for the time being, left both the communication and outer doors open, allowing the passengers to breathe some fresh air.

Initially, the man either didn't want to understand or perhaps had real difficulty grasping the meaning of his interlocutor's words. The policeman deemed to answer only after Stefan asked the question several times. His English, although broken, was surprisingly enlightening. "Drug," he said, making a wry face. "Heroin, cocaine, much drug," he repeated before turning his back to Stefan.

For a long time, nothing happened. Only the pine resin's sweet fragrance borne on the wings of a gentle breeze periodically arrived in hot perfumed waves, occasionally accompanied by the arrogant buzzing of the odd wasp, lost in its inadvertent search for easy food or shelter. Vigorous crackles of the cooling engine also infrequently disturbed the somnolent atmosphere, imparting imperceptible tremors to the cabin floor.

Just when Stefan, exhausted after his sleepless night and early morning start, was ready to succumb again to an almost unbearable desire to sleep, the approaching voices of a group of men and a gentle knock on the open exterior door aroused him to expectant attention. The warden got off to join the people outside and, after some animated discussion, let in three elegantly dressed gentlemen carrying expensive suitcases. In fact, one of them, the one with a head of curly black hair and an athletic bearing and who behaved like their leader, carried only an attaché case. His suitcase was carried by the youngest of the group, apparently his aide, a slightly plump, profusely sweating fellow. Freshly shaven, the new passengers were dressed in formal suits and white shirts, their jackets matching their well-cut and impeccably ironed pants. All three wore multicolored silk neckties.

"Probably some officials going to Athens," Stefan commented aloud, waking Lia from her uncomfortable napping.

The group entered in a flurry of greetings, bringing with them a refreshing mixture of fine fragrances and the aroma of good quality tobacco. Oblivious to the somewhat dejected atmosphere that reigned inside the compartment and acting upon the directions of the one who appeared to be the senior among them, they took over three benches, one exclusively for the storage of their suitcases. The newcomers acted with confidence and seemed to be in control of everything. Even the burly policeman hurriedly renounced his feeble attempt to close the communication door at the energetic intervention of a group member, prompted into action by the apparent boss. Once all had settled comfortably, the guard spoke into his radiotelephone gear to the driver, who immediately started the engine. The van left the fortress by the same route it had come and, bumping and jolting, returned to the main highway.

It was getting hot. The newcomers took off their jackets and, after some chatting among themselves, opened one of their suitcases, unveiling an astonishing assemblage of utensils, jars, and various other containers. Producing a shaker, a bottle of water, Nescafe, and sugar, the junior aide applied himself to expertly preparing instant coffee. He topped the frothing preparation with small ice cubes from a wide-mouthed thermos and poured it into big mugs under the close supervision of his elder colleagues. During the operation, which he followed with a critical eye, the apparent boss kept his hands busy, perfunctorily fondling a string of big shiny amber beads. He occasionally added a word to the flood of advice the third man showered upon their younger associate. When the coffees were ready and each of them had a mug, the senior man passed around a pack of Dunhill. They all lit cigarettes and gleefully started smoking, emitting appreciative grunts.

The men enjoyed themselves for some time, drinking coffee, talking, and laughing, seemingly having great fun. They hadn't yet finished their coffee when the leader walked over to the front bench and, after offering cigarettes to the other two passengers who had been quiet until now, endeavored to talk with them. The elder one wasn't too communicative and looked worried; but the rough boy struggled to answer, without much success. He blushed and stammered until the leader, clearly disappointed, left, quizzically raising his eyebrows. He approached the soldier next, who, when offered cigarettes, lit one of his own. For a while, they had a lively conversation, often dotted with laughter and followed by varying signs of amusement from the other members of the trio. It was during a pause in the discussion that the smiling leader turned to Stefan and asked him a question.

"I don't speak Greek. I am sorry, but I don't understand you," Stefan said apologetically.

The man pointed to his chest with his index finger, "Haralambos," he said. Then he pointed at Stefan and waggled the other hand in a questioning manner. For anyone from the Balkans, the meaning would have been obvious: "What is your name?"

Stefan told the man his name, but his curious interlocutor wasn't satisfied and wanted to find out more. Haralambos knew neither Romanian nor English, and Stefan didn't speak Greek. The language barrier notwithstanding, they managed to carry on quite a meaningful conversation, based mostly on body language, in which the hands played the main role. They also used a limited vocabulary of words similarly pronounced or closely related in both their mother tongues.

When it became clear to the Greek that Stefan and his family were political refugees, he immediately ordered four extra coffees for *roumanois,* the Romanians, and generously treated them to Dunhill cigarettes. As compensation for nonsmokers, Ana and Val were offered several packages of Greek chocolate.

Whatever Haralambos obtained from Stefan, he explained with many words to his colleagues. It appeared that the soldier understood some English and was able to help with the translation. The burly policeman stood in the doorframe, eager to listen but only sparingly intervening in the animated discussion, which at times went on in parallel.

Thessaloniki lies about five hundred kilometers from Athens; the travelers, blind inside the van and unable to divert themselves with the changing landscape along the route or with other distractions, had plenty of time to get better acquainted. At the instigation of Lia, who was puzzled by their fellow passengers' goodwill, Stefan asked Haralambos about his destination.

The man pointed first to the middle-aged dark fellow. "Kosta," he said. Secondly, he poked the junior's chest: "Ioannis." Then he turned his finger to himself and described a sort of a circle in the air that included the other two. "Kriti," he said, continuing an undulating gesture with his hand, meaning sailing to Kriti.

"Kriti? Do you mean Crete? Are you going to Crete? What for?" Stefan asked, accompanying the questions with the appropriate hand waggles.

The answer came in the form of a complex gymnastic exercise. Haralambos pretended to dig with an invisible spade, thrusting something into the ground.

"What's that?" Stefan wondered.

"Maybe that means work . . . in the garden," Val shyly suggested.

"Yes, yes. Work," the soldier said. "Me too . . . Crete . . . work," he concluded.

"*Neh*, yes," Haralambos agreed.

Everyone was suddenly talking and gesturing, and in the next half hour, with the combined effort of the whole group and a lot of hand waggling, an intriguing, unexpected picture emerged. Stefan and his family, to their utmost surprise, gained a new understanding of who their fellow passengers actually were. Initially, they thought it was a joke; yet as the story unfolded, they had to accept what they heard as the plain truth.

Haralambos, Ioannis, and Kosta were convicts—*prisoners* was the word the young soldier used. They had carried out a successful armed bank robbery together, initially managing to get away with an incredibly large sum of drachmas. But after being caught, they had been sentenced to fifteen years in prison. Now in their second year of imprisonment and due to good behavior, they were being transferred to Crete for work in the fields. He was himself a prisoner, explained the soldier, sentenced to a couple of months of disciplinary outdoor work.

Asked about his own misdemeanor, the soldier struggled with the language and told in faltering English an entangled tale about getting unconsciously drunk during the recent national holiday. In his drunkenness, he took his training officer's motorcycle for a joyride without permission. Apparently, he had never ridden a motorcycle before, got confused, lost his balance, hit a tree, and crashed the accursed vehicle, which became an instant write-off. When caught, instead of apologizing and repenting, he fought with the military police patrol. It was a rather sad story, he confessed, as everything happened because of bad luck and poor quality wine.

The other three fellows, who had already heard his adventures, listened while smiling good-humoredly and occasionally teasing the storyteller. "Pallikaras. Pallikaras. A brave. A hero," they shouted and laughed. This didn't seem to bother him as he took their amicable ironies in stride.

Although they were compassionate, Stefan and his family were dumbstruck and could not immediately find anything to say, so the conversation lingered. They had never been in such company and didn't know the appropriate behavior. Taking advantage of that momentary lull, Haralambos glanced at his Rolex wristwatch, approached the warden, and spoke with him privately behind the communication door. Shortly, some guttural radiotelephone chattering, broken by static, could be heard over the rattling engine noise; and the van pulled off the road, slowly coming to a halt.

Through his peephole, Stefan could see a tiny restaurant with tables and garden chairs sprawled along the road in the luminous shade of lofty chestnut trees. An open fire, temporarily sheltered by the lush foliage of grapes hanging from light trellises, was smoldering on a primitive fireplace made of loose bricks on one side of the shabby building beyond the tables. A woman dressed in black kept herself busy with pots and pans around the fireplace. From a loudspeaker installed in a wooden box under the eaves, loud Greek music poured out in an incessant flow of rhythmic melodies. There were no customers or other people in sight except for the burly policeman and a tanned man girded with a clean white apron, talking convivially in the bright midday sun. The cloudless sky was chalky white; and on the highway, traffic moved tirelessly in a continuous swish-swash, exuding irritating burned mineral oils and gasoline fumes into the hot air.

Kosta picked up a tune from the radio and started humming it with delight, his eyes closed in rapture. In no time, Ioannis joined in, adding words to the tune, and Haralambos supported them by skillfully whistling. They formed a good trio and obviously enjoyed singing along. The policeman came in, followed by the man with the apron who carried big flat plates with steaming food and quite rudely interrupted their budding entertainment. However, he was greeted with good cheer as the men found the food to their taste. The irresistible odor of spices and the appetizing smell of freshly grilled lamb filled the compartment, causing Stefan to feel the painful emptiness of his stomach.

"I am hungry," Val said, licking his dry lips.

"I am, too," Ana said.

"Everyone is hungry, dear. Unfortunately, we don't have anything left. We must wait until we arrive in Athens, I am afraid." Lia tried to appease them although she wasn't sure what was waiting for them in Athens.

"Don't think about food," Stefan stoically advised them. "You will feel much better."

"I cannot think of anything else," Val said. "We haven't had a decent meal for three days."

Haralambos followed their discussion with discreet interest. He walked a few paces between the benches, carrying his plate and fork, and sat beside the soldier, engaging in friendly talk as he gulped mouthfuls of lamb and vegetables. The soldier turned to Stefan, "Haralambos ask you not eat?"

"We will eat in Athens," Stefan answered.

"Not Athens," the soldier, prompted by Haralambos, said, "you not eat now?"

"No," Stefan said and made a gesture of counting coins. "We don't have Greek money."

The young man dutifully translated to his countryman, who shouted something. The policeman appeared in the doorframe with an inquiring frown on his face. A rapid exchange of words ensued, and the burly man withdrew after Haralambos gave him some banknotes. The guard soon reappeared with two plates, accompanied by the waiter carrying three more. Haralambos directed them to serve the Romanians and the soldier.

"No, no. Sorry. You are very kind, but you shouldn't do this. We are not that hungry." Stefan declined Haralambos's offer, accompanying his words with proper gesticulation. He was awfully embarrassed, indeed upset.

Stefan's ancestors were proud people who had always lived by their own means. In their code of honor, there was nothing more despicable than begging. He and his people would work, fight, or die—but never beg. The shame he felt at being treated like a beggar hurt almost physically. Haralambos was a sensitive man and had acted from pure goodness of heart. Yet that was another matter, and Stefan would have preferred to starve to death rather than survive on someone's charity.

Haralambos perhaps intuitively felt what went on in Stefan's mind because he came around, graciously shifting his square frame from one bench to the other. He put his arm around the Romanian's shoulders and patted him on the back. He spoke in Greek, pointing to Ana and Val and using his fingers to make the gesture of eating from the plate, his left hand cutting across the stomach to show he understood they were hungry. His smiling cronies repeated the gestures, also urging them to eat.

"You friends," the soldier said. "Haralambos say, you friends. You eat, you friends. No eat, no friends. Friends eat!"

"We must eat. We cannot insult them," Lia said.

"Yes, Mama, we must eat," Val agreed, taking a morsel from the plate. "This tastes very good."

"Yes, yes. Eat," the soldier said, talking with his mouth full.

"*Kala, kala.* Good, good," Haralambos said.

"All right, all right. Thank you very much," Stefan said, bowing slightly toward their benefactor as he noticed the soldier had done. The senior inmate smiled, displaying a row of beautiful white teeth. His pleasure was obvious.

The waiter appeared once more with a plate filled only with meat, which he handed to Lia. "What for?" Stefan asked.

The waiter talked to Haralambos, and they both laughed, telling the soldier to translate. "For dog," he said.

The food was undoubtedly good. The lamb was freshly grilled on the spit, and the baked potatoes were delicious. Lots of oregano and fat black olives spiced the huge mixed salad, something new for the Romanians' palates. What they most enjoyed was the bread, a special treat after their two days of fruit diet. It was freshly baked, still hot from the oven. They ate everything in almost religious silence, without too much ado. Even Stefan wolfed down the food, forgetting his scruples for the time being. Only Carina couldn't be drawn from her torpor, and her portion went to Val, who gladly finished it in no time.

The rough boy, who had for some time restlessly fretted, turning left and right in his seat, timidly stood up and walked to the warden's cubicle. He came back with a big grin on his round face, carrying a loaf of bread clutched close to his chest. On the way to his place, he slowed his pace, wantonly eyeing the women. The boy's dazzling green eyes almost popped out of their orbits, contrasting with the unhealthy purple of his complexion. He turned to look back several times.

"*Tourkikos*. Turk," muttered the soldier in a hostile tone, intently watching the boy. He resumed eating only after the boy had sat down and, for a long time after, retained a grimace of annoyance on his young face.

The waiter came in and picked up all the dirty dishes when he correctly guessed that everyone had finished eating. He spent some time amicably talking with the policeman and with his customers. The waiter also addressed Stefan, who inquiringly looked to the soldier for help.

"Food good?" the young man translated.

"Yes, very good. Thank you," Stefan answered to everyone's conspicuous satisfaction. They repeated after him, "Very good, very good," and all laughed happily. Even the warden smiled and looked pleased although nobody had given him anything to eat.

As long as the van was stationed under the chestnut trees, the atmosphere inside the compartment was acceptably warm. When it returned to the highway, taking its steady course toward Athens, it became exceedingly hot. The burning sun heated the exposed metallic carcass like a furnace, and there was little air circulation in the interior. To quench their thirst and cool themselves, Ioannis made another round of iced coffee for his buddies. Upon orders from Haralambos, he again treated the Romanians and the soldier, disregarding their weak protests.

Haralambos left his fellow inmates and perched familiarly on the edge of Stefan's bench to drink the coffee.

With the cooperation of the young soldier as before and with a plethora of expressive gestures, they sustained an animated discussion in which even Lia and her children were involved. The convict asked details about Stefan's children: their ages, their interests, and the schools they had been in. The Greek then told them about his own family, which he painfully missed. Artemis, his wife, was a tall shapely woman. She was beautiful and took good care of their children, but it was hard on her now, all by herself. Haralambos had two boys he was proud of: a six-year-old and a four-year-old. Upon his release from prison, they would be men in their own right, and he wondered if they would remember him. The thought that they had to grow up without him distressed Haralambos. He also had a little girl, born after his imprisonment and still a baby as he indicated by gently rocking an imaginary bundle in his arms. When he talked about his daughter, an unexpected tenderness softened his rugged face.

It was at that point that a violent emotion overtook Haralambos. He leapt to his feet, eyes closed and arms opened wide, with the coffee mug still in one hand, and started singing. He began almost whispering, and then his voice grew louder in a long crescendo. It was a wailing song, and although he didn't understand the words,

Stefan could feel its crashing sadness. He instantly succumbed to its wild, soul-stirring charm. The Greek sang it in a trancelike way, slowly turning around in between benches, heartstruck for the moment and oblivious of anything other than his deep inner turmoil.

This touching episode didn't last. His two cronies surrounded him with soothing words, and as quickly as it had started, Haralambos's melancholy vanished. They broke into noisy laughter, and Kosta changed the tune to a lively dance song. Presently, all three were snapping fingers, clapping hands in time to music, laughing and dancing in the narrow passage, accompanied by the soldier who first followed the scene with a mischievous glitter in his eyes and then began energetically kicking his feet.

A wild glee overcame the rough boy from the front bench, who stood up in a burst of uncontrollable enthusiasm and would have joined in if his older companion hadn't prevented him with a stern rebuke. Nevertheless, he continued to stand, gazing in bewilderment at the Romanian women and swaying erratically from side to side like one of those tamed brown bears gypsies used to display at country fairs all over the Balkans.

The noise also awakened the dejected-looking albino youth. He emerged from his cocoon with sleepy eyes and appeared at first completely disoriented. Ioannis, who noticed the boy's confusion, tried in vain to talk to him in between songs. After one more try, he left the boy alone with a dismissive shrug, shaking his head in disbelief. "*Allofron.* Deranged," he told Kosta, poking at his temple with a tobacco-stained index finger.

Haralambos, tie fluttering, turned to the Romanians and, still dancing, strove to entice them into the swing or at least into singing. One of the songs, which he and his friends seemed to favor, had an easy enough refrain. It began with the line "Opa, opa, ta buzuki," and although they didn't know what that meant, Stefan and his people soon had learned it by ear and sang along with the others, totally forgetting about their uncertain future. They got in the mood, clapping hands and snapping fingers; and the song miraculously acted like a soothing balm, annihilating the effects of fatigue and heat. Next, all together, they sang Zorba's famous *sirtaki*, then another song and "Opa, opa, ta buzuki" again and again, immersed in an apparently endless sea of friendship and merriment.

The singing seemed to have gone on forever, when the van came to a rough stop, causing the dancing men to fall one on top of the other and the songs to die in the sudden commotion.

"Athinai! Athens!" The warden shouted and hastily unlocked the outside door where someone was heard knocking.

An old severe-looking policeman with a magnificent gray handlebar moustache got on and stood in the compartment's open door, critically considering the human cargo in front of him. He was in full uniform, wearing the regular cap and carrying a big caliber pistol, the butt of which stuck out from the gray leather holster strapped to his belt. The burly warden who had accompanied them from Thessaloniki meekly peered over the newcomer's shoulder with a searching look, as if he was seeing his charge for the first time.

"Who is Stefan Popescu? Popescu and family?" the newcomer asked in an official tone.

Stefan fidgeted uneasily in his seat and then reluctantly stood up. "I am Stefan Popescu, and this is my family," he said tracing an imaginary circle around his people.

"Show me your passports, please." The policeman spoke with aloof formality. He studied the passports at length and then put them in his pocket. "You must disembark here immediately." He entered the compartment and glanced around. "Where is your luggage?"

"This is our luggage," Stefan said, pointing to their belongings amassed behind the last bench.

"And these are ours too," Lia said, indicating the little bags stashed underneath the seats.

"Take everything with you, and get off," the policeman commanded, stepping outside in order to free the exit.

Haralambos asked a question, which the policeman answered only briefly, giving him a cursory hostile glance. It was clear from their body language that the convicts and the rest had to stay in the van. Nonetheless, seeing that the Romanians were hastily moving their belongings and preparing to leave, the inmates pressed around them, eager to give a helping hand. During the ensuing bustle, Haralambos unobtrusively approached Stefan and presented him with two cartons of Dunhill cigarettes, a can of Van Houten cocoa powder, and a paper bag filled with chocolates that had magically materialized from the same inexhaustible suitcase. It was impossible to refuse as the man didn't want to hear any excuses. Afterward, in the refugee camp, Stefan and his family enjoyed those treats for several weeks. In the meantime, Kosta and Ioannis swiftly passed the bags to Lia and to her children, who had already gotten off.

When Stefan, loaded with a small bag and carrying the last suitcase, was ready to leave the compartment, the soldier nervously shook hands with him. Drops of perspiration rolled down his young clean-shaven face, and a sudden blush rose to the root of his crew cut. "*Adio*. Good-bye, friend," he said with a muffled voice, without looking at Stefan.

Then it was the inmates' turn to surround Stefan, talking excitedly and slapping his back. "Friend, friend," they repeated as the soldier had taught them. They all hugged Stefan, and Haralambos kissed him on both cheeks, making the sign of the cross upon his forehead. "Kalo taxidhi. Kali dhinami. Bon voyage. Good strength," they said to Stefan with changed voices, unable to hide their sadness.

"Good-bye, good-bye, my friends," Stefan repeated mechanically as he got off. He could barely contain his feelings. It was definitely more than he had asked for.

Finally, the entire bewildered family, tired and emotionally drained, stood in the vibrant heat of the afternoon on the burning dusty sidewalk in front of the police station. Huddled together, with Ana holding Carina in her arms and with their luggage spread around, they waved good-bye to the departing company.

Their ex-fellow passengers, bunched in the narrow door at the back of the bus, shouted good wishes and sang the lively "Opa, Opa" refrain, waving up a storm. When the truck's engine started, the burly policeman with the submachine gun slung on his back hurried to make room for himself inside by pushing the inmates who jammed the doorframe. They jokingly resisted for a short while.

The vehicle was already slowly moving when they good-humoredly helped the warden get on. The door noisily slammed shut, and the bus vanished away with a cloud of dust and exhaust fumes.

The old policeman grabbed Stefan by the arm. "Come inside the station, please," he said. "You should never fraternize with such people. They are bad people. Very bad indeed," he concluded, patting his moustache and looking at Stefan with reproof.

Stefan wondered, *If such were the bad people of Greece, how would the good ones be?*

In the Quiet of the Evening

As it happened, that October was unusually warm and dry in Attica. Although one could have noticed the warning signs of autumn, a somewhat tamed version of the summer was still stubbornly hanging about.

The change was already in the air as the days had become shorter, predicting the estival season's imminent end. Diaphanous clouds, unseen since springtime, had reappeared recently here and there, daring to put on a modest show. They shyly announced their arrival through a hazy veil hanging over the faraway mountains. Every day, they moved closer, insidiously descending along adjacent valleys toward the plains below. Some mornings, assuming more definite contours, the clouds had ventured offshore, materializing on top of the nearby islands, only to vanish without trace in the afternoons. The weather's gentle changes of mood notwithstanding, the days and nights were still hot and clear along the Aegean coast. Often, much too hot.

Early night found Stefan siting on the balcony in front of the open door, his legs stretched, and resting on the balustrade. He absentmindedly watched the stars fading as the moon rose beyond Makronisos Island. The balcony ran the length of the building, each room having access to it; but for the moment, he was completely alone, enjoying the agreeable sense of privacy that was such a rare luxury in the camp. He liked the quiet hour when evening met night and when the little town seemed to hold its breath before erupting into an incredibly effervescent nightlife.

From the harbor came faint engine sounds and muffled shouts. They originated in the spot where tremulous reflections of dancing lights in the dark waters marked the Kea Island ferry's mooring.

Further down, the dense night appeared to be populated with a swarm of crazy fireflies. Then the first moon rays reached the continental side of the narrows, drawing a silvery seam along the craggy hills and exposing the jagged ruins of the old dilapidated Turkish fortress. The deserted island, visible a few minutes before only as a huge black silhouette in the shape of a sleeping dinosaur, suddenly took on an eerie look as it lay forlornly surrounded by glowing mist. Moments later, the channel separating the island from the mainland came to life under the moonlight, like a theatrical stage when the reflectors are suddenly switched on. The fireflies died instantly, swallowed by the blaze, magically transformed into small black needles sliding back and forth on melted copper. Those were the nocturnal fishermen who now were hurriedly taking to the sea, their small crafts equipped with powerful floodlights in order to attract the fish.

From the silvery hills came a breath of wind, gently sweeping offshore the stagnant, foul-smelling air trapped between buildings during the day. The scarlet, brown, and gold leaves that littered the streets gathered in small drifts by the curbs or crowded round tree-trunks, rocked and swirled under the vacillating light of streetlamps, like multicolored weaves in a Fauve painting. Chased by miniature dust twisters, they took short flights, accompanied by ragged newspapers and other light garbage. Caressed by the breeze, the palm trees outside the refugee camp's wall began eagerly fanning their featherlike branches.

Years ago, when they were engineering students, foolish and madly in love, Stefan had made Lia, his bride-to-be, the most extravagant promises. Carried on by passion and letting his imagination run wild, he described in minute detail the luxurious villa he would build for her on the shores of the Mediterranean. He spared no expense in his imaginary project, and no material was good enough. Exotic wood, fancy tiles, marble columns, and glazed bricks would adorn his castle in the air. His depictions were so real that she could almost feel the touch of that silky, noble stone baked by the southern sun. With exaggerated accuracy, he sketched for her on scrap paper vast terraces and wide stairs lined with huge palm trees leading to the sea. He had a particular talent to make her believe, mesmerized to the point of actually sharing his daydreams. Sometimes, contagiously enthusiastic, he himself—more often than not—believed in the realization of his promises. Not so like Lia who, despite liking this easy form of evasion from the dullness of everyday life, felt deep in her soul that those projects would never happen considering how remote the possibility of traveling abroad was for people of their condition. She was too anchored in the present to let herself be fooled by dreams when the reality at hand was so strikingly different.

At the time, Romania enjoyed the unenviable privilege of being one of the newest East European communist states. In the "workers' paradise," under the dictatorship of the proletarians, nobody except the big shots from the nomenklatura, leading members of the almighty Party, could choose where they wanted to live or travel. Even for those political oligarchs, living abroad when not on government business would have seemed preposterous. To the average citizen, the Mediterranean was definitely out of reach, a realm to dream of, situated at an impossible cosmic distance incomparable with the actual earthly one. Dwelling on its paradisiacal shores was as unconceivable an idea as living on the moon, everything on the other side of the Iron Curtain being off-limits for them.

Similarly impossible in the first years of communist rule was building a modest private house, not to mention a villa. Even owning a modest house was sinful, almost equivalent to a crime, and simply having one for the exclusive use of a single family was unimaginable. As a consequence of the past war's devastation and due to decades of government neglect accompanied by massive migration from the country to the cities, housing availability was minimal. Lodging became a much-sought-after commodity and the object of high speculation on the black market. A medium-sized apartment usually had to provide shelter for several families, some occasionally sharing the same room if it was big enough to divide with curtains, blankets, or other similar improvisations.

These were the reasons why, after graduating and getting married, Stefan and Lia considered themselves lucky to get as living quarters what before "the revolution" was a small kitchen—three meters on each side, with a sink in a corner and a stove in the other. That was their bedroom, living room, dining room, and kitchen all in one. It was used as a study when Stefan enrolled in his doctoral program and as a darkroom when he took on photography. What in the beginning was supposed to be a temporary solution gained permanent status, and they were still living in the same place after their two children were born a year apart. Their already modest abode took on, out of necessity, the role of children's bathroom as well as nursery. But all that was history now, and as impossible as it would have seemed only two months before, they lived on the shores of that legendary Mediterranean, albeit in a refugee camp and not in a villa.

The camp was a complex of various whitewashed concrete buildings surrounding an inner court where a few lanky mulberry trees struggled for survival. Most of the space—except for the roomy kitchen, the stores, a couple of offices and the washrooms—was partitioned in dormitories of different sizes. Some were bigger rooms, which people of both sexes, who didn't know each other before, had to share. If those were crowded, life wasn't always pleasant. The administration generally tried to keep refugees of the same nationality together and sexes apart, when possible. They also gave preferential treatment to families with children, who were allotted separate rooms. People like Stefan and his family, sheltered in the second and third floor dormitories of the main building, enjoyed a magnificent view overlooking the town and its sleepy harbor with the ever-changing sea, the sun-scorched islands, and the eroded hills in the background. The camp was quite clean, the food acceptable, and the atmosphere—although not always overly friendly—tolerable.

What was most surprising for Stefan was the profusion of marble. For the first time in his life, he saw it used casually and in such an extravagant manner. He was an experienced professional who had seen many oddities in his practice but nothing like that. The main building's stairs were made of solid marble, and the floors were tiled with the same material. It was lavishly used even in the washrooms, where it often became ignominiously soiled when some refugees neglected to flush the Turkish-style toilets. Marble appeared to be quite a common feature in the local geology—the hills, the fields—under a superficial layer of dirt, and the rocky shores were more or less made of it. It was so cheap that in the absence of freight, cargo boats would load it as ballast. In the fields—he learned from working on a farm—it was a nuisance, any attempt at cultivation having to start with the removal of considerable amounts of rock, all of which was, in fact, marble debris. It took some time to accept this reality, but even then, waking up in the morning with sunshine glowing on the sugary white floor was for him a source of pleasant childish wonder.

Many years later, in Canada, when reminiscing with friends about their episodic camp life, he never let an opportunity pass to point out jokingly how faithfully he always kept his promises. If he didn't actually build his wife a luxurious villa in Greece, he would boast, at least, he took her to live there, in a place that almost—but almost—matched his youthful specifications, including marble floors and palm trees.

Behind him, Stefan heard the gentle scraping noise made by Carina's claws on the floor, followed by intense sniffing and sneezing at the door. Someone had entered the unlit room. Presently, his wife and Ana emerged on the balcony after turning the lights on. The women had been out shopping, and their arrival had awoken Val, who slept in one of the four beds. They all shared the same room as they had years before, and life in common had left much to be desired. The only consolation was that this time, the inconvenience would hopefully be for a shorter time.

Val pulled himself out of the bed with conspicuous displeasure. He joined the others on the balcony, yawning and stretching, his eyes still sleepy.

"Wake up, man," Ana greeted him. "You are wasting away your life sleeping. Come on, wake up."

"I am so tired," Val said, yawning and letting himself fall on a chair.

"Why are you tired, lazy boy?"

"Leave him alone," their mother said. "Val had a long workday today."

"I see . . . The boy is a working man. That's how you become a millionaire, they say, through hard work," the girl teased her brother. "Now you must be rotten rich. Where is my present?"

"Rich? You must be kidding. I haven't seen any money yet. Agamemnon will pay me at the end of the week, and anyhow, he pays me only a few bucks a day. And the work? Oh God, I barely could stand on my feet in the afternoon. Delivering thousands of bottles is not an easy job. I forgot how many times I jumped up and down from that truck, loaded like a donkey. Hard work, you said? This is really very hard work. You have no idea what hard work is. You just babble . . ."

This was his first day on the job, and the boy wasn't yet used to its hardships. Refugees weren't allowed to work, yet unofficially, most of them did menial jobs for the locals in order to earn pocket money. Stefan worked on a farm, and Lia worked with her daughter in a hotel or occasionally in a restaurant.

"You are a selfish brat who doesn't want to share the dough with his little sister," Ana said. "Wait until I'll get rich. Then I'll teach you good manners. Dread that day," she said, trying unsuccessfully to make her voice sound threatening.

The spaniel came to Stefan and put her cold nose in the palm of his hand, which hung lazily aside the chair. She gazed at him with that worshiping look cockers are well-known for.

"You are hungry, aren't you?" Stefan asked, stroking the golden red curls on the nape of her neck. He turned to the children, who were still teasing each other. "Ana, stop squabbling, and let us prepare something to eat," he said, regretfully leaving the comfortable position on the balcony, followed closely by the dog. His quiet moment was gone.

Soon, they had the electric hotplate running and several fish sizzling in the frying pan under Lia's watchful eyes. From the outside came the appetizing smell of fresh baked bread, and Val was dispatched to fetch some. The bakery was next door to the camp, and the telling smell always let refugees know when a new batch came out of its ovens.

Ana laid the table with unmatched plates and silver of different provenance on a colorful tablecloth from home. The eclectic assemblage she used was mainly inherited from people who had already left the camp. In a corner, on an upturned wooden box, Stefan busied himself making the salad.

Someone knocked at the door, which then opened slightly. Carina watched quietly, knowingly wagging her tail. A dark bearded head with curly black hair showed up in the opening and was greeted with joyful exclamations. It was Abdur, their young Afghan friend.

"May I come in?" he asked, smiling.

"Of course, Abdur. Come in, come in, please. Welcome," Stefan said. "Carina, leave him alone," he admonished the dog for her overly enthusiastic welcome.

Abdur was a man of medium height, well-proportioned, and athletic. His appearance was like that of a modern, youthful Othello. He moved with a graceful ease, like a powerful, confident lion. The son of an Afghan anticommunist general executed by the Russians, Abdur, only sixteen at the time of his father's death, had managed to escape from the squalid prison where they were detained together. After many detours and perilous adventures, he eventually reached the safety of Greece. Kabul is a long way from Athens, and it took him over two years to complete the journey across difficult mountain ranges and not-always-friendly borders. Only seven months older than Stefan's son, his escape prematurely aged Abdur; he already had some gray hair.

In spite of her master's rebuke, Carina followed the young man, feverishly sniffing his shopping bag and only later regretfully withdrew to her blanket under Stefan's bed.

"Did you have supper, my son?" Stefan asked.

"No, Father. I worked late, missed the camp dinner, and just finished shopping."

From the beginning of their acquaintance, the young man had become very attached to the Romanian family, and they had immediately adopted him. Not a day had passed since without him visiting in order to share the latest gossip or only to hang around with them. In their company, he found understanding and warmth, things he was deprived of and perhaps had longed for some time. Brought up in a close-knit family where the father was seen not only as the supreme authority and teacher but also as an admired role model, he recognized instinctively in Stefan something he had lost earlier in life. He would come every so often to Stefan for advice or just for a male chitchat; and a special friendship, going much deeper than the usual camp socializing, had soon developed between the mature man and the outgrown teen. There was reciprocal affection and respect in their relationship.

"Then you will have supper with us. Ana, put out a plate for Abdur," Stefan said.

"Thank you, Father. In this case, we should also eat from my food," the Afghan said. "I have some cooked rice here. It won't last till tomorrow." He unpacked his bag, giving Lia a casserole dish and a Styrofoam container. "Here are also a couple of *souflakis*, which we can have instead of appetizers. They are still warm, I hope."

"Good, then we will start with them," Lia agreed.

"Do we need tomatoes?" he asked. "I bought about two kilos."

"No. Keep those. They will surely last a few days. You can eat them tomorrow."

"Yes, keep them. We don't need more tomatoes. We have enough salad. Look, I just finished it," Stefan said. "Isn't it colorful and tempting?" He always felt irrationally proud of his salads.

The door opened with a bang as Val came in loaded with three loaves of bread precariously held against his chest and a heavy bag in his left hand. From the bag emerged the necks of many beer bottles, dripping condensation.

"Here is the bread, Mama, and there is your change," he said. "I bought the beers with my pocket money."

"Oh, wow! How generous of you. See, Mama, the rich boy has finally decided to give us a treat," Ana said.

Noticing Abdur, Val chose to ignore her malice. "How are you doing, old Pathan?" he asked instead. Val purposely mentioned the ethnic association, knowing how proud of his Pathan ancestry their young friend was.

"Good, good," the Afghan answered. He was conspicuously pleased although he didn't want to directly acknowledge it. "You've made some money today, I gather."

"Not really. I worked for Agamemnon. He doesn't pay you very well, you know." The boys hugged, slapping reciprocally on their backs. "Good to see you, man," Val said.

"Don't believe him. He is such a miser," Ana said.

"No, he is not. I know Agamemnon. He is pretty tightfisted. Last time, when I worked for him, he paid me so little that I decided never to do it again," Abdur said, his hand still on Val's shoulder. "My brother is not a miser. He is as generous as he can afford to be."

It was common knowledge in the camp that a few employers would take advantage of refugees, making them toil for almost nothing. In contrast, the majority of locals were a generous lot, rewarding their workers more than once with extra food, drinks, and clothes on top of the normal wages.

"Supper's ready," Lia announced. "Come on, guys. It is time to eat."

Before coming to the table, Stefan fed the spaniel, filling her bowl and placing it in the usual corner. "This dog eats too much," he commented. "She gets too much food and too little exercise."

"That's not true, Dad. She swims every day with us, and she is not fat. Look at her shape. She is as slim as a sponge diver," Ana said. She was right. Carina would sea-dive everyday, picking up pebbles from the bottom of the cove where the family went swimming.

They sat at the table, ate their food, talked, and drank cold beer. Through the open door, the sweet voice of Nana Mouskouri could be heard from a distant radio, mixed with other urban noises, soulfully singing a stirring love song. It was the forerunner of what was yet to come. Taverns scattered across town opened presently for the evening, and a multitude of loudspeakers suddenly came alive, blasting Greek music at the top of their electronic lungs. The sounds swept wildly through the streets like a furious tsunami, spilling over the roofs and treetops and rising high in the sky, filling the night with a cacophonous medley that would go on till early the following morning. Greeks are gregarious, and each night, the restaurants were full to the last seat with reveling crowds. Years later, Stefan was still wondering when those hardworking Greek people rested.

Suddenly, the smell of burnt coffee filled the room. Every time Ana made it, the coffee boiled over, and the pleasant aroma followed her around while she handed them mugs.

"How was work today, Abdur?" Lia asked, sipping her coffee.

"Not very busy. Fewer Afghan refugees are arriving these days. It's a consequence of tougher measures taken by Turkey, I believe."

Abdur was a polyglot and worked casually as a translator for the refugee relief agency in Athens. He had an innate talent for languages and, having been educated at the American college in Kabul, his English, learned at an early age, was faultless.

"Turks are coming now in ever-growing numbers." He paused to take another sip. "Mainly communists. All sorts of communists: Maoists, Marxists, followers of Enver Hodgea the Albanian, partisans of the Soviets, and you name it. The military junta is chasing them ruthlessly, and they are leaving Turkey as if fleeing the plague," he said.

"What will happen with them?" Stefan asked.

"They will probably end up in this camp," Lia mused.

"More than probably," Abdur confirmed.

"That's bad news," Stefan said. He hated the idea of having left-wing fanatics as next-door neighbors.

"The biggest problem for the people at the agency is how so many people with such different views will live together in one place. All those factions are fiercely opposed to one another and fight to death among themselves," Abdur said.

"Let's hope they exterminate each other before coming here," Val muttered.

Outside on the balcony, people talked aloud and then burst into noisy laughter. The voices came closer, and two men entered the lighted area in front of the door. It was Luca, a Romanian, with Váci, the young Hungarian. Recent newcomers, they both lived in a room next door and became fast friends, perhaps because Luca, originally from Transylvania, spoke Hungarian fluently.

The cocker approached and, recognizing the guests, stretched out on the floor close to the open door and relaxed.

"I have to tell you this one," Luca said, bursting with excitement. "It is a good one. I just heard it today. It is about Ceauşescu." He meant to tell a political anecdote about the Romanian dictator.

Malicious gossip and anecdotes were the only way people of Romania could express their outrage at how many scandals had marred the communist regime, or criticize the leader's ineptitude. They voiced their opposition by making fun of everything and everyone, including themselves. Such productions of popular wit would spread like wildfire, permeating the entire society. It was the national sport, albeit a very dangerous one. A person accused of spreading political anecdotes was liable to get many years in prison, which only few could have survived. Thus, fear was everybody's permanent companion. Everyone learned early in life how unwise it was to express political opinions in public or make certain comments even in front of one's own children. It was equally dangerous to confide in friends or relatives, who—under torture—could easily become sources of destruction. It was said that every fifth Romanian was an informer, either voluntarily or involuntarily. Some were paid, others did it for favors. Telephones were bugged and tapped routinely, and the rumor was that newer models recorded even when not in use. The reason Stefan hated communism most was because it killed human trust and made true friendship impossible.

Luca began to tell the anecdote, first checking the balcony to make sure they were alone and lowering his voice. He drew his head between his shoulders in an attempt to make himself less conspicuous. All Romanians did the same without even being aware of what they were doing. It was a second nature to them.

"Please translate to Abdur," he asked Stefan. "Your English is better than mine. Váci already knows it. I just told him in Hungarian."

"I will, I will," Stefan answered. "Do you want some beer before you start, or do you prefer coffee? The beer tonight is Val's treat."

"A beer of course, especially if it is Val's treat. Did you hit the jackpot, man?" he asked the boy.

Val looked half pleased, half embarrassed, and smiled sheepishly. He opened two bottles and passed them to Luca and Váci without answering.

"You know how bad things are in Romania these days," Luca began. "All the major public works are impaired by mismanagement, lack of vision, and poor workmanship. Nature is not cooperating either. This fall's rains, unusually heavy and accompanied by widespread floods, have silted several big artificial lakes from the Arges Valley hydroelectric system. To make things worse, some dams built of dirt collapsed, burying cultivated lands and numerous small localities under torrents of mud. It is like in the legend about Master Manole." He paused to give Stefan time to translate and took a sip from the bottle.

The legend Luca mentioned was about a master mason who, in the fourteenth century, allegedly built a church, a unique monument of late Byzantine architecture, still in existence. According to the legend, no progress was made on the building for a long time. Regardless of how carefully the masons worked during the day, the walls of the church crumbled overnight; and in the morning, the men had to start anew. As the strange phenomenon persisted, Manole and his coworkers decided to propitiate the evil spirits with a human sacrifice. The victim, the story goes, was the master's young wife, who they immured alive. Her sufferings and pleas for mercy, as well as her husband's distress, are the subject of a moving ancient ballad. Extremely popular, it was studied in schools across the country, and almost every Romanian knew at least parts of it by heart.

"Ceaușescu decided to surpass Master Manole by sacrificing himself," Luca said. "The plan was to build the dictator into the foundation of the biggest dam while he would deliver one of his long speeches. It would have to be a grandiose mise-en-scène, unique in human history, a feat to be remembered forever. But as everyone knows, the dictator always gestures during his speeches, madly waving his hands. And when the builders started pouring, the mortar wouldn't stick to his body. After two days of countless efforts, the Comrade was only up to his knees in concrete. Having exhausted the entire country's cement production, they had to call off the event."

They all laughed, including Váci. The spaniel woke up and stretched, yawning noisily. Pricking her long ears, she peered intently along the balcony, into the night.

"You know so many political anecdotes, Luca. Romanians, it seems to me, have a special sense of humor. It must be fun to live in Romania," Abdur said. "In Afghanistan, we just fight, fight, and fight. Ours is a very dangerous life."

"Make no mistake, young man. Life in Romania is not fun. Telling anecdotes could be as dangerous as any fight. Ridicule is a powerful weapon," said an unfamiliar voice coming softly from the dark side of the balcony.

The dog silently went outside, but didn't leave the lighted area in front of the door. Only then did they notice Dăscălescu, standing in the shade at the border between light and dark. He was a Romanian recently brought from Athens, where he had spent some time in a hospital. Nobody knew him well, but the buzz was that he had escaped and made the trip to Greece, tied somehow with ropes under the chassis of a long commercial vehicle. He was discovered in Thessaloniki when the truck was unloaded and put on a ramp to be washed. Being continuously exposed to exhaust fumes and without water and food for three days, he arrived severely sick.

"What do you mean, sir?" the Afghan asked. "What's so dangerous in an anecdote?"

"It is. Of course it is dangerous," Luca said.

"In Romania, it is a crime to tell political anecdotes, my son," Stefan confirmed.

"People lost their lives for this very sly piece of humor," Dăscălescu said.

The dog didn't move, obstructing the newcomer's way. "Carina, go to your place. Go, go!" Stefan said, and the spaniel did as she was told, repeatedly looking back and shuffling her paws.

Dăscălescu stepped into the full light. He was a tall stern-looking man, strongly built with cold blue eyes and gray hair. "I can tell you a story about that, but first, I need a match. I ran out of matches. Can someone help me, please?"

Váci offered his lighter, and Dăscălescu lit a *Papastratos* pulled out of a little metal box he kept in his pocket. He drew a couple of quick puffs to make sure the tip of the cigarette burned well and returned the lighter.

"You keep it. I don't need the lighter. Please keep it," the Hungarian said with a smile, which made him look handsomer than he really was. "I have too many lighters anyway. Seriously, you can keep it," he insisted.

Váci apparently had an inexhaustible supply of fancy lighters decorated with glamorous naked girls, which he indiscriminately presented around. As unusual as his generosity was, nobody dared ask where those lighters came from. He produced another lighter. "See here? I have a similar one for me." He winked, lighting a cigarette.

"All right, you convinced me. Thank you. I owe you a drink," Dăscălescu said.

"Drinks, I always accept with pleasure," Váci replied. "Speaking of drinks, may I have another beer, Val?"

"Would you like to have one yourself, Mr. Dăscălescu?" Val asked.

"No, thanks. I don't drink beer."

"What about your story, sir?" Abdur said.

"Oh, yes. My story. It is not actually mine. It is the story of an unlucky guy. Let's call him Peter." Dăscălescu paused for a while and inhaled deeply several times, watching the tip of his cigarette. He had a gloomy look, and his face was of an unhealthy yellowish pallor.

"This happened in Bucharest. One morning, Peter took the bus to go to work as usual. The bus was late and therefore overcrowded.

Squeezed in the crowd and unable to turn around, Peter overheard a guy behind him whispering an anecdote in someone's ear. It was the anecdote you just heard from our colleague," he said and pointed to Luca with his cigarette. "Of course, he couldn't see them because it was still dark, before sunrise."

"The anecdote was perhaps new for you guys," his hand made a circular, inclusive gesture, "but it is no longer new in Romania. Everyone, including the people around the dictator, once enjoyed it—except for himself and Comrade Elena, the dictator's wife, who was outraged when she heard the story. She took it personally and ordered the secret police, the securitate, to spare no means in finding out and severely punishing the author and those who spread it. Peter didn't know that, or he would have been more careful. Instead, the first thing he did that morning was to share the anecdote with his colleagues at work. He was a technician and worked with three other men in the planning office of a small factory.

"It was a quiet day, and after the initial fun of the new anecdote, they worked on their projects for a while. Then one of the men, whose name was Urzica, the only Communist Party member in the room, went out to the stores to pick up some materials for his project. Not long after, the phone rang on the desk of one of Peter's colleague. He was the senior technician among them, an older man close to retirement.

"'The director wants to see me immediately,' the man said and stood up.

"'What for?' Peter asked.

"'I have no idea. It was that girl, his secretary, who made the call.'

"'Maybe it is about your long-due promotion,' the other colleague teased him.

"'Do you think that the director has nothing better to do? From the girl's voice, it must be something else, but I couldn't make out what it was,' he said and left the room in a hurry.

"Less than half an hour later, the phone rang again, this time on the other colleague's desk. The man was also urgently called to the director's office. He looked worried when he heard what the caller had to say.

"'Something is happening up there,' he told Peter before closing the door.

"Left by himself, Peter tried to concentrate on his work, but couldn't. His drive was gone. None of his colleagues came back and, as the time passed by, he began feeling a sort of unexplainable anxiety. Something is cooking, he thought. Something probably went wrong, but what? It was lunchtime now, and in spite of his mounting nervousness, he felt hungry. They normally worked eight hours straight without breaks. And because they often had to stay longer hours, everyone brought lunch from home, eating it on the job, at their desks.

"That day, Peter's wife had packed him a tomato, some bread, and a chunk of feta cheese. The food was carefully wrapped in a piece of old newspaper, and as he was unpacking, his wife's image came to Peter's mind. He felt a sudden warmth flood his heart. She was a sweetie, so good and caring. Like a mother, he thought. Although being an orphan from birth, he didn't really know what a mother's love was like. They had been married for two years and were still very much in love. Currently, they were going through hard times as she had to stay home with their newborn baby. We will manage until she is able to get back to work, he thought, feeling optimistic for a minute or so. But the anxiety returned, and to forget it, he went on with his lunch preparations.

"Peter had a small plate in one of his drawers, which he now put on the desk, pushing aside the project papers he worked at. Next, he cut the tomato and arranged the slices around the cheese. Feta cheese was a rarity, being steadily exported by a government hungry for foreign currencies. Even good tomatoes were scarce. His wife's cousin, however, was an accountant at a state-owned dairy farm and could get first-quality feta and tomatoes anytime. They certainly weren't procured by strictly legitimate means. The food looked appetizing, but Peter never found out how it tasted. For at that precise moment, the door was flung open, and three men rushed in.

"Two were strangers, but Peter knew the third well because the man was the most feared person in the whole factory. This was

Comrade Ionescu, the secret police officer in charge of everyone and everything, the eyes and the ears of the Party, as such people were called.

"One of the newcomers closed the door and leaned on it. The other positioned himself close, behind Peter, while Ionescu took a chair and sat on it in front of the desk, smiling sardonically. This was the worst thing that could have happened, thought Peter, frozen by fear. And for the first time in so many years, he noticed how small their office was.

"'Sorry to interrupt your little lunch, Peter,' apologized Ionescu with unctuous irony as he helped himself to a piece of cheese. 'Excellent cheese,' he said appreciatively. 'These two are securitate workers,' he said, speaking with the mouth full. 'They are friends of mine, and they want no harm if you are clever and helpful. In fact, we know all about you, so don't be shy about telling us the truth.'

"'I don't understand,' Peter mumbled, overwhelmed with fear.

"'He doesn't understand. The comrade is innocent like a virgin. Can you believe that?' Ionescu said to his men.

"Without notice, the man standing behind Peter violently slapped his head with a heavy hand. Peter's head banged the desk, and for a moment, he blacked out. He returned to his senses utterly confused, as if waking up from a bad dream. 'This idiot thinks we are stupid,' Peter heard the man saying.

"'Be careful. Don't upset my friend. He's got a very short temper.' Ionescu's voice was almost benign. He helped himself to a chunk of bread and two tomato slices. 'You don't have salt, do you?' he asked in a matter-of-fact manner. Peter wanted to get up and bring the salt, which was kept in a paper bag on the windowsill. But the agent behind pushed him down by the shoulders, and he couldn't move. 'Don't bother,' Ionescu said. 'Now look here, Peter, we don't have too much time to lose with you.' His tone was official. 'We are quite busy these days, and we know you are a bloody enemy of the people. Comrade Urzica already informed us about your unpatriotic behavior, describing the horror he felt when you spread hostile propaganda about our beloved leader. Your colleagues have also confessed. Your fate is already sealed. However, we might choose lesser punishment if you cooperate.'

"'Mr. Ionescu, comrade, please. I am not an enemy. I am, I am, I am,' stammered Peter, who couldn't remember the proper word.

"'Stop it! We know who you are,' Ionescu shouted. The man behind him grabbed Peter by the hair, giving his head a shake and banging it twice on the desk. His swollen forehead was already tender, and the new abuse was terribly painful. He saw green stars on a black curtain. 'A bloody bandit you are. That's what you are,' the officer barked.

"'No, no,' Peter said. 'I respect and love our great and most eminent leader. I swear on my mother's grave. I do.'

"'If that is so, then quickly answer my question. Who told you that stupid anecdote?' Ionescu took another piece of cheese. 'This cheese is excellent. Here, have a bite,' he invited the man standing behind Peter's chair. 'The only thing we want to know is who told it to you. And that's all.'

"So that was the problem, Peter thought, the anecdote. Now he knew what their trouble was and realized in a flash how big his own trouble was. 'I heard it in the bus this morning,' he said aloud.

"'Don't give me that stupid excuse,' Ionescu barked.

"'It is not an excuse, Comrade Officer. It is the plain truth. The bus was crowded, and I overheard a guy telling it below his breath. It was dark at that time, and I couldn't see the storyteller.' Despite the mounting headache, Peter could again control himself and spoke confidently.

"'I see,' Ionescu said. 'You know what? You are a liar. Nobody in his right mind would tell such stories on a bus. You are covering up for someone. This is what you bandits always do.'

"'No, no. I am not a liar. This is the truth.'

"'Yes, you are. And where I will send you, they know how to make you confess,' Ionescu said, finishing Peter's lunch.

"'If I knew, I would have told you immediately. Honestly, this is the truth. I heard it on the bus,' Peter tried desperately to convince the officer.

"'Shut up! That's enough,' Ionescu cut him short and addressed the agents, 'I can't spend the whole day here. Take him with you. At the headquarters, they know how to properly handle such trash.'

"'But, comrade, I . . .' Peter didn't finish because the man standing behind grabbed his neck, pulling him up. Peter felt dizzy and stumbled when the agent dragged him to the door.

"'By the way,' Ionescu said instead of good-bye, 'when you will return, you must tell me where you find such fine cheese.'

"The man at the door greeted him with a punch in the lower ribs, hurting his spleen, and Peter nearly fainted. They carried him outside where a car was waiting. One of them opened the car door and pushed Peter inside. He didn't wait until Peter was completely seated and slammed the door, smashing his leg.

"'Careful! You are going to jam the bloody door,' the driver shouted.

"The agent swore copiously, reopened the door, and kicked Peter's leg inside, then pushed him further in and sat beside him. The other agent was already seated. And Peter, squeezed uncomfortably between the two, had no room to move. Ionescu came outside the building and handed a big envelope to the driver. 'Keep an eye on the bandit,' he said.

"It was one of the last sunny days of the fall. The clear sky had a transparent blue-greenish color you see only in Bucharest. In such days, one feels like the heavens are opening wide toward infinity. The light has a soft golden quality, and the autumnal atmosphere gives you an irresistible urge to get out of the city, to escape, to be free. The air was pleasantly warm, balmy. And although his leg hurt and his head ached, Peter thought that soon his wife would take the baby for a walk in the sun, waiting for him to come home. Inevitably, this pleasant image was quickly replaced by anxiety. What would happen to them now? Perhaps it would be a long time before he saw his beloved again.

"Peter didn't have too much time to spend with dark thoughts because the car entered an underground parking and came to a halt. There were several other cars and lots of busy people in what appeared to be one of the securitate's garages. The agents dragged Peter out of the car and pushed him roughly through the crowd. Peter limped badly, and each step made the pain worse. They took a dirty, foul-smelling elevator, which—to his surprise—instead of going up, went down. When the door opened, they emerged in a narrow, well-lit corridor in front of a small desk where four men in uniform were standing. Another man, also in uniform, sat at the desk looking into some papers. All five were armed, the standing men with submachine guns and the seated clerk with a big caliber handgun in its worn leather holster. A strong smell of cigarette smoke, urine, and something else he couldn't define floated in the stale air.

"The agents talked with the soldiers, and after looking into his papers, the man at the desk directed them to take Peter to interrogation room number 5. Limping painfully along the gray painted corridor, Peter noticed with horror that the doors they passed were of solid metal with peepholes, and several had small square barred windows. Behind some of those doors, people were shouting, screaming, or moaning. And the corridor was filled with frightening noises, inducing in him an unpleasant feeling of insecurity and fear. His heart sank.

"Interrogation room number 5 was a tiny windowless office with bare gray walls, sparsely furnished with a desk and three chairs. There was nothing else in the room except a telephone on the wall and the fluorescent lamp in its flimsy fixture hanging from the ceiling. One of the agents went out and returned with another two men in plain clothes. When the agents who brought him in left the room, Peter understood that the newcomers were the interrogators.

"The older of the two sat at the desk and opened a slim file he was carrying. The man motioned Peter to sit down, which he did reluctantly, suffering excruciating pain from his injured leg. The muscle tissues must been awfully smashed and swollen, and he felt the sock and the shoe wet with blood, but he didn't have the courage to check.

"'I am the officer assigned to your case. Sit down please,' the man said. 'What's the matter? Are you sick?'

"'No,' Peter answered, 'my leg hurts.'

"'Why is that?'

"'Getting in the car . . . the door . . .' Peter began.

"'Just a small accident, Comrade Major,' the second man said, 'Comrade Marin, the agent, reported to me about that. There is nothing of concern. The prisoner resisted and had to be restrained, nothing important.'

"'I didn't resist . . .' Peter explained.

"'You shut up! Speak only when asked. Understand?' the man barked, raising a hand, ready to hit him.

"'Slowly, slowly, Sergeant,' the officer said.

"'Yes, Comrade Major,' the sergeant meekly answered. He gave Peter a dirty look, spasmodically opening and closing his fists.

"The sergeant was an ugly-looking character. Of medium height and squarely built, he had a big fleshy broken nose matched by two little porcine eyes peering nastily under an unusually narrow forehead. In his youth, he had been a promising boxing champion. But money, drink, and women ruined his budding career. This job he had now suited him well because he was allowed to practice his boxing skills successfully—and with no risks—on a broad variety of human types. More importantly, the job didn't require anything intellectual, a domain in which he was rather weak.

"'You are accused of spreading defamatory propaganda,' the officer said, browsing through the papers. 'Is this true?'

"'I only told my colleagues an anecdote I heard in the bus, if that's what you mean by spreading propaganda,' Peter answered.

"'Yes. It is precisely the same thing, and this is a crime against the state. You know that?'

"'I understood that from Comrade Ionescu.'

"'Who is Comrade Ionescu?' The officer looked in the file. 'Oh, yes. Lieutenant Ionescu. He is my colleague in charge of your factory. He reports here that you are covering up the person who told you the anecdote, a fact Comrade Urzica, a coworker of yours, confirmed. Attached is his signed confession. Why did you do that?'

"'I heard the anecdote on the bus,' Peter answered.

"'Really? Tell me how it happened,' the officer urged him.

"Peter told him the story from the beginning. He also went into details about his arrival at work and how he shared the anecdote with the colleagues. He kept silent about Ionescu and the henchmen, fearing that bringing up their bad treatment toward him would antagonize his interlocutor. The officer listened and asked a few questions, taking notes. Peter liked the man and answered honestly. He thought the officer unbiased.

"'Are you married?' the officer asked suddenly.

"'Yes, I am.'

"'For how long?'

"'A little more than two years,' Peter answered.

"'Do you have any children?' the officer asked again.

"'Yes, one. A baby boy,' Peter answered, and the image of his wife with the baby waiting for him in the sunny street flickered through his mind.

"'Too bad. You made a big mistake, Mr. Peter, and we have a problem here.'

"Used as a form of address, the word *mister* was a sure sign of Peter's status. Enemies of the people were not considered dignified enough to be called a comrade. *Mister* was the official appellative used for criminals in general.

"The officer paused for a minute or so, looked thoughtfully at Peter, sighed, and picked up a sheet of paper from the file and showed it to him. 'See this? This is the information written by your colleague Urzica. It affirmatively states that you are covering up someone who told the anecdote. We need a name. Can you give me that name?'

"'No. I can't. I am sorry. I couldn't see, not to mention recognize, who was the person. The bus was awfully crowded,' Peter answered.

"'This explanation, in the light of your colleague's statement, cannot be accepted. Do you understand that?' the officer insisted.

"'Urzica is a liar, Comrade Major, he . . .'

"'Urzica is a member of our Communist Party and, by Lieutenant Ionescu's account, a trusted person. You should be more careful than to accuse him of being a liar.' The officer's voice was quite severe. 'Better remember who told you the anecdote. Give me a name.'

"'I don't know the name. I heard the anecdote in the bus. I already told you,' Peter said in an exasperated tone of voice.

"'Don't shout,' the sergeant said and stepped on Peter's foot. Peter couldn't repress a moan.

"'Easy, Sergeant,' the officer ordered.

"The major was a painter by profession, a talented and sensitive man. After graduating in fine arts at the end of the war, he went into painting icons and frescoes and acquired some recognition for his early work. He put in his frescoes a freshness, which—mingled with true spirituality—meant perhaps to open a new era in Romanian religious painting, the critics said at the time. Unfortunately, the new regime banned the construction of churches, and the young painter was reduced to restoration work. This was done on a small scale with government funds and mainly for propaganda purposes, in order to maintain monuments that attracted foreign tourists or were praised by internationally recognized specialists. The sites were under the secret police's tight surveillance, and the young painter got to know many of the plainclothes officers in charge, occasionally obliging them with information about people who frequented those churches. The securitate workers liked him because he was easygoing and helpful. They became good friends, spending many evenings at nearby restaurants, sharing after-job drinks and having fun. When one of the big museums was broken into and precious old icon paintings stolen, they recommended him as an expert. Eventually, he entered the ranks, becoming one of them.

"Life was good for securitate officers. They got the best houses, double salaries, and had access to closed-circuit shops where they could buy goods inaccessible to the average citizen. As a technical expert, he rarely had to deal with interrogations and suspects. Only now, due to the extreme urgency of the present witch hunt, was he given such a dirty job, which he disliked. Yet an order is an order, and the colonel's words at yesterday's meeting had left no room for discussion. 'No detainee should leave the interrogation room without giving a name. It is an order. Keep in mind that we have only three days to find out who is the jokesmith. If we fail, all of us will be axed and sent to foot patrol. Comrade Elena was adamant in this regard,' the Colonel had said.

"'Well then. Can you give me a name?' the officer asked again.

"'I don't know the name. Please believe me. I would gladly tell you if I could. I swear on my mother's grave. I don't know. I don't know who that guy was.' Peter was desperate. 'Please believe me,' he implored.

"The major checked his wristwatch. It was getting late. He had just remembered the tickets he had. Ullanova, a famous Russian ballerina, was in town to dance in Tchaikovsky's *Swan Lake* that night. No matter how much he loved ballet and wanted to see Ullanova, the way things were going, he wouldn't be able to make it. The officer was caught on the horns of a dilemma. On the one hand, he was inclined to believe Peter, about whom he had already formed a definite impression. The guy could not or would not produce the information they were looking for. On the other hand, the Colonel's order was quite clear, and he had to obtain a name. A most annoying situation, especially considering the new girlfriend he had invited to that night's show. She should be waiting for him, so young and attractive, he thought pensively, lighting a cigarette.

"'Sergeant,' he said, 'I have to make a phone call. Take the prisoner to the waiting room. We should give him a little time to think it over.'

"'Yes, Comrade Major,' the sergeant said and snatched Peter brutally by one arm.

"Peter stood up. The pain in his leg was more than he could bear. 'I can't walk,' he said.

"'Yes, you can,' said the sergeant and grabbed him with both hands. The sergeant was strong and easily supported him, but every step required an agonizing effort from Peter. They were at the door when the officer seemed to have an afterthought.

"'Sergeant, give him a little preparation. Not too much. Understand?' said the major, who knew well what he had ordered.

"The waiting room was at the end of the corridor, and when they arrived, Peter felt completely exhausted. The pain in his leg, the headache, and the turmoil made him feel he was in a living nightmare. He craved a pause, a quiet moment to allow him the time to gather his thoughts, to regain strength. He hoped to find it in that room. Unfortunately, there were no chairs, not even a bench, in that windowless, poorly lit room. There was a toilet in a corner and a sink. On the messy, wet, and slippery floor were spread pell-mell a few rags, a dirty pail, a blanket, ropes of different sizes, several pieces of lumber, and other objects Peter couldn't identify. An awful stench prevailed.

"There was also a man in the room, smoking and looking like the sergeant's twin brother. He didn't move when they entered but stood and expressionlessly stared at them.

"'Look what I am bringing in for a little preparation,' the sergeant said. He pushed Peter towards the man.

"Peter stumbled, lost his balance and would have fallen if the man had not caught him. He held Peter with a hand and, with the other, punched him in the face. The smashing of his nose cartilage resounded painfully in Peter's shattered skull. He felt broken teeth in the mouth and the strange salty taste of the blood gushing out. Instinctively, he tried to back up to protect his face with the arms and was met by another blow, this time in the kidneys. The sergeant expertly applied it from behind to produce as much damage as possible. Peter gave a loud cry.

"'Don't push me, bandit,' the sergeant shouted.

"'This guy is crazy,' the other man said, punching Peter successively in the face and under the belt in quick sequence. Both men continued to hit Peter, who swung like a punching ball from one man to another until he blacked out and slumped facedown to the concrete floor.

"'This guy's got no guts,' the sergeant said then spat on the floor and lit a cigarette, offering a second one to his partner. Obviously, they needed a break after such brisk exercise.

"'What do you expect?' the other man answered. He kicked Peter a few times and pushed with the feet, as people do with logs, in order to turn him face up.

"Peter lay unconscious, disfigured and bleeding. The sergeant took the pail and emptied its contents on the beaten man. The cold water worked, and Peter started moving slowly. With great difficulty, he lifted himself on knees and elbows, his head hanging low, close to the floor. He mumbled unintelligibly and breathed heavily. The blood was dripping from his nose and mouth, spotting the dirty floor with red.

"'Hey, mister! Wake up! This is not a dormitory,' the sergeant said and laughed.

"The other man dropped the cigarette butt, extinguished it carefully with the sole of his shoe, and then—with a swift movement—kicked Peter in the stomach. Peter fell on the side with a groan.

"'Stop messing up my floor, mister,' the man barked. 'I will teach him a lesson,' he told the sergeant and threw the wet blanket on Peter's motionless, contorted body. Then he grabbed a short length of thick rope and started hitting Peter indiscriminately, over and over again. 'Don't mess up my floor, don't mess up my floor,' he repeated after every blow, white froth forming at the corner of his ugly mouth.

"The phone rang and the sergeant rushed to answer, signaling the man to stop. 'Yes, Comrade Major. Yes, immediately,' he assured the caller. 'The major wants the arrested back immediately,' he told his colleague. 'Let's take him there. Quick, quick.'

"They poured a pail of water over the inert body. This time, Peter didn't move. When nothing happened even after the third pail, the men dragged him to the sink and put his head under the wide-open tap, drenching it with cold running water. Finally, Peter started coming to. In a hurry, the men tried to make him stand, but his legs wouldn't support his body. They tried a few more times, swearing and punching him, without success.

"Unsupported, Peter's body fell to the floor like a broken doll. He didn't open his swollen and blackened eyes. His face was terribly tumefied, and blood flowed in a continuous narrow stream from his nostrils and mouth. A weak groan came from between his broken lips, accompanying every breath.

"'Stand up, mister!' shouted the sergeant in his ear, shaking Peter roughly by the arm, 'the comrade major wants to talk with you.' Peter didn't appear to understand, and it was obvious that he wouldn't be able to walk either.

"The phone rang again.

"'Don't answer,' the sergeant said. 'Let's carry him there.'

"The two men dragged Peter along the floor, pulled him up, and propped his body against the wall, beside the sink.

"'You grab him by the legs, I will grab from under the arms,' the sergeant ordered. In their hurry, they somehow let Peter go too early, and his body slipped and fell with a twist. In its falling trajectory, his head met with the edge of the sink and hit it hard, producing a muffled metallic sound before banging loudly on the concrete floor. Peter stopped groaning and was now bleeding copiously from the ears and from a wide open wound in his skull.

"The phone was still ringing.

"'Don't bother,' the sergeant shouted to his colleague who wanted to answer the phone. 'Grab the bandit, and let's go.'

"The major was waiting in the front of the open door when they came to the interrogation room carrying the beaten and bleeding body.

"'What the hell have you done?' the major irritably asked.

"'A little preparation, according to your orders, Comrade Major,' the sergeant smartly answered as they put the unconscious man on the chair, holding him from both sides. Peter's head fell on the desk, where the blood started gathering in a quickly growing pool.

"'This is not a little, Sergeant. What do you want me to do with this mess?' the major asked.

"A group of men stopped in front of the open door, and one of them came in. The major and the two men straightened up and gave him a respectful salute. Without support, Peter's body slipped off the chair and fell like a sack on the floor, with a thump.

"'What happened, Comrade Major?' the newcomer asked. 'Leave him there,' he said to the two subordinates who jumped to put Peter back.

"'The sergeant had misunderstood my orders, Comrade Colonel.'

"'I can see that, Major. Who is this man?'

"'One who allegedly heard the anecdote on a bus and pretended not to know the source, Comrade Colonel.'

"'On a bus? Which bus?'

"'Yes, Comrade Colonel. This morning on bus number 36, and . . .'

"'Just a moment, Major,' the colonel stopped him. 'Stănescu, come here,' he called to one of the people waiting outside. A young man left the group and entered the room, coming to attention. 'Stănescu, can you recognize the man on the floor?'

"The young man knelt beside Peter, intently examining his disfigured features. 'I can't be a hundred percent sure, Comrade Colonel, because he is all messed up. But he might have been the one just in front of me on that bus when my prisoner told the anecdote,' said the young man. 'Your case is dead, Comrade Major,' he concluded and stood up. 'The rigor is setting in, Comrade Colonel,' he reported.

"The colonel ignored what Stănescu had said. 'See that guy there, Major?' he pointed to one of the men in the group waiting outside. The man's face was swollen, bruised, and he had a black eye. 'That's the guy who told the anecdote this morning on bus number 36. Lieutenant Stănescu arrested him soon after.' He turned around and left the room. The lieutenant followed suit and carefully closed the door after him.

"The major put the papers in the folder. He gave the two subordinates a cursory glance, checked his wristwatch, and then lit a cigarette. 'Call the doctor, Sergeant. Clean up the mess, and bring the certificate to my office,' he ordered. After all, if everything went well and the traffic wasn't too heavy, he might be in time for the ballet, he thought. 'I guess that takes care of everything,' said the major aloud and left the room in a hurry."

After he finished the story, Dăscălescu remained silent, as if absorbed in his own thoughts. He was still in the doorframe, where he had stood from the beginning, half turned toward the town below. The light of the full moon, much higher now in the sky, gave his drawn face a ghostly pallor. He looked older and tired than he really was: a middle-aged man with gray hair and shriveled features, tormented by some secret suffering.

Nobody made any comment. They just fumbled with cigarettes and lighters, eventually coughing to mask their feelings. The noise of the happy town poured incessantly through the open door like an inexhaustible waterfall.

"Poor Peter," Lia whispered in the end with a deep sigh. "Poor people."

"Yes. Poor people scythed like hay—a wasteful, bloody harvest," Dăscălescu said as if waking up from a dream.

"Poor little baby, left without father," Ana said, her voice veiled by sadness.

"So many unknown martyrs," Stefan whispered, overwhelmed by emotion.

Suddenly, it was silence in the room, if one ignored the town's background noise. Abdur stood up, looking preoccupied, and walked to the table and put his mug among the dirty dishes. "That truly was a moving story," he said. "How did you learn all those details, sir?" he asked Dăscălescu.

"Good question, young man." Dăscălescu's voice sounded stronger and confident now. He lit another cigarette and checked his wristwatch. "Tomorrow, I have to catch the first bus to Athens. There is a new church in Brahami, and I've got a painting job to do there. I must run," he said and left as abruptly as he had come in.

FIRST INTERMEZZO

The rough Turkish boy went to the Canadian Embassy in Athens. The boy was almost nineteen but seemed older because of his big frame and square shoulders. Only the childish expression of his dazzling, incredibly green eyes—always inquiring and wondering at the world's marvels—gave him away.

He showed up at the door, wearing a confident expression on his round, chubby face, which was spotted by a bad case of acne. While he talked, his cheeks turned crimson, accentuating the sickening dark purple of the awful pustules and giving him a fierce look. He wanted to see the consul, he explained in halting English.

They didn't let him past the receptionist, a middle-aged Greek woman speaking cultured English with an Oxford accent. "What for?" she asked. "What do you want from the consul?"

He wrinkled his forehead that glistened with perspiration and gave her a smile intended to be engaging. "Me go Canada . . . emigration . . ."

"What's your profession?" the woman asked, unimpressed by his smile.

"Communist," he answered with naive pride, forcing his voice to sound mannish and looking around to make sure people had heard it. "Me communist."

"I didn't ask that. What do you do for a living? What kind of work you do?"

"Oh, that . . ." he said, sudden understanding illuminating his ravaged face. "Revolution, street fight," he continued, punching an invisible adversary and making gestures as if throwing stones. "Bad, criminal policeman . . . fascist government . . ." The boy straightened up and took a deep breath, expanding his thorax. "Me for people," he concluded, pounding his large chest with clenched fists, producing a deep, wild sound.

Soul Searching

A strong wind pummeled the shores of the Aegean, chasing white horses across the channel. The breakers thundered along the shore, crashing on the rocky cliffs and splashing white foam and salty spray high in the air. Even the friendly cove where they usually swam in the afternoons, so cozy and quiet at other times, was now a boiling cauldron, prey to uncontrollable wild forces. Its turquoise crystalline waters had been replaced overnight by angry masses of gray-green steaming fluid. As if in a bad dream, the tamed, purring sea of tourist lore had metamorphosed into a growling beast animated by destructive fury.

At the cliff's edge, it was difficult to withstand the pressure of the wind; but the air was warm, and the sky was cerulean blue and transparent. Defying the elements, Stefan stubbornly stayed admiring the *tableau vivant* unfolding in front of him. Moved by its savage beauty, he applied himself to record in his memory the Odyssean imagery: the picturesque roaring sea and the distant colorful islands, which appeared much closer than they really were. As far as he could see down the coast, every detail was perfectly clear, for the unrelenting wind had removed all traces of dust and moisture from the atmosphere. The closeness was an illusion, but the wind was real, and he shortly had to climb down to seek shelter.

After crossing sun-scorched, weedy fields, Stefan came to the first cluster of houses, chaotically sprawled on the town's outskirts. Following one of the well-beaten, dusty paths, he emerged onto a wide street bordered by hibiscuses trained like trees. Turning a corner and walking briskly, he passed in front of the textile factory where the hum of machinery went on undisturbed even at that late hour. Soon the street joined a public walk paved with concrete slabs running along the sea up into the harbor. The promenade he now entered, populated with benches scattered under young orange trees loaded with unripe dark-green fruits, was the habitual haunt of quarrelsome dogs living in noisy packs. Abandoned by tourists, they subsisted on the generosity of local people, who occasionally fed them amid a concert of barks and squeals. Silent for the moment, the canines slept under a few skimpy bushes and paid no attention to him.

Here in the sheltered bay, there was no wind, and the misleading tranquility of the harbor made Stefan wonder if the raging storm he just witnessed was real. The long-forgotten ancients who had chosen the location of the port thousands of years ago had known very well what they were doing, he thought gratefully.

For more than an hour, Stefan loafed about the deserted sea walk. He felt depressed, his mind prey to the gloomiest anxieties, and didn't want to upset his family in the camp. To put things in perspective, he always needed to be alone.

It all began after work when, on a sudden impulse, he had gone to the post office and phoned his parents in Romania. The news from home was bad as his father had recently fallen sick. Stefan knew that his mother also wasn't in good health, having suffered lately from chronic heart troubles. She would now have to carry the burden of her husband's illness alone because help wasn't readily available. Added to the shortage of food and fuel endemic in communist Romania and without owning a car, caring at an old age for sick family members required almost superhuman physical and financial resources that his mother couldn't afford. Stefan, their only child, was aware of the situation and felt guilty.

Stefan's problem was rooted in love. He loved his father and, on a more intellectual level, genuinely admired him. Descended from free peasant stock, with recorded ancestors going back more than seven hundred years, his father had inherited a balanced attitude toward life and the world, compounded with a strong character and thirst for knowledge. His honesty, both professional and social, was well-known among the country's academics. An educator and noted scholar all his life, he had lovingly passed on these qualities to his son, together with a healthy respect for hard work. As a semiretired emeritus professor, he continued his scientific activity despite old age, failing health, and increased material difficulties inherent to the life of those ruled by bankrupt Marxist governments. In his late seventies, he had been energetic and outgoing until the political secret police started pestering him and the stress of their unwanted attention proved to be too much for his already fragile constitution. His son's defection was no doubt the last drop in a long series of health-undermining events. This unexpected consequence of his well-intended action now weighed heavily upon Stefan, who dreaded anything that could hurt his father.

With his mother, it was even worse, because Stefan was truly the apple of her eye. She was ready to sacrifice everything for him: her comfort, her time, and her money—even her life—if necessary. It was more than he deserved, Stefan objectively admitted. He would often remember her as she was in his early years, a loving mother and beautiful young woman who renounced the pleasures of social life for the sake of her child. After his birth, she had stopped going to the parties she used to frequent before and where, admired by men and envied by women, she sparkled with wit and charm. People who Stefan met on different occasions and who knew his mother from the past would endlessly praise her. "Seeing her dance was a breathtaking experience," or "Your mother had the unreal ease of movement of a fairytale character," or "She was a graceful conversationalist, an outstanding personality," they would often conclude their reminiscences, making him feel embarrassed and proud. His mother also quit playing tennis, her beloved hobby, when he first got sick with one of those contagious diseases of early childhood. She never played tennis again, always staying with him, caring for him when sick, watching him sleep, teaching him manners, helping with homework, preparing exquisite foods, or inventing games and toys to entertain him. Things went smoothly between them for many years, well into his teens. Then suddenly, Stefan and his mother had a hard time adjusting their relationship when, budding into manhood, he affirmed his emerging personality. In her deep love, she found enough understanding to forgive him time and again when he hurt her. Remorseful, Stefan acknowledged her efforts and most of the time tried to avoid direct confrontation.

Maintaining a well-balanced relationship proved to be even more difficult after he got married and had children of his own. For years, his mother couldn't get used to the idea of another woman in her son's life. This put a lot of unnecessary strain on their otherwise united family. Luckily, Lia was a conciliator, endlessly making concessions to her mother-in-law for the sake of common happiness. Soon, it became obvious that there was no love lost between those two. Caught in the middle, Stefan acted as a lightning rod, struggling to deflate potentially explosive situations and placate both women at the same time, which wasn't always easy.

The years passed, and with advancing maturity, Stefan learned how to control his own impulsiveness and that of others as well, getting better at his balancing act. He managed to maintain an uneasy truce so the families could help each other when sickness afflicted one of them or when the chronic penury reached acute levels as often happened in the Soviet system. On such occasions, waiting in enormous queues and spending long hours, sometimes days, on the street outside stores in order to get only trifles of essential supplies required concerted efforts. Even the children weren't spared. After returning from school, they would take their turn in the lineups in order to allow the grandparents, who started in the early hours of the morning, a much-needed rest. The parents would relieve them after work, and later, the elders would resume their place in line. This merry-go-round went on year after year, requiring resilience and good health, especially during harsh winters. In the absence of young family members, ill health was a liability with catastrophic repercussions, and so was old age. By defecting, Stefan had deprived his parents of their precious lifeline. It was his fault, and he had to face the consequences.

The more he thought things over, the guiltier he felt. Yet the truth was that his parents had once had their chance to avoid all that misery. It was at the end of the last war when his father was invited to teach at a French university. For a year or so, despite heavy Russian military presence on its soil, Romania enjoyed limited independence under a transitional democratic government; and everyone, including his father, thought the political situation would improve. Deceptive promises made by various British and American envoys convinced wishful-thinking Romanians that the Soviets wouldn't be allowed to take over their country. It was a time of democratic resurgence, and the burning desire to rebuild their country after the ravages of war was on every patriot's mind. It was his duty to stay home and help the reconstruction effort, Stefan's father believed. Accordingly, he naively postponed his departure for another occasion, which never presented itself because as soon as they seized power, the communists closed the borders. That sealed the professor's fate, his dedication to the country being rewarded by Stalinist-type slavery.

At the time these critical events took place, Stefan was an eager and idealistic adolescent. Good at school, he had a lot of free time to read, mainly about exotic lands and high adventure. Stimulated by such enticing literature, he daydreamed about daring faraway expeditions. Like many of his generation, he believed that North America, with its Wild West and its marvelous technical progress, was the promised land. In his youthful enthusiasm, Stefan would have given anything to immigrate there and urged his parents to leave the country. When that prospect died, he was bitterly disappointed. Only several years later did he realize that as tempting as living abroad might have been, emigration was never in his father's mind. Well-versed in history, the professor knew there was always an end to every regime, and he hoped for the fall of the Soviet Empire. Sooner or later, Romania would eventually be free again, he repeatedly told his impatient son. In the meantime, an intellectual's duty was to make sure that sciences progressed in their country and the real values of Romanian culture were preserved for that hypothetical future. A die-hard nationalist and a staunch patriot, he often used to say that there was nothing more precious one could give his country than his own life and that one must be devoted to one's homeland up to the last breath.

Love and admiration for his father notwithstanding, Stefan's opinions suffered a radical transformation as he came of age. On the one hand, Stefan continued to believe in his father's principles for a long time. On the other, everyday, he had to pay lip service to the new rulers and their philosophy in order to survive. According to their definition, patriotism meant unconditional love for the Soviet Union. Stefan abhorred this concept as he witnessed the continuous plunder of Romania's resources by the Russians. Also, he had to show continuous enthusiasm for Marxist-Leninist ideology in a display of bombastic verbosity contradicted at every step by the reality of daily life. To keep everything and everyone under control, prisons, torture chambers, and labor camps mushroomed all over the country as the totalitarian system's expansion eradicated any real or imaginary opposition. A network of spies and informers recruited from every strata of society was at work to keep those odious institutions busy at all times. Thus most of Romania's best—subtle philosophers, great writers, the finest poets, professionals of every kind, students, and even farmers—were rounded up by the repressive secret police under Soviet supervision and sent to perish in the infamous gaols. Even relatives and friends of his family became victims of the regime's witch hunt.

Stefan himself narrowly escaped imprisonment three times: first as a high school student and then twice during his university years. He was lucky, but his classmate Mircea was not. Arrested when he was only fourteen for singing a satirical song about the inept leaders, the boy spent the following three years in prison without a trial. Terminally ill when released, Mircea died a few weeks after his return home, just days before his seventeenth birthday. His emaciated face and grayed hair, as he lay in a shabby coffin in his parents' dinning room, told Stefan more about communism than any slogan of the official propaganda.

It took Stefan time to reach his own conclusions. The permanent exercise of insincerity, essential for individual preservation, eliminated reciprocal trust from any kind of human relationship. It was a life full of falsity and contradictions; and that, associated with the never-ending bootlicking, made him sick. As his frustration increased, he asked himself every so often what was behind the abstract concept of homeland his father loved enough that he was ready to sacrifice his life for it. In the meantime, Romania and its society went through radical changes. Private property gradually disappeared, taken over by the state, and private initiative was totally suppressed. The vast majority of the population lived in government-owned housing, ate food bought from the government's stores, dressed in clothes produced by government factories and sold in its outlets, and traveled by public transportation. The same factotum government employed everyone who was able to work. Bureaucracy reached mind-boggling levels, with the most irrational results. For the people, existence was bleak and insecure, always on the verge of poverty and with scarce hope for the future. In contrast, an oligarchy of political opportunist upstarts lived in extravagant luxury. If the country had previously supported one king, now there were several hundred, all hungry for absolute power and determined to keep it at all cost, surrounded by sycophantic public adulation. Were they part of that homeland which he was taught to love and for which he should be prepared to sacrifice himself? Stefan didn't believe so. Neither were worthy enough of such sacrifice the torturers, the spies, the obtuse and corrupt bureaucrats, nor the impudent staff of the bribe-ridden public services. The remaining amorphous masses also didn't account for much, nor did the new unprincipled intelligentsia.

If not the people, then perhaps it was the earth that could make the supreme sacrifice worthwhile—the land of his ancestors—with its rich plains, lush rolling hills, and scenic mountains basking in the generous sunshine under lovely blue skies. Yet none of these belonged to him anyway, and he couldn't even dream of building a house for himself and his family no matter how modest a spot he might choose. Not to mention the continuous rape of the country's riches in the name of proletarian internationalism and the irrational development of a monstrous industrialization that brutally altered the landscape and destroyed the environment. In only a few years, the country's famous natural treasures such as the primeval mountain forests, the wild and unique Danube Delta, and many others became almost extinct due to sheer mismanagement. *To love what?* Stefan asked himself. After all, there were many other beautiful places in the world; and in order to enjoy them, nobody asked you to give up your own life in exchange. *The only thing one needed in order to enjoy those places was freedom, whose symbol was a passport,* he thought.

The final straw came one day when a posse of four securitate officers broke into his father's home and started a search without prior notice or warrant. The old man was working on one of his scientific papers when they banged on the door. The commotion terrified Stefan's mother who, as a consequence, suffered a heart attack. She nearly died, but the professor held his ground and didn't sign a sham statement, which would have incriminated him. The search went on for fifteen hours, during which his parents were not allowed to leave, eat, or drink; and no medical assistance for his mother was called until they were done. Pictures were taken off their frames, carpets were turned upside down, bedding and clothes were searched and piled up in the middle of the rooms, and every piece of paper, including thousands of books from the professor's library, were thoroughly examined. Stefan remembered the day very well because Margaret Thatcher, at the time the British opposition leader, was visiting Bucharest. Ironically, the same evening that the search was taking place at Stefan's parents' home, Thatcher attended a banquet given in her honour by the Romanian dictator, during which she heaped praise on the bloodthirsty bully for "his respect of human rights."

The securitate officers subsequently continued their inopportune visits, sometimes taking his father with them for long interrogations, although they couldn't find anything significant against the old man. It never became clear what all the nasty trouble was about. The events, however, critically affected the professor's health; and he visibly started aging much faster than before.

If something like that could have happened to a man of his father's honesty and stature, what could anyone else expect? Stefan asked himself. If it had been obvious from the start that no value was recognized by the system, now it was proven that even a lifetime of exemplary work wasn't appreciated. Sacrifices and dedication were of no consequence when paranoia pushed the leaders to make haphazard use of their absolute power. From their perspective, everybody was expendable; therefore, repressive excesses would periodically put talent and creativity to waste just to keep the crowd regimented. The "beloved homeland" was a Moloch that mindlessly devoured its young and at best was an empty concept devoid of meaning. Instead of being governed on a just-contract basis, the new oligarchy saw society as a herd of milking cows. All the country's resources and wealth were supposed to belong to the people, while—in fact—the control was concentrated in the greedy hands of the dictator and his cronies. Citizens were allowed to enjoy life only through their representatives while demagogic slogans preached abstinence and patience with the never-ending privations. Everyone was asked to make sacrifices for the glory of the communism, except for a chosen few. After much soul-searching, Stefan finally realized how stupid he was to give his unique and precious life for such blatant crookery. He was no longer young, and a good part of his life had already been wrongly spent, Stefan concluded. The time had come to put an end to this foolishness.

His father, sensitive to what was happening around him, was not at all surprised by Stefan's change of heart. Although he disagreed with the latter's conclusions and what he heard went against his deepest convictions, the old man would never have interfered in his son's life. Although the professor openly cautioned Stefan about the dangers and difficulties of what he saw as risky endeavor, his personal feelings or well-being were never mentioned in their rare and limited discussions. At issue was his son's happiness and not his own, and Stefan felt that he had free hand to do whatever he thought appropriate. It took years before the opportunity to escape presented itself, and by then all of them were older, already struggling with the ineluctable problems of advancing age. He had taken the irrevocable step—finding out that his father's tacit understanding was of little comfort. It didn't give him extenuating circumstances and didn't help in the least to ease his guilt. Even his father's unwillingness to take a chance, when presented with one in the past, was irrelevant now. Unfortunately, there was nothing Stefan could have done to bring events back to their remote starting point, and this simple truth hit home.

Evening was setting in; and the prolonged walk, if it hadn't eliminated his woe, managed somehow to appease Stefan's remorse. The storm had abated a little, and already, a few early walkers had put in an appearance. The factory shift had probably ended because presently, a noisy crowd surrounded him, disturbing his train of thought. Caught up in his mental turmoil, he wasn't aware of his fatigue until it suddenly overcame him. He felt mentally and physically exhausted. Although he couldn't find complete peace, it was time to go home.

He took a shortcut along the wide alley behind the police station and was walking under the tall palm trees when he heard someone calling him. The street appeared empty; and at first, in the falling darkness, he couldn't see anyone. After being repeatedly called, he noticed a man in shorts and a white undershirt seated barefoot at a table by the sidewalk. The man gesticulated invitingly; and Stefan made for the table, where he recognized Thanasis, the policeman, off duty and casually dressed. The young Greek, although neat and trim as usual, looked completely different without his impeccably clean and always freshly ironed uniform.

A bowl of salad, a loaf of bread, and several small glasses were on the table; and a conspicuous demijohn was underneath it. Thanasis, judging by his half-empty glass, was enjoying himself in the cool of the evening. "Have a seat, sir," he invited Stefan. They were on quite good terms, and the policeman often dropped by for a coffee or a chat with the Romanian family. Since enrolling in an adult education program, he would occasionally consult Stefan for help with his English homework. "Where have you been, sir?" he asked. In spite of being friendly and warm, he never exceeded a certain polite formality in their relationship.

"I went for a walk," Stefan answered unenthusiastically.

"What's the matter? You don't look happy." Thanasis lifted the demijohn and filled one of the spare glasses before returning the bulging narrow-necked bottle cased in wicker under the table. He handed the glass to Stefan. "Try this good Greek medicine. It cures anything, sir." His fine face was illuminated by a broad smile.

The intensely sweet smell of anise tickled Stefan's nose and palate. He liked ouzo although it was new to him. He had never had the opportunity to taste it until another sympathetic Greek policeman offered him a drink in Florina. It was during the memorable day of his defection, and to Stefan, ouzo had since remained associated with the taste of his newly acquired freedom.

They clinked their glasses. "Ya mas! Health to us," toasted Thanasis.

"Ya mas!" Stefan answered, taking a mouthful of the aromatic liquor. "This is quite strong," he commented after the first gulp.

"It is. A relative of mine makes it in his village. Did you have dinner?" asked the Greek.

"No. I went for a walk after work."

"Then take some salad and bread. It is not good to drink on an empty stomach." The policeman's voice sounded concerned. "What's bothering you, sir?"

"My father," answered Stefan. "I phoned Bucharest and found him quite sick."

"Oh, no!" said Thanasis. "That's not good news. Surely you have got other brothers and sisters to take care of him. Haven't you?"

"No! And Mother is not in good health either. She is not young, that's the problem." Stefan looked at Thanasis with dejected eyes.

"I understand," said the policeman, speaking slowly and watching Stefan thoughtfully. "Take some salad, sir. Here, with this piece of bread," he said pushing a chunk in Stefan's hand. The bread was fresh and still a little warm.

Thanasis refilled the glasses to the brim. "Let's drink," he said and solemnly lifted his glass. "May the Lord restore your father's health."

They drank in silence. When the last drop was gone, Stefan tried the salad. The vegetables were fresh and tasty, with buttery feta cheese generously spread over the oregano-spiced greens. But he didn't feel hungry and, after a couple of mouthfuls, couldn't eat anymore. Yet the pleasant warmth induced by the ouzo flushed his cheeks, and a sort of mild detachment from the present and its troubles took hold of him. Someone inside the house turned on the light hanging above the table. Thanasis poured another round from the demijohn.

"Please don't fill mine," Stefan said. "Soon, I will be so drunk that you will have to carry me home."

"No, no. You won't get drunk from so little, if you eat. Why don't you eat? My *horyatiki salata* is the best Greek salad you can get in this town. I am a specialist. Ask anyone, and they will tell you." The young man was all smiles again, pushing the bowl and the bread toward Stefan. "It is very good. Just try it, sir. Please."

"I like it. I honestly do. I tried, and it is very good. Thank you. There is nothing wrong with your salad. It's me," Stefan struggled to explain. "I cannot eat right now." He didn't want to hurt his host's feelings. Absentmindedly, he took a sip from his ouzo. "I love my parents a lot. And it breaks my heart to know they are alone, old, and sick. If they died, I would never forgive myself. Never. That's all. You perhaps cannot understand."

There was a long moment of silence. Then without warning, Thanasis leapt to his feet, his face crimson and screwed into a scowl. He hit his broad chest a few times with a clenched fist. "I don't understand, you say? You really don't know what you are talking about. You have no idea how it is to have the entire family wiped out," cried the Greek, a ferocious look distorting his handsome face. "I know better than anyone what that means. Mine were all killed, massacred. My good father, my beloved mother, my dear older brother, and two beautiful sisters. The beasts slaughtered my baby brother in my mother's arms. Do you know what that means? Do you know how it feels?" He paused briefly to catch his breath, fixing Stefan with bloodshot eyes. "I suffered so much you wouldn't believe. I thought it would kill me. Oh, God! Oh, God, how can you tolerate such crimes?" His voice faded, ending in heavy sobs. He sat down exhausted, holding his head in his hands, tears spilling uncontrollably from under his eyelids and running down his shaven cheeks.

Thanasis's unexpected outburst of grief startled Stefan. He watched him in utter silence. He had, for the moment, forgotten his own worries. Moved by compassion, he put his arm around the policeman's shoulders. "I am sorry, Thanasis. I am awfully sorry. I didn't know about your family. What happened?"

"The Turks killed them."

"The Turks? Where? Why?" Stefan could not believe what he just heard. His own people had suffered under, fought with, and were killed by the Turks. That happened in past centuries when the Ottoman empire conquered the Balkans. Both Thanasis and he were too young to be part of those events.

"Seven years ago in Cyprus," answered the Greek, wiping his eyes with his handkerchief, struggling to compose himself and taking a long sip from his glass. "I am a Cypriot. Do you understand now?"

Stefan remembered the dramatic Cypriot struggle for independence, the subsequent bloody fight between the Greek and Turkish communities, and the ensuing division of the island. Yet he could not have imagined that things had been so bad. "I am really sorry, Thanasis. I didn't know they killed civilians during those skirmishes. I thought it was just the armed factions that wrestled with each other," he said.

"No. It was more than that. There were gangs of hooligans on both sides roaming through the countryside without control or restraint. I was studying in Athens at the time and only later found out how bad it was. One day, a gang of Turks came to my village. My father was in the vineyard. He was lucky—they shot him on the spot. The others endured much worse. The hoodlums rounded up the entire population and locked them in one of the local cooperative's wineries. They broke into the cellars, got drunk, and started raping the women and girls. A small group of young prisoners was forced to dig a hole behind the main building. That was when some teenagers escaped. The terrified boys found a hiding place in an empty vat, abandoned in a dark corner of the cellar, and witnessed the atrocities that followed. The fresh hole was only a couple of feet deep when the gang leader ordered the people to be brought out of the winery and shot. The bodies were thrown into the shallow excavation, and the executioners covered them with earth. Several people, only half buried, weren't dead and screamed for help, imploring mercy. The killers didn't pay any attention to their pleas and continued to cover them with dirt until it was quiet." The Greek paused, breathing heavily. His face was ghastly, wet from his tears. He stared absentmindedly in Stefan's direction with haggard eyes. It was obvious that the scene he had just described was still unrolling on the invisible screen of his imagination.

What could Stefan say? What could he do to appease his friend? Thanasis's suffering impressed upon him the unfathomable depth of people's souls and the infinite capacity of humans to bear pain. Who could have guessed this young man's tragic burden, knowing him only as he went about his daily job with kindness and efficiency, always cheerful, apparently undisturbed by anything? Obviously, no man alive was exempt from pain. Here was someone hit by a terrible calamity, still mourning his family, a man who—in spite of everything—was able to put on a good face and carry out his duties as eagerly as his ancestors, the Homeric heroes, had done in the past.

"And now," said Thanasis with offended exasperation, "the Turks are coming here, and I must protect them." It was true; every day, more and more Turkish refugees were brought to the camp. These were the members of banned left-wing movements who had escaped to Greece in order to avoid imprisonment or the death penalty. Turkey was on the brink of civil war, and the military junta installed in Ankara had decided to put an end to the apparently never-ending radical squabbling and rioting. In the eyes of the junta, no measures were harsh enough when it came to getting rid of the troublemakers, who ran for their lives. Throngs of them were leaving their country in a big hurry.

"Perhaps they are not the same people," Stefan said timidly.

"Perhaps. Who knows?" answered Thanasis. "I saw some of the newcomers' files. Most of them are communists of various affiliations: pro-Soviets, pro-Maoists, and God knows what else—all of them ready to cut each other's throats. A few are wanted in their country for murder. What do you think about that?"

"You know why I am here, don't you? I don't like communists. If anyone asked me, they should have been sent back. I don't want them in the same refugee camp with me. On the other hand, you must remember how much your Cypriot ex-leader, Archbishop Makarios, loved communists. He was one of those world statesmen who cultivated their friendship. And he didn't even make a secret of it," said Stefan.

"That's nonsense. Makarios was a saintly man, a Christian, and a hero. His ideal was the union of Cyprus with Greece, the *enosis*. He was the very heart of it. He was not a communist. Believe me, sir." The young Greek spoke with conviction and ardor.

"I didn't say he was a communist." Stefan's tone was conciliatory, almost apologetic. "However, I recall the archbishop's visits to Romania, where he was always received with great fanfare and lavishly entertained by the dictator. The population was herded into the streets of Bucharest and forced to acclaim him on his passage from one banquet to another. I know it because I was one of those people waiting long hours for him to pass by. Every time he arrived or left, Makarios embraced Ceausescu in front of the cameras and in his speeches called him his beloved friend. Meanwhile, Romanian priests and religious people were detained, some of them tortured and killed. I never heard Makarios taking a stand in their favor. They, not Ceaușescu, should have been his friends in Christ, shouldn't they?"

"Maybe he didn't know about those priests."

"Maybe. Perhaps in seeking support for his cause, Makarios had to make countless concessions. Politics is a dirty business. But this is irrelevant. The point I was trying to make was that the Turks you have here are more than probably not the same as those who ravaged your island. Protecting these ones, not that I like you doing it, doesn't mean you are protecting your family's killers," Stefan said.

"Considering their files, they could be even worse. Don't you think so?" Thanasis looked inquisitively at his guest.

"That's a completely different story, my friend. You must surely be aware that the Canadians, in order to process our recent immigration application, have asked for my criminal record from Bucharest. From the same people I tried to escape, do you understand? I wrongly assumed that we were out of their grip. I was mistaken. They still hold us in their claws. We have been awaiting the answer for almost three months now. A lot depends upon it. In fact, my entire family's future does, and I am awfully concerned what the outcome will be. The Romanian authorities, you see, can put anything in my record, even murder. Who can prevent them? How will I be able to defend myself against false accusations if the records have been doctored? I will probably never know what they kept on me in their secret files . . . May I ask you, what would your reaction be upon being given such information? Would you believe me or them?"

The Greek gave him a furtive glance and didn't answer. An initial fleeting look of surprise was soon gone, yet mixed feelings continued to alter his facial expression in quick succession, like the play of changing reflections on still waters. He knew as well as Stefan did that police everywhere work without exception with the evidence at hand. Thanasis respected Stefan and would have had great difficulty dismissing a claim of honesty made by him even against official evidence. There was also the old reciprocal sympathy between the Greeks and the Romanians and their no less common and ancient hatred of Turks. Things were terribly complicated. Deep inside, he acknowledged that the Romanian's rhetorical question was a valid one, and this realization clearly put him out of his stride. He fumbled with the glasses and poured another round. Thoughtful furrows appeared between the policeman's eyebrows. That and his serious, concentrated composure were the only signs that something unusual was going on in his mind.

It was now dark in the alley. The velvety sky above was alight with stardust twinkling and shimmering sharply over the tops of the palm trees. Somewhere, a door was slammed noisily, producing a resounding bang in the quiet of the evening. An angry female voice shouted a rebuke, and a child started crying.

Stefan checked his wristwatch. "It's late. I should go home," he said.

"Let's have this last one, sir." Thanasis pushed forth Stefan's full glass.

"Okay, if it is the last one," Stefan lightheartedly agreed as, considering the turmoil he had gone through, he now felt unexpectedly better. *After all,* he thought, *the Greek medicine had worked its promised magic.*

At the far end of the alley, a shapeless, uncertain black shadow detached itself from the dark background, first slowly, then quickly progressing in their direction. It twisted and changed its shape every moment, sometimes completely vanishing into the alley's darkness, only to pop up magically after a few seconds. The apparition introduced an intriguing and mysterious flavor into the laidback atmosphere. None of them could make out what it was. The suspense didn't last too long. Soon, they heard whistling, humming, and hurried footsteps on the sidewalk; and a man materialized out of the night. He walked briskly, guardedly singing an unfamiliar Oriental tune. Thanasis and Stefan watched the approaching stranger.

"It might be one of the Turks," Stefan ventured in a low voice. He had been having difficulties seeing in the dark lately and was just guessing.

"No, no. It is Abdur," Thanasis murmured. He put his glass on the table, and both men relaxed.

The Afghan greeted them effusively. He had been on his way to the camp when he noticed the pair sitting at the table and he came only to say hello, he explained. Abdur appeared excited and happy. He refused the drink Thanasis offered, starting instead to nibble salad from the bowl without invitation.

"Father, can I come to work with you tomorrow?" he asked, addressing Stefan and helping himself to more salad while Thanasis watched him with an amused expression. He knew the Afghan well, and they were sort of friends.

"Why not? Theodoros is always in need of an extra hand," Stefan answered. Theodoros was the owner of the farm where he lately worked every day. "I cannot guarantee that he will hire you, but we can try, my son."

"What about packing tomorrow? Are you ready? Isn't it the day after tomorrow that you are supposed to fly to the States, Abdur?" Thanasis asked. "You shouldn't work tomorrow."

"I renounced," Abdur answered, laughing carelessly. "And I need money. That's why I must work."

"You renounced what?" Stefan asked, shocked by what he had just heard.

Refugees awaited their flights with yearning, trepidation, and justified anxiety—and Abdur was no exception. After lingering for many months in the camp, flying out was the culmination of their dreams, the big day when the luckiest among them were given a new chance at life. For those who left the camp, it was the fulfillment of their cherished hopes of freedom, normality, and happiness in a new country. In the life of refugees, this was a major event, perhaps the most important day of their lives. To willingly give it up would have been madness, and so far, it was unheard of.

"I changed my mind. I am not in a hurry to go to the States right now. It would be better for me to hang about a little, I think." Abdur kept smiling broadly as he spoke. "I love Greece, you see, and I like you guys. Why leave so soon?"

"Abdur, my son, this is . . ." Stefan tried to find a mild word to express his disapproval.

"I know, I know. It sounds crazy." Abdur didn't let him finish, a carefree smile illuminating his dark complexion. "I'll be okay. Don't worry."

"I guess it is that blonde," Thanasis said. "Isn't it, Abdur?"

"What blonde?" Stefan asked.

"He knows who I am talking about. I saw them a few times on the beach." The Greek looked at Abdur with mock severity. "Come on, man, tell us the truth. It is for that girl that you have renounced America, isn't it?"

"She is beautiful!" Abdur exclaimed. His face was radiant.

"I know the story," the policeman said with bitterness in his voice. "I went through this a few times myself. Blonde is beautiful. Don't you have that saying, Abdur?"

"It's not what you think." Abdur wasn't smiling anymore, and he answered with certain reluctance. "We are very much in love. It is serious."

This is probably a joke, Stefan thought. He had finished his ouzo and stood up. His body was stiff and needed some stretching. After all that ouzo, he felt optimistic and his mind was sharp and clear. "Who is she? If I may ask."

"A Swedish girl from Stockholm, Father."

"Greece is packed with Swedish girls this time of the year, all blonde and looking for fun," Thanasis laughed at the Afghan.

"This one is special. She is not like the others. She is an angel," Abdur retorted.

"I know. Mine were all special." Thanasis again laughed bitterly. "In the beginning, I even didn't dare to touch them, afraid that they would disappear forever like the mythical nymphs. I looked at those girls in awe. They seemed to be, as you say, apparitions from heaven. But then, when the light goes down . . ."

"No, no. Monica is different. We will get married," Abdur burst out enthusiastically. He couldn't hold back the news anymore.

"My God! You are a really bad case, my friend." There was a note of exasperated compassion in Thanasis's voice.

"Do you really want to get married? Are you serious?" Stefan, who could hardly believe the story, asked.

"Yes. Why not? We will get married, and I will move to Sweden."

"And where is this angel, this Monica of yours?" Stefan inquired. *Perhaps life would be easier in Sweden for someone like Abdur,* he thought. Maybe changing his mind wasn't such a bad idea. Happiness is relative and elusive. Better to enjoy it as long as it lasts. Who had the right to tell Abdur what was good for him? Could anyone make him happier? Not he, Stefan, for sure.

"Right now she is flying to Stockholm. I just came back from the airport. The poor girl was desperate. She was crying her way to the airplane. I was afraid she would get sick. It took a lot of persuasion to soothe the sweet child." There was emotion in the young man's voice.

"And you expect her to return here?" Thanasis was blankly incredulous.

"No. Her family is sponsoring me. She took all my papers with her and will arrange my visa and my work permit there, in Stockholm. I will join her as soon as the papers come back. We will get married in Sweden."

"May God protect you, Abdur," Thanasis said gravely. "What I need the most is a drink to wash down your news. You should have one too. Unfortunately, you don't drink ouzo. This is too bad because one of these days, you will need it. Lots of it. What about you, sir?" He looked inquiringly at Stefan, who shook his head.

He didn't want another ouzo. His family was waiting for him. By now, Lia must be really worried. "I must go," he said. "Thank you for the treat, Thanasis."

"Are you feeling better, sir?"

"Yes, much better. You were quite right. The Greek medicine works. Thanks again. Kali nikhta. Good night." They shook hands, the Greek standing and bowing formally.

"I am coming with you, Father," Abdur said. "See you tomorrow, Thanasis."

"Okay, I'll see you tomorrow then. Don't get too excited about that girl."

Thanasis stood still and watched thoughtfully as they strode away, the rhythmic sound of their quick steps fading in the distance, until the darkness at the end of the alley swallowed them and the night was quiet again.

MEN OF GOD

Stefan was in a hurry, walking with long, confident strides on Calea Victoriei, the oldest and once the most fashionable among Bucharest's grand boulevards. Despite the last war's calamities and the many recent changes, the large and contorted avenue hadn't completely lost its stylish, glamorous charm, still being the home of several museums, commercial outlets, and administrative agencies. He enjoyed its special atmosphere as he strolled along bathed in the pleasantly warm midday sunshine, indifferent to the anemic displays of the mostly empty shop windows. It was spring, and the air was fresh and fragrant with the euphoric scent of blossoming lilacs.

He stopped at a street crossing, waiting for the green light. On the opposite side, tall lanced wrought-iron fences set in solid stonework surrounded the royal palace's massive complex of fine buildings, renamed the Palace of the Republic during the troubled epoch the Soviets brought upon Romania. The white Transylvanian marble that covered its walls, weathered by years of exposure into a honey yellow, glowed faintly in the mellow vernal light.

After the communists, with the help of the Red Army, forced the king to abdicate in 1947, the royal palace was transformed by one of the first republican decrees into a national museum, a repository for the country's most valuable works of art. Some of those treasures initially belonged to the exiled royalty. Yet the collection's bulk consisted of what was subsequently confiscated from art-loving citizens who had the misfortune of putting their

---

108

money into paintings and sculptures instead of wasting it on more ephemeral gratification. The result was a splendid display, and Stefan had spent many Sundays with Lia in the tall rooms and vast halls, absorbed for hours on end in rapt contemplation. In the beginning, access was free and the entertainment great.

But this, like many good things, didn't last long. After being invited to visit several foreign countries, Ceaușescu got a taste for royal pomp and suddenly decided in the early 1970s to use the central and southern wings of the palace for staging his increasingly numerous formal engagements. That section of the complex immediately became an off-limits territory, populated only by the dictator's henchmen, a mixture of prosperous-looking officials from the protocol services, contemptuous plainclothes secret police, and distrustful securitate officers in uniform. To keep up appearances, the national art collection was not completely removed; instead, it ended up crammed into the northern wing, a sparingly built postwar addition. Since the museum was now short of space, most of the artworks went into storage.

For the dictator, this arrangement was especially convenient. The huge, multistory building of the Central Committee of the Communist Party, where he spent his office time, lay just a few hundred meters across from the palace. In between the two, there was a wide square created after the war by removing a block of demolished ruins, a grim reminder of the American and German aerial bombardments—Bucharest having had the unenviable privilege of being targeted by both the US Air Force and the Luftwaffe. Even the Russians attempted to attack the Romanian capital by air during the hostilities, but their poorly built airplanes weren't able to touch it. It was under that newly created space, rumor had it, that secret underground corridors had recently been built. Now Ceaușescu could walk with his retinue from one building to another without the outside world knowing his whereabouts. The new owners had also built a modern three-thousand-seat conference hall, connected to the palace, where the Party usually held its important meetings. The location was very handy as the dictator, who liked to hear himself talk, never missed an opportunity to deliver a lengthy speech when the occasion presented itself. There was a meeting and a speech almost every other day. The palace also provided an escape route if the need arose, as his security advisers assured him.

Ever since a man who was refused permission to emigrate had tried to burn himself alive in front of the central committee's headquarters a few years earlier, the square and adjacent streets were heavily controlled. Only people with special permits and authorized vehicles, recognizable by their license plates, could approach the Party's headquarters. Consequently, the square was empty most of the time, undisturbed by the traffic flow on Calea Victoriei. Pedestrians were allowed to use only the opposite sidewalk, under the watchful eyes of soldiers in full battle gear positioned at short intervals behind the high wrought-iron fence of the palace. Hanging about wasn't tolerated in the area, and if someone was noticed loitering along the boulevard, the offender was shortly brought to order in no uncertain terms by a couple of plainclothes officers always on the lookout.

The traffic light went green, and Stefan crossed the street. As he passed along the palace's fence, he eyed the officers scattered in pairs throughout the square and patrolling the sidewalks. Over a dozen unmarked police cars were stationed strategically on the other side of the street, and a few more were grouped behind the university library. The concentration of so many secret police always made him uneasy. It wasn't fear, really—for after so many years, he had gotten somewhat used to these men's dangerous and conspicuous presence—only a sort of indefinite weariness. Pedestrians were scarce because it was a midweek workday, and few people could take advantage of the good weather.

Stefan passed by the first gate of the palatial courtyard and had a good view of the whole square, the buildings, and the boulevard. It was a fine sight, and he slowed down, thinking how nice it would be to take a photograph here one day. Then he remembered the police; one could get in trouble if seen fiddling with a camera in that neighborhood.

About a hundred meters or so ahead of him, nearly in front of the central committee's headquarters, a passerby stopped at that precise moment and jumped on the stone base of the palatial fence. The man climbed up on the iron structure and opened his raincoat, exposing a white strip of fabric with something written on it, which he quickly unfurled. He then hung from the fence like a fly in an entomological display.

Stefan realized with mixed feelings of excitement and apprehension that he was involuntarily eye-witnessing a single-handed political demonstration. An exasperated dissident was trying to send a message to the leadership in a move that equaled suicide. Nobody stopped to look at the man, too afraid, of course, to get involved. Anyhow, the whole thing didn't last more than a couple of minutes.

Instantly, the traffic lights at all the entrances to the square turned red, and the area was completely sealed off. In seconds, several cars crazily dashed at full speed from their strategic parking positions around the square, burning their squealing tires in a cacophony of roaring engines and gnashing brakes. The cars jumped over the curbs, drove onto the sidewalk, and stopped at the base of the fence, almost crashing into it and each other. In the courtyard, a group of soldiers with bayonets at the ready came running, rhythmically thumping their boots on the flagstones. A swarm of men poured out of the cars, frenziedly climbed the fence, and pulled the demonstrator down, his resistance easily overcome. In the blink of an eye, the dissident was swallowed by the repressive tidal wave and vanished in the tumult, while the mechanical bedlam of withdrawing vehicles subsided as quickly as it had arisen.

When Stefan arrived at the spot where the event had just taken place, only one car was still stationed, both open doors facing the curb. There were four or five men in it, and they watched him suspiciously. He couldn't believe his eyes. Everything around was incredibly peaceful. Nothing appeared to have changed. For the moment, he was somehow the only pedestrian on that section of the boulevard. It was unreal. *Perhaps I dreamed all of this,* he thought distractedly, glancing at the fence in the vain hope of seeing some sign of what had happened. But there was no longer anything to be seen.

"What are you looking for, comrade?" an officer asked sternly. A tall young militiaman in a blue-gray uniform was talking to him. Years ago, after the communist takeover, the prewar police—branded as an oppressive tool of capitalism—was dissolved and replaced, following the Soviet model, by the so-called popular militia. In fact, it was the same organization, using the same kind of people and methods, or—worse—dressed in a different uniform. In due time, the old policemen had been replaced with a new generation of communist creatures recruited from among misfits and sluggards, a bunch of ruthless and corrupt bullies who were best avoided.

"I was wondering what was going on," Stefan replied.

"Nothing's going on, comrade. Do you understand?" the militiaman haughtily barked.

"I thought there was a man there . . ." Stefan pointed the fence. *What on earth made you say such a stupid thing?* he thought, instantly regretting his imprudence.

"What man? What are you talking about? Do you know him?" The officer's voice took a menacing tone. "Give me your identity book. Come on, quick."

He didn't have the identity book, Stefan remembered with horror. It had been retained at the special militia office for foreign travel when they gave him the passport. And the passport was currently in Athens. The Greek police had it. They kept his Romanian passport in exchange for the Greek political asylum card. Images of Greece flashed through his mind. How free and happy they all were in Greece. He couldn't show the militiaman his political asylum card because that qualified him as a traitor. Why was he back in this hell?

Static noises mixed with nasal voices could be heard through the car's open doors.

The officer's walkie-talkie suddenly came alive with a crackle, and one of the men seated inside the car shouted, "Comrade Lieutenant, we are recalled to the base." The officer turned for a moment to speak with his colleague.

Stefan didn't wait to hear what the militiaman had to say because his mind was focused on how to make a quick escape, and all his senses were absorbed by the immediate need for action. He withdrew with a series of imperceptible movements and, after a few quiet steps, broke into a run, weaving in and out of the scarce pedestrians. Someone shouted unintelligibly behind him, and he heard heavy footsteps coming after him. He didn't turn back and continued to run even faster along Calea Victoriei.

Where the palatial courtyard ended, there was an opening between it and the next block of buildings, an area that continued with a succession of broad green lawns separating the palace and the adjacent conference hall from the neighboring streets. From the sidewalk, a short wide flight of stone stairs descended gently between beautiful magnolias in full blossom to the old Cretzulescu church. Built several centuries ago by a family of rich landlords, the Cretzulescu boyars, the church was—in the new era—a neglected heritage building surrounded by old trees and thick bushes. Damaged by the devastating 1977 earthquake, it had been closed since then, subject to never-ending repairs because in the Romanian workers' paradise, money was scarce for God's houses.

Stefan jumped through the bushes, scratching his face, and furtively went around the church, which was covered with tall messy scaffolding. In the summer, the air around would have been filled with the high-pitched cries of scores of swallows nesting under the church's roof, incessantly hunting for insects; but now it was too early in the season for them, and it was completely quiet. Strangely, no worker was in sight, and the place seemed deserted. Avoiding heaps of various construction leftovers haphazardly scattered about, he approached a dilapidated, weather-beaten wooden structure half hidden by the trees. So far, nobody had followed him up there. *Maybe they had lost him,* he thought wishfully. Piles of garbage blocked access to what appeared to be a storage shed.

Cautiously, Stefan opened the door. It made an awful noise, the squeaking sound reverberating from the walls of the church. Although the hinges were rusted, the roughly joined door was fairly solid. Inside, it was dark, dusty, and crowded with all sorts of building materials, mixed smells of wood, paint, and mortar pervading. He sneaked in and secured the primitive bolt. Then finding a heavy wood beam, he propped it against the door's planks. He was panting and felt quite exhausted.

Voices and footsteps approached, and someone knocked at the door. Stefan held his breath, forcing himself to stay still.

"He is not here," a male said in English.

"He must have been, not long ago," a female replied.

This is another one of their tricks: trying to mislead me into believing they are not the militia, Stefan thought.

Several people paced in front of the door, talking unintelligibly. After a pause, someone tried to open the door.

"This is locked from inside," a woman said. Although her voice sounded familiar, Stefan couldn't identify it.

They renewed their attempts and began boisterously knocking at the door, which shook violently in its frame.

"Deschide. Deschide usa! Open, open the door!" the woman shouted.

Stefan panicked, the prospect of being arrested paralyzing his reason. Covered in cold sweat and breathing heavily, he feverishly moved toward the end of the shed, hampered by things he couldn't see in the dark, and banged his head badly. He tried to squeeze in and hide under some loosely stacked boards but didn't fit in the small opening between them. Desperate and hopeless, he sat on the ground with his heart aching and the veins at his temples ready to burst. If caught, he would be a dead man.

Everybody in Romania, even children, knew that militiamen had no qualms about torturing and beating innocent people to death in order to extract incriminatory confessions at any cost. Subjected to unimaginable and inhuman violence, the majority of their victims would sooner or later succumb and, in the vain hope that it would put an end to their torments, would agree with everything their torturers, specialists in inflicting excruciating pain, asked of them. That was, however, an erroneous assumption as the torturers wanted more people to be involved and always continued their "investigations" until either the interviewee died or they had enough "evidence to unmask bourgeois plots against the working class," thereby justifying their existence.

The pounding and shouting at the door didn't stop. Looking in the dark for a hiding place, Stefan opened wide his scared eyes. With instant relief, he found himself in the refugee camp, in his own little room. In the waning light of the day, he could see the faint contours of sparse, familiar furniture: the children's bunk beds, the tiny table, and the two beds side by side on which he rested, stretched across, with his forehead pushing hard against the metal frame.

"Open the door. Stefan, open the door, please!" his wife shouted.

"Vin. Numai un moment. I am coming. Just a moment," he sleepily replied. Stefan stood up, the piercing pain in his chest still stabbing and, although not completely awake, shuffled to the door and turned the light on. The sweaty, unpleasantly cold shirt stuck to his torso, making him shiver slightly.

He had left his key in the lock, and Lia couldn't open the door. She was waiting outside impatiently and now quickly entered, accompanied by Father Agapitos.

"I am sorry," he apologetically told his wife, who gave him a slant reproving look. "I was awfully tired and had complete forgot the key . . . Good evening, Father," he greeted the visitor.

Agapitos was a Greek and, as out of place as he might appear in an all-Orthodox Greece, a Roman Catholic priest. He was the pastor of Ayia Praxedes (Saint Praxedes's), a church that Stefan and his family regularly frequented. The church, a historic monument, was tucked away on a low headland at the far end of the town, under tall and dusty palm trees overlooking the Aegean Sea and the harbor. It had beautiful old frescoes unfortunately damaged by a leaky roof. For centuries, the town had been home to a thriving community of Italian miners and traders assimilated, as happens with long-term cohabitation, into the local Greek population. They had built the church in the affluent past. Most of their descendants had strayed from the main fold, and nowadays, the small surviving congregation was unable to provide the means for the upkeep of a too-costly heritage.

The priest was strongly built, energetic, and optimistic. His presence always radiated a particularly buoyant enthusiasm one would not expect from someone in his late seventies. He had an inexhaustible reserve of that enthusiasm and unselfishly shared it with the refugees regardless of their beliefs. Father Agapitos's encouragement and advice had saved many from depression or even worse. His face reminded Stefan of Saint Paul from a Byzantine fresco he had seen years ago in an old Romanian monastery. Agapitos had the same aquiline nose between two ardent eyes presiding over a square jaw and expressive mouth. His domed forehead graced a balding head set on top of a stocky body. Stefan liked him and enjoyed his visits.

"Good evening, Stefan. Did we wake you?" the priest asked.

"Actually, you did. Yet this is a good thing . . . You delivered me from a hellish nightmare. Quite an unpleasant one . . ."

"Wow, your shirt is all wet on you, dear," Lia observed. "Better get changed. Quickly."

"Was it about going back home and being followed by police?" Father Agapitos casually inquired.

"What a surprising question, Father. That's exactly how it happened in my dream. I have already had this nightmare several times. It keeps recurring quite often. Part of it is perhaps a souvenir from my real life. The turn it takes in my dreams is unreal and awfully disturbing. The police are chasing me, and there is no escape. I always end up cornered, terrified, and I wake up sweating profusely, with a severe heartache." He shivered, recalling his dream, at the same time feeling greatly relieved. It was so good to be in the camp, out of reach of those dreaded people. "Thank God you came."

"He scares me," Lia said, "he moans and sometimes even hurts himself in his agitated sleep." While talking, she handed Stefan a clean shirt. "Here, take this and give me the sweaty one."

"Would you mind, Father, if I changed my shirt here?"

"Not at all. Go ahead . . . During my years of working with refugees, I heard many of them complaining about similar nightmares. That's how I know and why I asked you about it. Such dreams, it seems, are quite common among people like you. It is the

—
116

anxiety, the trauma of your escape. Who knows? Apparently some continue to have such nightmares long after they leave the camp. God, it seems, wants to remind you by contrast how lucky you are to be free. People so easily forget . . ."

Lia pushed a chair toward the priest, "Have a seat, Father."

Stefan had to take off his wet shirt and, for the moment, was too busy to say anything although he didn't agree with his guest's explanation. In his view, the tormentor was God's traditional enemy, but he wasn't in the mood to start a theological controversy. "We certainly should not forget soon," he muttered under his breath. "Every one of us knows too well why we are here. Some things one never forgets." He finished buttoning his shirt and pulling up a chair, sat at the table, and faced the Pauline likeness. "How are you, Father?"

"I am fine, thank you. But what about you, Stefan? How are you managing with your Turkish neighbors?"

It was a legitimate question because recent massive arrivals of refugees had swollen the camp's population to uncomfortable proportions, the two dozen or so escapees from communist countries being swamped by over a hundred hardcore leftists from Turkey. Throngs of unshaven, mustached, and bleary-eyed men were crammed into every available space, extra beds being brought in daily by the overburdened administration and quickly installed on top of the existing ones. There were now ten Turkish émigrés crowded into a room at the end of the corridor vacated by a Romanian family of four who had recently left for the States. The newcomers kept quiet for the time being, and none of the expected skirmishes among opposing factions had yet happened. Some almost never left their rooms during the day, being engaged in what appeared to be unending political debates that they held, surrounded by dense clouds of cigarette smoke. Others chain-smoked in the courtyard, crouching along the walls to take advantage of the sparse shade or chattering on and on in small clusters, adversely eyeing each other.

If one approached such a group, the discussions abruptly stopped, and people wearing the worried expression of those sharing very important secrets met the intruder with a hostile silence. In the evenings, they all congregated at the nearby cafeteria, seated for hours around tiny tables sprawled on the sidewalk while sipping coffee from thimble-sized cups. The cafeteria was right across the street from the local headquarters of one of several Greek communist parties, and the Turks listened with conspicuous rapture to lithe Hellenic versions of heavy Russian revolutionary songs orchestrated by Nikos Theodorakis. The Greek parliamentary elections were only weeks away, and as the electoral campaign reached its heights, so did the ideological war of decibels. Disregarding the potential damage to the ears of their countrymen, the communist-owned loudspeakers, set at maximum volume, boomed appropriate slogans and enticing music around the clock in a deafening attempt to stir the comrades into action.

"So far, they are not too bad," Stefan answered. "The only thing that really bothers me is their passion for Radio Moscow. They spend their nights listening to it, and the noise makes me nervous. I cannot sleep well in the sounds of the international."

A frown of disgust shadowed the Pauline serenity for a moment, and Agapitos waggled his hand in a gesture of tired discontent. "Did you tell them to stop it?" he asked.

"We tried, delicately, but to no avail," Lia said. "We didn't want to antagonize our neighbors. Some are quite fierce looking."

"And malevolent, that's for sure. You should be very careful with them. Especially you, Lia, and your daughter should be on your guard at all times," he said. "Do you know that a delegation of Turks complained about me to the administration?" Agapitos paused, looking in turn at Stefan and Lia with an offended expression on his honest face. "Their colleagues don't want me in the camp, they said. These people ignore the fact that the Conference of American Catholic Bishops has a major share in the sustenance of this camp, and one of my duties is to see how well is it run."

"They cannot stop you, can they? It is us you are coming for, not them, isn't it?" Lia asked.

"They threatened that something bad might happen to me if I continued with my visits. Can you imagine that?"

—

"Well, Father. When I questioned you about the appropriateness of Catholic organizations sheltering and feeding communists, you took me to task. Remember? You said that my comment was not worthy of a good Christian and rebuked me," Stefan said.

"This is true, and I still believe so." Agapitos warmed up. "We must be charitable toward people in need, no matter their religion. Any victim of persecution is our brother, even if he is a Muslim. We are all of us the sons of God. We cannot be insensitive to their sufferings and needs . . ."

"Sorry to interrupt you, Father," Stefan said. "This is nice in theory, but here, we are dealing with a completely different situation. These are not Muslims—they are militant communists, anarchists, and the like, who openly declare themselves enemies of God and ready to physically destroy not only any religion or social order but the very faithful themselves. Belief in God makes one an opponent in their eyes. And opponents, according to Marxist-Leninist theory, must be exterminated without mercy. We can tell you many tragic stories from Romania . . ."

"I know, I know. Don't think we are not informed, Stefan. We have heard about the terror and persecutions taking place in your country."

"And about the labor camps, the torture chambers, and the killings . . . ?" Stefan asked.

"We have heard about those too," Agapitos acknowledged, but his voice was not so confident now.

"You probably never heard what happened to our priests and bishops who didn't recant their beliefs," Lia said. "Have you ever heard about Bishop Vasile?"

"What about Bishop Vasile? I personally met him a long time ago. We were friends, you see. What happened to him?" Agapitos suddenly sounded concerned, his eyes shining with awakened interest.

"Bishop Vasile was a friend of my father, who knew him from his university years," Lia said. "Both were Transylvanians and initially frequented the same university until Vasile decided to become a priest and was sent to Rome to complete his studies."

"That's right. We spent three years together at Angelicum Athenaeum. When I arrived in Rome in 1928, he was already there. That was when I first met him. Those were some days . . ." A smile lit up Agapitos's austere features and mellowed the Pauline severity as he remembered his youth. "We soon became quite good friends. It was with sadness that we parted company at the end of our studies, when we had to leave the Eternal City. For several years, we continued to write each other. Then as usually happens, our letters became fewer and far between. Only now I realize that we haven't corresponded for decades."

"So you knew him? How small the world is, Father," Lia pensively said. "I remember him from my childhood when, before the communist takeover, he used to visit my parents quite often. Although in 1948, World War II was finished. Stalin's never-ending fight with God wasn't, so the Romanian communist government was ordered by the Soviets to restrict—indeed—to suppress religious life. They began with the non-Orthodox. First they arrested Vasile and five other bishops of Catholic Byzantine rite, the so-called Uniates, and transported them into the mountains to an abandoned summer guesthouse of the Orthodox patriarchate.

"The dilapidated building was transformed into a temporary prison surrounded by double fences of barbed wire and guarded by a detachment of numerous armed soldiers. The prelates were kept isolated, each in a separate room under permanent surveillance. The new Orthodox patriarch was a Marxist fellow traveler, a buddy of a man named Gheorghiu-Dej, the communist dictator of the day. He took the Uniate bishops into his custody in an attempt to make them recant their beliefs and allegiance to the pope, whom the new rulers stigmatized as an instrument of the most hated Anglo-American imperialism. They would have no freedom if they didn't convert to Orthodoxy, the patriarch warned the unyielding clergymen.

"For many months, the prisoners' daily food was reduced to only a few morsels of badly cooked polenta and water. It was winter already, and they had neither heat nor warm clothing, and some of the bishops suffered much as they were long past their prime. They all became famished, and the older ones got sick, yet they didn't lose heart and spent most of their time in prayer and contemplation. One day, the patriarch came with his suite, a bunch of aides and sycophants, and treated his prisoners to a lavish banquet where the finest food and wines were served. Ballet chorus girls and an orchestra were brought in from the Bucharest Opera for entertainment. That would be how they would be treated from now on if they renounced their stubbornness, the patriarch said. He was unpleasantly surprised and expressed his outrage when no defection resulted."

"When was that?" Agapitos asked.

"Sometime in the spring of 1949, I believe," Lia said, "but I was only ten years old and can't be sure." Then she went on with the story. "Following this aborted attempt to entice them to disown the pope, the Uniate bishops were moved to a sixteenth-century monastery not far from the capital. Several Orthodox priests who similarly refused to cooperate with the communist regime had also been imprisoned in that venerable cloister.

"Days without any food alternated with indoctrination lectures and meetings with officials who tried either to cajole or scare the unyielding clergy. The patriarch gave up after another half a year and, being unable to break their resistance, handed them over to the secret political police.

"In the summer, the prisoners were scattered among various old and remote detention institutions of bad repute or new forced labor camps that had been hurriedly set all over the country. Vasile and three younger bishops were taken to Bucharest to one of the infamous interrogation facilities, and each of them was put up into a separate damp underground cell. After that, they never saw each other again." Lia paused abruptly. She was short of breath and overwhelmed by a sudden, uncontrollable emotion.

"Does anyone know what happened to Bishop Vasile afterward?" Agapitos asked, unrestrained sadness darkening his face.

"Well," Lia continued with a conspicuous change of tone, "we don't know what exactly happened to any of them. We do know where Bishop Vasile is buried."

"What do you mean, buried?" Agapitos cried. "Vasile's dead?"

"Yes, he died indeed." Tears glittered in Lia's eyes. She wiped them away with her handkerchief. "He was killed. Tortured and killed." She again wiped her reddened eyes. "My mother heard this story from Father Fenyes, a Hungarian. Fenyes came from the same small town where my mother was born, and he trusted her because they had known each other since childhood. The government, in order to foil international criticism, allowed some limited religious freedom to minorities such as the Transylvanian Hungarians, for instance. And Father Fenyes was, at the time, in charge of the Roman Catholic cemetery in Bucharest.

"One night, Fenyes told my mother, a group of securitate men came to his little house at the gates of the cemetery and rudely woke him up. They brought a corpse with them and ordered the priest to bury it without delay. The body was in a makeshift, shabby coffin that was much too short. And bare feet and one hand were hanging out. The deceased was a man in rags who had died a violent death. His hair was pulled out from the head. And the scalp, negligently put in place, left part of the skull bones exposed. His once long beard was scorched, the lips swollen, broken and blackened. A number of front teeth had been knocked out and were missing. His cheeks were badly cut and the flesh partially charred. One eye had popped out of its orbit and hung along the tumefied, unrecognizable face. The victim's chest was covered with numerous small circular burns, probably made with cigarette butts. And long narrow blisters, some open and still bleeding, furrowed his belly. One of his legs was completely smashed, a mass of crushed bones and tattered muscles, really. There were no fingernails left on his hands. And all his fingers were crushed, the hands being a mass of bloodied, raw flesh. The entire poor, wretched body was covered with countless wounds, blood, and dirt."

A long pause followed, heavy with sadness and pain. Lia, her face turned toward the window, couldn't continue and was quietly crying. For several minutes, nobody said anything, and it was as if time had suddenly stood still. The complete silence of the room was disturbed only by the distant voice of Nana Mouskouri forcefully coming through the closed windows. She was once again singing, with all the power that modern electronics could provide, Manos

Hadjidakis's "Ta Pedia Tou Pirea," otherwise known to the Western world as "Never on Sunday."

"Did they tell your mother's friend who the dead man was?" Agapitos asked, almost in a whisper. "What did they tell him? When someone is buried, they have to record the death somehow. Don't they? How are you so sure that it was Vasile?" Agapitos, in denial, hoped that the dead man wasn't his friend. He could not and did not want to accept what he had just heard.

"They told Father Fenyes that the man was a Catholic priest who had died in a car accident. The securitate officers didn't give him the name of the man, only his initials, and rushed the priest to carry out the burial that same night. Their crew hastily dug and closed the grave and didn't allow the body to be washed or cleaned. Later, a wooden cross bearing only the bishop's initials and the year of his death was made for the grave by some charitable parishioners. Father Fenyes told my mother that he recognized Vasile, without any doubt, by a peculiar scar on his left arm, the result of an operation done earlier in his life in order to mend a fractured humerus bone."

Lia appeared unable to talk anymore. She just stood by the windows, looking outside into the deepening night, once in a while distractedly wiping her eyes. Agapitos murmured a prayer with closed eyes. Great pain distorted his usually serene facial features. Stefan kept silent. The voices of several people talking and laughing, an occasional happy whistling, banging doors, and noisy steps could be heard from the corridor. It was the usual dinnertime din in the camp.

"Requiem aeternam dona eis, Domine, et lux perpetua luceat eis," Agapitos concluded his prayer and made the sign of the cross.

"You wouldn't believe, Father, what happened shortly after that," Stefan said.

"What happened?" Agapitos spoke almost indifferently and with a hoarse voice. He looked much older now.

"After a while, one way or another, people found out about Bishop Vasile's burial place and started coming to pray at his grave. Ordinary people, you know? All kinds—Orthodox, Lutherans, even Jews, not only Catholics. Soon, pilgrims came in throngs as rumors spread that their prayers were answered. And apparently, some miraculous events took place. It was difficult to find out what was true and what was not, because the secret police repeatedly tried to stop this kind of worship—arresting, beating, and bullying some of the worshipers. In spite of their efforts, the crowds continued to grow as more people appeared to be ready to suffer for their beliefs.

"Banning access to the grave didn't work either, because pilgrims still came, gathering in the adjacent alleys, disturbing the normal cemetery services. The authorities threatened to close down the cemetery, but the measure wasn't implemented for fear of international outcry, so people continued to flock to Vasile's resting place. The cemetery's administration was forced to build several metal structures to hold the hundreds of burning candles and numerous bouquets of flowers the faithful brought in daily and piled up around the grave."

"Did anyone check the truth of those rumors? Did the Catholic authorities make an inquiry?" Agapitos eagerly asked. The priest seemed to feel strangely better, as if he was regaining his habitual vivacity.

"We don't know," Lia said. "Such things are not discussed openly, and even if the bishop of Bucharest had started such a process, nothing of that sort would be broadcast. Any information of that nature is banished, and to spread it is considered propaganda against the ruling party and its dominant Marxist-Leninist ideology. In fact, even discussing it is considered a criminal offense."

"What we heard were always secondhand stories and rumors. We never met anyone who had benefited personally or had received grace after praying for help through Bishop Vasile's intercession," Stefan said.

"This is terribly distressing. My poor friend suffered so much and had such an awful death. Such terrible events are, however, to be expected—martyrdom being something our church was confronted with from the beginning—and we cannot but follow the example of our Lord. I am sure that God who sees and knows everything had a bright place for a martyr like Vasile." Agapitos crossed himself again. "May God rest his soul and make him part of his everlasting light."

"Stefan," Lia said, "why don't you tell Father your story?"

"My story? Which one?"

"About your prayers to Bishop Vasile."

"I don't think it is important."

"What story? What are you guys talking about?" Agapitos asked.

"I am not even sure if it is a story to be told, Father. It is something I am still struggling with, and as far as I am concerned, it is not significant."

"Come on, Stefan, tell Father the story," Lia said.

"Tell us the story, Stefan," Agapitos urged him. "Now you made me curious. Has it anything to do with my friend?"

"I am not sure if it really has to do with him. This is the problem, and that is why I am so reluctant."

"Anyhow, tell us what happened. Lia already knows it, and I am a priest. Don't worry, nobody will find out about your story."

"Ah, Father," Stefan said, "it is not that sort of thing. You will immediately realize that. There is not too much to tell either. It started about a year ago. One day, I went to a funeral. And after the service, I wandered around and by chance came to the area where Bishop Vasile was buried. One couldn't miss his grave because of the huge number of burning candles, the piles of flowers, and the people jamming the alley at some distance from the graveside. I also easily singled out several plainclothes securitate detectives, a bunch of well-fed thugs incessantly joking and laughing, searchingly looking around. I lit a couple of candles and unobtrusively prayed for a few minutes. As you can imagine, I didn't want to attract too much attention."

"What did you pray for?" Agapitos asked.

"I asked Vasile to pray to God on my behalf and ask for our liberation. I wanted help to get out of the hell the communist dictatorship meant to me, to us, in general. At the time, I was desperate because I couldn't see any way out of that awful situation. I continued to privately pray to Vasile every evening or during my numerous sleepless nights."

"And then against any hope, in less than a year, we managed to escape," Lia said.

"It seems that your prayers have been answered. This is a miracle, Stefan." Agapitos cried. "Don't you think so?"

"This is the problem. I don't know why, but I cannot believe that. I don't consider myself worthy of a miracle, and then I cannot really see where the miracle is."

"You are here, Stefan. You are out of the communist hell, as you call it. Don't you see it?" Father Agapitos insisted, his eyes shining with excitement.

"Well, I wanted my country to be free . . . I didn't ask for help to escape."

"Yes, you did," Lia said. "Didn't you dream of climbing Mount Everest? How would you climb Everest from a Romania under communist dictatorship, eh?"

"Of course I dreamed of climbing Mount Everest. That was my dream from early childhood. That's not the point. I also dreamed of going to the Red Sea, to Arabia, to Polynesia, and many other places. This is a completely different thing," Stefan heatedly contradicted her.

"No, it isn't. *You* wanted to be free, not the country." Lia could be defiant and blunt, especially when she thought, perhaps not always correctly, that the truth was on her side.

"This is not true. The closest would be to say that I asked for both our people's and my own liberation and yours, among others, as a matter of fact. You know that, Lia, and . . ."

"Don't get excited, guys," Agapitos intervened. He had something else on his mind. "What Stefan really meant is not at issue. The fact that you don't consider yourself worthy, Stefan, is also irrelevant. God bestows his grace according to his own plan as he sees fit for our salvation. We don't always know what we are asking for and what God's answer could be when we pray for a special favor. If it happens, such a miracle is a private matter. To believe in it is not an obligatory act of faith. One is free to accept or reject a private revelation of this nature."

"Maybe you are right, Father . . . I still cannot believe it happening to me." Stefan obviously wasn't ready to change his opinion.

"Don't worry. It will come one day. God will open your eyes. Now I want to say a requiem mass for the repose of my friend's soul. What about if you two come over and join in with a few prayers of thanksgiving?" Agapitos produced a small worn-out notebook with purple covers from a hidden pocket of his discolored cassock and leafed through it. "It cannot be tomorrow, Friday. It is already booked. Also, during the weekend, it is impossible. What about Tuesday evening at seven? Can you come?"

"Why not?" Stefan answered. "What do you think, Lia? Can we go?"

"Of course, dear, we don't have anything for Tuesday evening. What plans can two people like us have?" she admitted with short self-deprecating laughter.

"We are set then," Agapitos said with finality and stood up. "I must go now. Thank you for your stories today. I got more than expected from you . . ."

Nobody could tell if Agapitos had more to say because whatever it could have been was lost in the uproar that followed. The noise in the corridor reached a new height. And the door opened with a jolt followed by deafening brouhaha as Val, Ana, and Abdur came in, laughing and talking at the same time. They brought an excited Carina with them.

The dog impatiently pulled on the leash. And Ana, who held her distractedly, let go. As soon as she felt free, Carina went straight to her corner and began to drink greedily from her bowl, loudly pushing it and splashing the water around.

Even without the spaniel's contribution, the room was, for a minute or so, in the eye of a miniature storm, the previous quiet replaced by a flurry of exclamations and noisy greetings. The youngsters liked Agapitos, who always had words of encouragement and advice for them. In spite of the age gap, they were pleased to be in his company. Even Abdur, who had occasionally benefited from his help, greeted the Catholic priest with deference.

"Are you leaving because of us, Father?" Ana teasingly asked the priest after the first wave of enthusiasm had subsided.

"Of course not. It is unfortunate, but I must go," Agapitos answered. "I must inspect the kitchen to see how old Savas is managing the work. I will see you soon, perhaps Saturday. It is Saint Praxedes, our church's patron saint holiday. I hope you will come to the solemn mass."

"Father Agapitos," Ana asked again, "I heard about the blessing of the automobiles. When is it? Is it this Saturday, by any chance?"

"Blessing of automobiles?" Lia stared at Ana with inquiring eyes under raised eyebrows.

"Yes. Ana is right. We have this unique custom of blessing automobiles following the holy mass on Saint Praxedes's day. The parishioners bring their cars and park them in a circle around the church. I say several prayers and a blessing and then go around and sprinkle their vehicles with holy water. After that, they blow the horns in a noisy honk of thanks. The ceremony will be held this coming Saturday. You can also bring your own little car. You are coming anyway for the mass, aren't you?"

The cocker approached the group of people with her wet muzzle dripping water.

"Oh, Carina, you naughty girl. Come here!" Stefan called. "Careful with the dog," he said to the others, "she is all wet." He grabbed a rug and knelt on the floor beside the spaniel. Before he could do anything, she gently poked her muzzle into his face. "Aye, Carina. Stay quiet. Don't be cheeky." He dried her thoroughly and stood up.

"Good dog," Agapitos said, searching in one of his pockets. "Don't come too close to me." Finding what he was looking for, the priest gave Stefan a dog biscuit in the shape of a bone. "I know the rule and won't feed somebody else's pet. You give it to her."

The spaniel cautiously sniffed the biscuit, then unhurriedly took it and retired to her corner.

"Mama, let's go to mass Saturday. I want to see the automobiles' blessing," Ana said.

"I don't see why we shouldn't go to that mass," Stefan agreed.

"You should come. Although Praxedes is not a well-known saint, her day is a church holiday. You don't have much to do here Saturdays, anyway," Agapitos said and rushed to the door. "Sorry, folks," he apologized, "I can't stay any longer. I must run. God bless you all."

"May I come too?" Abdur asked. He held the door open for the priest.

Agapitos was already running in the hallway. He turned his head without completely stopping and looked back. "Why not? You can even pray if you wish so. Allah waahid—God is one. You know that, Abdur? Don't you?" Then the priest continued to run until he disappeared around the corner at the end of the corridor.

"True, Allah waahid. Laa Ilaha Illa Allah . . . There is no god but God . . ." the Afghan shouted after him and closed the door. When he turned toward the others, Abdur's handsome face was flushed and his eyes shined fanatically, animated by a sudden burst of religious fervor.

SECOND INTERMEZZO

Stefan, Luca, Val, and Selim, one of the Turkish refugees, worked in pairs in Theodoros's orchard. They picked up stones, cleaning the land, and planted olive trees. That morning, the farmer brought in a fresh load of saplings from the nursery. They had to hurry because the young trees piled in his pickup truck wouldn't stand the rigors of the Attic heat. But it was hard to dig holes in the rocky ground, and they had to use crowbars and pickaxes, making only little progress.

Stefan was teamed with Selim. He was a rather dark good-looking fellow in his early thirties with thick shiny black hair and sported a fine black moustache. Of medium height, he had a wrestler's narrow hips and broad shoulders. The previous night, he, accompanied by the rough Turkish boy, had called on Stefan, whom they never had spoken to before and, without any introduction, begged him to take them to the farm next day. They badly needed work. Selim's wife was sick at home in Istanbul, and he wanted to send her money, the young man explained with imploring, moist eyes. The rough boy was also looking for a job in order to make some pocket money. Stefan, of course, couldn't promise anything on the spot, except to take them to the farm.

In the morning, Selim showed up alone as the rough boy, who had changed his mind, sent word that he was too tired to work after an all-night political debate. Stefan gave Selim a ride in his Trabant, which he recently brought from Thessaloniki; and Theodoros, when asked, readily agreed to try the man.

Soon after they started the first hole, Selim took a break and lit a cigarette. Stefan continued digging with the pickaxe. When the tool met a rock, sparks and stone chips flew. The Turk smoked skillfully, seated precariously on the wooden handle of a shovel laying flat on the ground. He gazed somnolently about, paying no attention at all to Stefan who, a few times, had to switch tools and use the crowbar in order to dislodge some stubborn rocks. Then Stefan endeavored to clean the hole of debris. "Sorry," he said to Selim, pointing the shovel, "I need that."

The man idly shifted his bottom a few inches away on a patch of sun-scorched grass, just far enough to free the shovel's handle. "Look," he said nodding at the back of the house where it was a small parking area, "big house, lots horses, many cars."

Through the slender silvery trees, the vehicles could be seen glimmering in the sun. He stretched his open hand, fingers apart. "Five cars. I thinking Theodoros big capitalist."

In fact, with Stefan's car, there were six vehicles parked together. One was the pickup truck loaded with olive saplings, another a medium-sized tractor, and the third a broken-up Impala, a shell really, in which Stefan and the crew would have their lunch served when it rained. Theodoros had also a tiny BM roadster kept on blocks. He had gotten it a few years earlier for nothing from an Englishman, a tourist in transit, who had wrecked the car in a traffic accident. In his free time, Theodoros undertook to restore it but never got enough time to finish. The farmer's family used the fifth vehicle, a roomy, relatively new Citroen for their errands and outings.

Stefan, who was shoveling dirt and stones from the hole, straightened his aching back, wiped the sweat from his forehead, and gave Selim a wry smile. "Theodoros is a small hardworking farmer. He is not a big capitalist," he said. "They have only one family car. The rest are utility vehicles necessary to his work and two nonfunctional wrecks. He pays us good money, so you had better take the pickaxe and give me a hand."

Selim silently considered him with incredulous eyes. He slowly removed the cigarette butt from his mouth and conscientiously buried it in the dirt, then unhurriedly stood up and stretched. "This thing very heavy," he muttered, weighing the pickaxe in his hands before starting to dig. He worked without enthusiasm, pausing every so often. As they took turns, Selim left Stefan to do most of the heavy digging.

When a hole was deep enough they, had to bring topsoil to fill it and plant the sapling. As soon as the second hole was finished, Selim went to the toilet instead of helping Stefan with the planting. More than half an hour elapsed, yet he did not come back. An exasperated Stefan went scouting about and found him crouched in the shade of the stable block, smoking. "Come on, man," he said "we have work to do. You can't let me do the whole job singlehandedly. Can you?"

"I tired," Selim answered in a weak voice, "my hands hurt."

"I know, I know. It happened to me, too. It takes some time to get used to it." Stefan tried motivating him, "Look here," He showed the guy his palms with conspicuous yellowish calluses. "I didn't have them before. It hurts in the beginning, but it is good money."

By noon, the pair had planted only half as many saplings as their colleagues. When Theodoros's wife brought them lunch, they all sat together under the patio umbrella behind the house and ate.

They were having coffee and a smoke when Theodoros appeared from the orchard with a worried expression on his face "You must hurry, guys!" he urged them. "It is very hot today, and the saplings are already withering. I covered them with a tarpaulin for now. Please don't let me down. I can't afford to lose them." He didn't wait for an answer. "I have to turn on the sprinklers," he said over his shoulder as he hurriedly walked in the direction of the barn.

The men started to move, piling dishes on the tray and shifting their feet under the table. Stefan, coffee cup in hand, stood up. "One last sip and I am ready," he said.

Val jumped to his feet. "I just finished. What about you, Luca?" he asked.

"Ready. Let's go," the man answered, returning the lighter and the rest of the cigarettes pack in his breast pocket.

—
132

Only the Turk continued to sit without showing any sign of haste, busying himself to light another cigarette. He acted as if nothing of what was going on around touched him in any way.

"What are you doing?" Stefan asked. "Another cigarette? These two have planted twice as many trees as we did. We should hurry. Didn't you hear Theodoros?"

Selim took several puffs from his cigarette before answering. He looked up at Stefan, standing ready to go. "Theodoros is a bloodsucker, capitalist exploiter," he said. "I intellectual, proletarian intellectual, not animal."

"So am I," Stefan said, "a highly qualified scientist. Yet here, because I need money, I am a farmhand. Theodoros pays us for farm work, not for our intellect. He pays us fair wages. He is not an exploiter."

Selim stretched his hands, turning them palm up, "See?" In the palms of his hands, there were a few fresh blisters, some broken, the blood dried between the ragged skin. He looked at them with disgust. "I artist. It hurts. This is no good for me."

"But the money is good for you," Stefan retorted. "Work is not easy. It hurts me too. I have pains and aches all over my body, yet we have to finish the job." He pulled his pants up with a reflex gesture. "Come on, man. You asked me to bring you here. We had better go back to work," he said and walked briskly toward the orchard. Selim followed him after a while, dragging his feet and taking his time.

The afternoon was excruciatingly hot. The planting went slowly because Selim avoided digging and carried only light loads of topsoil with the wheelbarrow. When Stefan asked him to work harder, he just ignored him. They had to cool themselves several times, showering each other with the garden hose. Every time they had a shower, Selim took also a prolonged break, smoking and peering thorough semiclosed eyes at Stefan who diligently dug hole after hole, sweating profusely.

One time, Stefan, who by now had resigned himself to finishing the job without much help from his younger mate, joined him for a smoke. He sat besides Selim, directly on the ground. "You said you are an artist, eh?"

"Uh-huh!" the Turk answered.

Stefan combed his damp hair with his fingers to stop a lock of it obstructing his view. "What kind of artist are you?" he asked. "Are you an art student?"

"No need for school. Why study? I talent, great talent." The Turk was obviously annoyed by Stefan's question. "I great caricaturist. I draw beautiful cartoons. Political caricatures. Very strong caricatures. I big artist." Selim pointed to his own chest with nicotine-stained fingers holding the cigarette he was smoking, "Yes, I very great artist."

They smoked in silence for a while. "How long have you been a great artist?" Stefan asked again.

Selim carefully pushed the ashes off the tip of the cigarette with his little finger. "Five months. Five months with a communist newspaper," he said pompously. "I great painter, too."

"Great painter?" Stefan was on the brink of bursting into crazy laughter. "What subjects did you paint?" His curiosity was now stirred, and he wanted to know more. "Are you an abstract or a figurative painter?

"Don't know. Next year, I try something great. Next year, I know." Selim looked disparagingly at Stefan. "You understand? Next year, I very great painter."

"I see," Stefan said, standing up with a grimace on his tired face. His lower back hurt. "I am not a great artist. I am only a scientist and so must go on digging."

In the late afternoon, the last sapling was finally planted, the topsoil around its delicate trunk well compacted and the rocks neatly piled up at the end of the tree row. The young olives threw long, narrow shadows on the reddish ground; and every object, every pebble, even the smallest, looked bigger under the oblique rays of the setting sun.

It was that magic hour of the Greek afternoon when the light enhances every detail, even the less significant, giving it solidity and a sort of personality of its own, which resonates irresistibly with the human soul. It makes one feel like being ready to sing a song of love, goodness, and friendship or to fly to the sun and bathe oneself in its radiant warmth. This supernatural drunkenness lasted only a short moment and then from the surrounding mountains—for Theodoros's farm sat in a flat depression among the foothills—the cool of the approaching evening came down like the breath of a faraway gentle giant. The accompanying thin shadows descended from the hills and came nearer.

"I am going to the washroom. Please take the garden hose and water the last trees we planted," Stefan said to Selim, who had already lit a cigarette. Stefan's back ached badly, and he was in a hurry to go to the washroom.

"I finished work," the Turk sharply responded.

"You didn't. I dug the holes and planted the trees. You just watched me and smoked. The least you can do is to water them. It is your turn." Stefan had delayed for quite a long time to answer nature's call, and he never had too much patience to spare for bums either. He raised his voice: "Take that bloody hose, and start watering right now. Otherwise, you will be sorry." He was already running. "I'll be back in a minute!" he shouted.

Afterward, he strolled back through the orchard, between the geometric rows, admiring the military alignment of delicate, slim olives standing at attention like the soldiers of a young army in silvery-gray uniforms. *Quite a good job*, he thought with pride. If nothing happens to them, these trees will be here for hundreds of years. This is something to be proud of.

Suddenly, his peaceful thoughts were disturbed by angry cries. It was Theodoros, at the very end of the newly planted area, swearing and cursing in a medley of English and Greek. Luca, Val, and Selim stood by, looking sheepishly at the red-faced farmer, who went on ranting and gesticulating furiously.

"What happened?" Stefan inquired when he was close enough.

"What happened?" the Greek shouted at the top of his voice. "This guy drowned my olives. That happened. Look, look what he's done," Theodoros said as he pointed to the end of the planted plot where several saplings had fallen to the ground and rested now in a shallow pool of muddy water. "He spoiled my saplings. That's what he did."

"Selim left the watering hose unattended," Luca said.

"What a bloody fool," Stefan mumbled under his breath, painfully aware of the futility of his efforts.

In the meantime, the water was fast receding, leaving behind a thin layer of red-brownish slime; and even as it vanished underground, some more saplings came down, leaning precariously on one side and exposing their delicate roots. Theodoros broke off his harangue, dashing to their support, trying to straighten them up and keep the falling ones upright. His attempts were doomed to fail though; too many trees were affected for a man to be able to singlehandedly restore order. While he was running in frenzy from one tree to another, his foot slipped and he fell into the mud.

"Are you all right?" Stefan asked, helping the frustrated Theodoros stand up. When he heard the other's affirmative answer, he continued, "Calm down, man. We'll fix them. I'll make stakes, and we'll tie them up. We'll refill the holes if we need to."

"That would be great. Thank you," Theodoros answered, brushing his wet jeans with both hands to get rid of mud, "but tomorrow will be too late."

"Not tomorrow," Stefan said. "Now. We won't go home until we finish." He had decided to rescue those olives without delay. "Right, boys?"

Luca and Val resignedly nodded in agreement. Surely, there was no enthusiasm left at the end of a long, hot day; and they were tired and hungry. Yet they sympathized with Theodoros, who was a good man and whom they liked. The last thing they wanted was to hurt him. Also, there was no doubt in their minds about the urgency of rescuing those saplings, and whatever grudge they bore, they kept it to themselves. After all, it was one of them who had made the mistake—they felt—and it was their responsibility as a team to fix it.

Selim, however, had no qualms about voicing his discontent. "I late. The day finished and I . . ." He tried to say more, but Stefan didn't let him finish.

"You, Selim, take the wheelbarrow and fetch some soil," Stefan barked at him, "and don't dare to bring only a handful or to make yourself scarce." The other man still wanted to say something. "No argument, Selim. This mess happened because of you. Now move, keep moving," Stefan, who was quite upset, urged him.

For the next hour or so, they worked without respite. Theodoros gave them a pile of cheap lumber, leftovers from some earlier fencing job; and they made stakes, planted them beside the suffering trees, refilled the holes with topsoil, and fastened the saplings to the stakes with brown garden twine. They all worked side by side, including Theodoros.

This time Stefan made sure Selim didn't play hooky. Whenever the guy slowed down or appeared to search for his cigarettes, Stefan would urgently demand something to be done without delay, thus keeping everyone—Selim included—on their toes. The Turk hated the whole situation and left his colleagues in no doubt about it. Yet he had no choice because all, without exception, toiled very hard.

The golden Mediterranean evening yielded to soft, balmy twilight as they finished with the last olive tree. There was again order in the orchard when they gathered around Stefan's little car, waiting for Theodoros to bring their wages.

The Greek came out of the kitchen with the banknotes in hand. Through the open door, they could see his wife busying herself around the stove. The appetizing smell of fresh moussaka tickled their taste buds, making them suddenly realize how hungry they were. Theodoros handed everyone his share. "I added a bonus for your extra work," he said, "and if you don't mind, we would like you guys to have supper with us."

The supper was good and rich. Theodoros, although he didn't drink very often, opened a bottle of smooth and fruity red wine that exquisitely matched the food. Once their appetites were satisfied, the wine soothed the fatigue of the day, which in the end had melted into a pleasant, gentle tiredness.

When they set off for home, dusk had already fallen, shrouding the familiar landscape in impenetrable black; and going to the car, they hunched up under the slight chill of the night. None of them was eager to talk, and Stefan drove all the way in complete silence. He parked the Trabant across the street from the camp, under the huge locust tree. In the camp, all the lights were ablaze, and the glow sprawled far into the street. In contrast, under the tree it was dark, and they could barely see each other's faces.

"All right, my friends, we are at home," Stefan said with a satisfied sigh. He got out of the car with a slow, cautious movement, careful not to stretch his aching back too much. "God, how tired I am," he complained as he locked the door. "Tomorrow, we'll go at the same time if this is okay with you guys. What do you think?"

"I'll be here," Luca muttered, yawning noisily.

"Me too," Val smiled impishly, imagining how great a day without work would be—an unconceivable dream in the existing circumstances.

They were now walking lazily toward the camp's gate, just emerging into the brightly lit side of the street. "Me not going," Selim belligerently said, pronouncing the words intently.

"Why? You don't like the money, or what?" Stefan good-humoredly asked, mellowed by the pleasant dinner at Theodoros's.

"You dirty capitalist instrument. I not work with you," Selim excitedly uttered. He stopped, pointing an accusing finger at Stefan, his handsome features contorted in an ugly grimace by conspicuous hatred. "I artist . . . You and Theodoros, bandits . . . You and Theodoros go to hell." His voice reached a high pitch, the words almost choking him; and as he spoke, froth gathered at the corners of his mouth. "You fascist pigs!" he shouted, then turned his back with a jerk and ran into the yard, hands erratically dangling.

Stefan stopped in the middle of the street. Everything had happened too fast for his tired reflexes. He hadn't had even the time to get angry. "What was that?" he asked without addressing his question to anyone in particular.

"They are a weird stock, these commies . . . That's his way of saying thank you, I guess," Luca mused. He spat in disgust on the dusty pavement. "The guy makes me sick."

PROBLEMATIC IDENTITIES

Váci sat in sullen silence in the middle of the courtyard under the mulberry tree. The camp was quiet for once, and the Hungarian was alone, struggling with a conspicuous fit of ill humor. He looked like someone whose hopes have unexpectedly collapsed as a consequence of a terrible calamity, his fair complexion much darkened and devoid of its usual cheerfulness, his blond hair in crazy disorder, his eyes bloodshot and vacant. On the bench beside him was an almost empty bottle of seven-starred Metaxa he occasionally brought to his mouth with a careful, slow motion, thirstily taking a big gulp. Then he replaced the amphora-shaped bottle on the bench, each time with increasing care and concentration.

It was just minutes before twilight, and the pale golden sky progressively metamorphosed into a delicate lilac blue. The late afternoon air was warm and dense with spicy fragrances, and from the big locust tree across the street came the shrill chirping cries of countless male cicadas. But Váci was drunk and couldn't care less about the color of the sky or the deafening chiming of these noisy insects. When Stefan returned from town, the Hungarian didn't even care to answer his friend's greeting.

Noticing that something was wrong, Stefan crossed the courtyard and came to Váci. "What's up, man?" he asked.

Instead of answering, Váci uncorked the bottle of brandy and passed it to Stefan with a shaky hand. "Drink," he said.

"I am fine, thank you," Stefan tried to avoid a drink he didn't want. He had his own worries and for the moment wasn't in a drinking mood.

"No, no. Drink. Drink!" Váci insisted, shoving the bottle into Stefan's hand. "Do you think that a Hungarian's brandy is not good enough for a stinky Wallachian?" he asked offensively.

Although they initially spoke English, Váci pronounced the offending expression, which was traditionally meant as a chauvinistic insult, in Hungarian. Those words always made Stefan's blood boil. He resented that expression emotionally and physically, with every fiber of his body. It painfully reminded him of the centuries of persecution, humiliation, and suffering some of his people had been forced to put up with. Yet he liked Váci and repressed his annoyance, deciding to accept the drink for friendship's sake.

Stefan raised the bottle to eye level to check how much was left in it, tilted it to his mouth, and took a deep draught of the amberlike liquid. Then he took another one. The brandy tasted good. As the smooth fluid descended in his stomach, he felt the wave of warmth that followed it and, almost immediately after, its soothing effect. "Don't be rude, my friend," he said in a conciliatory tone, returning the bottle. "Better tell me what happened."

Váci made a vague gesture with his hand and took another shot of the quickly-diminishing liquor.

"Come on, what happened?" Stefan insisted, this time in Hungarian. He had gone to university in Timisoara, a middle-sized Transylvanian town where Romanians mixed with minorities such as Hungarians, Swabians, and Serbs. His first girlfriend there was Hungarian, and as they say, there is no better way to learn a language than with a lover. In the years after he moved to Bucharest, his Hungarian became rusty because he didn't use it. Since the arrival of Váci and his companions at the camp, however, everyday practice had considerably improved his conversational skills.

"Oh," Váci said, gesturing with the now-empty bottle, "you wouldn't understand." He spoke with difficulty, as if he were chewing glue.

"I certainly will, if you would care to tell me," Stefan said with a faint smile on his face. He was in a better mood after that brandy.

László, another young Hungarian refugee, popped up in the open door of the main building, looking around searchingly. Seeing the pair under the mulberry tree, his face lit up with recognition and joined them.

"Drink," Váci said, passing him the bottle.

László took the bottle, carefully considered it in the fading light of the evening, and then put it back on the bench. "I can't. There is nothing left," he said, his voice tinged with a mixture of amusement and regret.

"I have two more bottles in the room. Bring another here," Váci drawled.

"I don't think I will. You are drunk," László said. He was good-humored but firm.

Váci brusquely stood up, unsure, on his feet. He gave László a dirty, disdainful look. "Fetch me the bottle. Go this very moment, go, go!" he cried. "Do you hear me?" He staggered perilously and would have fallen if Stefan hadn't supported him with a steady hand.

"I am a Hungarian nobleman. And you, László, are a nobody." Váci pointed his finger at László. "I will tell my servants to whip you if you don't do what I tell you. Go right now," he said and collapsed on the bench in a state of prostration.

"What happened to him?" Stefan asked.

"We have got a big problem," László answered. "We don't have proper documents, and the Canadians won't accept our application for landed immigrant visas."

"What kind of documents?"

"We don't have any. None, nothing."

"What do you mean? Nobody can travel these days without documents."

"We did," László said and laughed. "Yes, we did it," he repeated with unconcealed pride.

"You, mister, are completely mistaken," Váci's drunken voice sounded arrogant.

"Really? How come, Your Lordship?" László questioned him. His tone was sarcastic.

"One day, you will get that whipping. Have no doubt, for you deserve it." Váci hiccuped noisily. "You have forgotten . . . We have documents . . . Unfortunately, the Canadians . . . don't like them," Váci answered, speaking between hiccups and with long pauses, obviously searching for words. He fumbled feverishly in his pockets. Finally, he produced a piece of crumpled paper, laid it on the bench, and struggled clumsily to straighten it. The only thing he managed to achieve was messing up the piece of worn-out paper even more.

"Stefan. Stefan," a feminine voice called from the main building.

Stefan looked up and saw Lia standing on the second floor balcony with a mug in her hand.

"The coffee is ready," said his wife. "Would you care to have some?"

"Yes, of course. Could you bring it here?" he asked. Then pointing to the two Hungarians, he added, "Bring some for the company too, please."

"Ah, coffee. I love coffee," Váci cried. Distracted by the thought of good coffee, he relaxed his grasp, and the light breeze blew away the piece of paper, which landed on the ground. "There it goes, my bloody document!" he shouted and tried to catch it, almost falling off the bench himself.

László picked up the document and neatly flattened it on his hip, delicately smoothing its wrinkles with the palm of his hand.

"Give me that," Váci demanded.

"Does anyone want coffee?" Lia asked, presenting three steaming mugs on a piece of plywood she used as a tray. The smell of fresh Greek coffee enveloped them, pleasantly stimulating their palates and making them forget everything else for the moment.

"Excellent coffee," Váci said after a couple of quick, greedy sips. "My dear lady, you are the greatest of the Transylvanian noblewomen I have ever known." He stood up, swaying a little with the mug precariously held in one hand; and with exaggerated respect, he took Lia's hand, bowed, and noisily kissed it. Then exhausted by the effort, he didn't protest when Stefan and László helped him to sit down.

"I think you are right, Váci. My mother always told me we are a noble family," Lia said, accompanying the words with a self-deprecatory laugh.

"Where is my precious document?" Váci panicked, suddenly remembering his paper and worriedly looking around.

"Here," László handed him the paper, now carefully folded.

"See, Lia? This is my precious document the Canadians don't like," Váci said with a drunken smile.

"Why? What's wrong with it?"

"They say I am not what is written in it." Váci sounded hopelessly distressed.

"What's written in it, for God's sake?" Stefan asked.

"Compressors," László laughed bitterly.

"Compressors?" Lia and Stefan asked in unison.

"Yeah! See for yourself." Váci gave the paper to Stefan. "Read it."

It was a printed form, a shipping invoice emitted by the state-owned Magyar Compressor Manufacturing Factory from Budapest and confirming a shipment of high-pressure compressors to be delivered to the Greek Worldwide Shipping Company in Thessaloniki. There was no mention of Váci's or László's names in it.

"I don't understand," Stefan exclaimed.

"That's exactly what I told you," Váci triumphantly said. He didn't hiccup anymore as the coffee seemed to have somewhat dispelled the worst part of his drunkenness.

"That's not an identity document," Stefan said.

"Mine is similar," László intervened. "These are the only papers we have."

"László, give me a cigarette," Váci commanded. "You see, Stefan dear, we are not what you would call average people," he continued after his friend handed him an already lit cigarette. "First, the communists have confiscated my family's houses, land, and other possessions and stripped us of our title. My young mother died of bitterness and privation. Brought up in wealth and luxury, she could never recover after the loss of everything she had inherited. She never got used to the lifestyle of proletarians or to Marxist rule. Then the Russian occupation forces shot my father during the 1956 uprising. I was a child of five at the time. When years later, I tried to get into medical school, they didn't let me. There was no room for scions of rotten exploiters there, they said. I had to do something to survive. Only menial and dirty jobs were available to me, like sweeping floors or collecting garbage. That wasn't my ideal, my friends. In my view, the government had stolen my property, so I decided to get even with them. I never touched any private property, only recovered what I considered mine from the state. The communist state, that is. With the ever-flourishing black market, I did quite well for a few years. One day, I met László. You haven't seen him work. He is a fine draftsman with a marvelous hand and an accomplished engraver. He is, of course, very low class and dumb as a stone; but he has talent. In other times, he wouldn't have dared to approach me as his place would have been in the stables among my serfs. Only in the new era of . . ."

"Don't believe him. He is a shameless liar," László unceremoniously interrupted his friend's story. He was conspicuously not amused. "He just pretends to be a nobleman. I know his mother, a peasant woman from Alföld, our agricultural province. Medical school, he says. What a joke. Why are you always telling people these lies?"

"Watch your tongue, László, or I will punch your bloody nose." Váci's aggressiveness rose as his drunkenness diminished.

"Only if you are able to stand up, man," László laughed at him.

"Remember that whipping I promised? It's coming . . . That woman was one of my parents' servants. Although I told him many times, in László's woodenhead, there is no room for reason. She was a most generous woman, I must say, who brought me up. May God bless her! She formally adopted me, but she is not my biological mother . . . Where was I?" Váci looked inquiringly at his audience. "Oh, yes! I met László. Well, we set up our own personal mint and printed beautiful hundred-*pengö* bills. Lots of them. We became rich in no time."

"The faster we made them, the easier it become for the militia to catch us red-handed," László said in a singsong.

"If you hadn't had the stupid idea to fall in love with that undercover militiawoman, we . . ."

"Oh, Váci! It was you who got drunk and showered the gypsy musicians with new hundred-*pengö* bills, which made us so popular. And you were also the one who picked up that militiawoman in the little restaurant in Budapest. Remember?"

Váci shook his head in mock despair. "There is nothing to be done with you, László, you are such an incurable asshole. The smallest fly in this world has more brains than you." He gave his friend a severe, disapproving look. They had probably debated the matter many times before, and László didn't push it. "The fact is we were thrown in jail. That happened last spring. We were still in the first stages of investigation, if you know what I mean, when the fall came. That brought a welcome change to the everyday maltreatment. You guys must be familiar with the way communists would round up everyone to help with the harvest in the fields, the forced labor disguised as voluntary work."

Of course they were, Stefan and Lia acquiesced, nodding their heads in silent agreement. In Romania, every citizen from primary school to the age of retirement was forced to go into the fields and work without pay for several days during the harvest season. On many occasions, they also had had to toil under heavy rain or in falling snow, trampling through the mud to pick up corn or dig out potatoes. Nobody was exempt, only the bedridden and the disabled. Surely, in Hungary, things couldn't have been any different.

"The first day, we were taken to the cornfields in the outskirts of Budapest, not too far from the main railway marshalling yard," Váci continued. "I remember that day vividly because it was sunny and warm and we were outside for the first time in four months. The fresh air gave me a sort of pleasant light-headedness. Three of us stuck together: László, Stanislaw the Polish student, and I. Stanislaw was caught trying to illegally cross the border into Austria, and we became friends in jail. Our job was to pick the corn and pile it up in between the rows, ready to be loaded into trucks. The work area was huge, and the guards couldn't watch everyone, so we wandered farther and farther until we reached the end of that field. There were many railway tracks with parked boxcars of various sizes scattered all over, and a long freight train stopped at a red light. An older man was checking every car, affixing lead seals to the door locks. László and Stanislaw stayed hidden in the cornfield while I went to talk to the man. He could easily see who I was because of my rough twill striped coat and badly bruised face. I asked him if he had a spare cigarette, and he gave me a whole package. We had a smoke together."

"'Where is the train going?' I casually asked him."

"'To Greece,' he said and added that some of the cars were not sealed yet, but he was going to bring more seals from the office to finish them."

"Then he left, and I called my friends. It was child's play for us to get into one of the unsealed cars loaded with compressors and lie low among the big pieces of machinery. Later, the man came with someone else to finish sealing the doors. And soon afterward, the train started rolling."

Váci extracted a box of Dunhill from his pocket, offered cigarettes to his audience and, after passing his lighter around, also lit one for himself. "I am sure he knew we were somewhere inside that train. He was a good man," Váci said, looking thoughtfully at the glowing tip of his cigarette as if he could see the man's face there. "If caught, he would have been in big trouble. A remarkably good old man. God bless him!"

"We would also have been in big trouble if caught," László said. "The guards were allowed to shoot escapees and kill them on the spot."

"Yes," Váci agreed. "Our lives had no value. Fortunately, they didn't get hold of us before the train left. But our ordeal wasn't finished yet. Sooner or later, the guards would have found out about our escape. And surely, the police were warned and looking for us everywhere. To get to Greece, the train had to cross several borders. And at each of them, we could have been discovered. Also, a freight train moves erratically, spending a long time just waiting in all kind of forlorn places. And we had neither food nor water. At the beginning, to appease our hunger, we chewed tobacco from the cigarettes the old man had given me. They didn't last long and made us sick, but the worst was the lack of water. When the train crossed into Bulgaria on the fourth day, we were starved, thirsty, and confused. To make things worse, Stanislaw got a bad fever. He started raving, and we had difficulty keeping him quiet. The noise could have attracted the attention of the border guards, so we had to silence him quite roughly. What saved us was the rain, I think. It rained continuously during the following days while we were crossing Bulgaria. We put our coats out through a gap we had managed to open with bare hands between the boards forming the wall of the car. When they got soaked, we squeezed them well into our mouths and drank the water. During the nights, it was bitterly cold. We shivered continuously in our wet coats, and that prevented us from sleeping. In the end, László lay prostrate on the floor, barely groaning from time to time. Stanislaw was unconscious, totally silent as if he were dead. I lost count of the days and lived in a sort of painful dream, hallucinating every so often.

"One morning, the train stopped. And as I was dozing in a state of half consciousness, I heard people speaking an unknown language, which was not Slavic. Too weak to walk, I crawled to the door and shouted for help. No matter who they were, we needed their help if we wanted to survive. My voice wasn't strong enough, and it took a long time until someone heard me. That caused quite a big commotion outside. People were running, someone shouted, and finally, the door opened wide to a bright, sunny world. Blinded for a moment, I couldn't see anything. When I could see again, there were several men dressed in uniforms, with rifles and submachine guns at the ready. On a high pole, not far away, the Greek flag fluttered in the wind. Greece, Greece? I asked. And when they acknowledged, I tried to get off but rolled instead to the ground and passed out."

"The only thing I remember vaguely, as if it was part of a dream," László said, "is that I was lying on the grass. And this young soldier, probably an army nurse, inserted a needle into my arm. I didn't feel anything. When I woke up next, we were in a military ambulance going God knows where."

"The Greek border police were good to us," Váci continued. "They revived me, and someone brought a nurse who cleaned my wounds. Falling off the car, you see, I had hurt myself badly and I was bleeding like a stuck pig. He gave me water to drink and a little food. Not too much, because this could have been dangerous. Then the nurse rushed to help Lászlo and Stanislaw, whom the guards carried into the shade of nearby trees, laying them on a grassy patch. Sitting on the embankment and too weak to move, I asked the men standing by if this was Greek soil, pointing between my feet. They said yes and smiled. Then and there, although shaky and clumsy, I knelt, lifted up my hands to God, and kissed the earth, thanking him for my liberation. I cried uncontrollably, like a baby."

Váci's voice changed. He paused and furtively wiped his eyes with the back of his hand. But the tears couldn't be easily stopped.

"Before the soldiers took us to the ambulance, something prompted me to grab a few shipping invoices from the stack accompanying the compressors. We traveled as compressors anyhow. Didn't we? And after all, they were the only official documents we could have had. They really were our travel documents," Váci concluded.

It was dark now, and the stars were shining like diamonds on the high black vault stretched over their heads. The security light at the gate and the lamps over the exterior doors were already on, splashing the yard with big patches of light. Outside their reach, harsh deep shadows hid the details of the buildings, giving the familiar place a mysterious, exotic look accentuated by the palm trees silhouetted against the starry sky.

From one of the first-floor bedrooms where the Turks were lodged, the easily recognizable nine notes from the melodious beginning of the Internationale came loud and clear. A baritone voice echoed by the opposite buildings announced to the world in Russian that Radio Moscow was broadcasting.

"I wish someone would smash their bloody radio," Váci said, suddenly aware of the disturbance. "Shut off that stupid radio!" he shouted at the top of his voice. "Shut it off, you bastards, or I will break it into pieces!" he shouted again, his voice booming through the quiet of the night. Instantly, the volume went down, and the speaker's voice almost died. Something could still be heard, but it was just a babbling whisper now.

"They seem to love that bullshit propaganda very much. Why the hell don't they go to live in one of the communist countries?" Váci rhetorically asked. "Why do all these Turkish leftists only immigrate into capitalistic countries? They are flocking into West Germany, they try to sneak into Switzerland, and they are courting Sweden to accept them as refugees. Their dream is Canada and the States. Why? If they like communism so much, why they don't immigrate into those countries that are already communist to see how it is for real?"

"They like the theory, not the real thing," laughed Lászlo. "You should see them listening entranced and with gaping mouths to that rubbish the Russians broadcast to gullible foreigners. I can't believe it."

"Honestly, Stefan," Váci said, "I would gladly have changed my place in Hungary with any of them any time."

"I know," agreed Stefan. "I would have, too," he laughed bitterly. "Nobody volunteered for that exchange . . . I always dreamed how wonderful it would have been to be a communist in an affluent, capitalistic country cashing in on unemployment or living on welfare and getting taxpayers' money for propaganda during election campaigns."

The gate opened with a loud squeak, and two men entered, talking animatedly. Their faces were in the dark, silhouetted against the street light. They approached the group slowly. Those two were Abdur and Stanislaw, still talking when they came close enough to be recognized.

"What's new in Athens, guys?" Lászlo asked.

"Good news, boys. South Africa will take us in without documents," Stanislaw answered.

"Will you go to the Skunk State?" Abdur asked contemptuously.

"We cannot be too choosy, you know," László said.

"We can't afford to be stupid either," Váci grumbled.

"Come on, Váci. Their offer is quite generous: money, free housing, and bursaries for studies. A nice package," Stanislaw enthusiastically said.

"Of course, if in exchange, we agree to kill their blacks," Váci said with a trace of bitterness in his voice. "What's the catch?" he wanted to know.

"There is no catch. The consulate in Athens will get our documents through diplomatic channels. That's not our problem anymore. Since the American embargo, they have excellent relations with the communist bloc." Stanislaw spoke with confidence.

"It is true. These days, the Russians routinely buy South African gold and diamonds. They seem to be on very good terms," Stefan confirmed.

"I thought South Africa was opposed to communism," Abdur said. "Their government keeps that Marxist leader, Mandela, in jail. Apparently, he is not the only one, is he?"

"Don't be so naive, my son. International relations and internal politics are not the same thing." Stefan said.

"What about our criminal records?" Váci asked.

"They don't care about police records—I was told by the consul in person. She is a nice woman. I explained our situation. They simply don't care," Stanislaw said.

"What do you have to sign? Did they tell you?" Lia was curious.

"An application, the travel document, normal papers. Why are you asking?'" Stanislaw appeared puzzled by Lia's question.

"Because Stefan and I, for instance, have been asked by the Canadians to sign a statement giving up our claims to professional status in case we are accepted. We had no choice, this was a mandatory condition. And Canada is apparently the best in the treatment of immigrants. Every country would impose upon you some conditions from the very beginning. What are those in South Africa?"

"I don't know. They didn't tell me anything along those lines. I don't think there are any such conditions . . . At least, I don't believe so." Stanislaw wasn't so sure anymore.

"We can lightheartedly sign off our professional privileges as far as I am concerned," László noisily laughed. "I have nothing to lose."

"Maybe not professionally, László. There are many other things you can lose and be sorry about afterward," Lia said. "I am already sorry for what I signed, but we cannot spend our lives in refugee camps waiting for a perfect country, which doesn't exist."

"That's true. Same here. And after all, what else can we lose?" László asked.

"László, don't be stupid." Váci's voice was still tired. "If you sign a contract with their bloody military, you instantly lose your hard-gained freedom."

"Only for a few years, and they pay awfully good money, I hear. So what?"

"You might lose your dear life, smartie. You don't need too much for that. A little bullet like this in your blockhead would be enough." Váci demonstratively lifted two fingers a quarter of an inch apart, bringing them close to László's eyes. "Only that much—and you are gone forever into the evergreen hunting grounds of the Great Manitou, as Winetou the Apache used to say. Understand now?"

"The consul didn't mention military service at all. If you want, we can ask her. Just to make sure. I want to go to South Africa. You guys do whatever you like," Stanislaw said.

"Right now, I want to eat something. I am terribly hungry," Váci said and stood up. "Tomorrow, we will talk with your South African philanthropists and then start from there." He threw an arm around Stanislaw's shoulders and guided him toward the main building, walking surprisingly well, followed by the whole group. "In Afrika sind mädchen braun," he started, crooning a German tune that was quite popular at one time.

"In Cuba sind mädchen braun," corrected Stefan, who knew the song.

"Who cares, my dear Stefan," Váci said, speaking over his shoulder. "You can love and die in Africa as well as in Cuba."

The group arrived at the door, under the bright fluorescent light, where a multitude of moths and other nocturnal insects swarmed in a suicidal frenzy. Many were already littering the ground, dead or agonizing. Váci turned, showing them to Stefan.

"See, beings are naturally dying everywhere around us. Compressors, however, don't die. They are sent to the wreckers to be destroyed."

Armchair Revolutionary

The Canadian immigration officials required a complete medical checkup of every applicant for landed immigrant visa. Therefore, the organization for refugees that was taking care of Stefan and his family set up appointments for them with various medical specialists. To begin with, one morning, they were sent to have their chest X-ray examinations done.

The radiologist's office was at his home in Kifissia, the posh quarter of Athens. It was an impressive villa surrounded by a vast garden densely populated with trees and ornamental bushes. When they arrived, several sprinklers were spreading clouds of watery mist over the lush vegetation with rhythmic hisses. Minirainbows flew around in the wake of the shimmering water jets as they drifted back and forth between noble varieties of roses. Drops of dewlike moisture glittered on the fleshy petals of beautiful flowers in spite of the scorching heat.

There was nobody at home, so they had to wait, standing on the sidewalk in the meager shade of the tall stone-and-iron wall enclosing the property. It was awfully hot, but the atmosphere was fragrant with the delicate perfume of the roses, mixed with the stronger smell of pines and humid soil. Surely, it was cool among the artfully trimmed bushes and under the trees; and it would have been, of course, more pleasant to sit on a bench in the garden. Unfortunately, that wasn't possible; and during their long wait, the

Romanians—when they got tired of standing in one place—paced up and down the sunny street instead.

The doctor arrived home in a shiny black Mercedes more than three hours past the time set for their appointment, when his would-be patients had almost given up any hope of seeing him that day. He opened the main gate and the garage door by remote control and slowly drove inside. After carefully locking the door and the gate, the man walked at leisure through the garden, taking his time to look at the flowers. He finally came to the small wrought-iron gate where they were waiting for him and eyed them without hiding his contempt.

A chorus of "Good afternoon, Mr. Doctor" welcomed him, but he didn't answer. The doctor was a short older gentleman with neatly combed graying hair and a thin, finely-trimmed moustache descending around his mouth over a well-groomed goatee. He had a dignified appearance and obviously knew how to keep his distance.

"Are you those people sent by the organization?"

"Yes, Doctor," answered Stefan.

"Show me your identity books," the doctor haughtily demanded, considering them with cold eyes and reluctantly stretching his clean, manicured hand through the close-welded iron bars of the gate in order to get the documents. The man didn't care to hide his hostility. He checked their names carefully, comparing their faces with the pictures in the identity books, also looking into a dainty black notebook with gold-rimmed pages pulled out of his jacket's inner pocket. Only after he seemed satisfied did he unlock the gate. "Come in, follow me." He spoke brusquely without looking at them.

They crunched behind him over the gravel path toward the house, across that paradisiacal Eden exuding beauty and serene freshness. He stopped in front of the short flight of wide marble stairs leading to the intricately carved solid oak door. "Wait here . . . I have to open the door . . . Today is my staff's day off," he murmured without turning around or stopping. Then he continued to walk and disappeared around the corner of the building.

Another quarter of an hour elapsed before the latch clicked and the front door was cracked open. They saw him peering from the doorframe. "You can enter," called the doctor, who was now wearing a freshly pressed and starched white medical smock.

He led them through the entry hall and a vast waiting room furnished with expensive-looking furniture. Oriental rugs were spread over the shiny parquet floor, and numerous good-quality paintings enlivened the room. Half-drawn roll shutters kept the interior pleasant and cool. French doors extended across the entire back wall, and when the doctor opened one of the frosted glass panels, they could see into his roomy office. There was a huge desk, several tall bookcases lined with expensively bound books, and a white black-spotted Great Dane that was sleeping in an armchair. The dog morosely opened his eyes and yawned without showing any intention of moving.

"Shall we wait here?" asked Stefan, preparing to sit on a leather couch in the waiting room. In order to be able to catch the first bus, as was usual for a trip to Athens, they had woken up at four o'clock in the morning; and he was already tired after standing in the heat for several hours.

"No. Not here," the doctor hurriedly answered. He opened a small side door and led them through an unlit narrow corridor into the kitchen. The kitchen was smelly and hot. "Here. You wait here," he said. Then pointing to one of the four doors in the kitchen, he told them to undress in the room behind it before coming to the X-ray examination room.

"Where is that room?" Stefan asked. He resented the Greek's insulting behavior.

The doctor was already in the middle of the corridor, apparently returning to his office. "Here!" he shouted and opened a side door, which he left ajar after vanishing behind it.

"I will go first," Stefan said, "to see how it works."

He opened the door shown by the doctor. It was heavy, made of solid metal; and after opening it with some difficulty, he found himself in the house's incinerator room among garbage bins, brooms, mops and dustpans. Feeble daylight filtered through a small smoky window, giving the place a gloomy, repellant look. A thin layer of fine ash and dust covered everything, and an old garbage smell persistently hung in the stuffy atmosphere.

"This is not a dressing room," he told his people, after returning to the kitchen. "There are no hospital gowns either. There is not even a coat hanger in that dirty hole."

"Mama! I won't ever undress in that pigsty," Ana said as she peered inside the incinerator room. "I don't want to mess my clothes with soot. Even the smell is enough to make me throw up."

"Val, close that door, please. And come back here," Lia called her son who, curious by nature, had gone exploring.

"I'll take my shirt with me," Stefan decided. "Val will come after me, and you girls go in together and undress in the examination room," he said and left.

The doctor wasn't in his examination room. The modern white X-ray machine with shiny levers and black knobs surrounded by slick electric cables purred menacingly like a big cat, winking hostilely with its warning lights. Stefan, his shirt under one arm, stood motionless in the middle of the room, expectantly glancing over some strategically sprawled screens, and waited for a couple of minutes. "I am here," he said loudly in the end when his patience ran out.

The doctor opened another sliding door and came in. Stefan could see into the office where the Great Dane was asleep in the snug armchair. In the fleeting moment the door was open, Stefan saw a painting on the opposite wall. It was a quadruple portrait. He thought he could recognize the men in that picture but discarded the idea as too improbable.

"What do you want?" the doctor asked brusquely. Stefan felt his animosity.

"I am ready."

"What do you want to do with the shirt?"

"I shall put it somewhere here."

"Why didn't you undress in the room I showed you?" the doctor asked irritably.

"That room is dirty. We are not used to such a place. And as a matter of fact, there are neither coat hangers nor hospital gowns in there," Stefan said and resolutely added, "I preferred to keep my shirt with me."

"I see. That room is too dirty for you . . . for your clean shirt," the doctor said with a sneer.

"Yes, it is indeed," Stefan confirmed. In spite of feeling frustrated, he restrained himself. He didn't intend to antagonize a professional who was not inclined to treat them with civility. Among refugees in the know, the rumor was that medical certificates were decisive in obtaining the much-sought-after landed immigrant visas.

"All right, then leave it on that," the doctor said, indicating a little chair beside the X-ray machine while frowning with undisguised displeasure. Grumbling, he retired behind the solid protective screen with a tiny square window in it and began fiddling in earnest with his equipment.

When the examination ended, the doctor reappeared, holding a flat metallic box loaded with the exposed films. "Go back, and when all are finished, bring everyone into my office," he ordered Stefan.

"What about the hospital gowns?" Stefan asked. He was at the end of his tether now.

"Hospital gowns? What for?" The man's voice was high-pitched, and he appeared to be scandalized.

"For the girls, sir. Otherwise, how do you want to examine them?" Stefan asked, giving him a dirty look.

"Oh, the girls. Yes, yes. They do need hospital gowns . . . Right." The doctor seemed to have had a sudden change of heart. He opened a third sliding door, hidden behind one of the screens; and Stefan saw a clean elegant changing room with whitewashed walls and a wide curtained window. Several neatly ironed hospital gowns were stacked on a small table, surrounded by half a dozen modern utilitarian-type designer chairs. Along the wall, there was also a good-sized rack with numerous empty coat hangers. On a low coffee table, glossy multicolored magazines and newspapers were ready to provide entertainment to more important patients than a handful of refugees.

The man pulled two gowns from the stack and handed them to Stefan. "There. Take your gowns. Tell the women to leave them afterward in the kitchen." He unceremoniously pushed Stefan toward the exit. "Go now. Go!" he said.

Later, the Romanians gathered in the waiting room outside the doctor's office, and Stefan knocked on the French door. Getting no answer, they waited several minutes until the doctor called them inside. When they entered, the dog was still lying idle in the only armchair in the room. His master sat at the desk on a high chair, scribbling in a register book.

To his utmost surprise, the painting on the sidewall confirmed Stefan's previous impression. The four characters in the expensively framed quadruple portrait were Marx, Engels, Lenin, and Stalin. It was one of those standard propagandistic depictions of the dialectical materialism's icons familiar to everyone who had lived in the communist bloc. He stepped a little closer in order to sneak a better look, but the doctor made a warning move, raising his right hand, in which he held his fountain pen like a weapon. "Don't come too close," he said. "The dog is indisposed."

He began to fill in a questionnaire by asking their first names. Both Stefan and Lia had three first names, and it became obvious that the doctor didn't like that. "Why does anyone need three first names? Only the mobsters have so many aliases," he grumbled, talking to an invisible listener. "No wonder there is so much crime in Greece nowadays. What can we expect if we give shelter to all kind of schemers and racketeers?"

Stefan could feel his blood pressure rapidly rising and the anger overwhelming him like an irresistible tidal wave. His head felt very hot, and his tanned complexion became flushed under the effect of strong emotion. "Sir," he said with extreme politeness and calculated slowness, "these are not aliases. These are baptismal names: two names of saints, one given by each grandmother, and the third is a Latin name in honor of our Roman ancestors. Customarily, the godfather chooses the third name. As a matter of fact, we are not gangsters, and we don't want to stay any longer than necessary in your country. We are political refugees. Do you know what that means, political refugees? That's what we are. Do you understand, sir? We are political refugees . . . as is stated in this Greek identity book . . . See that?" Stefan's face was crimson, his forehead covered in cold perspiration, which glistened as he bent across the desk to show his document to the man. "We are not gangsters. We are honest people—legally acknowledged refugees."

"Don't shout," the man said. "I know what you are." He pushed his chair back and looked hard at Stefan. "What have you done in Romania that you had to flee from your country?" His tone of voice was inquisitorial.

"Nothing, sir. We have done nothing wrong. As a matter of fact, I was a scientist, a pioneer in my field. And Lia was a highly regarded professional. The reason we left our country was the lack of freedom, the everyday abuse of human rights, and the paranoiac tyranny perpetrated by the leadership."

"How can you dare say that, when your leader is such an outspoken democrat, a freedom fighter? We know and admire Ceaușescu, your president, for his boldness, for his position on international issues. A great man, a good communist leader." The doctor had spoken with unbridled enthusiasm. His entire demeanor had suddenly completely changed. He had forgotten his examination register, the examination itself, and the fact that he had a professional duty toward his visitors. The subject seemed to be closer to his heart than anything else.

"Everything is relative, sir," Stefan said. "What do you mean by 'a good communist leader?' I see you have here a portrait of Stalin. Would you call him a good leader after he slaughtered tens of millions of his own people?" Stefan paused to regain his breath. "It is common knowledge that he killed even some of his closest comrades, Trotsky and Kirov, among several others . . . perhaps even Lenin. After all, Ceaușescu is not what you think. He is a decoy to lure Western politicians, a puppet of the Soviets. He is starving the whole country in order to enrich his clique and his family. On his orders, bloodthirsty henchmen torture and kill without remorse those seen as potential opponents. There is neither freedom nor democracy in Romania."

"Sacrifices are needed to secure a bright life for the future generations. Communism is the future . . ."

"You want to convince me that 'blood is part of the political surgery,' as someone has said. It would be a futile exercise, sir, because I know all the slogans," Stefan cut him short, laughing bitterly. "Communism is the springtime of humanity. Communism is the proletarians' paradise—from everyone according to his abilities to everyone according to his needs. Work is a duty of honor. Proletarians of the world, unite . . . What a sinister joke. Do you want me to continue? I know all of them by heart. They are the claptrap we have heard day in, day out, since the end of the Second World War. It is the fodder of the political bureaucrats in every country of the communist bloc. I am sick and tired of those empty words. Nobody believes in them except idealistic intellectuals from the Western world. Those from the communist bloc were brutally exterminated a long time ago," he said.

Then he suddenly remembered: "Romanians aren't allowed to travel freely abroad. And even moving inside the country is forbidden, except for those on government business or, of course, if one can afford to bribe the approving bureaucrats. And by the way, do you know, sir, how it feels when you have a microphone in your bedroom or your phone is bugged? I know too well because it happened to me for a long time under your admired Ceauşescu. Is this freedom?"

"Well, well. Who knows what you have done?" The doctor laughed mischievously. "If one raises a hand against the people, one must pay the price. Perhaps you were a rich bourgeois, a scion of the exploiting classes, an enemy of the proletariat, or a spy. What do I know?"

"That's true. You don't know. I am a proletarian myself, and all my adult professional life was selflessly dedicated to the country. Actually, until recently, I sacrificed my life for the good of the people and never had a house of my own or any other property. Only a few months ago, we were able to buy a shabby little car for which I was on a waiting list for seven years. My only mistake was to promote new ideas in science, to develop new research avenues . . ." Stefan was short of breath.

"Don't get excited," the doctor said. "It's not good for you. Mistakes happen everywhere. What is a life when the future good of the whole of humanity lies in balance? I would gladly give my life for such a worthy cause." He popped up, stretched, and stood on the tip of his toes, trying to get taller than he really was, his heart inflamed by revolutionary enthusiasm. "What is the value of one's life in comparison with the triumph of communism? A trifle!" he shouted with all his might, as if he were on stage at a public meeting.

The Great Dane, awakened by his master's loud voice, growled menacingly and stared at Stefan with bloodshot eyes. Perhaps the animal shared his master's convictions and didn't like fugitives from the ungodly paradise.

"Let's go," Lia murmured in Romanian. "Don't you see the guy is a fanatic? Let's get out of here."

"Don't be in such a hurry to give up your life, sir. Life is too short, I found, to be wasted on an illusion. From our experience, people like you are usually the first victims of the new regime," Stefan heatedly retorted. He couldn't resist the urge to continue the debate.

"I can't believe you. This is a calumny. You speak like that because you are a turncoat," the doctor said aggressively. "Your presence here among us is indubitable proof of that."

"Stefan, let's go," Lia insisted. "It is late. Come on, let's go home."

"Just wait a moment. Give me one more minute, please," Stefan said in Romanian to his wife, and then turned toward the doctor. "I'll give you an example, a fact that perhaps you don't know. The man you admire, Ceauşescu, a mere bloody dictator himself, publicly revealed several years ago, when it was convenient for the promotion of his own career, the atrocious manner used by his predecessor, Gheorghiu-Dej, to get rid of the ex-president of the Party, Pătrăşcanu. Every day, Gheorghiu-Dej personally prescribed the number and severity of head blows to be given to Pătrăşcanu by torturers wielding heavy wooden clubs. These were intended to kill him, not immediately, but slowly, over a period of more than half a year. And so it happened. Pătrăşcanu was the founder of the Party, a loyal communist, and a faithful Marxist-Leninist. What makes you think that someone like you would be spared?"

"My honest life, my unspotted professional record, and my unblemished reputation are well-known. My trademark is dedication to the people. Nobody can find any fault with me. There is nothing secret about me, and my opinions have been repeatedly and publicly expressed. Everyone knows what my convictions are and where I stand." He spoke peremptorily, looking with pride and disdain at Stefan. "I would never be a deserter of the great cause."

"Maybe you wouldn't. I don't know you, sir, and wouldn't discuss that. But what about your property?" Stefan asked, smiling impishly.

"What about my property?" The doctor looked genuinely surprised. "What are you talking about?"

"Property is based on crime and theft. Don't you remember what Marx said? The first thing a Marxist regime would do would be to confiscate your house and nationalize your practice. What do you have to say about that? Would you agree with such measures?" Stefan eagerly awaited the response.

"Now I see what you mean. To tell you the truth, I could not be happier. No more taxes to be paid, no more expenses to keep the business running, no costly investments in equipment and all the associated worries. I would be totally free to dedicate my time to my real calling. I am looking forward to being part of such a revolution and benefiting from such a happy turn in my life."

"There was no revolution in Romania, just a takeover by a handful of Soviet puppets brought upon us by the bayonets of the Red Army. The confiscation of property was not done by popular request—it was spoilage done under duress. The witnesses were thousands of murdered peasants and landlords of all categories thrown into unmarked common graves. Even if you somehow avoided the bloodshed, you wouldn't have a house to live in or a source of income after a Marxist revolution. Everything has to be in the hands of the state. How would you make a living?" Stefan asked.

"I have another house in Athens and one in Corfu, where I, with my family, spend summers," the man said. "I would work for the state and get a steady salary, not an always fluctuating income like now. Upon my retirement, the state would give me a pension, and I wouldn't have to worry about my old age. There is no safety or stability in capitalism."

"Can't you see, Stefan? The man is spoiled rich and bored, looking for excitement in his dull life. Let's get out of here," Lia, who had become impatient, whispered in Romanian. "Let's leave. I want to go."

"Just one more moment, Lia, please. Please," Stefan begged her and turned again to the doctor. "Don't be mistaken, sir. There won't be any private property left in a communist state. Your three houses and your private practice will put you in the hated category of past exploiters, and no job will be available to you except menial, unskilled, low-paid physical work. You will be lucky if they don't lock you up in an extermination labor camp." There was pity in Stefan's eyes when he ended his last sentence. "I knew people who had that unenviable fate, whose sole fault was their professional proficiency, success, and naivete."

"What you describe is a fascist state. The dictatorship of the proletariat has deep democratic roots. We will take care that nothing like that happens here. Ours will be a free New World without exploitation, where all people are equal, well fed, and cared for," the radiologist declared with emphasis.

"May God help you, sir. After almost forty years spent in the communist system, I doubt you would have even the chance to survive such a revolution. As they say in Romania, 'What is born from a cat always eats mice.' The evolution of events in all the communist bloc countries shows that no exception to the Soviet model is possible. Have you red *The Gulag Archipelago* by Solzhenitsyn by any chance? Didn't the extent and bestiality of oppression he describes make you wonder what all that was for? That wasn't fascism—it was the first communist state, the proletarians' paradise on earth. Those atrocities were the direct result of the genuine theories of Marx, Engels, and Lenin in action. Would you categorize that as fascism?"

"Solzhenitsyn, you say? That sly servant of the American millionaires? A second-rate writer. I don't have any use for his garbage. He hated Stalin, a great leader. As I already told you, mistakes do happen everywhere, but they don't account for systematic oppression. They are accidents in the course of history, perhaps regrettable, but not the rule. We won't need repression because people will be with us, not against us. We don't need God either, because we have knowledge and experience," he said, pointing to the crammed bookshelves. "Do you see these books? I have studied them from cover to cover. All the great geniuses of socialism are here, the mightiest brains in the world." He looked triumphantly at Stefan.

"Whatever you want to call him, sir, and in spite of your disbelief, Solzhenitsyn tells the truth. What he is presenting and similar facts I know from personal experience, are not isolated mistakes. As you correctly defined them, perhaps unwillingly, they are the result of systematic and purposely organized oppression. And this whole mess started with Lenin. But he only cracked open Pandora's box. The follow-up came naturally by itself. I mean the reign of the inseparable triad of dictatorship, oppression, and corruption. The Marxist-Leninist theory is perfect, we used to say back home. It is the daily practice that is killing us." Stefan felt drained and would have preferred to be somewhere else.

"I firmly believe you are wrong. You are either poisoned by American imperialistic propaganda, or perhaps you are spreading your hostile calumnies in order to get attention and therefore benefit from capitalistic support. No honest proletarian would ever have fallen as low as you have," the doctor said, taking a deep breath and stretching, standing on the tip of his toes, unsuccessfully trying again to get taller than he really was.

The exhaustion finally caught up with Stefan, who remembered why they were there, the certificates they needed. He felt foolish for letting himself get dragged into such a useless, perhaps damaging, debate. However, he couldn't prevent himself from continuing. "If you ever have your revolution, sir, remember my words. Unlike me, you are a rich bourgeois, a capitalist employer of paid labor. and therefore someone automatically labeled as an exploiter. And in all fairness, this is what you are. Any communist government will see you as such in the long run, no matter what you are willing to do for them. As far as I am concerned, I would always prefer liberal bourgeois freedom to any form of dictatorship, including that of the so-called proletariat . . . I apologize, sir. We shouldn't have had this discussion. I am really sorry," he said in a conciliatory tone of voice.

"No, no! We definitely should have. It strengthens my belief in the final victory. I am not afraid of debates. Who do you think you are to be able to change my scientifically reached conclusions and my deepest beliefs based on philosophical analysis? The braying of the stupid ass cannot disturb the serenity of Olympus, we have said since ancient times here in Greece. No matter how many pygmies like you try to sling mud at us and stop progress, communism will prevail, and the working class of the whole world will one day enjoy a true paradise here on earth. That day it is not so far away." He sat on his high chair with a sigh of satisfaction. "Yes, we will soon have our paradise on earth."

The doctor had spoken with conviction and then began in earnest to complete his notes.

"Who can foretell the future?" Stefan said. "Yours is a nice dream, generous perhaps, yet a real 'opiate for people.' The 'geniuses' who started it were clever and crafty. However, their only mistake was that they endeavored to fight the Christian religion on its own grounds and have promised a paradise here on earth, as you said. And that's the biggest fallacy of all. And so I rest my case."

Stefan was fed up with this sort of political nonsense and didn't want to continue anymore. According to his own past experience and knowledge, life was a strenuous pilgrimage through a shadowy valley of sorrows with only short periods of lull in between never-ending struggles. From his perspective, no earthly paradise was in sight; and not only that, but it was also an impossible utopia. He decided that it would be better to change the topic.

"May I dare to ask, sir, when we will get our certificates?" he asked in a subdued voice after a long pause.

"I'll send them to the organization in a couple of days. Don't worry, our discussion won't influence the results. After all, I am a professional. As a communist, I would have preferred you to acknowledge your mistake and renounce your deviation. We want the conversion, you see, not the death of the sinner."

The radiologist put down his expensive fountain pen embellished with gold ringlets. "You people can leave. I don't need you here anymore," he concluded the interview. Although his tone of voice was finally dispassionate, his dislike of them was still evident from his entire behavior. Perhaps he unconsciously felt their presence to be an irrefutable proof of his beloved socioeconomic system's failure, a fundamental negation of those cherished theories he so confidently proclaimed, creating an irresolvable dilemma for which he viscerally hated them.

The doctor led them to the front door through the elegant waiting room and across the empty, darkened hall without saying a word. He opened the main door in an enmity-filled silence and let them out, locking it after them in a hurry with a series of loud metallic clicks. In his haste to get rid of them, he didn't even bother to answer their good-byes. They could still hear the rattling sound of his security chain being latched while they crunched back over the gravel path to the exit. The electromagnetic latch remotely unlocked the gate with a buzz, and they were off.

The shadows thrown by the trees were longer and slightly deeper now. The sun was visibly lower in the sky, heading toward sunset somewhere behind the surrounding hills. At the end of the street, dust specks swarmed like golden minuscule flies in the oblique sunrays filtering through the sparse foliage of the pines. It was still hot, and the entire family was hungry and thirsty.

"What a nasty old man," Val exclaimed as they walked briskly down the street in the direction of the nearby bus station.

"I was afraid he would set his dog on you, Dad," Ana confessed and took his father's hand as if she wanted to protect him from an invisible enemy.

"What on earth came over you, Stefan, to get involved in such a stupid debate?" Lia asked. "I thought you were smarter than that."

"I am sorry. I shouldn't have done that. It could be, of course, bad for us," Stefan acknowledged.

"That's what I meant. I will never understand why you meddle with such fanatics when you know how useless it is. How can you spend so many words to no avail? The guy is so short-sighted that he cannot see the tip of his nose. Didn't you notice that? Also, he could easily be a communist agent. And then what happens?" Lia was upset and let it be known.

"Okay, okay! I already said I am sorry. He could also have been an informer for the Greek secret police, the CIA, or any other Western agency trying to find out if we were genuine dissidents. Who knows? In this screwed up world of ours, everything is possible. After all, the man was rude all along. Didn't you see his haughty airs, his arrogance? We are not obliged to swallow every bastard's garbage, and more so if he is a rich bourgeois living in luxury while preaching the virtues of proletarian revolution. We haven't escaped from hell only to agree with any left-wing sucker who wants to convince us that that was the true paradise," Stefan said hotly.

"Mama, don't be so hard on Dad. He is right," Ana said. "This doctor treated us like scum. Remember the dirty hole he wanted us to use as a changing room? If the doctor is such a people's man, why is he so conceited? Dad had every right to tell him the truth." Stefan's daughter gave him a hug. "Good for you, Dad."

"In a way, I felt sorry for him," Stefan said. "He might well be one of those misguided people of goodwill who, in their naivete, work hard to unleash the beast that will devour them first and then the rest. A completely impractical intellectual, I must say. We had some individuals like him before in Romania. Not anymore, though." Stefan couldn't repress a bitter laugh. "They had no idea what class warfare is, but surely, they all found out before they died."

"I thought we had finished with the theory. Haven't you guys had enough of it? I am starving, and nobody seems to care," Val cried, angry at their apparent lack of interest in more mundane matters.

"Val is right," Lia agreed. "The breakfast was quite light today. We didn't have lunch, and dinner is still at least five hours ahead."

"Don't get excited, guys. In the morning, I noticed a little tavern across the station. We should have something to eat there before taking the bus. It is my treat," Stefan said.

Not long after they had finished a copious meal and relaxed from the day's excitement, they all were enjoying quiet coffees in the empty restaurant while Lia and Stefan had a smoke. Tourists were scarce in the middle of the slack season, and it was too early for the Greek patrons who would show up only during the late evening hours. Even the waiters were having a break at that particular time of the afternoon. Three of them slept around the kitchen as the Romanians had discovered when they looked in the deserted tavern for someone to take their order. For the moment, Stefan's family were the sole customers.

"How did you guys like the broiled chicken?" Stefan asked

"Excellent, and the size of my portion was quite satisfactory," Val declared without hesitation.

"This is amazing," Ana teased him. "I can't believe my ears, Val."

"Do you know," Lia pensively said, quelling their squabble with a wave of her delicate hand, "I don't remember having eaten such juicy roasted chicken since I was nine years old. We lived at the time in Arad, the town where I was born. And some evenings, father would take my mother and me to the theater. There was a little restaurant close by where we would dine every time after the play. In the wake of the communist takeover, the restaurant was nationalized. Chicken became a rarity, and even when found, the quality was appallingly poor. Some people swear that a different species of hens—much smaller, bonier, and foul-smelling—is bred nowadays on the state-owned farms."

"Oh, come on, Lia. According to our radiologist, this is American propaganda. The difference was perhaps only in your devious mind," Stefan teased her.

"I am serious, Stefan. Remember the queues we used to attend to after work? At the end of several hours of waiting, we felt lucky when we could buy an ugly, sick-looking bird—purple—as if it had died of some terrible disease." Lia said. "And this happened in a country famous before the war for its poultry."

"What about the smell, Mama? When you boiled it, the whole kitchen smelt of rotten fish. Remember?" Ana frowned in disgust.

"You people are making me sick. Stop it!" Val cried, aggrieved by unpleasant memories.

"It is time to go home. Let's move," Stefan said and stood up. "Forget about the past. Think positive. Try to imagine our wonderful life in Canada instead."

"You're right, Dad. And by the way, when we have that huge ranch in Canada we always are talking about, will you please buy me a Great Dane? One nicer than the doctor's? Will you, Dad?" Ana asked, looking at him with her beautiful eyes.

"Of course, dear. I will buy you the best breed in the entire world," her father promised. Promettre c'est noble, it is noble to make promises, the French say. Keeping them is another story. He should have known better as he could never have earned enough money to buy that ranch they all dreamed of, but for the moment, Stefan honestly believed what he had just said.

An Engagement Party

Thanasis had invited Stefan and his family to a party scheduled to take place in one of the local taverns. Some relatives of his were getting engaged, he said, and the young pair wanted to celebrate this happy event among friends.

At first, Stefan tried to excuse himself. Neither he nor his family had ever met the groom or the bride, not to mention their relatives and friends except Thanasis. And from what he had told them, it wasn't really clear what the policeman's relationship with the pair was, if any. As always, Stefan hated to intrude and didn't want to spoil what he believed to be someone's private affair. But the young Greek begged him for days, becoming increasingly gloomy when Stefan continued to refuse. In the end, upon Lia's advice, he gave in and accepted the invitation in order to avoid upsetting the young man, who was taking the refusal as a personal insult.

It was a Saturday; and as Thanasis had promised to pick them up in the late evening, they were waiting for him in the camp's courtyard, dressed up in their best clothes. The entire family had left their room earlier and was now gathered about the bench under the rickety mulberry trees, the adults smoking, the youngsters carelessly joking and laughing. Since it was their first invitation to a party in Greece, there was a feverish expectancy about them as of students waiting for the summer break.

Night had already fallen, and in the absence of the moon, it was dark outside, except for those few areas of the camp's grounds brightly lit by security lamps. The Milky Way, hanging over their heads from the feathery tops of the tall palm trees, glistened like gold dust thrown across the black deep of the cosmic space. Billions of stars were remotely shimmering in apparent cold placidity, tirelessly announcing to the mostly indifferent humanity below the faraway birth and death of countless worlds in swirls of fire and radiation Armageddons. In spite of all that was going on in the universe, it was pleasant on earth in the warm, windless Mediterranean night.

From the surrounding buildings, with most of the windows wide open in a futile attempt to get some cool air, came muffled noises: an isolated cough, scattered meaningless words from unintelligible chatter, and the Radio Moscow speaker's drony voice persuasively indoctrinating the Turks who were congregated for the night in several of their dormitories.

Stefan felt unusually tired at the end of what had been a long, busy day. Although it was his day off from the farm, he had worked the whole morning and a good part of the afternoon with a construction team, digging foundations for some Athenian millionaire's villa. He would have preferred to be in bed at that hour instead of having to go partying. Unlike him, Lia and the youngsters were all excited, barely able to contain their eagerness.

"What do you think, Mama, will we have any opportunity to dance at the party?" Ana asked with shining eyes and flushed cheeks, her expression gay and restless. It was obvious that the prospect enchanted her.

"I didn't know you were such an expert in Greek dancing," Val remarked.

"Oh, dear," Ana replied emphatically from the tip of her lips, putting on airs, "there is no dance in the world I cannot grapple with. Just wait and see."

"I would like to learn a Greek dance," Lia confessed. "They are so lively."

"Ah, Mama, I would love to see you dancing Zorba's dance with Dad." She looked enquiringly at her father, "will you dance a *sirtaki* with Mama?"

"I am too exhausted for something like that, yet would certainly enjoy listening and watching *you* dance." Stefan said. "I am old and tired," he continued, yawning and feeling really exactly that.

"Dad, you are always saying that," she said. "But you look so young, and you really are young. This is quite a poor excuse. Isn't that true, Mama?"

"He is young to me, that's for sure. Nevertheless, sometimes, he can be very tired. And in such an instance, I won't deny him a much-needed rest. This is a special occasion though, and we should be happy Dad was able to come with us tonight. I hope that soon, after a good sip of ouzo, he will get in a better mood," Lia said, gingerly stroking her husband's curly hair. "Won't you, dear?"

"I might. I will try to do my best. The last thing I want is to upset Thanasis. It is for him that I am making this effort," Stefan said, feeling guilty for his lack of enthusiasm. After a moment of suspense, as if moved by an afterthought, he added, "And, of course, for you . . ."

Talking excitedly, they didn't notice the man, who had entered the courtyard, walking softly like a cat through the velvety shadows of the night. At first, they didn't even recognize him as he was elegantly attired in a well-cut blue-gray alpaca suit with a matching silvery tie. Gone were his regular uniform and the stereotyped image of him they were used to. Freshly shaven and with a slick haircut, he looked more like a young, gentlemanly model stepping out of the pages of a fine fashion magazine. They all watched him in silent surprise until, rather slowly, they realized who he was.

"Why, this is Thanasis," Stefan was finally able to say. "You are so dapper. For a moment, I didn't recognize you."

"How come?" Thanasis feigned astonishment. "It's the same me."

"No," Lia said. "You are not the police officer we know so well. You are an elegant gentleman."

"Mama is right," Ana confirmed enthusiastically and blushed.

"In comparison with you, we look like a band of ragged gypsies," Val confessed his ego's secret hurt.

"No. That's not true. You are decently dressed. And you all look quite"—he paused to find the proper word—"respectable."

"Perhaps. Yet not nearly as stylish as you," Val said. He didn't sound appeased by the policeman's compliment.

"I am one of the family, and I have to be more up to the occasion than others." Although flattered, their friend seemed uneasy about the compliments he was getting.

"We had better go. It is a bit late," he urged them.

The Salamanis's Tavern, where Thanasis took them, was a modest establishment huddled in one of the old, narrow streets just across the main square, at a pleasant walking distance from the camp. Its window, half covered for the occasion by a makeshift poster, was brightly lit. The hand-written sign in Greek, adorned with artificial roses that the owners had obviously hung themselves, stirred Stefan's curiosity by its unusual look.

"That says there is a private engagement party going on inside," Thanasis felt obliged to explain.

Through the open door, lively Greek bouzouki music overflowed into the street, mixed with the din of excited human voices. The familiar bitter-acrid odor of olives and the sweet licorice smell of ouzo welcomed them inside. Now several fine French fragrances prevailed in that rich bouquet, adding more spice to the already exotic atmosphere.

The arrival of Thanasis and his companions was greeted with joyous cheers. Several young men dressed in their finery surrounded them, talking simultaneously with unrestrained glee, and openly ogling Ana. Then the newcomers were shepherded to the middle of the room and immediately introduced to the feted pair, two rather young people.

The fiancé was tall, slim as a reed, and had a mane of rebellious black hair descending to his shoulders. He greeted them with a broad smile behind a fat moustache, which could hardly conceal his still lingering adolescence. His fiancée, elfishly small, was nevertheless very much a proper woman with big brown eyes over olive cheeks and vivid red smiling lips. They seemed to be very much in love, overly excited, and enjoying being the center of everyone's attention.

There were perhaps two or three dozen people of both sexes in the tavern. Some stood about, and others were seated around two long tables. These were temporary arrangements made by joining together small square restaurant tables to form a sort of reversed letter L, with the shorter arm parallel to the counter located at the far end of the room. Numerous guests, mostly men, were jammed in the central space free of tables, drinking, smoking, and chatting cheerfully at the top of their voices.

Moving with ease among the crowd, Kirios Salamanis (the owner), his wife, and a confused looking teen, Takis the waiter, busied themselves generously serving ouzo with or without ice.

After many lengthy explanations in both Greek and English about his guests, Thanasis slowly guided the Romanians to the opposite end of the room. They were sat side by side at the smaller of the two communal tables, greeted with a flurry of jokes they didn't understand, and met with encouraging smiles, happy exclamations, and laughter. Immediately, the waiter served everyone the ubiquitous glasses of ouzo.

An impressive looking man, perhaps in his late forties, sat across Stefan. Thanasis greeted his elderly countryman with conspicuous deference. "This is Mr. Stefan, the Romanian, and these people are his family," the young policeman said, making the introductions. "And this is my boss, Kirios Yamandakis."

The man held out his hand and energetically clasped Stefan's. The Romanian remembered seeing him briefly, once or twice, when calling for business at the tourist police office. He had a small, fine, but firm hand.

"I am glad to meet you and your wife, sir." The Greek raised his glass in an informal salute. "Ya mas! Health to us!" he said, followed by the others.

In silence, they drank the strong, aromatic liquor; and during the ensuing pause, Stefan noticed a table set aside, standing by the wall at his left. The two sleazy characters seated there, somehow out of the great turmoil going on in the restaurant, were as different from the rest of the crowd as someone could be. One of them was a hippie with long, oily, sun-bleached hair and an overgrown beard. He was dressed in a long peasant shirt worn over a pair of tattered, dirty corduroy trousers and wore no shoes. His companion looked like one of the local fishermen freshly arrived from the sea, with a two-week stubble and fish scales all over his discolored overalls. The seaman was wearing folded-down waders. Both characters seemed to be having a good time by themselves and behaved as if they were alone on a desert island, oblivious to the increasingly rambunctious hubbub surrounding them.

"Who are those two?" Stefan whispered in Thanasis's ear. The strangers were seated pretty close, and he didn't want his question to be overheard.

"Englishmen, friends of the groom," the Greek whispered back.

Stefan, who thought his question misunderstood, would have continued with the inquiry if at that moment something else hadn't caught his attention. A pair of tourists in skimpy garments and shod in lousy flip-flops had just entered the tavern. The bulky athletic man, dressed only in some ugly Bermuda shorts, was well past his prime. Trailing in his wake was a very young-looking woman with discolored, almost white, blonde hair wearing a tiny monokini and a halter top that was too big for her. She seemed overly self-conscious and had a hard time preventing her small breasts from popping out of her low-cut top.

The waiter barred their entry and tried to persuade them to leave, or so it appeared, agitatedly pointing to the hand-written sign in the window. In spite of his insistence, the two intruders didn't seem to accept being turned back. Soon, what was a more or less polite discussion developed into an argument that threatened to get out of hand.

"That is an American university professor spending his sabbatical here," Thanasis said, nodding in their direction. "I know him quite well."

"You must be kidding," Stefan said. "He doesn't look like any of the university professors I know. Look at the scruff of his neck—a retired wrestler, I should say."

"No, no. Take my word. He is a genuine one and is also quite a well-known writer with left-wing leanings . . . I saw his credentials." Thanasis was serious. "The man recently split with his wife of thirty years for that girl you see. When the wife went home to get a divorce, he decided to stay. He met the girl here." The policeman stood up, looking around. He got hold of Kirios Salamanis, who happened to be passing by, resolutely grabbed him by the sleeve of his shirt, and insistently whispered something in the owner's ear.

The restaurateur immediately rushed to the door and spoke soothingly to the tourists, gesturing toward Thanasis. Dragging his feet, the sulking waiter retired to the kitchen while his boss led the pair to the only empty table in the room, one of those small affairs used by busboys to store dishes and silver. It was stashed between the counter and the other small table taken by the two English hobos, right behind Stefan's chair.

After seating his companion, the stranger came to Thanasis with honeyed words of gratefulness. A big smile wrinkled his well-tanned face as he inserted his body in between Stefan and the policeman. He leaned on the table, his large sunburned chest covered with bushy gray hair, and spoke in the latter's ear. Effluviums of strong male fragrances and suntan lotion surrounded him. The Greek was apologetic and apparently embarrassed by the man's exaggerated show of gratitude.

"You are right. I saw the sign, but I thought there might be some exceptions. Sorry for the misunderstanding," the stranger concluded loudly.

In the meantime, Kirios Salamanis brought to the newcomer's table two glasses, a bottle of ouzo, a plastic water bottle, and a bowl of ice cubes, which he dropped in front of the blonde.

"James, what is this?" the girl mewed.

"I don't know, darling," the American said. "I'll try to find out. I didn't order anything yet." He straightened up and accidentally stepped on Stefan's foot. "Sorry about that, pal," he muttered and gave Stefan a mouthful of Colgate-white teeth, one of those artificial well-practiced smiles, pretending to be friendly.

"It's all right, although I don't know what *pal* means," Stefan said. His limited vocabulary failed him as there was no *pal* in it, and he didn't understand what the man wanted to say. "It's all right, really. Just don't fall on me," he warned the newcomer and was rewarded by an ugly look as the smile disappeared for an instant like a faraway landscape behind a curtain pulled in haste.

The man turned again toward Thanasis as if Stefan didn't exist. "Who do you think ordered that drink for us, Officer?"

"I wouldn't worry about that, Professor," Thanasis said. "Everything is on us."

"I can't accept that," the man heatedly raised his voice and looked provocatively around. "I want to pay. I always pay my bills. We are not beggars."

"You don't have to. I told you already—this is a private function for friends and relatives only. You are our guest tonight, not a customer. Everything you and your lady friend drink or eat is free. If you don't like what they served you, just tell Takis, and he will try to accommodate." Thanasis smiled conciliatorily and motioned for the waiter.

"We are not relatives, and I want to pay," the man insisted.

"That's what I told them myself, but nobody listens to me," Stefan complained in a jocular, faked meekness.

"Now that's unbelievable," the man said looking down at Stefan with a half-searching, half-angry look. Still irritated after what had happened at the door, he couldn't decide what to make of this unexpected generosity.

"That's what Greek hospitality is all about," Stefan quipped.

"Who the heck are you?" the man asked in a gruff manner. He sounded ill-tempered. "Are you a relative? Your accent is not Greek, I gather. What kind is it?"

"No, sir! I am a foreigner, the friend of a friend . . ."

"Mr. Stefan is a political refugee from the camp," Thanasis murmured.

"A political refugee? Are you Russian?" asked the American with sudden interest.

"No," Stefan answered, "Russians are Slavic people. We are your forgotten Latin friends."

"You must be a Mexican, then. Am I right?"

"No. I am a Romanian."

"Romanian? Are you really a Romanian? What on earth is Romania?" he asked.

Stefan was taken aback. His capacity to understand English was limited, based mostly on reading, and he was slow to grasp rapid speech.

"I'll tell you what it is. It is one of those small Russian republics. That, it is. I was right to call you a Russian."

The man is probably joking, or perhaps he is trying to provoke me, Stefan thought. "It is all right with me," he said, "I would, however, be careful not to say that to a Romanian. I am stateless, a political refugee, as you've been told. And I don't care anymore. Romanians, on the other hand, like to believe they are a sovereign nation, an independent Latin enclave among Slavs and Hungarians."

"Aha! That's all the same to me," the man exclaimed, straightening up and looking at Stefan with a sort of infantile superiority. It took Stefan a few years to learn that for some obscure reason, that was the attitude many Americans would assume as soon as they realized the person they were talking to was a Romanian. "You people are like one of my fingers," he said and continued stretching his hands wide apart. "Here is Poland, East Germany, Hungary, Romania, Czechoslovakia, Bulgaria, Albania, Korea, Vietnam, and Cuba." Then he clasped his hands in a double fist and held it under Stefan's nose. "And that is the Soviet Union. The Russians have swallowed all of you and now are digesting slowly. What do you have to say?"

"Not much, unfortunately," Stefan answered.

The man, ready to join his companion, turned his back to Stefan with an air of lofty disdain. Satisfied at having the last word, he gladly dropped the touchy subjects of Greek hospitality and wounded dignity.

Stefan tapped him on the shoulder. "Excuse me, sir! There is some truth in what you've said. Except that it is so only because of your people's blunders. It is their fault, not ours. What do you have to say?" He tried to copy the other's accent.

The American jerked as if bitten by a wasp and faced him. He looked annoyed. "My people's fault? You must be raving, fella."

"Surely, you know what I am talking about. You do remember Yalta, don't you?" Stefan stood up, feeling suddenly hot and itchy.

Lia, who silently followed the discussion, delicately pulled at his sleeve. "Don't get excited," she said in Romanian. "Calm down, Stefan."

"Don't worry. I don't get excited that easily," he whispered back.

"I know you, dear," she muttered with a sigh.

"As a matter of fact, I do remember Yalta," said the American. "So what? If you folks didn't like Yalta, why did you accept it? There were anticommunist movements in Hungary, Poland, and Czechoslovakia—but never in your country. You must have liked the communist rule." The shorter man looked up defiantly at Stefan. "You folks must have really liked the Russians."

"As a matter of fact, we didn't. And there was opposition, even a budding guerilla war in my country. Our people were ready to fight if it hadn't been for Averell Harriman, your envoy. He came and told our politicians and the king to stay put and wait. The United States wouldn't allow the Soviets to take over Romania, he emphatically said. 'The government of the United States of America is the guarantor of your freedom. Don't do anything that can eventually upset Stalin, and we will defend your independence,' he promised them. They believed him, and the whole country cooled down, waiting for the Americans. And you know what happened?"

"What?" the American belligerently asked.

"The king was forced to abdicate. And those politicians, as well as every potential leader, were soon jailed and exterminated. And the rest of the population is still waiting even now for you, the

Americans, to bring them freedom." Stefan had spoken passionately and ended by raising his voice over the background noise.

The nearby revelers became instantly silent, staring enquiringly at the two men. Reassured by police chef's benign countenance and the calm mien of Thanasis, they resumed their socializing after a moment of suspense.

"You are too loud, dear. Tone it down a little," Lia murmured in Romanian.

"I am sorry, sir," Stefan said apologetically. "I stupidly allowed myself to become upset. I am awfully sorry." He felt remorse for having raised his voice and wanted to sit down and forget about the whole issue.

Unexpectedly, the American's mood changed. "I didn't mean to upset you, man. Don't take the whole thing so hard on yourself." His tone of voice was now almost soothing. "Those countrymen of yours should have known better than to believe Harriman, the son of a rotten-rich capitalist who financially supported Lenin's revolution while sucking the blood of American workers. A wolf in sheep's clothing, I should say," he concluded acidly.

"Please excuse me for meddling in your discussion, gentlemen," the hippie intervened firmly with a deep, throaty voice. "I just overheard what you were talking about. You are both mistaken. The culprit wasn't Harriman. He was merely a messenger, a tool. The mastermind was our dear Winnie Churchill."

"I wouldn't be surprised," the American hurriedly agreed. "Your Winnie was another enemy of the proletarians who fraternized with the Soviets, getting friendly with Stalin in particular. I still remember him, once sending in the army to break the backs of striking British miners."

"You've got that right, sir. My Dad was a Welsh coal miner, and after that strike, he could never forgive 'good ole Winnie' for what he did. His lordship's gross lack of sensitivity to human suffering was well-known, and my father and his mates have hated his bloody name ever since."

"What has that to do with Romania, gentlemen? Churchill was our protector. We loved him, indeed worshipped him. He is one of my personal heroes," Stefan said. "He tried to get us out of the Soviet influence in the late forties, if my memory is right, which brought Stalin's wrath upon him. I was in high school at the time and still remember one of Stalin's mighty speeches warning Churchill 'not to poke his piggy snout in our socialist garden,' calling him a political failure and all kind of names."

"Ha, ha," the hippie laughed with his whole mouth, opening a pinky chasm in his bushy face. "Piggy snout, you say? What a clever use of words. Stalin wasn't totally stupid after all . . . That must have been after Winnie's speech at Fulton. That speech was only dust in the eyes of the naives. What I am talking about happened long before, in Moscow. In 1944."

"And what important event happened in Moscow?" Stefan asked.

"Didn't you read Churchill's memoirs called *The Second World War*? You should have, because Winnie candidly reports in the sixth volume how he gave Romania to Stalin over a glass of vodka," the hippie answered.

"I didn't. Churchill's memoirs are forbidden in Romania. The possession of forbidden literature can be punished with several years of jail. The only book by him I could find and risked reading was *My Early Life* translated in Romanian and published before my birth. A good book, well written. Churchill was a great man. I cannot believe what you're saying about him. It must be a calumny. You are probably biased in your opinions because of your father's bad experience," Stefan concluded, sitting down. "Sorry, but I just can't, sir."

"I read those memoirs, and what this man tells you is true. Churchill exchanged Romania for Greece. That shows you where Romanians ranked in his list of priorities. You better believe it," the American said as he walked to his table with an air of haughty arrogance that seemed to be second nature for him.

The hippie lurched unsteadily in Stefan's direction with his glass in hand. A heavy bunch of keys hanging from his belt on a short chain jingled noisily at each step. He pulled up an empty chair, let himself fall on it among metallic clinking, and sat uncomfortably at the corner of the table, squeezed between Thanasis and the Romanian. He had taken a shine to the latter, it seemed.

"Listen, my friend, I don't want to hurt your feelings . . ." The hippie put a heavy hand on Stefan's shoulder and produced a loud hiccup. A pungent smell of alcohol, fish, and onion surrounded him; and Stefan drew himself erect in an unsuccessful attempt to put some distance between two of them. "You are a nice chap, and I mean no harm. Give me your address, and I will mail Churchill's book to you. It is entitled *Triumph and Tragedy*, a most interesting read. I am not kidding you."

"You don't have to send anything to me, sir. I will look for it myself. If what you are saying is true, there will be another death of a hero's myth," Stefan said with a hint of sadness in his voice.

"No, no. I do want to send you the book, because I hate to be thought a liar. Do you understand? Do you understand, my friend? Nobody ever said that John Alison Hewlett—that's me—is a liar."

"You can mail that book in care of the tourist police station," Thanasis's boss said from across the table. "We will pass it on to Mr. Stefan. Wherever he is at the time, we will know and send the book to him. Trust me."

"I will, I will," the hippie said, "I am a British customs officer, and as a matter of fact, a truly honest one. I have almost never lied in my entire life. Indeed, only very rarely and only in matters without importance, sir. I hate lies."

"All right, then. Thank you very much for the book, and forget about the incident. Let's drink to friendship," a repentant Stefan proposed. He didn't want to be a wet blanket. His attention had returned to the surrounding festive atmosphere, and he had realized how inconsiderate it was to start a political debate in a place like this. But the seed of doubt had unfortunately been already sown in his mind. *The accursed Englishman should better have kept his damaging knowledge to himself,* he thought. Now it was, of course, too late.

"You're right, my friend. To friendship! Bottoms up! Cheers." The Englishman emptied his glass with a gulp, oblivious to what was going on in the Romanian's mind. Then he pushed the empty glass toward the middle of the table in a desultory way and looked inquiringly around, searching for more drink.

With a meaningful nod, the police chief passed a bottle to Thanasis, who obligingly served the hippie. "There you are, sir," he muttered.

John Alison Hewlett took just a small sip this time. "That's the best liquor in the world," he said emphatically and turned around expectantly as if waiting for confirmation, "and it is one of the reasons I am here. The best climate, the best people, and the best drink." He looked inquiringly at Stefan. "What about you? What brought you here, friend?"

"Freedom, I wanted freedom," Stefan answered.

"Freedom? Why? Wasn't there freedom in Romania?"

"There is no freedom in Romania at all. The secret police are always looking out for nonconformists. At the slightest sign of disagreement, people are jailed, tortured, and often killed. Even humor can be dangerous. There is a joke about telling humorous anecdotes about the dictator and his scam rule. Whoever tells political jokes gets fifteen years in prison as an enemy of the people. Whoever listens to someone telling a joke and doesn't inform the proper authorities in due time gets fifteen years in prison as an accomplice. Those who don't tell such anecdotes can also get fifteen years for absenteeism from the country's social life."

"Really. That's bloody hell. How can this be possible? Who has time to watch people telling jokes?" The hippie didn't grasp the gist of the Romanian's anecdote, its black humor. He didn't even smile.

"That's not a problem. They say that every fifth person is an informer in communist Romania. Many are paid to watch the people. Others do it voluntarily for advantages, such as an extra room in their rented apartment, promotion at their workplace, or simply under threat. Some do it involuntarily, talking to the wrong people, others under duress during interrogation. Telephones are bugged. I used to be a scientist trying to promote new technologies, which was a bad thing to do. And one day, my wife discovered a microphone in our bedroom, hidden in the ceiling lamp. It stayed there for months on end until it disappeared mysteriously. Maybe the sleuths had moved it to another location. Who knows? You never knew who was watching, following you, and recording or informing about what you just said."

The Englishman took another sip from his glass. "Bloody hell. I wonder how people can live like that." He tried to look hard at Stefan, managing only to give him an evasive glance with alcohol-hazy blue eyes half shaded by locks of shaggy hair. "Why didn't you take away that mic?"

"No way! That would have been considered an acknowledgement of guilt. The biggest possible mistake. How did we live, you ask? Well, every evening, before going to bed, I spent time telling myself to keep my mouth shut while asleep. You know how it is—sometimes, people speak in their dreams, and a wrong word could easily be interpreted to incriminate someone. In the morning, I always woke up with a sort of hangover because overnight, I clenched my jaws until my entire skull ached." Stefan made a gesture with his hand as if he tried to push away the unpleasant souvenir. "Let's forget about it. Better tell me what brought you here."

"Ah, me? The same thing, my friend—lack of freedom."

"What do you mean by lack of freedom? I thought England was one of the strongest bastions of freedom in our world." Stefan was sincerely shocked with what he had just heard. "Where have your famous liberties gone? Habeas corpus, magna carta, and so on? Where are they?"

"No," the Englishman said, "you don't understand. It is not about that kind of freedom. I was a working man, an employee of Her Majesty's government. A working man is never a free man."

"I am not sure if we are talking about the same thing. The freedom I believe in cannot survive without responsibility. People must work for a living and for society's sake. Otherwise, how can they be part of the human family and sustain themselves?" Stefan felt that he was getting a little confused.

"That's what I meant. The working man is a slave. So I quit my job to taste true freedom. And to meet people." The hippie took a mouthful of ouzo. He was getting visibly more intoxicated. "The best drink in the whole bloody world . . . Do you understand now?"

"Not really. And how long do you hope to enjoy your personal brand of freedom? Perhaps you have other means of subsistence, and you don't need a job."

"No, my friend, I am not one of the idle rich." He emptied the glass. "So far, I have lived for about two years off my savings. Sadly though, what I was able to scrounge is already gone. Like sand sifted through a sieve, like my drink now . . ."

Thanasis, who followed the discussion with a quizzical expression on his face, poured another shot of transparent liquor into the Englishman's glass. "Aren't you working for Minas anymore?" he asked.

"I am," the hippie answered and shook the heavy bunch of keys. They jingled noisily. He showed them to Stefan. "See? This is the yoke of my newly found slavery."

"What kind of work is that?" Stefan asked.

"I am a caretaker at Minas's youth hostel. It is only a casual job that allows me to earn just enough to stay around a bit longer."

Out of the blue, it occurred to Stefan that, in a more general sense, being a caretaker at a youth hostel was not much different from being a customs officer. He had come to Greece to meet people, the hippie had said. Didn't he meet enough people at his job as a customs officer? After all, he was working with the public, meeting perhaps dozens, even hundreds, of people a day, wasn't he? What if the man was sent to Greece on a secret mission, to gather intelligence of some kind, especially among the youth? The two Greek policemen seemed to know the man too well for an average tourist. The modern world is terribly complicated. He should be more careful from now on with what he said. His deep distrust of governments recommended prudence. Suddenly, he felt hunted, annoyed, and unhappy. Luckily, the ouzo was having its usual mellowing effect, and his alarming thoughts began to slowly dispel. *I am getting paranoid,* he thought, and then he relaxed somewhat.

From the kitchen, the pleasant smell of freshly grilled lamb spread into the room as Salamanis and the waiter came in carrying big brass trays piled with steamy joints fresh from the oven. They began distributing plates loaded with meat and serving Greek salad in deep earthen bowls. The waiter handed the plates like an automaton and put one each in front of Thanasis and Stefan but stopped holding the third in the air. He was looking at the hippie, puzzled.

The Englishman stood up, leaning heavily on Stefan's shoulder. "All right, Takis," he said to the waiter. "It's all right. I am going back to my place, over there." He straightened up with difficulty and staggered across, carefully placing one foot in front of the other. Before collapsing on his chair, he turned to Stefan, sketched a vague military salute with two fingers brought to the level of his shaggy head where his forehead had to be, and haltingly said: "You'll get . . . that book . . . I promised . . . You have . . . my word, my friend!"

The surge of adrenaline, once exhausted, left Stefan feeling weak and drained; so he welcomed the digression provided by the arrival of food. The lamb was excellent—juicy and tender. Stefan loved the way it was cooked and spiced and began to eat with pleasure in spite of the late hour and his earlier dinner in the camp. The waiter had brought him a huge portion, and soon, it became obvious that he wouldn't be able to finish it all. Some red wine was also served with the meal; and presently, he decided that it was time to take a break, have a drink, and look around, glass in hand.

As everyone was busy eating, the noise of the conversations in the room had gradually subdued to almost a purr. Only the bouzouki music continued to blare as before, punctuated frequently by bursts of laughter and the clinking of glasses. Thanasis entertained Ana and Val, having great fun together. The police chief was talking to Lia, who turned excitedly and grabbed Stefan's hand.

"Listen here, Stefan! Mr. Yamandakis knows someone in Canada and is willing to put in a good word for us."

He didn't understand. The thought of the police chief giving them a recommendation sounded ludicrous. "He wants to give us what?" Stefan asked in Romanian.

"Don't be silly," she said in their mother tongue. Then she continued in English, leaning forward and looking at him, "Mr. Yamandakis assured me that we will get lots of help from his friend."

"The man is not a friend. He is my first cousin, Nikos, a Canadian born to Greek parents. His father is my mother's little brother" the chief, who had followed the dialogue, explained. "He is a lawyer, a legal counselor to a senator from Alberta. He lives and works in Calgary, although he often travels to Ottawa to participate in senate meetings. He is an important man who has a lot of power and connections . . . Here is his business card." And the chief showed them a card bearing the crest of the government of Alberta.

"Oh! Your cousin seems to be quite an important person." Stefan was impressed, but still incredulous and couldn't avoid a certain hesitancy when he asked, "How, er, how someone like us would be, er, able to contact such a, er, such a personality? We would, probably, er, never even come close to him."

"Don't worry about that. Nikos is a people's man." Yamandakis had noticed Stefan's hesitation. "My cousin gave me several of his cards so that I can send him people in need of help—worthwhile people. You know what I mean—really good people who deserve to be helped. I will write a few words on this card, and when you are in Canada, send it to him by post. He will look after you a hundred percent. Nikos is the most generous man I have ever known." The chief produced a fountain pen from one of his pockets and for a few minutes wrote diligently on the reverse of the Canadian's business card, signed it, then passed it over to Stefan. "It is in Greek . . . I warmly recommended you to my cousin."

"That's fantastic, isn't it, dear?" Lia exclaimed.

Like many other times when he had found himself in similar situations in Greece, what was happening to him now, after his innate incredulity was overcome by evidence, left Stefan gaping at the generosity of people who were actually complete strangers. He took the card and didn't know what to say, feeling touched and embarrassed at the same time.

"Thank . . . you . . . you . . . very . . . much," he stammered. "You are most kind." He looked into the chief's eyes, which followed him intently. "How do you know I am one of those worthwhile people? You could easily be mistaken by appearances." He preferred to parry his mounting emotion with a joke.

"It is my job to know the refugees under my care, Mr. Stefan," Yamandakis said, his face fleetingly illuminated by a faint sparkle of private amusement, which he managed to repress. "I am a professional psychologist, not only a policeman. Aided by the information we get, I rarely make mistakes in my judgement of people's worth. You are a good man, and I feel sorry that soon, you have to go elsewhere. It would have been better for us to keep you here, I think." And then with a short chuckle, he added, "Too bad you must go, only because you have chosen to do so."

Stefan felt a nuance of regret in the chief's pleasant voice. "Thank you again," he said, still moved. "I would love to live here. If you know my situation and me so well, you surely understand why we have to go somewhere else. Maybe one day, we will be able to come back . . ."

"Well, sir, I would be most happy to welcome you if that happened." He raised his glass, nodding politely in Lia's direction. "Good luck to you both."

They had barely finished emptying their glasses when suddenly, the music got louder. Someone had turned up the volume, and the people seated at the end of the long table began shouting excitedly and rhythmically clapping to the beat.

The fiancé stood up, climbed nimbly onto his chair, and jumped lightly on the table. He stretched his hands to the fiancée invitingly and, when she stood up, helped her to climb beside him. Then with arms high in the air and gazing into each other's eyes with concentration, they began dancing, skillfully avoiding the plates and the glasses.

The music became much louder, the clapping and cheering reaching paroxysm intensity; and then the waiter rushed in from the kitchen carrying a dozen plates, which he let fall onto the floor, where they broke, scattering countless shards with a deafening splat.

"I guess your friend Takis is in big trouble," Stefan shouted into Thanasis's ear in order to make himself heard.

"Not at all. This is one of our customs here—it is supposed to bring good luck," the policeman shouted back.

"That is cheap pottery, specially made to be broken at weddings. Those plates are used only on such occasions," Yamandakis explained, laughing heartily.

"Look, look, another set of plates is coming," Thanasis cried as a grinning Kirios Salamanis, this time bringing the earthenware himself, threw the plates to the floor.

The uproar that followed made the glasses hanging in the wooden rack over the bar and the bottles on the shelves rattle. Enthusiastic ovations shook the whole building when the music stopped, and the couple jumped off the table at once. To Stefan's utter amazement, nothing was broken on the table, no wine was spilled, and no food was spoiled during young couple's dance.

The end of the couple's jig was the signal for the beginning of the ball. The music started again in earnest, and guests of both sexes formed a wide-open circle by holding handkerchiefs. They followed the leader, an older man who was extremely agile for his age. He performed a series of amazing turns and elegant twists and jumps while the others followed, moving to the side smoothly with light, rhythmic steps. It was a simple, dignified dance; and the hieratic movements reminded Stefan of ancient rituals he knew only from reading.

"This is Kalamatianos," Thanasis said, "we must dance it." He sprang up as if summoned by the music and, ceremoniously inviting Ana, leaped with her into the circle, joining hands with the others. Another dance followed, and another, and then a third, when two giggling girls came to Val. They took the boy by hand almost against his will and forced him to get into the circle of dancers, with one of them at each side.

There was a short pause after several dances, during which everyone had to drink in honor of the engaged pair. The fiancé and fiancée embraced and kissed one another in a stormy round of tumultuous applause that rent the smoky air. Many more toasts, generous drinks, and lots of applause followed before the dancing continued.

When among laughter and jokes the circle had formed again, the convivial crowd appeared, in spite of repeated libations, to be more energetic than ever; and their dances continued to be as lively as they had been at first.

A group of young men and women—among them Thanasis, Val, and Ana—came excitedly to Stefan and Lia, who—together with

Yamandakis—stood in front of the table, still holding their glasses, now empty after the last round of toasts. The mirthful youngsters surrounded them in a flurry of smiles and chatter. The music was rather loud, and they all spoke and laughed at once so that for a while, it wasn't clear what was wanted from the elders.

"Come, dance with us!" Ana could finally be heard saying, dragging her father toward the dancing chain of people while the others came to her help with exhorting cheers.

"And you, Mama," Val insisted. "Come on, dance with us."

Stefan resisted. "I have no idea how to move my feet."

"You should tread at least a few steps. It is not so difficult," Yamandakis said. The chief's face was glowing with a broad smile. "Let's try together. I will teach you. Take your wife's hand, and let's dance." He motioned for the other young people to join in and started leading the group in a stately manner, showing the Romanians how to place their feet according to those unfamiliar Hellenic rhythms.

Their chain soon became interwoven with the other dancers' chain in a succession of intricate and complex figures. Stefan—swamped by the spirited mood of the gathering, encouraged by the goodwill of his partners, and enticed by the chief to sway to the music as everyone did—eventually shook himself free of his shyness. His initial reluctance was replaced by a state of rare elation as if all his worries and fears had melted away, absorbed into the overpowering common feeling of freedom and happiness. As the music went on and on, dance after dance, everyone joined in, continuing till the wee hours when the night began thinning into the milky-gray shades of the young morning.

The newly engaged duo had left long before the dancing stopped. Presently, most of the guests chatted in small groups; and only a few enthusiasts, including Ana and Val, were still treading a measure, humming merrily. It appeared that the Romanian teens were diligently learning some new steps under Thanasis's guidance. In the crude changing light, Lia looked exhausted, with black circles around her eyes; and Stefan himself felt tired, indeed beaten.

"Let's go home, Stefan," Lia begged. "I am smashed."

"So am I," Stefan agreed. "Children, let's go home! Mama is tired," he called. To his surprise, they acknowledged being tired too and appeared unusually keen to follow their parents.

Lia and Stefan looked for Yamandakis, who, in a group of elderly guests, was also getting ready to go home. They good-humoredly thanked him for his expert dance training before bidding farewell.

"Don't forget to call on my cousin," the chief reminded Stefan when they shook hands.

"Hey, *roumanos*! Hey, Romanian!" Stefan heard someone calling as he started shuffling toward the door along the main table. He turned around and saw a smiling stranger standing by the window and waving his hand.

"Buna seara Domnule. Good evening, sir," the man said.

"Mai bine spune buna dimineata. Better say good morning," Stefan answered. "Do you speak Romanian?"

"Yes, I do," the other said while slowly coming closer.

"How come?" Stefan asked as they shook hands.

"I am one of Markos's children."

"Are you really?"

"Yes, I am."

Stefan knew those children's adventures. It all had started a short time after the end of the World War II, when the Greek Civil War provoked by the leftists and waged by their military arm, the National People's Liberation Army, ended in defeat. Vafiadis Markos, one of their generals, had his base of operation in northern Greece and, before the collapse of the short-lived communist rule, had forcibly evacuated the children from his area to Romania and Bulgaria. Markos himself and his cronies fled to Romania. There, they were allowed to establish their headquarters in downtown Bucharest, in a villa confiscated from an aviation scientist by the name of Henry Coanda who, at the time, lived in England. A few of those children came to Romania with their parents, but many were by themselves and, upon their arrival, were relocated across the country to be generously supported by local authorities. They were enrolled in local schools, and almost all had finished by earning university diplomas. Stefan had had several colleagues among them, both in high school and at university. After graduation, they received good jobs from the Romanian government, free first-class housing, and rich stipends of various kinds. Although their life was much easier than that of the average Romanian, they soon tired of the dreary communist lifestyle. In the 1960s, when Greece decided to heal the wounds of the Civil War and Romanian communists agreed that the time had come to improve their diplomatic relations, those ex-child refugees had eagerly been repatriated.

"That explains your perfect accent . . . What are you doing here?" Stefan asked.

The man was a professional electrical engineer, now married with two children, he told Stefan in impeccable Romanian. He had come from Athens for the engagement party. After repatriation, he had difficulty settling down in Greece and had immigrated to Canada. Now he had a nice job, and life was quite good for him. He was even considering an early retirement to dedicate himself to the education of his young sons.

"Do you intend to immigrate to Canada as I heard from Thanasis? Is this true?" he asked.

"Yes, I do. As political refugees, we don't have too many choices, do we? Nobody seems to be willing to keep us in Europe," Stefan said.

"Don't feel sorry about Europe. Canada is the best country in the world," the Greek engineer assured Stefan. "The ten years I spent in Toronto were the most enjoyable in my entire life."

"It is probably true, if one has a proper job . . . My only worry is if I would find work," Stefan confessed. "It is not so easy nowadays, I have heard."

"Don't worry about that," the Greek enthusiastically reassured him. "In Canada, you don't have to work. The government showers immigrants with lots of money."

"I do want to work, man. For me, it is impossible to imagine a life without work." Stefan was scandalized at the thought of him living like a parasite at society's expense.

"Don't worry. There is plenty of work, and there are good jobs in Canada if you really want one. You don't need to bother, though, because you will get money from the government for everything. Believe me, Canada is a paradise."

"When are you going back?" Stefan asked.

"Going back? Where? To Athens? Why, I am going back this morning as soon as the party is done." The man looked puzzled.

"I didn't mean Athens. My question was when are you going back to Canada?"

"Oh, I won't go back to Canada. I am currently living in Athens with my family. We have a comfortable house, excellent jobs, and everything we need. Why should I go back? We are here for good," he said with a big smile on his satisfied face.

A shadow of doubt went through Stefan's mind. "If life was so wonderful in Canada, why did you come back?" he asked.

"Ah! Now I understand why you were asking . . . You Romanians are so quick-witted . . ." he derided Stefan. "One of my uncles died and left me some property here. Family ties and responsibilities, you know how it is. Families must always have the last word. That is why, my friend."

Stefan would have liked to ask more questions, but at that point, Val reentered the tavern and called him loudly, "Father, we are ready to go. Mama is wondering why you are not coming."

"All right," Stefan answered, "I am coming." He looked with obvious regret at his new acquaintance. "Sorry, I must go," he said. "I would have loved to talk longer with you, but as you just mentioned, families always have the last word . . . Thank you for the information anyway. It was a pleasure . . ."

"Here, take my business card. If you come to Athens, call on me." The Greek engineer tossed his card in Stefan's hand. "We might be able to arrange a meeting, perhaps a get-together or something," he suggested, making a vague characteristic gesture of dismissal with his outstretched hand.

"Come on, Father," Val called again.

"All right, all right," Stefan answered. He hurriedly left the tavern, having heard only half of what his new acquaintance had just said. His family and Thanasis waited outside and welcomed him with a chorus of protests. Caught in explanations and reproaches, he soon completely forgot the friendly professional.

The sleepy town seemed to rest under diaphanous snow. A late-rising waning moon covered everything in powdery whitish-blue light. The alternation of transparent geometrical shadows and lightened surfaces of buildings created an eerie landscape that gave Stefan the strange impression of walking dreamlike through a cubist painting. The air was fresh and cool, but he felt warm, his heart bursting with bliss. It could have been the effect of too much ouzo, although he was definitely intoxicated by too much freedom and friendship all at once. Every Romanian is born a poet, they say in Romania, and he was now in one of those poetical moods.

"O, millennial Greece," he declaimed emphatically, his voice echoing in the quiet of the silent street, "the mother of all civilizations. You are the fountain of freedom and democracy. Your sons and daughters are most generous hosts, and their kindness is the healing ointment that soothes my soul's wounds. Blessed be your lands forever!"

"Should I understand that you have enjoyed yourself, sir?" Thanasis smilingly interrupted his friend's sentimental rambling.

"Are you asking me if I enjoyed the party this evening, my friend?"

"Yes, sir. Did you enjoy it?"

"Oh, yes. Oh, yes . . . So much that if I die tomorrow, I'll die a happy man. Whatever happens from now on, I won't ever feel sorry because I have tasted again something lost a long time ago. These are the fruits of true freedom that we enjoyed tonight. Liberty tastes very good. And I am truly happy, indeed, perfectly happy. This is so far the climax of my adult life. What else is needed in a man's life after all that?"

Stefan was well aware that in many parts of the world, freedom, liberty, and happiness were empty words, more often than not masking terror and sheer slavery or making unlimited cruelties look good. He also knew that democracy is vulnerable, and freedoms are fragile. Even in the most powerful and free countries in the world, if people don't watch over it, democracy can easily be trampled upon and liberties snatched away in the blink of an eye. In every human, there is a little of both Dr. Jekyll and Mr. Hyde, although the proportion of each might differ widely. While souls yearn for the highest spirituality, the animal urge to enslave and dominate by any means always lurks dangerously in the shadows of many a human brain.

THIRD INTERMEZZO

When Stefan came back from work late that afternoon, Ilkay, the student from Ankara he had met in the English class, was waiting by the stairs on the first-floor landing. He was alone, unshaven as usual, the five-day stubble giving him the look of a pirate afflicted with an advanced stage of galloping consumption. Dressed in a faded camouflage blouse, commando trousers, and wilderness boots, the young man was gazing aimlessly at the opposite wall with vacant eyes, giving the appearance of having fallen in a trance.

While climbing the stairs, the Romanian could not get rid of the oppressive sensation of being watched. In spite of the guy's out-of-this-world impersonation, something warned Stefan his colleague had been waiting for him. This vague impression turned to certitude when the moment he saw Stefan, Ilkay's eyes lit up with a sudden glimmer of recognition. He lazily straightened up, leaving the banister against which he had lolled until then. "Good evening," he said in a whisper, "do you have a minute for me?"

"Me?" Stefan reluctantly asked, trying to gain some time. "Sure . . . Why not? What's the problem?" The intrusion did not exactly make him happy. Having just come from Theodoros's farm, he was hungry and tired but didn't want to show it, ever on his guard and cautious when dealing with his Turkish neighbors. He was especially careful since his earlier experience with Selim.

"No problem at all," Ilkay threw around a furtive glance. "We would like to talk to you for a minute in my room," he said in a muffled voice.

"Now? To me? What for?" Stefan's surprise was genuine, as he wondered who the *we* might be. Could that have been Ilkay himself? Was it the majestic plural? Or perhaps he spoke on behalf of a group of people? And if so, were they Turks only? Then what political color might they have, and what be their reason for approaching him? *That could be a tricky, even unpleasant situation,* he thought, suddenly alarmed by the student's conspiratorial airs. However, Stefan managed to hide his annoyance and keep cool, racking his brains to find possible ways out of what he perceived as a potentially awkward situation. Regretfully, for the time being, he could find none.

"We would like to ask for your opinion on a very personal matter." Ilkay now gently yet persistently pushed him toward the end of the corridor where he shared a dormitory with other Turkish refugees. "Don't worry, we won't keep you for too long," he said to his interlocutor as if to assure him that it was just a small thing.

As they passed the door to his room, Stefan remembered with a shrug that nobody was at home. It was too early for Lia and Ana to be back from their work in a hotel at Cap Sunion, and Val was out at a movie with Abdur. He would have liked to let them know what was happening, but given the circumstances, that was impossible. By now, it would have been too late anyhow.

When they entered Ilkay's dormitory, Stefan took in at once the dusty walls covered with the same kind of posters advertising all sorts of alcoholic beverages that adorned his own room, the double tiered beds lining the walls, and the people present. Three of them, including the rough Turkish boy—the one who had traveled from Thessaloniki in the police bus with Stefan's family—were around the table, smoking silently. The acrid smell of tobacco smoke and the stale odor of sweaty bodies hung in the air.

Stefan's immediate attention was irresistibly drawn, however, by a fourth character: a chubby young man seated on one of the beds by the windows, who busied himself with a Walter PPK, a handgun Stefan knew from his military training. The Turk was oiling or cleaning the weapon with a dirty rag. In front of him, spread on a newspaper, was an array of small tools, a tubular brush, and a minuscule oilcan. The fellow, apparently oblivious to the newcomer's entrance, held the open pistol against the light and looked with concentrated attention through the barrel. Stefan didn't know his name but recognized the youngster as one who had been involved in an aborted hunger strike a few days earlier.

A fierce-looking older man from the table barked a few words in Turkish, and the young fellow clicked the barrel in place, loaded the pistol with its clip magazine, hid the weapon under his belt, pulled his sweater over it, and quietly left the room. There was instant obedience and complete submission in his entire attitude.

"Over here, please." Ilkay motioned Stefan to sit, dragging an empty chair to the opposite side of the table. The others stared straight-faced at him while he seated himself across from them. Nobody talked, and only the rough boy smiled with his dazzling green eyes wide open. The third man, whom Stefan had never seen in the camp before, was wearing some heavily patched overalls. He offered the Romanian a cigarette from a crumpled package.

To Stefan, the whole setup appeared more like a court martial than a friendly meeting. The atmosphere in the room was anything but reassuring. He experienced the uncomfortable sensation of being brought to trial, and although he calmly lit the lousy cigarette with a steady hand, his anxiety grew. *My God,* he thought, *what I have done wrong? What is all this about?*

"This gentleman here," Ilkay said, pointing the older man whom Stefan had seen once or twice walking the corridors in the company of two athletic young Turks, one of whom always carried an attaché case, "is our most respected leader. An important personality in our country." The camouflage-clad student bowed toward the man, who nodded silently in acknowledgement. "The other two are very good friends of ours." The older man nodded again; and Ilkay, who apparently finished the introductions, took a seat at the far end of the table.

Stefan produced a forced smile, which he intended to be friendly. "I guess you know who I am," he said. "What I am expected to do for you, gentlemen?" He couldn't figure out why they had brought him there and was at a loss as to what attitude to adopt. The whole affair appeared completely bizarre, to say the least.

For a minute or so, nobody said anything; only the rough boy continued to smile airily. The silence grew heavier, and Stefan could clearly hear his heart beating. Then the older man stubbed out his cigarette in the overfilled ashtray with studied slowness and started talking. The man spoke Turkish with a sort of superior aloofness, addressing mainly Ilkay. He had a husky baritone voice, not entirely unpleasant bar a peculiar menacing harshness that was evident at all times. Those unexpected inflections in his voice had the effect of a faraway thunder in the middle of a clear, sunny summer day. Although he spoke for a couple of minutes, it was impossible to read anything from his unshaven face. When the leader had finished, it was Ilkay's turn to translate; and while he did so, the man gazed intently at Stefan. His almond, feline eyes peered out from under bushy black eyebrows with singular fixity.

"Do you have a daughter?" Ilkay asked. "Is Miss Ana your daughter?"

"Yes, she is my daughter. What's the matter with her? What's the problem?" Stefan asked, completely baffled. From his point of view, in the present situation, Ana was the last person to think about. He grew increasingly alarmed though, his uneasiness deepening.

"No problem, no problem at all," Ilkay hurriedly answered, raising both hands with palms turned toward Stefan in an appeasing gesture. "The fact is that our friend here" and he pointed the rough boy "is in love with her."

"Do you really mean that this boy is in love with my daughter?" Stefan asked incredulously, his voice suddenly high-pitched. The story sounded funny, even grotesque. It was so unexpected, an anticlimax really, like a cheap coup de théâtre in a bad play. "What's his name, by the way?" he asked as an afterthought.

"Yes, yes. He is very much in love. My friend's name is Ali, and he wants to get married to Miss Ana," Ilkay jauntily replied.

"Our most respected leader here"—he stood up, his boots noisily scratching the marble floor, and again bowed courteously toward the older man—"is heartily supporting Ali as he has known my friend and his family for a long time. That's why we invited you here. We want your opinion."

The man in shabby overalls grunted approvingly; and the rough boy, all smiles, with a tinge of happy expectation plainly visible on his face devastated by acne, looked from one person to another around the table. By an uncontrollable trick of his mind, the boy reminded Stefan of a hunting dog from his childhood, tongue hanging and dripping saliva, excitedly waiting for the usual reward even after an unsuccessful retrieval. That one was the most useless dog he ever had. Carina was more composed and controlled, and she had learned very early on that not everything that flies is food.

Unprepared for what he had just heard, Stefan didn't know what to say. In any normal situation, he would have laughed, considering the whole episode a bad joke. Yet this wasn't a normal situation and definitely not a laughing matter. His mind raced feverishly from one thought to another, tormented by contradictory impulses. On one hand, he felt better, knowing there was no political issue. A heavy weight was taken off his shoulders as an anticommunist refugee always had to be on the lookout for *agent provocateurs*, kidnappers, or hit men sent by their governments to get rid of fugitive dissidents. On the other hand, he could foresee tremendous complications, even danger, ahead. A marriage in the refugee camp, to start with, could have jeopardized, even annihilated, his family's chances to immigrate to Canada. Nobody could predict the consequences of such a foolish step. Also, he couldn't possibly agree to his daughter marrying a totally unknown, unfinished boy such as this one. He would never accept that. The main question was, did Ana share Ali's love? After all, the boy was too young, uncouth, and ugly. Ana was beautiful, certainly more sophisticated, and mature. Yet do such differences really count when love strikes? Who could know for sure? Love is blind, and the groom must be only a trifle better looking than the devil, they say in Romania. However, he trusted that if there was something between those two, Lia would have known already and told him.

Stefan, with a deep sigh, decided he had no use for Ali, whose love was probably only a teenager's infatuation with the first girl who crossed his path and happened to catch his fancy. He could see this happening easily in the camp, mostly a man's world, where one was forced into an existence full of repressed and unsatisfied desires. He was aware that no decent Greek woman would show any inclination to get involved with a refugee, least of all with a Turk. The boy was obviously immature and perhaps didn't realize that falling in love and getting married were not the same thing. It surprised Stefan that a seasoned man with such experience as the alleged leader couldn't see the absurdity of his protégé's request. But then was the leader a real one? What if he was only a fake? That possibility was always there, the incertitude complicating a situation already very hard to handle.

He looked at the old, gray-haired ogre who watched him with cold and, it seemed to him, ferocious eyes, his upper lip hidden by a ragged, nicotine-stained moustache. No help would come from that direction. *These are violent men,* he thought, *ready to contest everything. And it isn't a good idea to antagonize them.* He remembered the young fellow with his Walter PPK, probably hanging around somewhere on the other side of the door. Only God knew how many other firearms were in that room. Maybe all his hosts were armed even as they were talking. What can one expect from a gang of trigger-happy toughs—as rumors depicted them? He was completely defenseless and had the dreadful sensation of being paraded naked in front of strangers. Who would have thought that something like this could happen to him?

Stefan made an effort to relax, and in a flash, the souvenir of the books he had read as a teenager rushed through his mind: the unforgettable stories of Karl May, Pierre Loti, and many others he had enjoyed so much, time and again. He recalled what those beloved authors had to say about Turks: they cannot resist the sight of a pretty woman, they are touchy, and like nice talk. A good yarn can help one to win the day with them. Despite the tension and anxiety, he felt a sudden surge of relief, even exhilaration. The situation undoubtedly had its Oriental and adventurous flavor; and Stefan perversely enjoyed its absurdity, exoticism, and danger. It was almost like living one of the famed Arabian Nights stories.

"Marriage is an important matter and requires serious consideration," he finally said, carefully choosing his words. "I am honored by Mr. Ali's request and especially impressed with the support of such a great personality as the gentleman here." He paused, slightly inclining his head toward the older man. "I am sure Mr. Ali is an excellent person from a good family, but we don't know each other at all. And before discussing anything else, I would like to find out more about this handsome young man who wants to be my son-in-law. For instance, what's his profession?"

Ilkay spoke a few words in Turkish, and the rough boy excitedly jumped on his feet before answering. The older man grabbed Ali by his shirt and pulled him back in the chair, then said something to Ilkay, who translated for Stefan. "Politics. His profession is politics."

Stefan forced himself to produce another friendly smile. "Politics is surely very important. A most noble occupation, which, I learned from the communists in my country, one does voluntarily in the interests of people." He spoke with emphasis, accentuating the words *communists* and *people* and was elated with the effect, noticing how everyone around the table seemed charmed, their faces brightening. "I also learned from the communists," he continued, "that every man needs a working qualification, something one does for a living in order to feed his wife and children. For instance, someone can be a politician and at the same time a millwright, a welder, an engineer, a physician, an electrician, and so on. Has Mr. Ali such a skill in order to support his future family?"

Again, Ilkay translated to his mates; and the group launched into animated discussions for a while, the rough boy agitatedly stirring in his chair, his face purplish red. Eventually, the older man motioned his head toward Ilkay, prompting him to answer Stefan's question.

"My friend Ali is currently a politician, a communist. He has decided to dedicate his life to the cause and has no such profession as you mentioned. He hasn't finished high school yet, but he intends to continue his studies and become a lawyer. Our respected leader,"

Ilkay bowed as deeply as before, "said money is of no concern because Ali's family is extremely wealthy. As a matter of fact, my friend is ready to pay you in American dollars as high a price as you would ask for your daughter."

"You mean he wants to buy my daughter?" Stefan was both surprised and amused but acted as a scandalized father instead. "I would never agree to that. To sell my daughter? No, never. Never, you hear me? I learned from the communists that selling human beings is the most awful crime of all. Now you are daring to suggest that a communist is offering to buy my daughter? I cannot believe it. How can you people even think about something like that? And in the twentieth century. I, a father, to sell my daughter? Incredible." He stood up making an effort to look scandalized and upset. "I don't want to hear this anymore," he shouted.

The others also stood up, all talking at the same time. Ilkay was desperately struggling to translate, inadvertently mixing English with Turkish. Instant pandemonium had broken loose. It was bedlam. The door of the dormitory opened a crack, and the owner of the Walter handgun put his head in. He wore an inquiring, alarmed expression. His appearance lasted only a fleeting moment, for the young man hurriedly withdrew and disappeared like a shadow, closing the door silently when the leader barked a short order, dismissing him with an energetic sway of his hand.

Taking advantage of the confusion, Stefan made a move toward the door. He couldn't go far because the Turks surrounded him, barring the exit. Ilkay gently grabbed both his hands, trying to say something, while the rough boy circled around them, imploringly repeating, "Pleezee, mister, pleezee." For the next minute or so, they all did their best to soothe Stefan and more or less politely dragged him back to the table. Resistance was to no avail, he had to admit in resignation.

"Please sit down," Ilkay said. "Please sit down, just for one more minute."

"Pleezee, mister, pleezee," Ali repeated parrotlike.

"We good people, no problem," the older man who stood up beside Stefan said, resting a heavy hand on his shoulder. He kept a broad smile on his ferocious-looking face while he continued to speak in Turkish. Ali also wanted to say something, but the leader brushed him aside and shut him up. The man in overalls offered Stefan another lousy cigarette from the same filthy pack. Stefan reluctantly chose one, and four lighters were lit simultaneously under his nose. He narrowly escaped having his eyebrows singed in their haste to be helpful.

"Our respected leader," Ilkay began again with the habitual bow, "says it was a mistake. You misunderstood us. The money Ali offered is a present. This is an old custom in our country. He didn't mean to buy your daughter. We don't buy our wives—women are our comrades, not slaves." All nodded eagerly and sat down.

"All right, all right," Stefan agreed with a bored sigh. He was disappointed, for his trials weren't finished yet. "Of course, they are our partners," he said, "and because women are our comrades, any marriage should be based on love."

"Yes, yes, mister. I love Miss Ana. I love very much, very, very much. Pleezee, pleezee, mister," Ali cried looking at Stefan with dejected eyes, which were almost popping out of their orbits. He was bursting to say more, but the older man again silenced him.

"My friend loves your daughter very much, you can see that," Ilkay said. The others grunted approvingly.

"Maybe he loves her," Stefan said, "but love must be shared. Our women are free to decide whom they want to get married to. I would never force my daughter to marry someone she doesn't love. The question is, does my daughter love Mr. Ali?"

Ilkay's translation was followed by a long moment of complete silence. Everyone was looking inquiringly at Ali. The rough boy made a long face and murmured something close to the leader's ear. The older man gave him a quizzical look without making any comment.

"My friend didn't ask Miss Ana this question," Ilkay answered on their behalf.

"Well, my friends," Stefan said, "I think she should be the first to be asked. Don't you agree?" He was now treading on more solid ground and wanted to keep his advantage. "Did Mr. Ali speak to my daughter at all? Did they speak about love, about the future?"

"They met only twice, in the English class," Ilkay said. "They didn't speak much, and they didn't talk about the future or love."

"You see? Things are not that simple, but that's all right," Stefan replied, hardly containing his joy.

The rough boy hastily said something to Ilkay, who listened attentively, and then turned to Stefan. "My friend Ali thinks Miss Ana loves him because she always answers his greetings when they meet in the classroom for their English lessons. She even smiled at him once or twice last time, he said."

"Well, gentlemen, my daughter is a polite person. To answer your colleague's greeting is a civilized gesture. She always behaves like this and does the same with everyone, I am sure. A smile is also a sign of recognition. One cannot marry a woman just for a smile." Stefan stopped for a moment to clear his throat and to give more emphasis to what was coming. "There is a long way from a smile to love. In my country, we are used to something called courtship. If a boy likes a girl, he asks her out, they meet several times, they go to movies, they visit with their families and friends, and get to know each other. Only then, and if the girl is willing to listen, would they talk about the future and marriage. Sometimes, it takes months, even years. My daughter is too young for marriage. She hasn't come of age yet. Starting a family is a serious matter." He looked hard into the eyes of the leader: "We older people know that too well. Am I right, sir?"

The man didn't answer, quickly turning toward Ali with a question. Their dialogue went on for several minutes, Ana and Canada being repeatedly mentioned. In the end, a worried-looking Ali jumped up, wiped his sweaty forehead with the back of his hand, and pointed a finger at Stefan. "You go Canada?" he asked.

"Yes. This is true. We applied for Canada. Canada is where we want to go." He defiantly looked up to Ali. "So what?" He felt confident that the situation was under his control and decidedly didn't want to let himself be bullied by what he saw now as being a sex-starved teenager.

The rough boy came around the table to Stefan's side. "Me go to Canada," he said. "Me love Miss Ana. She my wife." He accompanied the words by fiercely pounding his chest with both fists.

Stefan stood up and stretched himself. He was taller than Ali, who, although sturdy, was a head shorter. He patted the boy's shoulder. "Don't get excited, man. I see you are an intelligent boy, and this is an excellent plan. We all go to Canada. There, you will study for a profession, get to know Ana better and, if she likes you, eventually get married. You are young, she is young, you both are young, and there is plenty of time for everything."

"Yes," said the boy. "Me go Canada, get married." He took Stefan's hand and shook it. "Thank you. Thank you very much."

Ilkay translated for the two other men in a flurry of words, and an ecstatic Ali wandered back to his chair.

On the spur of the moment, it occurred to Stefan as he was standing in the middle of the room considering the scene with wearied eyes that he had enough of this nonsense and it was time to leave. He was fed up with being a character from the *Arabian Nights* tales, feeling exhausted and hungry. He checked his wristwatch and realized why he felt so drained—it was more than two hours past his dinnertime.

"Sorry, gentlemen," he said, "I must go now. My wife is waiting for me, and I am starving." He made a suggestive cutting gesture with the open palm across his stomach. "I am hungry. See you later. Good night." He turned his back to them, briskly walked the few steps to the door, swung it open, and was out. They had neither the time to stop him nor to say anything. His abrupt departure had undoubtedly taken all of them by surprise.

The chubby fellow with the Walter handgun, squatting by the side of the door, was surprised too. He bolted up, lost his balance, and fell flat on his back. Stefan broke into laughter. "Be careful, my brave," he coaxingly said to the embarrassed young man who was struggling to stand up. "You could get into big trouble if that pistol you are keeping under your belt ever goes off by itself."

Stefan was still smiling when entered his room. They were all at home, and the family was waiting impatiently for him. Carina was at the door and tried to lick his hand, but he held it up, so she only touched it with her cold nose.

"Be good," Stefan said to the dog as she happily jumped around him, "don't make so much fuss." The spaniel continued with her enthusiastic welcome. "Stop it, don't be pushy," he said and petted her on the head. "That's enough. Now leave me alone, please."

The table was already neatly laid for supper; and on the hotplate, a pot boiled, sending a thin jet of steam into the air. The tempting smell of fresh chicken soup filled the room. It felt good to be home.

"Where have you been?" asked Lia, her melodious voice hardened by a tinge of exasperation. "I just started to fret and worry about you."

"You shouldn't worry, Mama," said Ana, giving her father a great mischievous smile. "He probably found a Greek girlfriend somewhere nearby." Although father and daughter loved each other very much, for the last few years since the girl had entered into her teens, their relationship had been a little edgy. Often and for no particular reason, she would say something outrageous to him, like now. This was why her behavior had many times badly tested his patience, and it was perhaps his mistake that he never had the heart to rebuke her. She jumped up and gave Stefan a burly hug and kissed him. "Mama was quite worried," she whispered into his ear.

Stefan gently disengaged himself from Ana's embrace. "Don't be cheeky, girl," he said, "because I can easily get rid of you." He glanced appraisingly at his daughter, a faint smile playing on his lips. "And in the process, we all can get filthy rich," he added teasingly.

"How come?" The girl looked at Stefan with beautiful shining eyes, her face illuminated by a sweet, slightly mocking smile.

"Well, I just got a serious offer to sell you to a prospective husband."

"You must be joking," Lia exclaimed, her voice still tinged by upset.

"Can you believe such a miracle, Mama? To get good money for our ugly duckling?" Val laughed, showing all his teeth. He was always ready to tease his sister. "That would be really something. Don't you think so?"

"How much did the man offer for me?" Ana sounded interested. "I hope you asked a really high price for me."

Stefan sat at the little table and poured some soup into his bowl. "Let's eat," he said. "I am awfully hungry."

"How much money, Dad?" Ana asked again. They were all sitting around the table now, busying themselves with their soup.

"You don't seem interested in finding out who the guy is," Val said. "I honestly wonder who could be so foolish as to throw his money away on you."

"Of course, I am asking about the money, dear, because I want to know my worth." Ana's voice was cutting. She didn't appear to take the matter too lightly.

"Actually, Val is right. Who is the fairytale prince?" Lia asked.

"You would not believe this. It is the rough Turkish boy. Mr. Ali is his name."

"Come on, Dad. This is impossible. That awful kid? The boy with the bad acne?" Ana sounded disappointed.

"Why, that is a really handsome lad. Ha-ha," Val teased her.

"That is the man, Mr. Ali," Stefan said. "Don't worry, sweetie, the deal is off."

"I cannot believe this. The boy must be out of his mind. I cannot stand him. Who put that idea in his head?" The girl looked really upset. She hadn't touched her food yet, and now she pushed her soup bowl away, making a disgusted grimace.

"That I was wondering myself. Was it you by any chance?" Stefan gave his daughter a half-inquiring, half-teasing look.

"Me? For God's sake, Dad . . ." With a cry, she stood up, kicking the table so that some soup spilled over. Tears welled up in her eyes.

"Be careful," Stefan cautioned her.

"Now, now Ana. You sit down and eat. Be a good girl, be my daughter I love. Don't make a mess of everything," Lia said soothingly. "Your father is joking. He didn't really mean it."

"But Mama . . ."

"I don't want to hear anything, dear. Here," Lia gave her daughter a handkerchief. "Dry your eyes, and eat. We will clear up this nonsense after dinner. We should all eat, quietly and civilized. Understand?"

Presently, Stefan finished with the soup. "This is not nonsense," he said with a stern frown, dropping his spoon in the empty bowl. The spoon made a sharp ding. Although he was unhappy things had turned sour, he decided it would be wiser not to make an overly big fuss of his displeasure. "The boy asked to marry Ana and offered to pay for her. This is a sort of custom in some parts of Turkey, they tried to convince me. I refused, and that's all. There is nothing more to discuss. The matter is closed."

"The boy is crazy," a red-eyed Ana pouted.

Stefan looked hard at his daughter. "You listen carefully to me." He patted Ana softly on the cheek. "You should be careful in the future when dealing with these hotheaded revolutionaries who are ready to give up their cause for a girl's smile." He paused a moment. "Now what's the second course? Shall we finish our dinner tonight or not?"

The Invisible Face

of the Moon

Stefan shifted the heavy shopping bag from his right hand to his left, impatiently unlocked the door, and rushed in. The dormitory was deserted. None of his family was at home, and their absence disappointed him. All the way to the camp, he had toyed with the idea of surprising them, imagining how excited everybody would be at the sight of him bringing in the Samos wine. In his mind, he had even visualized all of them, including himself, drinking it with fresh pistachios and walnuts. And now, instead of basking in their excitement and happiness, he had to wait until God knows how long to quench his thirst.

Stefan carefully put the four one-liter bottles and the futuristic painted tin of mixed nuts he was carrying on the table, and then threw himself on the bed with a resigned sigh. Uncorking one of the bottles was out of the question because he hated to drink alone. After all, he had brought the treat to be enjoyed together with his family. He knew how much they all loved that sweet wine and did not have the heart to deprive them of even a small part of that pleasure.

Stretched out on the bed, he felt sorry for himself. However, his despondent spell didn't last. It was warm and stuffy in the room, and presently, Stefan began to be bored with his bad mood. It didn't take him long to realize that it was time to open the doors to the balcony in order to breathe some fresh air. Yet being tired at the end of a long workday, he only reluctantly resolved to make the effort. And even then, he was hardly able to find the necessary motivation.

Stefan stood up lazily. He unlocked the French doors and shuffled outside the room. It was late fall, and the days were much shorter. In the failing light of dusk, the gray shadows of early evening had already begun to dissolve contours and distort perspective as if seen through the eyes of a Fauve painter. It was relatively quiet outside in the absence of a breeze, and the taverns were still silent at that hour. The foul air hung thick and heavy, loaded with tobacco smoke, and filling the balcony the way a pool of stagnant, pestilential water fills a dying marsh. As always, when he was not smoking himself, that stale odor made him sick.

After the first moment of disorientation, Stefan realized he was not alone. In the quickly advancing twilight, he could barely distinguish their faces but recognized Luca and Abdur seated on two of the several chairs scattered across the balcony, gesturing and arguing with subdued voices. Both were smoking, the former trying perhaps to convince the latter, who objected vehemently, to do something he didn't want to. At least that was Stefan's initial assessment of the situation.

"Good evening, guys," Stefan greeted them. "Why, are you really smoking, Abdur? What an event," he mockingly said. "I have never seen you smoke before. What's the occasion?"

"Don't ask, Father." Abdur dejectedly waved his left hand, the right being busy with the cigarette he was clumsily holding, and looked stealthily at Stefan with bloodshot eyes.

In the young Afghan's voice, there was a definite note of pain, a tonal alteration akin to despair, completely unlike the Abdur he had known so far. That voice, charged with grief, instinctively drew Stefan's attention. He grabbed a chair for himself, pulled it close to the pair, and sat down.

"What's up, guys?" he asked, noticing a big yellow envelope and a pile of official-looking papers spread on the concrete floor. In spite of straining his eyes, he couldn't decipher the writing in the poor, vanishing light. Minute failings like that always unpleasantly reminded him of fast-approaching old age. Disgusted by his weakness, Stefan turned his attention to Abdur, trying to guess what was troubling his younger friend. "Are you all right? You don't look too good, my son."

"It is nothing. Nothing at all," Abdur muttered with downcast eyes.

"The boy is in terrible distress," Luca whispered in Stefan's ear, speaking in Romanian. "His girl dropped him."

"His girl? Which girl?"

"I don't know. His girlfriend, I believe."

"Now, Abdur, my son. Tell me what happened," Stefan asked.

"Nothing, Father. Nothing at all."

"Come on, Abdur, don't give me this nonsense. Be a man, and tell me the truth. Don't be afraid. You know I am your friend. You know that everything you tell me dies here. It is not out of curiosity that I am asking. I just want to help you if I can." Stefan put his arm around the boy's shoulders. "Come on, tell me, my son."

"Monica," the young man mumbled. "She left me. She married someone else." Abdur raised a haggard face and looked for the first time straight at Stefan with big wet eyes, trying hard to hold it together. He was almost unrecognizable, his handsome features ravaged by sadness.

"Monica? Is this the blonde Swedish girl?" Stefan asked, remembering how not long ago Abdur had enthusiastically described the girl, almost worshiping her.

"Yes. Her folks didn't let her marry me. She mailed me back all my documents. Everything." He pointed to the papers spread on the floor and glanced at Stefan with wild eyes. "What I am going to do now? I wish I could die . . . Honestly . . . I would, if I could." He took several quick puffs from his cigarette. The smoke choked him, and he started coughing, tears spilling out from under his swollen eyelids.

"That's silly, my son," Stefan began reproachfully, intending to condemn smoking. But he decided to skip the reproof and offer something positive instead. "The world is teeming with beautiful girls, and you are quite young. As my mother would say:

'What is yours is put aside.' Sooner or later, you will find a nicer girlfriend."

"Never. I know that . . . I am finished . . ." Abdur recovered his breath and reached forward with a grunt to stub out his cigarette in Luca's ashtray that was lying on the dusty concrete floor. "Monica is unique, so good, so beautiful. I will never find another one like her."

"Yes, you will. Never say die, my son."

"That's what I tried to tell him," Luca intervened.

"I don't want another girl. Monica is my only love. She promised to be mine forever. It is only her I want."

"Then you have to fight for her, not mourn." Stefan felt he was beginning to lose his patience.

"I cannot fight," the wretched youth cried. "They have already forced her to marry a man of their acquaintance. It's a fact. It's done . . ."

"She is already married? When did that happen?" Stefan asked.

"Last Sunday. She wrote . . ."

"Did she say anything before?"

"No. She was always writing how much she was looking forward to marrying me. I can show you . . ." He bent forward, feverishly rummaging through the papers. Running out of patience, he picked up the first letter at hand and showed it to Stefan. "This came today out of the blue, unexpectedly, like a thunderbolt . . . What shall I do now?"

"I cannot believe that, Abdur. Sweden is a modern country. Nobody can force a girl in that country to get married against her own will."

"That's exactly what I tried to make him understand," Luca said.

"They did. They forced my Monica . . ."

"Now listen, my son. Don't take this the wrong way, but she was already married, or she didn't really love you. This might only be an excuse to get rid of you. For her, it was perhaps just a summer holiday's fun, a passing infatuation, or an exotic adventure.

She simply dropped you in the end. It is quite common. Do you remember Thanasis's warning?"

"This is a lie!" the young man shouted and, in a blind fit of rage, hit the railing with his fist. The heavy metal bar screamed in protest, and the railing vibrated and resonated with a muffled bang, the sound running back and forth along the balcony until it died down. "No way, Monica is not that type of a girl. She wouldn't do that to me." His voice was a heavy rasp and edgy. "She was the one who convinced me to make the change for Sweden. For her, I renounced my ticket to the States. I put all my hopes in her words and my future in her hands . . ." he ended in a husky whisper and paused, exhausted.

"Why don't you want to accept the obvious truth? She dropped you, my friend, don't you see? You are not the only one in such a situation, Abdur. Almost every man in this world has gone through something like this at least once in his life. It happened to me several times and to my friends also. If you want to listen, I can tell you many such stories," Luca volunteered.

"Thanasis is another one, remember? He told you the same thing, and I must confess that it happened to me too," Stefan murmured, a self-deprecating smile troubling his composure for a fleeting moment as he remembered a long-lost sweetheart of his youth.

After his emotional outburst, Abdur didn't say anything. He just sat in a state of prostration, as if blind and deaf to whatever went on around him. His present hard-earned wisdom nor the past experiences of his elders—no matter how painful—couldn't assuage his current, all-pervading grief.

"To come to his senses, this man needs a strong drink," Luca said. "A shot of ouzo would help, I think."

"He doesn't drink that stuff," Stefan thoughtfully murmured. "I know what Abdur really needs. As it happens, I have bought some Samos. I am going to open a bottle. Don't let Abdur go away," he instructed Luca.

Stefan rushed inside and, after a couple of minutes, returned holding an uncorked bottle, accompanied by his son, who was carrying four glasses. The youngsters, together with their mother, had been grocery shopping and had just arrived home, he informed his friends while pouring the golden honeyed liquid in glasses. He then offered one each to Luca and Abdur. Luca didn't wait to be invited twice and swiftly grabbed the glass. The Afghan, ignoring Stefan, didn't make any move to take his.

"You won't be so impolite as to keep an old man waiting on you as a slave," Stefan admonished his young friend, half severely and half mockingly. "I am a free man who doesn't like to be kept waiting."

"I am awfully sorry, Father . . . I apologize for being rude," Abdur said and stood up as if awakened from a heavy sleep, bowing to Stefan with hands joined in supplication. "You shouldn't do that . . . I am not worthy of your kindness, Father," the young man said.

"Come on, take it." Stefan forced the glass into Abdur's hand. Then he declaimed in a theatric manner:

Here with a Loaf of Bread beneath the Bough,
A flask of Wine, a Book of Verse—and Thou
Beside me singing in the Wilderness—
And Wilderness is Paradise enow.

This is from your beloved Khayyam. You should at least listen to old Omar, if not to me."

"I always listen to you, Father. You know that . . ." Abdur said apologetically

"Never mind, Abdur. Let's drink, my son," Stefan urged him. "To your recovery. To Abdur."

"To Abdur." Luca and Val went along with the toast.

"Look, Ana, those naughty boys dare to drink without us," Lia cried from the doorframe. Both she and her daughter were demonstratively holding upside-down empty glasses.

"As long as you will continue to wait up there, those glasses will surely be empty. Come here if you want to share some of this lovely wine with us. Come on, girls," Stefan called them. "Bring the other bottles and the corkscrew, please," he whispered to Val.

"Bună seara la toată lumea. Good evening, everybody! What's the happy occasion?" a melodious tenor voice asked in Romanian.

215

It was one of the newly arrived refugees, known in the camp so far only by his profession, not by name. He was a professional engineer who had received a bed in the dormitory Luca shared with the two Hungarians, Váci and Lászlo, and with Stanislaw, the Polish student.

"It is not a happy occasion. We are trying to make our young Afghan forget his girlfriend. She dropped him, and the poor boy is pining for her. But please, keep that to yourself," Stefan warned him in their mother tongue. "Would you like a glass of Samos wine, Mr. Engineer?" he continued in English. "We are short of glasses. Please bring yours, sir. Will you?"

For what he had learned in the camp from rumors conveyed by the refugees, Stefan admired the man. The engineer, a widower, had fled Romania together with his twenty-four-year-old daughter; and because he had previously worked for the state's railway organization, the two had decided to make a daring escape by the famous Orient Express.

In those years, most European passenger railway cars had several compartments, opening sideways onto a narrow corridor running from one end to the other; Romanian-made trains were no exception. There were also two built-in lavatories, one at each end of the car; and the roof was doubled in those areas in order to provide room for the water-tanks, which sparingly supplied washbasins and toilets. There was a small empty space left for maintenance in between the ceiling, the water tank, and the roof proper, just enough for a slim person to lie either prone or on their back in a rather uncomfortable position. Once someone crawled into that space, if an accomplice replaced the cover from the outside, it was impossible for the person squeezed in there to move, except to turn around or to come out eventually by kicking the cover off. As an expert designer, the engineer was thoroughly acquainted with that type of construction.

The two stowaways set off toward the end of August, the hottest month, which also coincided with the peak of the summertime holiday season in Romania. During that busy period, due to an increased influx of tourists from Western and Central Europe traveling to Greece and Turkey, more passenger cars than usual were attached to the Orient Express. This circumstance provided better chances for a successful escape, making it easier for them to sneak into Bucharest's overcrowded marshalling yard. His son-in-law helped them get inside their hiding places and locked them in. They expected him to follow later with a friend. The travelers took only a couple of thin sandwiches with them, as many as they could hold in their pockets, and a water bottle each.

The trip lasted three days and nights. Though in the middle of the day it was excruciatingly hot as the sun-baked sheet-metal roof was over sixty degrees Celsius, the nights were cold, especially when they crossed the Balkan Mountains. There was no room to stretch; and the engineer, a tall man, got crippling cramps, especially during the second night when he had a severe attack of sciatica, which caught his left hip and thigh. Turning was difficult; in his daughter's case, as she was six months pregnant, it was impossible. Because of her swollen abdomen, the poor girl had to spend almost the entire trip lying on her back. If by chance they touched the hot metal roof, it burned their skin and formed painful, suppurative blisters.

At their momentous arrival in Athens—starving, dehydrated, and gravely burned—the organization that cared for the refugees immediately put them in a hospital. After a month or so, both were transferred—with healed wounds and somewhat recovered from their ordeal—to a hotel where father and daughter had to share a tiny room. When the girl's husband in turn escaped and eventually arrived in Greece, the engineer asked to be moved elsewhere, thus allowing the reunited couple a little more privacy. Since then, his daughter had, in due time, given birth to a healthy baby boy of almost four kilograms, making her a hero among the refugees and him a happy grandfather.

"These two were drinking alone, and I invited them to join us. I hope you don't mind," the engineer said, displaying an embarrassed smile when presently reappeared with a glass, seconded by Váci and László.

The Hungarians had their glasses filled with some dark golden liquid, and Váci carried a half-empty bottle.

"What are you guys drinking here?" László asked.

"Samos," Stefan answered. "Would you like some?"

"No, thanks. We had brandy for starters, and we don't like to mix our drinks. Maybe later," Váci said, seating himself next to Abdur and sheltering his bottle underneath the chair.

László having silently agreed with his friend, Stefan turned to the engineer and filled his glass. The man sniffed the wine with closed eyes, took a delicate sip, noisily swilled it round his mouth and, after a pause, swallowed. "Ah," he cried, "this must be ambrosia, the true drink of gods. What kind of wine is it?"

"Samos. I already told you: the liqueur wine of the island of Samos." Stefan's answer sounded a bit ruffled.

"Don't get upset with me," the engineer said. "My family was in the wine-making business for over two hundred years, but I have never tasted anything like this."

"Do you like it, then?"

"Yes. Very much."

"I am glad you do. I like it too. In fact, since we became acquainted with it, of course only after our arrival in Greece, Samos has become my preferred wine. I would probably drink this wine to death if I could afford it," Stefan confessed.

"Why are you guys looking so gloomy?" Váci asked cheerfully. He obviously was in a happy mood. "What are they mourning for, Abdur?"

The Afghan didn't answer. He just drank the last mouthful from his glass and shook his head in a desultory way, fixing Váci with haggard eyes.

"'The eternal game of love and chance,'" Luca quoted loosely as knowledge of Shakespearean plays wasn't among his fortes.

"Don't talk to me about love, Luca, please. Love is a bitch and a witch," Váci frowned, making a grimace of disgust.

"Not everyone here is of that opinion," Lia said, smiling and raising her glass. "What happened to you? I hope this is only a passing bout of blues. Cheers, Váci."

"Are you the host of this sad party, my good lady? Then I won't dare to contradict you. I would never, but never, fight with a lady. With regard to the blues, I might confess that you are a fine connoisseur of the male soul, Lia. Cheers!"

"Well, my friends, why should we waste our time arguing about love? We all know how it is, except the very young. They learn, alas, sooner than necessary," Luca said, nodding his head in Abdur's direction. "I would like to tell you a story instead of repeating clichés. The tale has been in my mind the whole evening, and if I don't tell it, it will probably make me sick with frustration."

"All right, all right! For God's sake, man, nobody wants you to get sick. Go ahead, tell us your story," Stefan said, unguardedly laughing as he refilled his friend's glass. "We can't run away from you. It is too hot. Innocent victims, we are at your mercy."

All of them laughed except Abdur. The young man continued to be in the throes of depression, a sad figure lost in the midst of their lively get-together. He agreed in the end, to Stefan's relief, to drink some more wine. When Lia passed around the tin box of nuts, he even helped himself, taking a handful and munching them absentmindedly.

"Some of you know already, some don't. But before coming to Greece, I worked for a couple of years in Syria." Luca said. He sipped slowly from the wine and put a few pistachios in his mouth.

"Why, then, did you come to Greece from Turkey? That is where you came from, isn't it?" Val asked flippantly.

"Yes, of course. That was because I had no other choice as only Turkey has borders with both Syria and Greece. But this is another story." Luca made a gesture as if pushing something away and, during the short pause, helped himself to more nuts.

"The story I want to tell started some years before, when the Romanian government signed an agreement with the Syrians to design and build several grand-scale industrial complexes in their country. It was half propaganda and half business. You must have heard the slogan 'Communist Romania helps its brothers and sisters from the third-world countries in their struggle against Anglo-American imperialism.' Such deals allowed the Romanians to get hard currency by selling technology and qualified labor at dumping prices. That was also advantageous for their counterpart, the Syrians in this particular case, which got high technical know-how and advanced equipment for a fraction of the price being asked on the world markets. In the work I was concerned with, no matter how little our government paid me, it was still a lot more than my salary at home. For this reason, jobs like mine were coveted and couldn't be obtained just through connections and bribery because, as a rule, only married members of the Communist Party with children were sent to work abroad and . . ."

"Why, Luca. You told us that you had never been a member of the Communist Party. Now the truth is coming to light. Shame on you, liar." László cried maliciously. "Could you believe something like that, guys?" He rhetorically asked, looking around with an upset face.

"I am not a liar. What I told you is the truth. You should be patient and listen quietly. Otherwise, I'll withdraw to the dormitory and never speak to you again." Luca stood up, the picture of righteous indignation. "Shame on you, László, not on me!" he blustered.

"Come on, come on, guys! What is happening to you? Stop this nonsense." Stefan tried to pacify his friends.

"Luca had told me . . ." László mumbled.

"Shut up, László!" Váci snapped.

"It is László's fault. He is always negative!" Luca thundered.

"Come on, Luca. You know László, don't you?" Váci said. "He speaks without thinking, but he has a big heart."

"I'll kick that bastard's ass . . ." László angrily said but couldn't continue because Váci pulled him by the back of his pants, forcing his friend to sit on the chair.

"I'll punch your dirty mouth if you don't shut up, László," Váci said. "I am bloody serious."

"I am . . . I . . . I . . ." László stammered.

"You just shut up, please," Váci insisted, forcefully holding László down.

"Quiet, quiet, gentlemen! It is nobody's fault, just too much brandy and Samos. Stop this childish squabble, and please listen in silence. No more interruptions, please," Stefan ordered, trying to sound severe. "Okay now, Luca, tell us the story. If you have such an intriguing story to tell, you shouldn't be afraid of interruptions."

"Yes, you don't have to be afraid of interruptions," Abdur said dreamlike, as if coming back to life from a lethargic sleep. "Please continue, Luca."

"I am not afraid of interruptions . . . I am just . . . if you guys insist . . . This actually started long before I went to work abroad. I was born in Arad, a mid-sized town in western Transylvania, not far from the Hungarian border. Even today, the town has some Hungarian and German minorities. And during her pregnancy, my mother befriended the neighbor's wife, who was a Hungarian. Her husband had a mixture of German, Hungarian, and Romanian blood. As it happened, their confinement came at the same time. And both my mother and her friend gave birth to a baby boy each, only a few hours apart. It was only normal that we, the boys, became good friends. Franci—that was my friend's name—and I grew up together, played together, went to school together, and courted girls together until Franci's marriage. None of us had brothers or sisters of our own, but we were as close as one could get."

Luca paused for a sip and glanced around to see the effect of his words. So far, nobody had turned on the lights, and it was dark on the balcony. The town's bright illumination, however, sent glimmers of lights and mild dancing shadows upon the whitewashed buildings so that the faces of Luca's audience were enveloped in sepulchral, pale reflections from the walls, making it hard to read his listeners' expressions. It was quiet on the balcony, except for the town's background noises and the distant musical cacophony that restaurant loudspeakers had just begun to broadcast. He let out a dissatisfied chuckle, gulped another mouthful of wine, and resolved to go ahead.

"After graduating from the technical high school, both of us were sent to work at a factory manufacturing heavy machinery, which we had to leave the next year for military duty. In the army, our lives took different directions. I was sent to an armored vehicles unit and trained as an auto mechanic. Franci was selected for service in a special unit as a sort of commando. Everything they did was top secret, and he never wanted to talk about it. Once, however, when we had one drink too many, he mentioned training Zimbabwean Marxist partisans for guerilla warfare. That was all I could gather from him, and I never tried for more.

"I forgot to tell about Franci father's third cousin: this distant relative was a member of the prewar, insignificant Communist Party. And he left Romania just before the Second World War, taking refuge in the Soviet Union. At the end of the war, the man returned with the Red Army. He immediately got a leading position in his party and a ministerial job when the communists took over the country. Thus wherever Franci went, he was instantly recognized as a relation of that important comrade and got the best possible treatment. That also explains why, soon after finishing his military service and returning to the factory, Franci was appointed secretary of the local organization of the Communist Party.

"I don't have to tell you what that meant. Franci became the most powerful man in the factory. He had more power than the technical director or even the general manager, who were practically his subordinates. His power reached beyond the confines of that factory as he was also an influential member of the regional committee of the Party. Our relationship, though, remained unchanged for some time, the only difference being that opportunities for a friendly get-together became few and far between. My friend was an important and busy personage, and I didn't complain. In the beginning, he tried to persuade me to join the Party myself—there were plenty of advantages in it—but I loved to go fishing instead of spending hours between four walls talking nonsense during all sorts of boring meetings. He gave up in the end, disappointed with my stubbornness. After that, there was a tacit agreement between us to avoid political discussions when we were together. Although nothing else intervened, our past camaraderie became lukewarm as time went by. And later, I saw very little of him privately.

"For a short while during our high school years, I wooed a pretty mignonette, Maria, until she told me on one date that she had fallen madly in love with Franci and there was no chance for me. Unfortunately for Maria, Franci didn't share her infatuation.

Although she spared no effort to ingratiate herself with him, nothing had worked out by the time we went to fulfill our military duties. She was still unmarried and employed at the same factory when we returned. But she must have known by then that her hopes for a happy ending with Franci, if she continued nurturing any, were in vain.

"It was two years after his appointment as secretary, I believe, that Franci suddenly fell for a blonde doll seven years his junior. Her name was Zoia, after a famous Soviet war heroine widely popularized by the Russian book and movie *The Young Guard*. They had met at one of those dull political functions that Party honchos attended day after day. The girl had just graduated from high school and currently worked for one of the Party's organizations, a posh and well-paid sinecure. Like Franci, Zoia's father was also a big shot in the Party's nomenklatura, and his daughter enjoyed all the advantages such a connection could have offered. While most Romanian women were obliged to dress modestly due to clothing shortages and ideologically repressive taboos, she lavishly wore low-cut blouses of fine silk and very short imported miniskirts. Zoia's long, shapely legs were always shod in fashionable Italian high-heeled shoes or tall boots, and she was a knockout. According to the opinion of many, she had the kind of looks that make one think that a girl is all beauty and no brains. But love has to do with other things than brains, and Franci didn't seem to mind her lack of such endowments.

"In all truth, after he met Zoia, my friend became a different man. It was as if an incurable disease, a sort of madness, had gotten hold of him. He followed the girl wherever she went, and quite often, she spent long hours with him in his office at the factory. When that happened, nobody could approach Franci. And as a consequence, the consideration of many important issues had to be deferred until he found time to deal with them. People began grumbling about him neglecting his duties, yet nobody had the guts to openly criticize such a powerful man. It was close to Christmas when Maria came to my workplace for a chat one day and asked me to do something to stop Franci from making a fool of himself. She told me that Zoia had lived with one of her high school chums. In fact, they had become engaged when the fellow was called to fulfill his military duty a couple of months earlier. It was also rumored that the guy had left Zoia pregnant, Maria said.

"No matter how much I wanted to warn my friend, opportunities for a friendly talk were lacking. Our meetings depended on his schedule, not mine. As a high-ranking member of the Party, he lived in a sumptuous villa outside the city, rarely coming to our neighborhood to visit his parents or old friends like me. I was reluctant to directly interfere with such an intimate aspect of his life, and it took me a long time to plan the most appropriate way of passing on Maria's warning. In the end, Franci married the girl the following February, before I could have approached him. So I wisely decided to drop any further attempts to enlighten my friend.

"I was invited to the wedding dinner, which was a big affair, seating over three hundred guests in one of the Communist Party's closed-circuit restaurants. In contrast, with the acute food shortages that marred the life of Romanians at large, we were lavishly regaled with black caviar, venison, the finest wines, champagne, and genuine American bourbon. During that evening, it became obvious to everyone that Franci was in seventh heaven. When I went to congratulate him after dinner, he confessed that it was the happiest day of his life.

"Sometime in the early summer, Zoia gave birth to a blonde baby boy. Some ill-intentioned people argued that the delivery was much earlier than normal. But the incongruity, if any, was soon forgotten. The marriage seemed to be quite a success, and my friend exuded happiness and goodwill.

"Less than two years after Franci's wedding, I myself got married. That fall, I had felt lonely and old. Most of my friends were already married with children, and my bachelor status brought upon me a sort of tacit banishment from their circle. It seemed as if theirs was a world apart, haunted by severe money problems, chronic housing shortages, children's illnesses, and family worries unknown to me and which I was not qualified to be part of. Those shortcomings notwithstanding, I envied them. In my foolishness, I felt ashamed and rejected, indeed isolated, a pariah among my own people. Loneliness has more victims in the fall than the flu, they say in Romania. Shorter days, longer nights, and cold weather all get at you, making you crave warmth, especially bodily warmth, if you understand what I mean. Bachelors would wake up one morning during what we call the blind week prey to melancholy and get in a pernicious frenzy that ended either in marriage or suicide. That proved to be true for me too. With hindsight, I must say it was a mistake. At the time, it didn't look bad at all. I loved my wife, she thought she loved me. And the following year, at the end of an extremely hot summer, our first and last child, a girl, was born."

"Are you still married, Luca?" Abdur whispered. "You never mentioned having a wife or a child."

"Sort of . . . My wife asked for a divorce . . . last year. Currently, it takes more than five years to get a divorce in Romania . . . I was away for too long, and she found someone closer to home who loved her more than I did, she said. She felt neglected . . . Let's not stray from one subject to another, please. All right?" Luca took a deep breath and sighed long and sonorously.

"I am sorry, very sorry, Luca," Abdur murmured.

"Never mind, Abdur. Never mind, my friend . . . er . . . What I was saying? Oh, yes, my marriage. That's not important. What is important happened a week after my daughter was born. I remember as if it were yesterday. I was on the afternoon shift, and almost at the end of it, Franci came into our workshop. He spoke shortly to the manager, a young engineer, and—after exchanging jokes with some older fellow workers—came to the test stand where I was assigned at the time. He wanted to have a chat. 'Get dressed as soon as possible and meet me in my office,' he said. 'The manager was informed and had already given his permission,' he casually added.

"So I took a quick shower, changed into my town clothes, and hurried to the secretary of the Communist Party's office, a suite of three large rooms in the rambling administration building. The building was silent as usual in the evenings and empty, except for the security guard watching the main door. Franci was waiting for me in his luxurious office, alone, if not counting the unappealing company of Marx, Engels, Lenin, and Ceaușescu's portraits dominating the tall walls with their cadaverous faces, vacantly gazing from dusty, gilded frames. He motioned me to sit on a couch in front of his desk and produced from the depths of a sideboard a rare bottle of Dacia superfine cognac brandy. It was my preferred drink, and he knew it. Without a word, he filled two of the four glasses set on the tray in front of him. Then he carefully poured water with ice from a jug in the remaining two and, with a familiar gesture, invited me to drink.

"After we emptied the glasses, Franci rushed to refill them and began to talk. He awkwardly congratulated me on my newborn and asked for details about my wife's health and about the baby girl. My gut feeling was that he hadn't called on me to socialize. Surely, there was something else on his mind, something he wasn't comfortable talking about straightaway. Although our friendship wasn't what it had been in the past, I disliked him beating about the bush, and I let him know it without too much ado.

"'You are right,' he said, giving me an embarrassed smile, which I was familiar with from our childhood. 'I should have found time before for an old friend such as you. It is entirely my fault, and I have to agree that our relationship had suffered because of me . . . My job is so demanding that I barely have enough time to visit my parents.'

"He shouldn't have told me this because I knew precisely how often he visited his folks. Yet I was his friend regardless of how long we hadn't seen each other, and in my opinion, friends must be there when one needs them. I told him bluntly to forget about niceties and get to the point. Although it wasn't clear at the time, the fact was he needed me. I only realized later how badly he did.

"It was for the moment a secret known only at the highest levels of leadership, he finally told me, that soon several factories, including ours, would be engaged in a joint venture with the Syrian government. Syria was the Arab version of a communist dictatorship, and a team of numerous carefully picked workers and technicians would have to go to that country and help build a giant complex to produce triple super phosphate fertilizer, equipped with Romanian-made machinery. I never heard of the location he mentioned, a place soon to become an important part of our lives. The completion of the project would probably take a couple of years or more, and he was appointed as its general field manager. Several professional engineers and plainclothes securitate officers would be, of course, in charge of key technological, administrative, and intelligence positions under him as the supreme boss and the all-powerful representative of the Romanian Communist Party at the building site. He didn't want to go, Franci said, although both his father-in-law and his wife insisted, this apparently being the last step before a ministerial appointment in the government.

"I raised my glass and congratulated him. I was surprised that Franci wasn't as thrilled by the prospect of his advancement as one would have expected. He received my words with a rather worried face. He didn't want to go, he reiterated. He was happily married to a beautiful woman, and they had a lovely child. It was obvious that he would have preferred to stay home, enjoy family life, and take care of his boy. Why, then, was he not refusing the position, I asked. My friend mumbled something about allegiance to his important uncle, the big Party honcho, and alluded to owing a debt of gratitude toward his in-laws. Somehow, I got the impression that in the nomenklatura circles, it was impossible to refuse such a position without losing a lot of prestige and favors or jeopardizing other people's positions. Also, his wife craved the foreign luxuries one accessed only when abroad, I gathered.

"It was already late, and before going home, I had to do some shopping for my family. I explained the situation to Franci, pointing out that my wife was alone and still weak after the recent delivery, and asked point-blank what he wanted from me. It took him almost another half of an hour of mumbling, stammering, and drinking brandy until I could understand what his problem was. He needed someone he trusted to go abroad with him, and he wanted that to be me. The idea came as a shock. I lacked the qualifications for the job because I wasn't a member of the Party and had been married for less than a year. Never in my life had I ever dreamed of such a job. He had taken me completely unprepared for a life change of that magnitude. Still in love with my wife and eager to prove a good father, I didn't want to leave just like that, giving up my real happiness for some illusory advantages.

"Party membership was not critical for the job I was offered, he assured me. It was enough that I was married, and having a child was an additional great asset. Following his prior recommendation, I had already been approved for the position of assistant to the general field manager. Moreover, the securitate had, during the previous months, checked my background without my knowledge and duly cleared me. He just needed my agreement to have the decision made official. In the meantime, the administration had begun the formalities for a passport on my behalf, which he assured me would arrive shortly. While on location, the government would pay all my expenses such as rent, food, and travel. And the salary would be three times my current one plus an equivalent amount in US dollars paid monthly in Syria. Whatever I bought abroad would be duty-free on my return to the country.

"Having noticed my surprise and almost negative reaction to his offer, Franci literally begged me to accept, invoking our old friendship, not before he conspiratorially went around and checked all the windows to make sure they were securely closed. He also looked behind each door, which he afterward left fully opened so we could see anyone coming into the office across the empty rooms. After he had satisfied himself that nobody was listening, he unplugged all the telephone sets that crowded his desk and sat on the couch beside me, talking in a whisper. He couldn't trust anyone who has been suggested for the job so far, and that was why he had proposed me, he said. In all the years he had worked in the Party's organization, he had never found a single person, from the lowest to highest-ranking member, moved by so-called communist ideals, he confessed. All were bureaucrats or opportunists, fierce egotists from all walks of life using the Marxist-Leninist ideology, the proletarian slogans, and the repressive *apparat* to their sole benefit. He was fed up with the permanent lying, backstabbing, and never-ending ass-kissing required to survive in a leading position like his. And although he hated the idea of working abroad, in a way,

———

228

he was happy to get out of that stifling atmosphere. Perhaps there would be less politics and more honest, productive work, he hoped. Once on the building site in Syria, it would be up to him to set the tone, and that was why someone he trusted could be essential for implementing his management style.

"Part of that was dangerous talk, and I told him so. However, he was in such an excited state of mind that nothing could have stopped him. He knew the risk, he said, but I was his only friend and confidante. He couldn't have discussed this with anyone else, be they wife, parents, or in-laws. Those secret thoughts were his playing cards, and he had exposed them to me as a sign of unrestrained trust. In spite of his sincere openness and honest intentions, I doubted the new job would change anything for him. Also, I was skeptical about my future in working abroad. There was no guarantee or stability in those jobs, being continuously under the scrutiny of the secret police agents, with informers prowling about and Party bureaucrats watching behind the scenes. It was common knowledge that passports and visas could easily be here today and gone tomorrow. But he kept cajoling me, insisting and begging.

"To make a long story short, after recovering from the first shock and after long discussions with my wife and parents, I gave in to Franci's entreaties and accepted the job. Let's face it: such opportunities were extremely rare in Romania. Normally, it would have been impossible for a little guy like me to even get a passport, not to mention traveling to Syria and visiting Greece, Lebanon, and Egypt or Turkey on the way. The money aspect was also tempting. The only huge foreseeable difficulty was that we weren't allowed to take our wives and children with us at least for the first year or two. In that respect, Luciana, my wife, was adamant. She would not accept more than a year of separation. When told, Franci promised to do something about that because being a long-term absentee husband didn't appeal to him either.

"Two months later, we were in Syria, struggling to get acclimatized to the harsh environment, the fall being the warmest season there, and swamped with hard work. In the beginning, our progress was hindered day and night by all kinds of organizational and technical problems nobody was ready for. We were also in an entirely different society and culture. The fact is we never thought we would have to overcome so many difficulties. On the other hand, those difficulties kept us busy, and time just flew.

"I am not sure now when I overheard the first rumors about Franci's wife. Perhaps it was at the New Year's dinner, when some colleagues shared news from home that wasn't meant for my ears. Later, in the spring, my wife mentioned in her letters meeting Zoia accompanied by a young man who, she maliciously implied, behaved as Franci's proxy. Those disparate tidings didn't really bother me. People always gossip, and women have a tendency to be critical of their kin and misinterpret other wives' behavior, especially when they think they are misbehaving in the absence of their husbands. Then one evening in the middle of the summer, a troubled Franci came to my room and, out of the blue, asked me if I remembered Maria, our colleague.

"'Yes I do,' I said. 'She is still a friend of mine. What's the problem with her?' I asked.

"'Nothing, no problem,' he evasively answered. It just happened that he remembered her. Just like that. However, I knew him too well to believe such nonsense."

Luca paused and absentmindedly searched his breast pocket. "Where are my cigarettes?" he asked. "Has anyone seen them?"

"Take one of mine," Váci said, offering his pack.

"No, thanks. I need my brand," Luca insisted, "I am not used to Dunhill. They make me cough."

"Sorry, Luca," Abdur said in a meek voice. "I somehow got your cigarettes. Here, please take them back."

"Aha! I knew someone pinched my cigarettes." Luca grabbed the package and, after feeling it, took a cigarette out and lit it. In the ensuing glow, his face, distorted by an impish smile, became visible for a few seconds. "Thanks, Abdur," he said, "I was just kidding you. What do you expect from an old man? I had forgotten giving them to you."

"What about your friend Franci? Will we hear more about him tonight?" Stefan asked.

"Patience. I will tell you. May I have another glass of that wine of yours first? My throat is kind of dry."

"Of course," Stefan said and motioned Val to go around and fill the empty glasses.

"On the building site," Luca continued his story, "Franci and I shared a small apartment. And after almost a year of continuous living and working closely together, our old friendship had rekindled and was stronger than ever. We talked openly about everything, and there were no secrets between us, or so I thought. That night, it didn't take me long to find out what had happened. It appeared that during the day, my friend had received a letter from Maria in the mail. It wasn't really a letter, just a short note and three photographs showing Zoia in more or less compromising situations. The high school chum Zoia was engaged to before marrying Franci had finished his military service, Maria wrote, and was back in town, showing around his ex-fiancée. Arad is one of those small cities where most people know each other, and it is hardly possible to hide an extramarital liaison for long. Franci was quite upset. My friend knew Zoia wasn't a saint before their marriage, but he wasn't either, he confessed. They had agreed, he said, to forget the past and never betray their loyalties in the future. In the beginning, he wasn't too sure about her feelings as she was so much younger and foolish. After they got married, he never had any doubts, he said. Apparently, on one occasion, when he brought into discussion the possibility of an eventual split, she didn't even want to hear about it. She made him solemnly promise that if anyone happened to come between them, the matter would be discussed honestly and settled before becoming public. For Franci, that was proof of her commitment, and he also naively believed that having a baby so early in the marriage had been a sign of sincere love. Now it seemed his wife wasn't true to her word, and he wanted my advice.

"I didn't dare to ask Franci how sure he was that Zoia's boy was also his. What I said was that in my opinion, it is wrong to judge such delicate matters only by a couple of pictures. People going together to movies, kissing in the street, or embracing in parks are not necessarily having a love affair. Yet I agreed that a married woman with a child should act with more discretion, especially when her husband is thousands of kilometers away. I have always been in favor of temporizing, and my suggestion to Franci was to write his wife, asking her clearly to stop seeing that fellow. My friend was scheduled to return home shortly for his yearly statutory holiday, in fact, the following month. It would be better to assess the situation on the spot and decide with full knowledge of the facts, I advised him.

"I have no idea what he did with my advice. Certainly, until he took his vacation, we didn't have another such discussion. In the aftermath of the events all of us went through, I am convinced that he deliberately avoided me.

"During the month he was absent, Franci wrote me once although I didn't expect that much from him. It was a postcard describing his satisfaction being at home in our 'beloved mother country' with his loving wife and wonderful child. Romania was making tremendous progress under the leadership of the Party, building a great future for our nation, he said, quoting an overused slogan. Everyone welcomed him with open arms, many of his acquaintances inviting him and Zoia to lavish dinners and endless outings. I knew how loaded with presents he had gone home. It was a lot of expensive stuff for his family and especially for those important comrades from the nomenklatura who had supported him, and it wasn't any wonder that he enjoyed so much popularity. In his letter, he didn't mention any familial disagreement or marital problems, so I assumed everything was just fine. What I didn't realize was that he didn't write for me. He wrote for the censor's office."

"What do you mean by censor's office, Luca?" Abdur asked. "How did you get the postcard if it wasn't for you?"

A chorus of surprised voices mixed with bursts of uneasy laughter followed Abdur's question, resonating across the balcony. Luca couldn't continue. He was not prepared for that interruption and didn't know what to answer.

"Someone should explain to Abdur how censorship works," the engineer suggested.

"Abdur, my son," Stefan said with a wry smile, "forgive our laugh. It is not your fault. It is a nervous reaction more than a mere laugh. You must understand that in Romania, everything sent or received by mail passes through the censor's office. There are specially trained securitate agents who open every single letter and read it. His friend's letter was addressed to Luca yet went to its destination only after passing through that office. Do you understand now?"

"If the contents of his postcard had aroused the slightest suspicion, the securitate would instantly have taken what they considered appropriate countermeasures. These usually range from keeping a close watch on the writer and his correspondents to speedy detention, investigation under duress, and sometimes their physical elimination. Any sign of marital trouble in the life of people working abroad means a potential weakening of their commitment to the family left behind and implicitly an incentive to defection. The solution is to bring back and withdraw the passport of the person under suspicion. It is impossible to leave the country without a passport," Lia explained. "That's how the system works."

"To make you understand better, Abdur, I'll tell you a little joke we have about a folksy character named Bulă," the engineer said. "Bulă works in a factory. As a reward for his hard work and loyalty to communism, the management has decided to entrust him with a mission abroad. The departure day arrives, and Bulă is getting ready to go to the airport. He is in the bathroom, shaving in front of the mirror, whistling happily. In a burst of enthusiasm, he winks at his reflection and addresses himself, saying, 'Bravo, Bulă, you sneaky guy. Who could have believed that? You outwitted them.' He has barely finished shaving his left cheek when the bell rings. Half shaven, he goes to the door and opens it. It is a securitate officer. 'Comrade Bulă, you are not going abroad anymore. We don't trust you,' the man in uniform announces, 'give me back your passport.' After the officer leaves, Bulă returns to the bathroom and continues shaving. He looks reproachfully at his image in the mirror and says, 'Bulă, Bulă, you dirty traitor. You taught me a lesson. I will never

ever tell you a secret again.'" The engineer sighed. "Although this is only a joke, it is not too far from the truth," he concluded.

Nobody laughed. There was an unsettling movement of chairs instead; and then someone, perhaps Ana, turned the light on. A chorus of protests, which soon, however, died, welcomed the sudden passage from darkness to what everyone felt to be blinding, harsh light.

"I remember now that once, the Russians' Afghan puppets tried to set up something similar in Kabul on a much more modest scale," Abdur said. "The mujaheddins blew up that vipers' den."

"What happened next, Luca?" Val asked.

"Yes," Luca began again, struggling to catch his lost thread, "yes . . . It is as you guys said . . . Now let's go back to my story . . . When Franci returned, this time with his wife, it was my turn to go home. Zoia was allowed to stay with her husband in Syria for two months, and they looked very happy and conspicuously in love as if nothing had ever happened. In Romania, however, I learned that the situation was worse than I could have imagined.

"For me, that holiday wasn't a happy one. My wife's passport application had been rejected, and she wanted me to give up the position in Syria and stay home. Franci himself had had difficulties in getting Zoia's trip approved. It was only through her father's connection that she had gotten the permission to travel to Syria. Maybe next year, my wife would get herself the desired passport, I was told. That was just a vague possibility, not a promise, and therefore not satisfactory at all to Luciana. During my stay at home, there was no day without her crying a lot and she constantly nagged me. Perhaps there was something going on which I wasn't aware of. Even if there was, she never told me. I begged her, though, to be patient until the end of the year, a mere four months. Then if the situation didn't change, I would resign and come home, I promised, oblivious to what lay in the future. I was still hoping to get her an approval with Franci's help.

"Franci's shadow was another thing, which loomed heavily over my holiday and killed any hope of a quiet vacation. No later than the second day after my return home, I became unwillingly caught in the middle of a wasp's nest, and the buzz was everywhere. My parents, Franci's parents and relatives, Luciana, the neighbors, other friends, and acquaintances all were eager to tell what they knew. And they had a lot to tell.

"Since the return of that high school boyfriend of hers months before, Zoia had carried on a public torrid love affair with him. She almost moved in with the man, spending nights in a row at his place while her little boy was left in the care of his grandparents. Even during Franci's holiday, she managed to sneak out and meet the guy stealthily several times. When, before returning to Syria, my friend had to go to Bucharest for a special meeting, which lasted three days, she spent the nights with her lover. Franci seemed to be oblivious to all that and didn't want to listen if one of the numerous benevolent souls tried to open his eyes. He spent his days in what appeared to be blissful ignorance, maddening the people who cared for him with his numb detachment, and they always left him in disgust or plainly outraged. All kinds of gossip was going around, and what really disturbed me more than anything was what Maria had to say. According to her, the big brass in the Party and the securitate bosses knew every detail about Zoia's affair and were extremely concerned. And it had just recently been decided in those high circles that immediately after her return, Franci should be recalled and replaced. Maria swore she had heard this from a reliable source, very near to the main power brokers. The thing was certain, and she implored me, with teary eyes, to warn Franci.

"At the end of that unpleasant month, I went back to my job in Syria with a wavering heart. It was a busy time at the building site, and a big load of unsolved business was waiting for me. To compensate for countless morning meetings with local representatives, I had to spend long evenings in the office, my workday lasting quite often until midnight. Franci and I had agreed to let him and Zoia use the entire apartment as long as she stayed in Syria. There was always someone away on vacation, and I moved into a dormitory with other colleagues. The lack of comfort impeded my sleep. Too much work and not enough sleep did nothing to help overcome the stress that goaded me. I lost my appetite and began losing weight.

"Due to our busy schedules and to the fact that Zoia always accompanied Franci, opportunities for a private discussion were scarce. After waiting several days for an elusive occasion, I decided to resort to any possible stratagem in order to convey Maria's message to my friend. Soon, a favorable occasion presented itself as we had both been invited to a meeting with some dignitaries in the nearby town. On the appointed day, the Syrians phoned me early and cancelled it. Keeping the news to myself, at the expected time, I took one of the Jeeps, picked up Franci at his apartment, and set off. Our drivers were local people, and there were always some absentees, so it wasn't unusual for us to occasionally drive the company cars.

"I began unloading my news as soon as we had left the building site. After a few kilometers, Franci asked me to stop and pull off the road in the shade of a huge pistachio tree. At first, he tried to take the whole thing lightly, making fun of me. But I could tell from the look in his eyes that he was shaken. He realized how much I knew but didn't want to acknowledge it. It was fearfully hot, and an unnerving wind incessantly blew from the Syrian Desert, shrouding the arid landscape in a dusty haze. 'Really, Luca,' my friend reproved me, 'you shouldn't pay attention to gossipy women.' Maria wasn't a gossipy woman, I replied, she was sincerely concerned and loved him. 'Yeah,' he halfheartedly acknowledged, 'poor old Maria.'

"We talked for a couple of hours, each of us fretting in our own way under that tree, blown by the burning wind of the desert. The car had no air conditioning, and we kept the doors open to cool us, but to no avail. He asked me about what other friends had said. I preferred to pass on only what his close relatives had asked me to, and he didn't insist on hearing more. He made no comment, and then proposed going back to the building site. All the way, he brooded in silence over his own thoughts. Only once he murmured, as if only to himself, 'poor Maria, poor girl . . . how stupid I have been.' At the building site, we parted without words, and I drove to the garage and parked the car.

"The next day, Franci was his old self again, showing no sign of trouble or emotion. There wasn't any change in his public behavior toward his wife, the pair presenting the same loving image as before. Then in the week preceding her departure, Franci drove Zoia to town every day, spending several hours with her in what was seen by many coworkers as a wild shopping spree. They would leave early in the morning and return at night, overloaded with parcels and bags of various shapes and sizes.

"Two days before Zoia's flight home, my friend went alone to town to arrange her train and airplane tickets. His wife was scheduled to take a flight from Damascus airport, a two-hour rail trip away. In his absence, Zoia, looking more than ever the blonde bombshell, dropped by my office without notice. She was wearing one of those miniskirts and a loose halter top, which didn't leave any doubt about what was underneath. Since her arrival, there had been several complaints from the locals regarding 'her dressing habits violating Islam's moral rules of conduct,' but she couldn't have cared less. Zoia sat herself on my desk, pushing her shapely legs under my nose and leaning forward. I could see she had no bra. Between silly jokes and hysterical laughter, she asked me about acquaintances and common friends met recently while vacationing in Arad. My curt answers and lack of attention didn't deter her, and suddenly, she let herself slide onto my lap for a few seconds before swaying away. 'Luca, dear. Come to my place, and let's have fun,' she whispered in my ear."

"Oh, Luca, what a lucky man you are," Váci cried with conspicuous envy.

"Me? Why?" Luca asked, looking disoriented.

"That beautiful woman . . . She had a crush on you," László said, giving Luca a malicious smile, and then looking at Váci for confirmation.

"Are you crazy, guys? That was my best friend's wife!" Luca cried. "For God's sake, how can you even think something like that?" Luca was obviously hurt. "You must be out of your mind."

"Well . . . I didn't really . . ." Váci mumbled.

"It's your fault. It is your way of telling the story that . . ." László blurted.

"All right, guys. I would like to hear the end of Luca's story. Please, let him finish," Lia said.

"For your information, guys, far from believing it to be a piece of good luck, I didn't take advantage of the situation. To avoid some crazy trouble with her, I told Zoia to go home and wait for me there. Then I phoned for a Jeep and asked the chauffeur to drive me to the far end of the building site where one of our teams was busy pouring concrete for a foundation. I was still there late in the afternoon when Franci came home. In my opinion, that woman wanted to find out at any cost how much I knew and perhaps what I had told her husband and, most of all, how Franci had reacted. Her feminine intuition must have alerted Zoia that something had changed in their relationship. She had always been very much in control and confident, but for the first time in their married life, she was afraid of something she couldn't apprehend. It was neither infatuation nor vice that had driven her to make that pass at me. It was premonition.

"On the morning of her departure, Franci started quite early with Zoia and the voluminous luggage she had. He wanted to be alone with her and drove himself to the train station in an IMS, a mid-sized utility vehicle made in Romania. They stopped at the main office to say good-bye. I was already there, and he asked me to get ready for an afternoon meeting with the technical staff, giving all kinds of detailed instructions about what he wanted presented to them. He would be back in about three hours, he said.

"That was the last time I saw him. When Franci failed to show up on time, we initially thought he had changed his mind and had gone with Zoia to Damascus. As he wasn't back the next day either, the chief engineer, his deputy, assumed that something had gone wrong. He phoned Romania's commercial representative in Damascus, the Romanian embassy, and the headquarters in Bucharest. And soon, a team of 'specialists' arrived in a hurry. For a couple of months or so, our normal life was interrupted by a flurry of brainwashing meetings alternating with hostile inquests, every person on site being treated as a criminal and interviewed more than once, harassment being more important than work. Denunciations, false accusations, finger-pointing, and anonymous incriminating information on closest colleagues became rampant. Several scapegoats were easily found and sent back to Romania. It was as if all hell had let loose in our community. All was in vain. The investigators couldn't find any trace of Franci. He vanished with the car and was never found. Wild rumors about his premeditated defection would once in a while surface, locating him in Iraq, Iran, Turkey, or Lebanon and as far as South Africa, only to be proven wrong one after the other."

"What about his family in Romania? Did they hear from him?" Váci asked.

"No. Nobody ever heard anything. The securitate recalled their sleuths at the end of the third month, and the Syrian police gave up the search after a few more."

"Maybe some bandits killed them and buried their remains in the desert. With so many valuables in that car . . ." Val said.

"Did his wife disappear with him?" Ana asked.

"No. That is the funny part."

"What happened to her?"

"You won't believe that, Ana. He sold her."

"Sold her?" Ana cried. "How was that possible?"

"Your friend sold his beloved wife?" Abdur asked, and for the first time that evening, he looked fully awake and alert.

"Yes, he did. Without any doubt, Abdur," Luca answered.

"Yours is an intriguing story, Luca. Do you know what happened afterward to your friend's wife?" Lia asked.

"Yes, though I must confess that I don't know the exact sequence of events. Among several changes that followed my friend's disappearance was the arrival of a new general field manager, an *apparatchic* from the central committee of the Party. He brought his own assistant with him, and I was moved to a different job without further access to the main sources of information. As my friendship with Franci was no secret, I was put under strict surveillance, and my movements were restricted. Thus this part of my story is based only on hearsay evidence.

"From what I heard, Franci had installed his wife in one of the train station's waiting rooms on that fateful morning and returned to the car to fetch the luggage. Zoia had been waiting for some time when a group of local men came in and attempted to take her with them. She resisted energetically and made a tremendous racket, crying, calling her husband, and shouting for help. Attracted by the noise, the police promptly intervened and dragged the whole bunch to their headquarters. At the police station, the locals produced certain legal documents, and an officer explained to Zoia that Franci had sold her two days before for quite a high price. The procedure was correct and the deal legal. Those local men were the buyer and his relatives, acting in good faith. Zoia was now the legitimate wife of one of them, and according to the law of the land, she had to go with him. Later on, a colleague of mine who knew more details of the case from a securitate officer told me that Zoia's new husband had put her on the market. He forced her to work as a prostitute for rich clients recruited among his friends who were crazy about blonde women. Vicious beatings and starvation were the persuasion methods routinely used in that business. She went through hell for some time as it took more than ten months of diplomatic intervention, including the payment of a large sum of money, before Zoia was released from bondage and finally allowed to return home. Not before she had gotten a nasty venereal disease, my informer assured me."

"Wow! That was quite a story. Why did your friend do this?" Val asked.

"Revenge, sweet revenge," Váci declaimed.

"What a beast," Ana indignantly blurted.

"Have you heard, Váci? That's what we should have done to that bitch who put us in the hands of the police," László said.

"That might have been possible in Syria but not in Hungary, László dear," Váci acidly reminded his crony.

"How can someone do such a mean thing?" Ana asked. "Your friend, Luca, must have been a vicious brute."

"Oh, young lady, don't be so hard on the poor man. Great love can give birth to the greatest hatred," the engineer said.

"I would never do something so cruel to my Monica, although in our law, there are much harsher punishments for adulterous women," Abdur whispered loud enough to be heard by all.

"What do you mean, Abdur, by harsher punishments?" Val wanted to know.

"Er . . . er . . . stoning, for instance, among other things," Abdur answered in a low voice.

"Ugh," Val said, "how horrid."

"I knew my friend for a long time, Ana," said Luca as if he didn't hear Abdur, "and I hope he is alive and well somewhere. I don't believe he is worse than any other man. He loved that girl more than anything else in the world, and she betrayed him. Not only did she betray, she made a fool and a laughing stock of him. She grieved Franci, who suffered terribly, and the pain maddened him."

"Ah, my friends, people's souls are like the moon. They have a dark, invisible face. Most of the time, we show others only our bright side. Beware when, for some unexpected reason, the other face becomes visible," the engineer said.

"Certainly, there is some truth in what you are saying," Stefan acknowledged, although only moderately convinced.

"Of course there is," the engineer said. "And to prove my point, I will tell you a story, if you all agree. It is only nine o'clock—not too late, I think. Before starting, I would like to ask, if I may, this young man," he pointed to Val, "to fetch a few more bottles of Samos, which I would like to share with you. As anyone can see, there is nothing left in those empties. The new bottles are my treat. Today, I toiled in the harbor, unloading Portland cement from a cargo ship. And although I have a sore back, I am currently rich and awfully thirsty."

The Ever-Untrustworthy Cupid

The wine stall was nearby in the main square and always stayed open late, so it didn't take long for Val to fetch the engineer's treat. He was gone only a few minutes and returned carrying half a dozen bottles of Samos. The expectant gathering was smoking in silence, nobody having left so far.

There was not even a breath of wind, and the stagnant atmosphere smothered. The buildings couldn't radiate the heat stored during the day fast enough, and the camp compound sizzled like a well-stoked oven. It was impossible to sleep when it was that hot; and everyone was waiting for the wine, the engineer's story, and the blessed cool of the breeze, which would come later in the night.

"You all know that I am a professional," the engineer began after he and Val had uncorked a couple of bottles and filled everyone's glasses. "Mr. Engineer is what most of you call me, not knowing my real name."

His words were received with a muddled murmur of either protest or approval. It was hard to tell one from the other.

"You don't have to feel guilty. That's all right with me," the professional man assured his audience. "What you also don't know is that I am twice an engineer." He smiled shyly, raised his glass toward the light, looked at it with appreciative eyes, and then greedily swallowed half of its golden contents. "Divine," he sighed.

"What do you mean, twice an engineer?" Váci asked.

"Exactly what I said: twice an engineer. I will explain." He paused and gulped the rest of the wine. "Please bear with me until I pour another drink, my friend," he said. "I don't know where this thirst is coming from. My glass seems to be too small tonight."

"You hold two engineering diplomas, I presume," Stefan said.

"Absolutely correct! In vino veritas—the truth is in the wine. You are right. I earned two diplomas," the man said.

"You must be quite ambitious, sir, and . . . smart," Abdur said. He looked more awake now.

"It was dire necessity, not ambition, that made me go through university twice for the same degree."

"Lucky you. Not everyone was so fortunate. Some couldn't go to university at all. I, for example," Váci said without fully grasping what the engineer had meant.

"Not being familiar with your situation, I can't make any comment. On the other hand, calling me lucky just because I was obliged to toil twofold for the same degree is a little preposterous."

"Why did you have to study twice for your diploma?" Abdur asked.

"Very good question," the engineer said. "As you will shortly see, my misfortunes originated in my early high school years. I loved mathematics and physics, participating in all the competitions opened by *Gazeta Matematica,* that magazine of mathematics, which some of you from my generation might remember. At the time, flying machines also fascinated me more than anything else did, and I read avidly all that was connected with aeronautics. Thus my decision to become an aviation engineer had been made long before I finished high school.

"The wisdom of that choice was problematic though. When I entered the polytechnic institute, the war had hardly ended. And soon, after the nationalization of all private enterprises, the Romanian aeronautical industry was axed. Without the public's knowledge, the existing airplane factories were dismantled, and the technical documentation and production equipment were shipped to the Soviet Union. The remaining facilities were redesigned and equipped to manufacture machinery for agriculture. As a consequence, the number of students in aircraft construction was drastically reduced. I considered myself particularly fortunate when the institute accepted me among those very few, because of my good marks."

"If there was no aeronautical industry left in Romania, why did you insist upon working in that field?" László asked. "Wouldn't it have been better for you to become a specialist in something else—agricultural implements, for instance?"

"This is a pertinent remark, proof of good common sense, my friend," the engineer said. He looked with pleasure at László. "Of course, it would have definitely been better. The problem was that when one is young and in love with someone or something, there is little room for common sense. And I was living for and dreaming only of airplanes.

"I must confess that in the long run, it has been proven not to have been entirely a bad choice. When Romania adhered to the Warsaw Pact, the Soviets decided to allow us to have a small defensive air force, and a factory with one assembly line for MiG fighter jets was created in the city of Bacău just before my graduation. My engineer-in-training assignment there came as no surprise. The first three years were the best in my life. I loved my profession, and all my heart was in what I was doing, mostly research and development in preparation for the real thing: the assemblage of turbojet airplanes. Then the parts started coming in from Russia. Production work began, and finally, the factory brought out a small series of fighter-jets, which were duly commissioned.

"My happiness soon ended when it became apparent that those MiGs had some deadly faults. During the first training flights, several accidents took place one after the other, ending in the death of the pilots and loss of the airplanes. The flights were temporarily suspended, and an ad hoc commission of inquiry found that when such a jet turned around at a certain speed, the pilot was inadvertently ejected from the cabin and killed by impacting the tail of the airplane. Those unfortunate pilots were ejected together with their seat and parachute, which should normally have secured a safe landing if the ejection speed had been fast enough to clear the plane. The commission concluded that in every case, the ejection speed had been insufficient. It was just my bad luck to be assigned the job of finding what failed technically. With hindsight, I must say that there was no more dangerous or delicate task. Even flying one of those killer jets would have been less risky, I now believe.

"The accidents happened during one of those periodic political flare-ups that often raged throughout the communist bloc. I am sure you know what I am talking about. They used to call them 'sharpening of the class warfare,' and whatever went wrong was indiscriminately labeled as sabotage, the work of the proletariat's enemies directed by Anglo-American imperialists. Knowing that, I applied myself with utmost care to the thorough study of the existing documentation, having firmly decided to avoid the slightest finger-pointing. I didn't want to hurt anyone and never thought, even for a second, to cover myself, which, of course, was a big mistake. But that often happens when one is young and idealistic.

"During my research, I learned that a device called a booster was involved in the ejection of the pilot. The documentation mentioned it as an essential piece of equipment. Yet there was no picture, schematic, or description of that implement. Inquiring at the receiving office, I was told that they had never seen such a thing. We double-checked all the shipments up to that date and found no such item ever included in any of the waybills. Thinking that it was a translation mistake, I studied the original documentation, which was in Russian. The word they used was also booster, which even when written in Cyrillic is not Russian. Following an in-depth analysis of available data and more advanced literature research, it became clear to me that all the accidents had occurred for lack of boosters.

"For confirmation of what the elusive apparatus was supposed to do and in order to find its exact specifications, I spoke to my supervisor. This happened to be an elderly fighter pilot, a survivor from the war, a none-too-bright colonel of aviation, but a relatively good-hearted man and an ace. Officially, it was his job to help me get the necessary information. Talking to him, among other ideas regarding the booster, I advanced several hypotheses. One was the possibility of the device being bought by the Russians from a foreign manufacturer, perhaps from an English-speaking country. I timidly suggested that documentation in the original language would be a bonus because my knowledge of Russian was only basic, while my English was much better. I am not sure that he understood the technical aspects of the problem or their implications as at the end of our meeting, he lightheartedly advised me to put everything on paper. So I wrote a detailed report, gave it to him, and waited.

"About three weeks later, I was summoned to a special meeting with the Russian technical adviser. The event took place in a high-security building, built on an isolated spot of the factory's grounds, surrounded by barbed-wire fences, and guarded day and night by securitate units. All the technical documents, blueprints, and field manuals were kept in that building. Access to those materials labeled 'top secret' was restricted, and drawings or information sheets were released to us following complicated bureaucratic procedures and had to be returned the same day.

"When I entered the meeting room, the technical adviser, a Red Army general, was already there surrounded by a mixed group of Romanian and Russian superior officers, my supervisor included, all dressed up. To my surprise, I recognized several securitate uniforms in that gathering.

"There was seating for about hundred people in the room and a long desk at one end, covered with red cloth, for the presiding brass. A stern-looking portrait of Stalin hung high on the wall behind the table. Several slogans hung on the other walls, and I remember one: 'Freedom,' it said, 'is the understanding of necessity.' The officers sat at the table, and I was directed to sit alone in the area usually reserved for the audience. One of the securitate officers read from a piece of paper, asking me to confirm my name, professional status, and position in the factory staff. Then the Russian advisor spoke heatedly for a long time, and his interpreter followed with the translation. The interpreter's Romanian was quite poor, yet good enough to make me understand that I was accused of espionage in favor of the enemy and proliferation of calumnies about the Soviet Union. On top of that, even the deaths of the pilots, which had started the entire trouble, were attributed to me.

"Believing that there was just a misunderstanding, I asked for permission to answer, which was granted after a short consultation among the officers seated at the table. Using excerpts from my report, I tried to demonstrate that my approach was purely technical, not political, and that the accusations were therefore unfounded. The assignment was not my choice, I told them, and I acted on orders given by my supervisor, who was seated at the table among the presiding officers. Someone asked him if it was true. The man, unaware of danger, answered in the affirmative. Then the same officer ordered him to leave the table and sit beside me. Another officer stood up and announced that my supervisor shared with me all the previous accusations. In addition, both of us were now also accused of sabotage and conspiracy against the Romanian socialist state. The two securitate officers then came forward, viciously tore off my supervisor's epaulets with the insignia of his rank, and removed the decoration tabs from his uniform. We were immediately arrested and sent under armed escort to a transitional jail.

"I will spare you the details of my interrogations, which lasted several months . . ."

"You don't have to bother telling us how the communist justice system works. László and I know those transitional jails quite well," Váci said. "Their souvenir is still painful . . ."

"I could tell you a few things about the communist jail system in Afghanistan too, if you want," Abdur said.

"Guys, please. Let's listen to our engineer's story," Luca said.

"Patience, please. I will finish shortly," the engineer said. "After more than a year, I was taken to a secret military tribunal, thrown in a box with my ex-supervisor, several engineers from the factory's staff, and two workers. One of the workers was a veteran who, as a young apprentice, worked with our aviation pioneer Aurel Vlaicu on his first airplane built in 1905. The poor man was in his late seventies, pensioned off, and had been brought out of his retirement for his special skills. Neither the workers nor the engineers had ever in their lives heard the word *booster*. At the end of a mock trial that lasted a mere ten minutes, each of us was sentenced to fifteen years in prison. We had no right to appeal, and the sentence carried with it the loss of all our rights, including the annulment of our diplomas, professional titles, and work qualifications.

"Not long ago, I heard a rumor, which supposedly explained what happened with the booster. Apparently, the device was stolen by Russian intelligence from a foreign manufacturer during a top secret operation. To avoid complications, the use of those copies of the stolen original subsequently built in the Soviet Union was restricted to the domestic air force. When I made my report, the Russians were in the process of developing a new design exclusively for the MiGs they sold abroad. The new booster was slightly different from the stolen original, and it wasn't ready yet. Thus they sent the jets to Romania without boosters, intending perhaps to deliver them at a later date. The accidents and my report with its untimely suggestions had produced among those responsible for the deal embarrassment and fear of an intelligence leakage. Both the Soviets and their Romanian counterparts acknowledged this to be a potential political crisis with unpredictable international implications and agreed to hush the affair. We became the scapegoats, sacrificed in order to erase any tracks of it. For reasons unclear, the entire group, minus four who had died in the meantime, was liberated after only six years of detention by some obscure amnesty never made public. My ex-supervisor and the veteran worker were among the dead.

"Afterward, the only employment available to me as an ex-political detainee was in heavy industry as unqualified labor. The good thing, though, was that workers were allowed and encouraged to take evening classes at the technical university. I didn't waste any time and, as soon as it became possible, registered into the engineering program. For me, those courses were child's play. The learning pace was slower in the evening school system, and it took me another six and a half years to get my second diploma, thus becoming an engineer for the second time."

"I very much admire your perseverance," Abdur said. He spoke slowly as if searching for words. "Yours is truly a victory over that criminal system." He paused and looked straight into the engineer's eyes. "With all due respect, sir, I cannot see which is the dark side of the individual human soul." Abdur appeared to be as eager as ever and very much alive. He seemed to have forgotten his beloved Monica for the time being.

"You showed us collective evil at work, dark forces playing havoc with human destinies, yours included. I have had similar experiences in Afghanistan. My suffering was of a shorter duration, though . . . It is my fault, perhaps, but still I don't understand your point. Can you explain?"

"I must also confess my inability to see in your story that dark, invisible face of human individuality you alluded to," Stefan said. "Where was it?"

"You are both right, my friends," the engineer said. "The story I wanted to tell you is about other people, not me. That was just the introduction in order to show you how I came in contact with the poor chap who is the main character of my true story. Then I felt Váci deserved an explanation and let myself get carried away. As they say, 'The older one gets, the longer one's stories are.' Please bear with me once more and, in the meantime, help yourself to the wine. Don't be shy. We must finish this wine tonight because tomorrow, it will be stale and good for nothing."

"If that is so, can I have some wine?" Váci asked. "I have finished my brandy."

"By all means," the engineer, who was pouring wine into his glass, said.

He put the glass down and filled Váci's first. "You people cannot imagine how fortunate I feel at this very moment," he said, "sitting here among you, free as a bird, surrounded by good company, and sharing this marvelous wine with you." He looked dreamlike into the void for a minute or so as if trying to recapture in silence some lost images.

"In my years of detention, I never dreamed that such a life could exist or that a happy evening like this would ever be possible," he said. Then his face underwent a sudden change as if screwed by some inner pain.

Stefan would have liked to say something to show his sympathy, but his ingrained reserve didn't let him. There were many terrible stories being told in the camp, and one could never be sure if they were true or not. Each refugee had at least one personal horror tale. Unfortunately, one never knew, really, who the teller was: a genuine dissident, an undercover agent sent by one of the communist governments, or perhaps one of their henchmen fed up with his life as a torturer, bootlicker, or demagogue. The engineer was too new, and although Stefan thought much of him for his courageous escape, it would have been unwise to totally confide in anyone. As everyone knew, some words have very long legs and travel much further and faster than one can imagine.

"I couldn't have imagined such a good life either. I mean, the one we have here in the camp," Stefan said instead. "None of us, I believe, would have left our countries, our positions, our families—everything that can make a life full—without good reason. We have all suffered in one way or another—physically, psychologically, or both. What you said about being with us is true and touched my heart because I feel the same way."

"Ah," the engineer said, "you have no idea what this means to me . . . Even I find the life I went through sometimes hard to believe . . . Shortly after my trial, I was sent to Jilava. For our foreign colleagues here, I will try to translate. Jilava means "the dank," an appropriate name for an unhealthy place. It is a little suburban village in the outskirts of Bucharest, synonymous now with an infamous prison. Before the First World War, the army had built a circular line of forts to protect the capital in case of enemy invasion. It consisted of a complex of underground concrete blockhouses, bunkers, shelters and ammunition storehouses, and an extensive network of communication roads and galleries. Jilava became part of that defensive ring in spite of unfavorably high groundwater levels.

"During the war, when the need to defend the city became real, the entire concept was proven inefficient. This is why at the war's end, the fortifications had fallen into neglect. Some were simply left to decay, and some were destroyed, while others were converted for civilian use. A cluster of those facilities survived at Jilava for a long time, and after the Second World War, they were converted into one of the most dreadful penal facilities for political detainees.

"I spent almost four years at Jilava in a true house of death before they moved me to another place of bad repute, the Periprava Colony. We were twenty—sick, famished, and often trembling with cold 'politicals' locked up in a damp underground bunker half the size of this balcony. Our concrete box lay deep in the earth, under several feet of dirt. True to the bad name of the place, the water oozed through the walls partially overgrown with moss. During the spring thaw or after heavy rain, the floor became covered with floodwater, which sometimes reached up to our knees. There were neither windows nor ventilation in that building, except for a minute airshaft in the warden's office. That office was at one end of the bunker, where it was entered by the main door from a steep set of concrete stairs leading above the ground. The second door of the office opened into a corridor where two men could barely walk abreast. The corridor went along one side of the entire building, ending with a single Turkish-style open toilet. During the floods, the toilet would back up, the foul smell of rotten sewage infesting the already noxious atmosphere.

"Concrete walls divided the bunker into five little cells. The heavy metal doors of the cells, provided with peepholes, were usually kept double locked and, when open, gave access to the corridor. In every cell, there were four narrow bunk beds, paired off one on top of the other on each side of the door. The bunks were separated by a space wide enough for a man to stand. The use of the toilet was limited to a few minutes daily but wasn't necessarily granted on a routine basis. For the rest of the time, there was a bucket in each cell to provide for the physiological needs of the detainees. The buckets were emptied some days, in the morning.

"It is impossible to describe the stench, the lack of oxygen, and the infection polluting the atmosphere. We never had a walk, and I saw daylight only three or four times during my incarceration.

Once was when the man in this story died. Everybody knew him as Comrade Amăriuței.

"Comrade Amăriuței arrived one spring after my ex-supervisor, the aviation colonel, who coughed so badly that he no longer had lungs left, had been transferred to a hospital. At least, this was the warden's version. In reality, he was moved to the far end of the prison's grounds in a dilapidated brick building, an old cavalry stable, half morgue and half infirmary, where the administration isolated the dying in their last days. No medication was available, and the diet consisted mainly of a thin soup made with corn flour, which the patients—left to their own devices—had neither the energy nor the appetite to eat.

"His departure left an empty bunk in the cell, and we were anxious to see our future cell mate. He appeared preceded by a terrible commotion that disturbed the roughly enforced silence. Hysterical shouts, loud cries of pain, dirty cursing, and other awful noises could be heard through the doors as they reverberated back and forth across the concrete box. Those were the sure signs that the wardens were beating a detainee. Then suddenly, the hubbub broke out into the corridor and came to a stop in front of our cell. The door was unlocked and flung open, and we saw four or five wardens, almost one on top of the other, dragging a man's body covered in blood. With what seemed to be a great common effort, they managed to push the man into the door's opening, where he still resisted, with stretched legs propped against the frame. It was only when one of the wardens jumped on his belly while another hit him with a steel bar on the shins that he couldn't hold his position anymore and let go. The victim was finally forced inside, where he slumped to the floor in between the bunks.

"The warden on duty locked us in, and we could hear him talking with the other jailers as they walked toward the office. The man on the floor slowly regained consciousness, and when we rushed to help him, he precariously stood up, leaning on one of the bunks. His tumefied face was unrecognizable, covered in bloody cuts and open wounds, some still bleeding, the blood running down on the tattered, dirty shirt he was wearing. He pushed us aside and dragged

252

himself to the door where, with what appeared to be a superhuman effort, he began weakly pounding the metal cover.

"We tried to dissuade him as such behavior always brought a savage repression, but he stubbornly hung by the door handle and kicked whoever came close to him quite viciously. In the end, we had to give up and leave him alone. He gathered strength from God knows what resources hidden in that beaten body of his, and what initially was only gabble soon became a loud cry. His pounding on the door was shortly accompanied by very articulated shouts.

"'I want to report to the commanding officer! I want to be taken out to report to the commanding officer! I want to get out immediately!' he shouted in a high pitch. 'Open the door! Open the door immediately! I am Comrade Amăriuței, and I ask you to open immediately!' He continued to pound the door and to shout louder and louder.

"Knowing the warden on duty only too well, we were terrified by the consequences his daring could bring upon us and tried to quiet him. Every one of us joined in and demanded silence for the common good. 'Sh-sh! Shhh! Hush up! Stay quiet, please!' we whispered.

"'Don't hush me up, bandits,' he said and continued to shout and pummel the door.

"Then the warden came back, and the peephole opened with a jerk. He looked inside with bloodshot, angry eyes. 'If you don't behave, next time, when we take you out, we will kill you. Troublemaker bandits like you don't live long here,' he barked.

"'Criminals, murderers, vile servants of the bourgeoisie,' the man shouted back with renewed energy after a moment of suspense. 'I will soon show you who am I. I will make you fascists lick my boots. I am a communist. I am Comrade Amăriuței, not a bandit. Do you hear me?'

"'If you don't shut him up, you will all share in his punishment. Do you understand this, bandits?' the warden barked again, this time talking to the entire cell. 'Shut him up, or else. I will give you only three minutes. You know what follows if you disregard my orders,' he said and closed the peephole with a bang.

"We were three undernourished and sick shadows of men, while the newcomer was young and athletic. We couldn't fight him, so we tried to peacefully talk him out of his suicidal rebellion but without any success. When we attempted to stop him, he fiercely punched and kicked us—cursing and swearing—every time, afterward, returning to bang at the door.

"We didn't hear the wardens coming and knew they were there only when the door pushed by three of them opened violently, catching the newcomer in between the tiered bunks and the wall. They hit him with the door repeatedly, banging his head on the wall, while the warden on duty and another one began beating us. 'Under the beds, bandits. Under the beds,' they ordered and forced us to crawl under the bunks, kicking us with their boots and hitting randomly with their rubber cudgels.

"When the newcomer was finally silenced, they closed the door, letting him fall on the floor. There was very little room for all of them, and they had to take turns beating him, sometimes stepping on his legs, kicking him in the face, or smashing his fingers under their boots. In the end, they got tired. And after a last series of blows with their cudgels, the wardens retired, leaving him as if dead in a puddle of blood. 'This is just a mild warning for you, bandits,' the warden on duty barked before locking the door.

"For almost a month, we nurtured the young man back to life and succeeded through indescribable efforts. His recovery in our circumstances was a miracle. And in particular, it was perhaps the direct result of the selfless and dedicated care provided by our middle-aged cellmate, Tudor. As a modest ex-military orderly, Tudor, a peasant by birth, had little medical knowledge, the lack of which he successfully supplemented with infinite goodness of heart. His own mother couldn't have given to Comrade Amăriuţei more loving attention than he did.

"After our colleague became conscious again, he behaved quite normally until he regained some of his physical strength. Then it took a lot of persuasion to convince him to give up his dangerous behavior. Perhaps he accepted this only as a truce and due to his extreme weakness. Although in his own way he was thankful for our help, he showered us all day long with invectives and made it clear that we were part of two different—-indeed antagonistic—worlds.

"'You are enemies of the people and the dirty tools of Anglo-American imperialism. Our Party has every right to keep you here. You should have been executed long ago,' he would say even before he was able to walk again. 'I am Comrade Amăriuţei, a university professor, a high-ranking member of our glorious Party. I do not want to have anything to do with the social scum that you are.' And he continued to rant in this vein for hours, even if none of us was listening.

"He would relent only when we had to dress his wounds or feed him. It was during those relatively quiet breaks that we slowly got a glimpse of what his real personality was. He was gross and uncultured—almost ignorant—except for a thin smattering of Marxist-Leninist clichés he had picked up during his limited schooling. In the rest, he possessed a few confused snippets of both national and world history and a vague familiarity with the new realist-socialist literature. He always interspersed his conversation with demagogic slogans, the use of which appeared to be a reflex acquired through brainwashing.

"Comrade Amăriuţei spent a little over a year with us. During that time, we managed to rid him of some of his idiosyncrasies, indeed reaching a point when he would even laugh at some earlier pretensions of his such as being addressed with the formal appellation for instance. In the beginning, however, we had to be careful with him, because he took the smallest disagreement as an insult and reacted with unrestrained violence. He was young and strong when he arrived, his brutish force not yet diminished by the extermination regimen we went through. Any physical encounter with him could have had fatal consequences for every one of us. Unfortunately, some ideas were so deeply ingrained in his mind that nothing could have changed them, no matter how hard we tried or how dangerous their expression had proven to him. Among several, that was the case with his manic insistence upon talking to the commander of the prison and the firm conviction that his presence among us was a mistake.

"The story of his life was quite intriguing. He had neither a known father nor relatives. And Măriuța, his mother, had died when he was only a toddler. During childhood, he lived from whatever charitable folks had given him. There were several childless families in his village who would have liked to take care of the boy, perhaps even adopt him, if he had not developed quite early on an incurable restlessness. As if pushed by a demon, he was unable to stay in a place more than a couple of months, no matter how well they had treated him, moving from one household to another as his fancy took him. He also couldn't get used to the type of discipline that school meant and dropped out of the second primary grade. He wasn't what one would call a quick-witted boy yet was always willing to help and preferred to spend his days doing errands or menial jobs for whoever needed a hand. The villagers loved him for that, and he always had a place to sleep or eat and never lacked appropriate clothes as required by the seasons. When the boy was sixteen, he had fallen in with one of the senior shepherds and convinced the man that he wanted to learn the trade. He was already an athletically built lad, stronger than any teen of his age, exuding energy and eagerness. And from early spring, the shepherd took him into the high mountains to work with the flocks. That summer, he grazed the sheep on the alpine pastures or apprenticed at the shepherds' camp, struggling to learn how to prepare all sorts of dairy products, and only rarely came down to the village. He worked hard, and the shepherds liked him despite his lack of acumen.

"While the future Comrade Amăriuței was working with the sheep, the communists launched their campaign for the collectivization of agriculture. Teams of propagandists, accompanied by securitate workers, were sent to every village in order to help the local authorities set up collective farms following the Soviet model, the kolkhoz. Simultaneously, a small group of anticommunist partisans started operating in the mountains surrounding his village.

"Even from the start, the villagers had met that official land-grabbing scheme with hostility. As long as everyone could remember, their ancestors had been free landowners. And during past centuries, they had always successfully fought the numerous attempts to deprive them of their lands. To the negative reaction of the farmers, the Party responded with terror and repressive measures. The most outspoken villagers were arrested and sent to jail. Other opponents were savagely beaten or killed, while a minority took to the mountains to join the partisans in the hope that the Americans would soon come to bring freedom to their country.

"The partisans were poorly equipped and lived in primitive high-altitude camps. They continuously moved their quarters to avoid detection and relied on relatives and friends from neighboring villages for food and other necessary supplies. Although not many people knew where the partisans were positioned, they couldn't make any movement without the shepherds being aware. After all, the shepherds were their main food providers. The young Amăriuţei knew better than anyone where the partisans had their bases because, being the most junior among the shepherds, he was most often sent to them with supplies.

"In spite of their inadequate logistics, the partisans were intrepid and efficient. Familiar with the local topography, they soon managed to become a nuisance to the authorities. Occasionally, they made forays into the foothills to ambush and plunder the trucks that supplied the government-owned village stores and raided the offices of the newly set up collective farms, getting away with small amounts of money. So far, they had never killed anyone. And with the stolen money, they had helped the poor old people, widows and orphans. Their successes, no matter how limited, meant bad public relations for the political establishment. And the government, in order to stop the unrest from spreading, decided to uproot them. Therefore several securitate units, to the strength of a company each, moved into the area and sealed it off from the rest of the country. From that moment on, armed soldiers with specially trained Alsatian dogs permanently patrolled all the access roads. Some patrols disguised as tourists even ventured high into the alpine pastures, sleeping a night or two with the shepherds. Yet for quite a long time, they could not find any trace of the partisans.

"A small securitate special intelligence and investigations unit sent from Bucharest set up headquarters in the boy's village. There were about five men in the unit led by a Russian officer, an attractive blonde woman of about forty. And they were snooping around day and night, always watching the people. Farmers suspected of potential connections with the partisans and all persons entering the area were brought to the unit's office to be interrogated. That also happened to Amăriuței when one late summer evening, he came down from his mountainous temporary quarters to do some errands for the shepherds.

"It was routine procedure for the Russian officer to be present at all the interrogations, including the boy's. After more than two hours, nothing of value was extracted from him. And the man carrying out the questioning, bored by the youth's lack of wits, concluded the interview in frustration. Then something fateful happened with the woman officer. From what Amăriuței told me, it is hard to know if it was her flair or lust or perhaps both. My cell mate, you see, had never been exceedingly perceptive and, even when I met him, seemed to be confused about many things past and present. Certainly, something must have clicked in that woman's mind, for she showed a sudden peculiar interest in him. Instead of letting him go, she took the boy to the dilapidated village cafeteria. There, the officer treated him to a few beers, talking to him as she would with a mature man, never mentioning the partisans. They chatted as equals for a couple of hours, only about themselves. And she cajoled him into telling her the story of his life, continuously praising and encouraging him. The woman's Romanian was faulty, but her Russian accent gave her a certain childish charm that made one forget about the age difference. She had also been born to a family of peasants in a village like his and knew everything about life in such backward places, she told him. And afterward, they got along together marvelously well. Under her sympathetic gaze, he felt important and unusually proud of himself. When the cafeteria closed, the officer asked the boy to accompany her. It was already dark, and they walked arm in arm to the house she was billeted in. There, she invited him in for a last glass of vodka.

"They drank more than a glass. And then, without too much ado, he ended up in her bed. The Russian officer wasn't his first woman.

But the old, repugnant gypsy he had made it with several times before was no match for her. She was special, hot and soft, motherly and sexy, and gave him pleasures he hadn't experienced yet. He believed that was genuine love and felt himself an adult—somebody who had awakened such desire in a woman of her status must be a real man, he thought.

"In the morning, at breakfast—tired, proud, and happy—the boy wanted to look macho and boasted, without her asking, about his business with the partisans and not only about that. As a habitué of good people's houses, where he was always welcomed and benefited from their largess and charity, he knew their most intimate secrets. He told the woman officer everything, where those people kept illegal rifles and ammunition, where they had hidden produce from the government collectors, and who had hoarded gold coins and where they were to be found. Those coins were set in elaborate necklaces, heirlooms passed along for centuries, some containing up to hundred pieces, which girls and women wore at dances on big holidays or special occasions. The necklaces were part of their traditional folk costumes, their families' pride and treasure. And when the government declared the possession of gold coins against the law, nobody even dreamed of handing over what they kept mostly for ornamental and sentimental value. After all, the necklaces weren't stolen property, and generation after generation had toiled hard to put together and perfect those beautiful works of folk art.

"As a consequence of the boy's chatter, many of his past benefactors, including the shepherds, were presently imprisoned and the partisans destroyed. It was an easy victory and a great success for the Russian officer's special unit as the securitate forces led on secret trails by the young Amăriuţei, now for the first time called Comrade Amăriuţei, stealthily encircled the guerillas' dugouts. There were relatively few partisans, and all but one was killed in the unequal skirmish that followed. The last survivor, captured and tortured, was shot soon afterward in the nearby town's main square. His bloodied body, dressed in dirty rags and riddled with bullets, was left for several days where it had fallen for the entire world to see how the enemies of the proletariat are treated in the workers' paradise.

259

"Once, when he was in good mood, I asked my cell mate if he had ever felt any remorse for having brought such calamity on so many good people, especially on those who had been his benefactors. He had learned from his woman friend that they were bloodsucking exploiters and his class enemies, he told me. Everything they possessed was stolen from people like him, and he appeared to be genuinely convinced that such elements had no room in the new society. Any means to exterminate them, no matter how cruel, were totally justified, he said. My timid attempts to make him at least acknowledge the help he had gotten from those people made him utterly mad. He cursed and started calling me names, threatening to retaliate after his recovery for what he felt was a personal insult.

"Perhaps the village was no longer safe for the boy, or maybe it was just the woman officer's interest in him. But when the special unit returned to Bucharest, they took Comrade Amăriuței with them. With the woman's warm recommendation, he got a job at one of the Communist Party's centers and became a factotum, arranging chairs in the meeting rooms, hanging slogans on the walls, and herding people into the meetings. That was during the day. During the night, he continued his torrid affair with the Russian woman when she wasn't busy fighting the so-called enemies of the Romanian people.

"In spite of his limitations, Comrade Amăriuței proved to be a valuable acquisition for his employers. He had a stentorian voice, a good memory for slogans, and an innate talent for using them at the most appropriate times. He was promoted shortly and became a sort of prompter. When the speaker paused during a meeting, he shouted the necessary slogans and started clapping, and the docile audience followed. There were meetings everyday, and he was extremely useful and enthusiastic. As even the high-ranking communists were watched by the securitate, he did some moonlighting for them, directed by the Russian woman. He looked so naive, almost stupid and innocuous, that nobody really paid too much attention to him. And he could successfully eavesdrop at his leisure. Due to his excellent job record and with a good word from his girlfriend, after only six months, he was enrolled in one of the workers' special schools.

"No formal education was necessary in order to be accepted into such a school. The only requirements were the express recommendation of the Party and the candidate's ability to more or less satisfactorily read and write. Students graduated after two years, and then could enter any university as their diplomas were officially recognized to be equal with those that senior high school graduates got after twelve years of formal schooling.

"As soon as he graduated from the workers' special school, Amăriuţei had to satisfy his compulsory military duties and was conscripted into the army. He didn't spend more than three weeks in training though, because following some string pulling at high levels, he was transferred to a securitate officers' school somewhere in Transylvania. He didn't want to tell us what kind of school it was, but we figured out that it was probably a training camp for sleuths and spies. While there, he became a member of the Communist Party. He didn't stay long in the officers' school because during one of the periodical medical checkups, our cell mate was diagnosed with a congenital heart condition and discharged from the military. When he first told us, it was difficult to accept that he had a genuine health problem except perhaps a mental one. For physically, the young man looked more like an athlete than a sick person. We believed that exemption to be another of the Russian woman's maneuvers in order to bring him close to her.

"The fact is that at about nineteen years of age, Amăriuţei returned to Bucharest and resumed his semimarital life with the Russian woman. To begin with, he hung about for a few months, doing small surveillance jobs for the securitate in the student milieu before being enrolled in the Party's political university. Although not much of a student, he had an immense capacity to learn insipid political texts by heart, and nobody asked for more. During his university years, he didn't neglect his collaboration with the many friends he had previously made among the securitate officers and also continued his profitable love affair. The woman provided a comfortable home for him, satisfied his sexual appetite, and always watched protectively over him. When he graduated at the age of twenty-three, Comrade Amăriuţei was immediately appointed lecturer at the Polytechnic Institute of Bucharest and at the age of twenty-six became a full university professor of Marxism-Leninism. The entire world seemed to lie at his feet.

"In the year Comrade Amăriuţei was appointed a university professor, the Russians decided to withdraw their occupation forces from Romania, giving the Western world the false impression that the country was from now on its own. In reality, the political system and the ruling methods remained the same. If anything changed at all, it was that the dictatorship became tougher. To him, however, that withdrawal meant a true change, for his sweetheart was ordered to report back to her headquarters in Leningrad.

"For the first time in his life, Amăriuţei had to look after himself, get organized, and start living independently. He had no experience in such matters and initially felt at a loss for practical ideas. Two problems were especially nagging him: how to find a home and how to start a relationship with another woman.

"His search for a proper accommodation was luckily solved almost without effort. He was already part of the nomenklatura, the list of the influential communist élite, and a special housing office speedily found and allotted him two rooms with access to the kitchen and bathroom in what initially was someone's private house. Since most of the country's real estate had been nationalized, the building now belonged to the government. Yet the previous owners, a retired general and his wife, still lived on the premises as tenants.

"The two-story villa to which Amăriuţei moved his scanty belongings was inherited by the general from his parents. The property had been initially part of a patrician housing development known as the Cartierul Jianu, close to lakes and parks, currently favored by the members of the communist leadership for its luxurious looks and quiet setting. The house was generously built before the Second World War, in the best period of Romania's history, after the design of a well-known architect. It was by no means a big building, yet had everything to make a mid-sized family comfortable. This was, however, no longer the case. At the end of the war, a huge migration from the countryside to the cities, combined with the complete collapse of the private home building industry in the wake of nationalization, had triggered an endemic housing shortage. As a consequence, a different family now lived in each of the three upstairs bedrooms. The general and his wife lodged in the master bedroom and in addition had the sole use of the dining room and the library. A widowed cousin of the general and her son of twelve rented the second bedroom. In the third bedroom camped the general's mother-in-law. A couple of nonfigurative painters, friends of the general, with their two boys of eighteen and twenty, students at the university, occupied two small penthouse rooms used in the past by servants. The house had no true ground floor but a mezzanine, which contained the kitchen, a vast pantry, the dining room, a guest's restroom, the living room, and the general's library. The general's wife's brother, a structural engineer in his mid-thirties who spent most of his time out in the country supervising industrial building sites nominally lived in the living room. Everyone had access to the kitchen and shared the big bathroom upstairs, except the family of painters who had sole use of the service restroom with a sink and a shower. It was awfully crowded, yet the ex-owners were happy to still be among relatives and friends in what was once their home, while most of their neighbors had been evacuated, their houses being entirely taken over by high-ranking communists.

"In order to make room for Comrade Amăriuţei, the structural engineer was ordered by the Rentals' State Administration to move in with his mother and share the latter's bedroom, and the general's library went to the wine cellar. The Red Army's soldiers had ransacked the cellar of its noble wines in 1944 during what the official history called the friendly liberation of Bucharest, and since then, it had remained empty. The office that found the home for him cleaned, painted, and furnished the rooms appropriately so the comrade professor could start living comfortably and creating philosophical chefs d'oeuvre as soon as he moved in.

"If the finding of a new home went so incredibly smoothly, considering the quagmire in which the Romanian population's housing was at the time, finding a replacement for his lover was another story. First, Amăriuţei had to deal with her dramatic departure. The Russian woman officer didn't take the separation easily. She was about fifty, a critical age, and perhaps really loved her young stud. Whatever the reason, the perspective of losing him at that point in life had a devastating effect on her morale. For the last two or three weeks prior to her trip to Mother Russia, they couldn't even have good sex because she was continuously crying until she got sick from so much sadness. Crying also made her look old and ugly, and that irritated him. Then just a day or so before leaving, she appeared to have received some good news, giving her great hopes of a possible return. The change in mood reflected in her sexual appetite, and they made it as if there was no tomorrow until she got sick from an excess of happiness. Comrade Amăriuței was totally exhausted when he took her to the airport, and the prolonged good-bye jarred on his nerves. He was fed up with her and could barely wait to see his old sweetheart off. Oblivious to his lack of sensitivity, the Russian woman pledged to be back soon.

"His exasperation with the Russian notwithstanding, soon after her departure, Amăriuței got fidgety, feeling lonely and unsatisfied with his bachelor life. For some reason, he didn't receive any letters from his ex-sweetheart except for the first and only message she sent on a postcard upon her arrival in Leningrad. That was filled with love and promises. At the end of the second month of being alone and without news as well as for want of womanly warmth, he began hungrily looking around.

"His first conquest was a charwoman working at the Party's university. Late one evening, Comrade Amăriuței was ready to go home when she came in to clean his office, and they started talking. Although the woman was neither young nor beautiful, she appeared to lend an understanding ear to his needs and, more than anything, had particularly easy and engaging manners. One thing led to another, and they got hot and carried away and made it right there. The encounter was extremely uncomfortable because of the sparse, inappropriate office furniture and the stress of potentially being caught but, in the long run, could have nevertheless become a promising relationship. He had to give that woman up, though, when a friend from the securitate advised him to be more careful.

She was one of their agents, and her duty was to report on him. From that moment on, he spent his evenings alone at home.

"Comrade Amăriuţei didn't have anything to do at home. He wasn't much of a reader, writing was a dreaded chore, and he had no hobbies. After reading *Scînteia, The Spark*, the Party's daily newspaper, an obligatory routine for someone in his position, he tried to kill his evenings drinking vodka and smoking a Russian brand of cigarettes called Kazbek, something he had learned to like from the Russian lover and was skilled at. But in her absence, he discovered, most of the fun in it was lacking. After a while, at the end of his tether and unaware of the existing relationship among them, he tried to make friends with the other residents. All of them, except the general's wife, were overly polite and distant. And from their behavior, he couldn't ever have understood how much he scared them or guessed the intensity with which they hated him.

"One of my other cellmates, an older gentleman I will call Jean, happened to be a reputed law university professor who had also been a senator before King Carol II suspended the constitution, dissolved the parliament, and established his personal dictatorship. That relatively limited meddling with prewar Romanian politics was the reason why he had the misfortune of sharing his last days with me in our pestilential cell at Jilava. His and the general's parents had been lifelong friends, and the boys frequented the same schools until they chose different careers, one in the military and the other in academia. After we met Amăriuţei, Jean told me privately a lot about his childhood friend and his family. Those intimate details gave me a much broader understanding of the mess in which our new cell mate got involved.

"The ex-owner of the house into which Amăriuţei moved, the general, was tall and lean, a good-looking man of soldierly bearing, always impeccably attired. In spite of his age and graying hair—the man was already past his sixties—he impressed everyone with his elegant appearance and refined courtesy. That courtesy always had the effect of a heavy artillery bombardment on Comrade Amăriuţei, leaving him bewildered, speechless, and wounded. It shouldn't have to be that way because, as was common knowledge, the general himself had unassuming beginnings. Descended from an old but modest family of Greek Orthodox village priests, his grandfather, a cavalry captain, was the first to embrace a military career and died a hero's death in 1877 during the War of Independence fought against the Turks. His orphaned and poor son, the general's father, became by his own merits a military cartographer and a professor at the Superior School of War, the predecessor of the current military academy. Realizing early on that opportunities for promotion past his rank of major would be lacking in peacetime, at the end of the First World War, he took a rather guarded interest in politics. Making good friends among decision makers, he arranged to be appointed military attaché abroad and, until his retirement, with the rank of colonel enjoyed the pleasant and exciting life of a diplomat in posh places such as Rome, London, and Paris. Of limited ambition, he died a satisfied man during the Second World War.

"The grandson of the Independence's hero, the general, who was the third generation in that line of military men, began his career on the eve of the First World War. Thanks to his excellent academic record, as soon as he had graduated from one of the military high schools, he was sent to the Royal Military College at Sandhurst in England to be trained as an army officer. He returned to Romania a fresh lieutenant in 1917, just in time to take part in all the major battles that secured our country's victory against the central powers. Courageous and skilled, he managed to be wounded once, winning several medals for bravery, and at the end of the war found himself a captain.

"In between the two World Wars, the young captain returned to school, completed the required years of study at the Superior School of War, and became a staff officer. During those peaceful years, he enjoyed being a bachelor and never got married. He spoke both English and French fluently, was an avid reader, a good dancer, and a charming conversationalist who preferred the pleasures of the intellect to those of matrimony and the excitement of illicit liaisons to the quiet of a dull family life. When Romania entered the Second World War against the Soviet Union on the side of Germany, he was a lieutenant colonel in the general staff of the army. Sent to the front line, he soon earned the reputation of being an excellent strategist and was promoted, subsequently rising to the rank of a general.

"Since the Romanian army had liberated the provinces occupied by the Soviets two years before, many Romanians, including the newly ranked general, thought that it was a big mistake to continue fighting deeper into Russian territory. The general was not a dilettante and fully understood that in the given circumstances, it was impossible to just stop the hostilities. While the vast majority of his countrymen were content only to grumble, the general, risking his situation, wrote a confidential letter to the dictator, Marshal Antonescu, whom he admired, asking him to somehow negotiate Romania's withdrawal from the war. His well-documented letter, a lucid analysis of the local and worldwide situation, concluded by enumerating all the military and political reasons why Germany would eventually lose the war. Contrary to all expectations, the dictator never acknowledged receiving it, the only apparent measure, if it was one, being the general's transfer to the army headquarters in Bucharest. Later, after the general's predictions had been fulfilled and the country became a Soviet satellite, the marshal was shot as a war criminal after a mock trial. In the bloodshed that followed, his unacknowledged letter saved the general's life. He was one of the very few high-ranking army officers who got an honorable discharge and an early retirement—many others among his colleagues were sooner or later exterminated. Because of that letter, the new leaders liked to see the general as one of theirs, a friend of the Soviet Union and a sympathizer of communism, while in fact he was just patriotic and concerned with the future of his country.

"The general's retirement coincided with a period of uncertainty and radical change in Romania. Those were times when people went to bed unsure where they would wake up the following morning or went to work in the morning not knowing when they would see their families again. The depressing atmosphere and the boredom pushed the general to make a step he would have never considered before. He got married. His choice fell on the daughter of a recently deceased colleague at the Superior School of War. The girl's mother, from a family of lesser nobility with vast land properties, had been previously married to a prince with whom she had two daughters. When the prince died rather young, she remarried a handsome officer, the general's friend, and together had two more children, a son, the structural engineer, and a girl called Roxana.

"The prince's daughters, who at the death of their father inherited the title, had prudently moved all their assets to Switzerland before the Second World War and were currently living in Geneva. Their unlucky mother and stepsiblings who stayed in Romania were condemned to live more or less in poverty like everyone else except the leaders as happens in a communist regime. The mother, after all her lands and properties had been nationalized, had managed to get a menial job as a checker at the gate of a textile factory. Advantaged by his profession, the structural engineer had a well-paid job, being what the bootlicking press called one of the builders of socialism. Roxana, unlike them, although well-groomed for social life at a private high school for rich girls previously run by Catholic nuns, could neither get into university nor find a job because of her unbecoming pedigree. She was unemployed and in a sulk when fate presented itself in the appearance of her family's friend, the general, with a marriage proposal. Everything afterward moved quickly. And at the end of a discreet religious ceremony in one of the old, beautifully painted churches in Bucharest, the Stavropoleus, Roxana and the general were man and wife. The general, a ladies' man and a habitué of illicit boudoirs, should have known better, for his bride was thirty-four years his junior.

"If Comrade Amăriuței's coresidents were uncommunicative, the general's wife was especially cold, like an iceberg. In spite of her married years, she was—at twenty-eight—a mature beauty who walked with an air of exquisite elegance, ignoring everyone and everything, always trailing behind a cloud of French perfume her princely half-sisters sent her from Geneva. The woman excited him as much as her lofty disdain repelled him. Hurt in his manly pride, Amăriuței decided to capture her attention and get even somehow. In that respect, he had a lot on his side except for social skills and, when tried to speak to Roxana, she looked through him like nobody was there.

"This unneighborly atmosphere had already lasted for some time when, late one evening, less than six months before his incarceration at Jilava, Roxana knocked at Comrade Amăriuţei's door. As usual, at that hour, he was smoking Russian mahorka, with the bottle of Moskovskaya vodka and a half-empty glass in front of him. The room stank abominably of alcohol and coarse tobacco smoke. He was already mildly stoned and welcomed the woman with hazy eyes, in the beginning incapable of even recognizing her. Roxana, as if not noticing his drunkenness and the sordid environment, was all smiles. And although polite, her manners were friendly, almost casually familiar. She had run out of matches and asked him if he could lend her some. Without any invitation, the general's wife sat on an empty chair, waiting with a cigarette ready while he fumbled with the matches, finally managing to light one after breaking several others.

"Her husband was playing bridge with friends, she told Amăriuţei. An awfully boring game, she added when he asked for details. Then Roxana inspected the bottle, and he felt obliged to offer her a drink. Afterward, he couldn't remember what they talked about during that first evening. But when she left, he realized with a shock that it was past midnight.

"Three or four evenings later, she again came to visit, bringing with her a steaming teapot and two delicate cups of fine china on a richly ornate silver tray. The general's wife carried the heavy tray with inimitable grace and poured the fragrant liquid, serving him with exquisite elegance. She couldn't stand those gaming parties of her husband's, Roxana told the bewildered comrade. He was too simpleminded and already smitten with that woman to imagine a reason other than himself for her presence in his room. Awkward and uncouth to the point of rudeness, he struggled to sustain a spirited conversation and failed as the gift of polished conversation wasn't his forte. It soon became obvious they didn't have anything in common or to talk about, but still, she didn't leave until well after midnight.

When she was leaving and he ventured to kiss her, Roxana put her perfumed hand on his mouth instead. 'Later, maybe next time,' she murmured in guise of good-bye. The uncouth comrade couldn't sleep that night, unsettled by her promise."

The engineer stopped. He looked around, conspicuously surprised as if seeing his audience for the first time since the beginning of the story. They were all silent, waiting for him to continue, cigarettes glowing in the dark like tired fireflies. At that very moment, the breeze came as if by magic. First, it was a light puff of hot air, no more than one gets when an oven door is open in an overheated kitchen. The salty moist smell of the sea and the rotten stench of fish and seaweed followed it immediately. Then another light puff, this time a little cooler, swept the buildings, gently shaking the leaves of the mulberry trees. The engineer lit a cigarette and took a sip from his glass.

"I never was a pious man," he said, "yet in prison, my views on God, life, and humanity changed a lot. A man I met during my detention, a Jesuit priest who had already been in jail for seven years just because of his beliefs, opened my eyes. He told me once that in so many years spent in various detention facilities, he had heard countless confessions. In his opinion, all those people had gravely sinned in one way or another, which justified their sufferings. My cell mate Amăriuței had made several wrong moral choices in his rather short life and through his actions had inflicted a lot of hardship upon many people, including his own benefactors. What is more, he had no regrets. He was also indirectly responsible for the killing of people who hadn't done any harm to him. From the moment he tried to kiss Roxana, Comrade Amăriuței, without knowing it, was fast heading toward his own demise because divine justice always reestablishes the balance in a way or another."

"But sir, what about you?" Abdur asked, to everyone's surprise.
"What about me?"
"What was your sin?" Abdur asked again.
"Abdur is right," Váci cried. "From what you told us, you were innocent and still got so many years in prison. How does this agree with your priest?"

"Oh," the engineer said, "human and divine justice are two different things. Humans are sometimes just blind tools in the hands of the Almighty. A punishment that in the eyes of humans would appear unjust could be payment for something we, or maybe our parents, committed at an earlier time, which might have been a grave crime in the eyes of God."

"Do you know, then, what your crime was?" Stefan asked. "You were quite young when the whole thing happened to you. What could have been bad enough to justify such a harsh punishment from God, who is supposed to be a loving supreme being?"

"I cannot be sure . . . It is hard to say . . . How can I know the way divine justice works? Suffering can be a learning experience, a means to make us better. The priest I mentioned thought he knew why he was punished and said that our duty was to struggle to be perfect as our God is, and some of us needed to be corrected because otherwise, we wouldn't amend our actions. Maybe I am a slow learner. God only knows."

"What happened with you guys? You cannot find another time for theological discussions?" Luca complained with slight irritation in his voice. "I would like to hear the end of this gentleman's story."

"Luca is right," Lia said, "I would like to hear the end of the story too."

"It was my mistake. I am sorry for the interruption, sir. Please continue," Abdur said.

"It is all right," the engineer said. "Perhaps it was my fault too. Who am I to judge other people's sins? After all, it wasn't only my cell mate's or Roxana's mistake. One might say that it was the general's fault as well. Real life is more complicated than one might think. After eight years of apparently undisturbed and happy marriage, he blindly trusted his wife. And then there were those card games he played with his friends. He had been introduced to bridge in his youth, at Sandhurst. He liked it and quickly became an expert player and never since said no when the opportunity to play a game presented itself, especially in the troubled postwar years when quality entertainment was lacking.

"As some present here will remember, in the first decade of the new rule, all foreign movies and theatrical plays were completely banned except for the insipid Soviet productions glorifying the heroics of some obscure Russian braves or depicting boring exemplary lives of model workers in a proletarian utopia. Russian so-called works of art composed in the socialist realist style also swamped the repertoires of opera and symphonic orchestras. Even the works of our best Romanian authors were under reconsideration and therefore not available to the public. There were no places to dance, except the few off-limits nightclubs and bars open only to foreigners with passports or at some chosen factories where the occasional Saturday 'comradely reunions' were organized under Party supervision. That is why people of all ages preferred to get together privately and have fun playing poker, bridge, or rummy amid effervescent gossip.

"It was during such card games that people exchanged forbidden world news and the latest political rumor. What in normal times would have been an innocent pastime had become in the new proletarian era a risky business. Everyone was starved for news in Romania as the press was tightly controlled and every piece of information was edited until it fitted the Party line. The foreign broadcast stations were jammed, and no Western newspapers or magazines could be found at newsstands. They were available, of course, to a minority, a handful of people from the securitate or other special services. And from there, sometimes, the news leaked to the population at large. In a few remote areas of the country, the jamming stations were less efficient. And a few privileged locals could easily tune into the BBC, the Voice of America, or other uncensored news sources, afterward supplying their less advantaged countrymen by word of mouth. Once in a while, the authorities themselves would spread classified information as rumors when they thought it in their interest. Unfortunately, one never knew which was legitimate and which wasn't, and news mongering had led more than once to loss of freedom or worse. That was, however, part of the dangerous life we all shared.

"My cell mate, Jean, had frequented such parties before his arrest. And according to him, the evening always ended with idle speculation about when the Americans would come or about what the guests and their hosts would do when that happy event took place. The *convive* smoked and drank their last coffees before going home, assigning one another positions in postcommunist governments, discussing reforms and laws, or inventing power schemes without any real bases. It was a lot of wishful thinking as they waited for the Americans to come and reinstate them in their lost lands, houses, and positions. If it was winter, the Americans would come in the spring. If it was spring, they would come in the summer and so on. The Americans never came, but those people continued to dream year after year, if they managed to avoid arrest. It was like an incurable disease, a sort of national sociopolitical epidemic. One could have called the entire exercise farcical if death in a dreary cell hadn't so often been its final consequence.

"This was the case with the general's bridge parties. His friends, once influential people who were currently barely able to make ends meet after being pushed aside by the revolutionary tide, would dress in their fading suits and once-fashionable gowns and gather two or three times a week for a friendly card game and long political debates. They had set up, of course, just in case the Yankees came, their own shadow cabinet in which the general was the minister of defense. They didn't have any connections in the army, police, or higher administration. For any of the would-be opposition had long before been purged and jailed. It would have been too much to call their mostly academic debates a political plot as those men and women were really evolving in a void and never even tried to substantiate their ideas with actions, yet their gatherings were always alive with heated and noisy discussions.

"In those circumstances, the intrusive moving in of Comrade Amăriuţei had suddenly created a security problem for the general and his guests. To be sure that the newcomer was not eavesdropping, the general asked his wife to divert the man's attention by keeping him company during those evenings when their political friends came to visit. Roxana didn't like the idea, considering the man a fraud, low class, and repugnant. Only after the husband insisted repeatedly did she accept, but her involvement was perfunctory.

"That was in the beginning. Shortly, however, the woman in her became aware of the effect she had on the young man even before he realized what was happening to him and was flattered. She was young, easygoing, and eager for the forbidden fruit. He was young, good-looking, and strong. And in spite of his lack of intellectual luster, she found him acceptable. Lust and sex do not require mental prowess. And so not long after the first anodyne encounter imposed on her by the imprudent husband, Roxana's views on the matter seemed to have changed, and the inevitable happened. It is true that he was not a sophisticated lover, yet he had something she couldn't get from her husband or from the men in her husband's entourage, all of them past their prime. There was in Amăriuței a greedy sexual hunger, a brutality stirred by insatiable desires, which she had never experienced and now found pleasurable. And whatever he didn't know, she taught him. Completely lacking in imagination, he needed a lot of coaching. Every new trick she taught him brought delights he never thought of and liked. In his primitive mind, he still equated sex with love and wrongly believed those to be legitimate rewards for his own special merits.

"On the one hand, he mildly despised the sensual woman who, he thought, had so easily fallen for him, considering her little more than a whore. On the other hand, overwhelmed by passion, he had himself fallen in love to the point of becoming addicted to her, indeed enslaved by his senses. But he was so infatuated that this truth totally escaped his judgement. No wonder then that the memory of his Russian sweetheart soon faded away.

"Comrade Amăriuței's life couldn't have been much better except that unbeknownst to all involved, for some time, the securitate had had the general and his entire group of friends under surveillance. The political sleuths were well-informed about what was going on at those bridge parties. And one night, when the guests were ready to go home, the secret police raided the house. The building was surrounded with sentries in uniform, and armed guards in pairs were planted in every room. Nobody was allowed to leave the place in which they were found or to talk one to another while a swarm of plainclothes officers proceeded to do a thorough search of the entire house, from cellar to attic. The next day around noon, after the search was finished, everyone was taken into custody and transported by blinded vans to several unknown destinations.

"The night, when the search started, Roxana didn't come to visit as usual. Her unsatisfied lover had already been waiting impatiently for quite a long time when a pair of guards and three secret agents bumped the door of his bedroom. He had already drunk a few glasses of vodka and was in a bad mood, and thus told them in coarse language and rather impolite terms to get out. They treated him roughly, and his request to be allowed to phone the superior officers he knew was simply ignored. The intruders laughed at his treats of retaliation, and when he didn't stop shouting and tried to forcibly leave the room, they put an end to his insistence by beating him badly. Because of his aggressive behavior, he had the unenviable privilege of being taken to the securitate headquarters earlier than his housemates during the night and in a separate car. This was the first contact Amăriuței had had with the methods his friends routinely used on their, and previously also his, victims.

"From that moment, Comrade Amăriuței followed the painful pathways we ourselves did after our arrests: interrogatories under duress, days without food, and sleepless nights followed by more harsh interrogatories. What really brought him to the verge of madness, I believe, was how his past friends from the securitate had vanished from the face of the earth. Nobody seemed to have even heard the names of those superior officers he worked for, befriended, and partied with. They were nowhere to be found, and whenever he mentioned their names in order to confirm statements made during his interrogations, he was treated as a liar. As if this wasn't enough, his genuine lack of knowledge about what was going on at the general's bridge parties was labeled as unwillingness to cooperate and an attempt to mislead the investigation, which attracted more beatings.

"On top of that, there were some truly incredible and maddening accusations. On one occasion, for instance, the interrogator had shown our cell mate someone's damaging deposition clearly incriminating him. The anonymous writer pretended to have witnessed Amăriuţei accepting a position in the underground government set up by the general's friends, quoting some inflaming anticommunist speeches he had supposedly made in that entourage. As the young man never played cards or frequented any bridge parties, he denied those allegations and told the officer the truth but was not believed and was tortured. Concurrent depositions apparently made by the general and other members of the group and produced during the following interrogatories confirmed the anonymous information. Amăriuţei was not a fighter. And finally, unable to stand severe bodily pain, he gave in and acknowledged the accusation as a fact. That completed the dossier and sealed his fate, and he was dispatched to Jilava to await trial.

"As implausible as it may sound, he was still unaware of the gravity of his situation. Only when he was waiting for the transfer did some prisoners with whom he shared the securitate's dungeons open his eyes. When Comrade Amăriuţei understood in what sort of a mess he had put himself in, he wanted to change his deposition. But that was impossible. Frustrated and maltreated, he got into a bout of violence like the one we witnessed on his arrival, which always ended with him being mercilessly beaten. It is amazing how he survived so much abuse, perhaps only due to some congenital animal resilience.

"Jean, who as I said was a lawyer, became interested in the comrade's case and, later that year in the summer, when we were on better terms with our difficult cellmate, once asked him if he ever thought of using his alibi. From what the young man told us, during the general's parties, except on the night of his arrest, he was always in Roxana's company. If that was the case, her confession could eventually exculpate him from the false accusations. Perhaps he didn't want to tarnish her reputation, speculated Jean. Yet in the given circumstances, that could also have been to Roxana's advantage. Amăriuţei didn't know the word but when the meaning was explained to him as well as how an alibi worked, he got overly excited and made it clear that he had no qualms about exposing their love affair. He never thought the woman that important in comparison with his securitate buddies.

"It took some effort from Jean to make Amăriuţei understand the difference between a witness and an elusive protector. With even more effort, he also impressed upon the young man that it would be better for him to forget about his friends from the securitate whom he stubbornly insisted upon contacting. The officers had so-called conspiratorial names, the older man told his incredulous pupil, which they routinely used when on missions. And both the assigned and the real names were known only to immediate superiors or to a very few close collaborators. The securitate workers at large were ignorant of those various identities, a precaution meant to protect the agents. Even if, by some unusual piece of luck, they were known to the interrogators and had been advised about him trying to get in touch, his casual friends would have almost surely avoided any dealings with him, now a compromised person. A witness who is not responding voluntarily, however, if accepted by the judged, might be compelled to appear in court.

"Working gently on him for many days, the old lawyer managed to temper the young man's volcanic bursts of rage, which sometimes fringed on madness. I believe Jean saw it as a sort of challenge, like the taming of a wild beast, and he rose to the task. With infinite patience, he trained Amăriuţei and finally convinced him to formally ask for an interview with the political officer of the prison in order to 'complete his deposition.'

"The political officer was an important person, and our cell mate had to wait several weeks. In the end, the administration granted him the interview. Amăriuţei returned from that meeting all smiles. Apparently, the officer had promised to review his dossier and have Roxana called as a witness. In a rare gesture of gratitude, forgetting the class struggle, the comrade embraced the old emaciated lawyer, who was utterly weak, barely surviving, and who received the homage with unrestrained tears. Since becoming our colleague, even the young man had lost a lot of weight and some of his cocky aggressiveness after his athletic muscles melted down. He was looking rather gaunt, almost skeletal, as we all did.

"The general's group was brought to trial the following February. Four armed soldiers took Comrade Amăriuței to court one morning, urging him to hurry, and cutting short our good luck wishes. He was hopeful and appeared to have regained some of his early haughtiness. The old lawyer was by now so weak that he needed help to leave his bunk or to stand up during the routine morning inspections—his days with us were numbered. In spite of his rapidly declining health, he had spent the last weeks preparing the young man for the event. In all our years of detention, we never met anyone who turned a political trial in his favor. Yet if there was anyone who had any chance to do it, it was our cell mate, we thought.

"Usually, such political trials lasted less than an hour. But this was one in which the government wanted to make a big show, capitalizing on the known names of the people involved for propaganda purposes and drawing it out for three days.

"There was great publicity about what was presented in the official press as an unparalleled imperialist antigovernment plot, and the authorities even allowed foreign correspondents to attend—however, only for half an hour—when the trial began. We had no means of following the proceedings, cut off from the outside world as we were. Normally, any information took a long time to reach us. This time, it was different. The third day in the afternoon, the warden on duty paced the corridor, striking the metal doors repeatedly with his rubber cudgel as he passed by and, in the end, shouted loud enough for everybody in the building to hear, 'For all of you to know: the bandit Amăriuței has gotten twenty-five years of hard labor.' It was, in fact, a death sentence.

"Early the next day, the soldiers brought Amăriuței back. We were surprised to see him as people condemned to hard labor were always been sent directly from the court to the mines. Then we realized that the man was in a frightening state of shock. When they pushed him inside the cell, he stumbled as if in a dream and then stood between the bunks without seeing us. Our excited questions got not answers while he kept whispering as if talking to an invisible person, 'Twenty-five years of hard labor, twenty-five years of hard labor, twenty-five years of . . .' he would mumble without pause.

His face was haggard, and his expressionless eyes had the fixation of a sleepwalker. Our cell mate, Tudor, the one who used to be an orderly, gently motioned him toward his bunk. And with my help, we laid the man down without him protesting. Unlike before, he didn't put up any resistance nor did he stop his maddening monologue. He refused to eat, but we managed to make him take a drink of water. Late that night, he drank more water by himself and even slept a bit.

"During the rest of the little time he spent with us, Amăriuței never recaptured his mental balance completely. In a week or so, he recovered enough to tell us, even if only through snippets of information—which sometimes would degenerate in hallucinatory babbling—what had happened in court.

"He never paid attention to our questions, often repeating isolated sequences the way a broken record repeats only part of a tune. Roxana was a witness all right, he said, although she was the main witness of the prosecution, not his. The deposition incriminating our cell mate was hers as she betrayed him from the very start of the inquiry. That was not all. Through her depositions, she had also incriminated every member of the group, including the general and even her bedridden mother who, like Amăriuței, never attended even one of those parties. While Roxana was in the witness box, the prosecutor himself read her entire testimony. Then came the long testimony of a securitate colonel who had conducted the undercover operation that led to the arrest of the defendants. After that, nobody else had the opportunity to say anything.

"One exception to this regimented conduct happened on the last day of the trial, just before sentencing, when the general suddenly stood up and declared that all depositions had been obtained under duress and were false. He requested the court to record his protest and pleaded not guilty. The incident produced confusion and a lot of disturbance, and the presiding judge cleared the courtroom.

"After a short break, the court restarted its proceedings without the general—who was missing from the prisoners' dock—and the audience was reduced to a handful of uniformed securitate officers. The general's lawyer apologized to the court for his client's absence 'due to ill health.' In the end, everyone from the so-called antigovernmental plot got between twenty and thirty years of prison with or without hard labor as the court thought fit, except Roxana, who was acquitted. Jean, whose mind was still sharp in spite of his physical weakness, was quick to conclude that clearly something fishy had happened behind the scenes. From our underground cell, however, it was impossible to know what.

"For the following few weeks, Amăriuţei's behavior remained mostly unchanged. Something had changed, though, and it was his looks and his appetite. If Tudor hadn't fed him the way one does with spoiled children, he probably would have starved to death. His hair also started graying, his face got wrinkled, and he began to lose even more of his already diminished weight. A couple of times, he appeared to come out of his insanity, as if the arrogant, violent youth he used to be had suddenly awakened from a deep sleep. In those rare moments, he again harangued us in an unbroken monologue consisting of slogans and senseless statements. But those episodes were short-lived, and in each of those instances, he almost immediately relapsed.

"This was the situation one morning in March when during the inspection, Tudor and Amăriuţei were ordered to take out the pail and empty it in the toilet, a routine chore we took turns doing. That particular morning, the pail was overfilled with forty-eight hours of waste—as usually happened after some days, like the previous one—when the wardens did a thorough search instead of allowing us to do the cleaning. Somehow, enough tobacco for a cigarette or two had made its way in our subterranean hell, and the telling smell of smoke aroused the suspicion and retaliatory fury of the wardens. Although the search didn't produce any incriminating evidence, we were nevertheless punished by having to spend extra time in the company of our own waste.

"Our cell's turn had come. And when called, Tudor went out first into the narrow, crowded corridor followed by Amăriuţei, carrying the waste pail in between them. Other detainees were also carrying their pails to and from the toilet, and several wardens watched the action intently, shouting orders and insults. My cell mates were slowly clearing the human obstacles, carefully handling their load, when one of the wardens kicked Amăriuței in the buttocks. 'Move faster, bandit,' the warden shouted. He was one of the nastiest among our jailers.

"Taken by surprise, the young man stumbled along a few steps before regaining his balance, and in spite of Tudor's efforts, the foul-smelling contents spilled over. 'Put that pail down, bandit,' the warden barked. 'Take your shirt off, and sweep the floor with it.'

"'I am not a bandit. I am Comrade Amăriuței,' our cell mate said quietly, avoiding the eyes of the warden.

"'You are not. You are a criminal and a bandit, and you'll do what I tell you. Otherwise, I'll make you clean that floor with your own tongue . . .' the warden said, menacingly lifting the cudgel.

"'All right,' Amăriuței said louder this time, a hint of ferocity lurking in his voice, 'you will get what you asked for.' With a swift movement, he grabbed the pail with both hands, raised it up and, with unexpected easiness, turned it upside down over the warden's head, pulling it down to the man's shoulders. Everything happened in a trice, like a strike of lightning. The contents of the pail spread all over the warden's uniform, covering him with the pestilential mixture while he desperately struggled for air and blindly fought to get rid of the ignoble head trap. He had let his cudgel fall on the ground, and our cell mate took it and hammered the pail with it, increasing the man's confusion and making a tremendous racket. The other wardens rushed to help their colleague, but the crowd jamming the corridor slowed their movements. Whoever came closer to the scene was also repelled by the awful smell, the slippery floor, and the fierce-looking, unleashed Amăriuței. Everyone was shouting, detainees and wardens alike, and there was bedlam for a while. Not for long, though, as one of the jailers managed to sneak into the office and phone the administration, asking for reinforcements. The repression was unmerciful.

"First, we had to clean the mess, continuously harassed by a succession of brutalities, gross humiliation, and savage beatings. As a punitive measure, the entire group of twenty detainees was deprived of food for three days, with only a small drink of water every twenty-four hours. Amăriuței, as the main culprit, was punished more harshly in disregard of his obvious insanity. He was additionally given three weeks' confinement in a lock-up room called *carcera*.

"This was a six-foot parallelepipedal airtight box, with the sides of the square bottom about one foot and a half each, and in which two detainees were usually locked up at the same time. If there wasn't enough room for the pair, the wardens would 'help' by punching and kicking them with their boots before locking the door. *Carcera* had no window, ventilation, or light. The punished detainees couldn't lie down or sit. And because the partition rested on a concrete slab, during the winter, it was atrociously cold. They were taken to the toilet twice a day, whenever the jailers remembered them, and their food was reduced to a small modicum of bread and a little water once a day. After two or three days, the forced immobility would impede the circulation of blood in their lower bodies, and their legs would gradually swell. First, the kidneys and then the heart were affected. No matter how healthy the punished detainees were initially, after a week or so in the *carcera*, they would invariably get sick. Depending on their physical strength, after two or three more weeks of what the prisoners called with dark irony *mon caprice*, my fancy, the victims never came back into the cell, being sent directly to the 'hospital.'

"Although it was highly unusual, a week before the end of his term, two wardens carried Amăriuței into the cell and dropped him on my bunk. His lifeless body was dirty and smelly. Unshaven, with closed and blackened eyes, his bruised face had an ashen color, looking more like a death mask than a living being. What especially scared us were his legs, swollen to an incredible size. The skin was bluish, shiny, and overly stretched, almost ready to burst, and suppurating. Big drops of serum oozed out incessantly, rolling down in tiny rivulets. None of us had ever seen such a thing. It was scary to look at, and we were afraid to touch him. Tudor has heard that such swelling occurs in some heart illnesses, and that was a bad sign, but none of us knew anything about such ailments or how they were treated. Regardless of our impossible situation, we felt that something had to be done. And as the only one of us with some first aid experience was Tudor, he made a summary examination of our cell mate. The man was still breathing—in a weak, broken, and jerky manner. His irregular heartbeats were much faster than normal. There were no other signs of life in his body.

"The only thing we could do was to wash him, sparingly using our meager reserve of water, and keep a cold compress made out of a wet rag over his heart. After that, his heart rate decreased a little but still didn't stabilize. Tudor also tried to make him drink, without much success. At dinner, we reported Amăriuţei ill, only to be derided by the warden on duty. That day, we had received a sort of watery bean soup, which Tudor managed to somehow feed to the sick man. Soon afterward, our cell mate opened his eyes and tried to speak, uttering senseless sounds. He appeared confused and unable to recognize us and spent the rest of the evening in a state of prostration. Minutes before the lights went out, he fell asleep, or so we believed.

"Sometime early in the morning, Amăriuţei awaked us. For the first time since his return, he spoke clearly. He wanted water and drank a lot of it, yet he appeared to be oblivious to his surroundings and shortly afterwards relapsed into a kind of agitated unconsciousness. His shortness of breath accentuated. Periods of accelerated breathing were followed by complete cessation of it when he gasped desperately for air, making an awful, harsh noise. Sweat was seeping from all his pores. And his shabby, ragged shirt was drenched like that of someone caught in a rain. Then the pauses between breaths became longer every time he stopped, while his breaths got increasingly shallower. And at one point, he couldn't recover his breath anymore. And that was the end of Comrade Amăriuţei. The Great Equalizer who levels bad and good, rich and poor, had, as always, the last word.

"The lights were already on, and all three of us were awake.

"'The candle,' said Jean. 'Where is my candle?'

"I don't know what Hungarians or Afghan people do when someone dies, but we have this custom to light a candle. It is believed that the soul takes light from the flame and can then cross through the gates of darkness to the Almighty. Jean had asked us to prepare a candle for him in case of what he felt to be his imminent death, and we made one from some threads taken from our ragged clothes, braided together and covered in breadcrumbs. The result of our painstaking labors of many hours was not a true candle although it almost looked like one and burned slowly enough, albeit with quite a lot of smoke. As it happened, this one was not for Jean but for the late Comrade Amăriuței. Tudor was a master at hiding such things as the candle, some matches, or even a needle in order to elude the routine search during the morning inspection. And he was the one who now took it out of its hiding place and lit it. He put the burning candle in between the dead man's crossed fingers, which began getting cold and rigid as we prayed for his soul.

"The morning inspection found us praying. When the warden on duty opened the peephole, Tudor reported the death according to the regulations. 'I, the bandit Tudor, ask permission to report the death of the bandit Amăriuței.'

"The warden hurriedly closed the peephole. He didn't say a word and kept us locked up until everyone went to the toilet, the pails were emptied, and the food distributed. Hours after the inspection, the warden showed up, accompanied by an armed soldier who carried a folding canvas stretcher. We were ordered to undress the dead man and move him onto the stretcher, and Tudor and I had to carry the corpse out. It was at the beginning of April, and before we had surfaced from our underground hell, it had probably rained one of the fast downpours of spring.

"The sky was a stormy gray, the earth still soaked with rain, and the air fragrant with the smell of wet dirt, lilac, and young grass. Far away, on the other side of the barbed-wire fence, in the villagers' orchards, the fruit trees were in blossom. Their virginal white flowers contrasted brightly with the overall gray of the day. In daylight, the dead body, emaciated and skeletal, looked unreal like a nightmarish vision. We were ordered to put the stretcher down, and that was when the warden noticed the candle still burning. 'Take that thing down,' he barked.

"The fresh air gave us a sort of exhilarating drunkenness, a crazy indifference, and we disregarded his orders as if in a dream. We were too busy tasting the glorious, almost-forgotten spring in spite of the death, the regulations, the prison, and our frail, shivering bodies.

"'It is against the regulations. Take it down immediately!' he shouted again as none of us moved. 'Come on, men. Do what I tell you.' There was a certain desperation and impotence in his hoarse voice.

"He knew why the candle was there and, afraid to commit sacrilege himself, wanted us to despoil the cadaver of its guiding light. I suddenly realized that the monster who would beat or torture another man to death was afraid of the dead.

"'Better do what you were told . . . It is not worth the risk of a week in *carcera* for that beast,' the jailer said. 'God, if he exists, doesn't need the likes of his sort. He will go only to the devil, if he goes anywhere.' He laughed despairingly. Obviously, everyone at Jilava knew our cell mate's contributions to the victory of communism.

"Tudor looked straight into the rough jailer's face, as if to better see the marks of fear, with the air of mockery and distrust that only peasants can display when meeting strangers they recognize to be their own in city clothes. 'At least we gave him a chance, Mr. Warden. May God forgive him,' he said and made the sign of the cross.

"'All right, then. Back to the cell,' the warden ordered. 'You listen carefully to me, bandits,' he murmured through his clenched teeth as we went past him, 'I am a good man and will keep my eyes closed this time. Do not think I will not remember . . .'"

The engineer paused and sighed as someone taking a rest after a long and arduous effort. "That is it," he said.

"Wow. That was quite a story," Luca said.

"Why did that woman, Roxana, do so much wrong to so many people?" Ana asked. "I cannot believe something like that really happened."

"You better believe it, Ana. Perhaps she was forced, maybe tortured. Until one gets there, nobody knows how they will react to physical or psychological pressure," Stefan said.

"To incriminate her own mother? That seems too much to me. A sign of degeneration, I should say. There must have been something wrong with that woman," Lia said.

"I asked myself that question many times over the years," the engineer said, "without being able to give a proper answer . . ."—he sighed again—"until recently. It happened before we left. I found out that Roxana was married to a general from the securitate."

"That woman seems to have had a soft spot for high brass," Lia said.

"Yes. And guess what? He was the same colonel who was in charge of the undercover operation that ended in the arrest of her first husband. At the time of the events I just related here, Roxana was having an extramarital love affair with him, and it was just a matter of expediency to help get rid of the husband. He was an obstacle that had to be removed. In the process, everyone else also had to be sacrificed. It was a chain reaction."

"Phew!" Luca cried. "What a whore. She not only cheated on her husband, she cheated on her lover, too."

"A slut, a double-dealer, and a bitch," László said. "I would have killed her."

"One never knows what hides behind appearances," Stefan said.

"All of us are sinners. Those men paid for their sins. She might have been only a tool," the engineer said. He loved the idea of people being tools for divine retribution.

"Come on, Mr. Engineer," Lia said, "you must be joking. Roxana and her current husband, as I gather from what you are saying, are well-off and happy. They also had lots to account for and haven't paid anything, so far."

"So far." It was a hint of something in the engineer's voice. "Only so far," he repeated.

"What about your cell mate? Roxana made him believe she loved him. It was her fault. Why was he sacrificed?" Ana cried with a shrill voice.

"You are too young to understand," Lia tried to calm her daughter.

"I am not, Mama. The man had no sin."

"Think twice, dear. You are wrong," her mother tried again to reason. But the belligerent girl continued to mutter some disagreement.

"Amăriuţei was just a pawn. And her mother, because of her past wealth and 'unhealthy' social origin, was a liability. They both had to go to the garbage can of history, as Stalin used to say. Roxana pushed them just a little in that direction," the engineer said.

"There is no common sense, loyalty, or trust left nowadays in Romania. The new bosses brought to the surface the basest in humans, and I don't know how that process could be ever reversed," Stefan said with regret.

"Don't be sorry, Stefan. The same applies also to Hungary," Váci said, "and to the entire communist bloc. I can bet on that."

"That is not true, Váci," Lászlo cried. "There is nothing like that in Hungary."

"Do you remember that woman officer? The one who sent us to jail?" Váci reminded him.

"She was a paid agent," Lászlo muttered.

"If you look at it this way, the woman, Roxana, got her payment too," Stefan said.

"Maybe." Lászlo wasn't ready to fully agree yet.

"What do you mean by maybe? She got her payment all right," Váci said.

"Afghan women would never do such vile things," Abdur said.

"How can you be so sure? What do you know?" Váci looked inquisitively at Abdur, with a fine ironical smile on his face.

"I know for sure. Whoever does such a thing in my country becomes an outcast, especially a woman—anyone has the right and the obligation to kill her. She wouldn't live to see the next day," Abdur answered.

"Would she be stoned to death?" Val asked

"Probably. More likely stabbed or strangled. One way or another, she would have to die." Abdur spoke confidently. "There is no doubt about that."

"This is a bit too extreme," Lia said.

"I disagree, Lia. If it works, as Abdur says, it might be quite efficient. I kind of like the idea," Váci mused.

"Cu bâta'nveţi pe câni bontonul. With the club, you teach the dogs fashionable manners," Stefan recited.

———

"What was that, Stefan?" Váci asked. He obviously didn't understand what his friend had said.

"It is a verse by Cosbuc, one of our poets. He implies that using force, you can try to teach people like dogs to behave, though I doubt he favored the method. A friend of mine used to say that you could do everything by force to a human except good. Humans will always find a way to cheat even when one tries to do something in their interest. They will make a fool of any system, good or bad, no matter how harsh. We are the best example." Stefan paused and smiled. "Except that what we did was legitimate because we have restored our freedom, something the system had stolen from us."

Abdur stood up. He had his papers gathered in one hand and looked as young and sharp as usual. "Mr. Engineer," he said, "that was a truly enlightening story. I learned many things here tonight. But I have a lot of thinking to do before, hopefully, everything becomes clear to me. It just passed through my mind that recently I have neglected my duty. My people are still suffering under the same godless oppression you described, and I have forgotten them. My fighting friends entrusted me with a mission, and I let them down."

"Don't be so hard on yourself, my son," Stefan said, "there is a time for everything, especially when one is young."

Finally, it was pleasantly cool, the breeze blowing gently and steadily, promising a night of good rest. The engineer bade them good night and left carrying the uncorked bottles. The others began pushing the chairs. Val and Ana busied themselves picking up glasses and the empty bottles spread on the floor.

"I am coming with you to the farm tomorrow," Luca told Stefan.

Váci, who overheard him, stretched and let out a noisy yawn. "Stefan, dear," he asked, "what time are you going to that farm?"

"Seven-thirty, perhaps," Stefan answered.

"We will be ready by that time. Will you give Lászlo and me a lift?"

"Of course," Stefan answered. "What about you, Abdur? Are you coming as usual, my son?"

"I am sorry, Father. I won't come with you. Tomorrow is Friday, and I want to spend the day in prayer. My mind is still confused, and I need guidance. Afterward, *Inshallah*, if God wills, I might work again."

FOURTH AND LAST

INTERMEZZO

Before Christmas, many charitable organizations came to the camp bringing presents for refugees. Some offered cookies and cakes on big trays, or various assortments of bottled soft drinks in multicolored hard plastic cases. Others handed out neatly wrapped parcels in which were soap, perfume, shampoo, toothpaste, and small packages of coffee. Whenever that happened, the camp swarmed with noisy refugees. There was always a lot of elbowing, pushing, and good cheer, especially around the distribution point.

Also before Christmas, the Canadian consul's wife organized a big party for refugees at her home, a large rambling villa on a hill in well-to-do Kifissia. After they ate their fill—pampered with exquisitely smoked salmon, fine cheddar cheese, and plenty of good Tim Hortons coffee—the guests were invited to the basement to take their pick from what was stored there.

That area of the villa looked like Ali Baba's cave of *Arabian Nights* fame. A vast open space was furnished with several big cupboards, and numerous chests of drawers packed with all kinds of clothing, coats, and shoes. Three smaller rooms were stuffed with an assortment of large cases, and huge crates crammed to the brim with accessories such as bags, belts, gloves, shawls, hats and caps. Although some goods were new, others had been previously owned

---

and came from donations. Yet everything was in pristine condition as their affluent owners had never used most of the items.

The refugees who attended returned from that party all smiles and with glowing faces, barely able to carry their booty. It was an unforgettable event, and long after it, the Canadians' party was still fondly remembered and talked about in the camp.

One of the two Communist Parties in town sent a group of activists and organized a pre-Christmas gathering in the camp's recreation room. They served cheap cigarettes, coffee, and mint tea. Mostly Turks crowded the place, steaming cup in one hand and cigarette in the other, talking animatedly, surrounded by clouds of smoke. Stefan flatly refused to go, but Lia and the youngsters didn't want to miss the excitement and went there out of pure curiosity.

The room was adorned for the occasion with two red banners bearing slogans written in big, white lettering. One read: 'Proletarians of the world unite!' 'Communism is the springtime of humanity!' proclaimed the other. Three Party delegates presided near the end of the room under the banners, sitting at a small table draped with a piece of red cloth. Their leader happened to be the richest merchant in town. The man owned several rented houses, a gas station, and five different stores that sold almost everything. He lived in a new, modern, American-style villa with a gorgeous sea view. The refugees knew him quite well as many worked for him in one of his various thriving businesses, and he was notorious for paying poor wages.

When the organizers thought the crowd had appropriately warmed up, the leader stood up and began a spirited speech, extolling the virtues of communist government. Expanding upon what appeared to be his pet subject, he brightly described an idealistic communist future as he saw it and soon got lost in adjectives and the grand scheme of things. The Turks, however, swallowed his words with gusto; and he repeatedly had to stop because bursts of applause continuously interrupted him.

Mr. Ali, the rough Turkish boy and Ana's aspiring suitor, appeared from nowhere, sneaking through the crowd to get closer to Lia and her children. He smiled at them, his round face illuminated with pleasure when the Romanians nodded back, acknowledging his greetings. The boy overflowed with energy; and every time the audience applauded, he jumped and cheered, making a lot of noise.

The Romanians, however, listened placidly and didn't participate in the uproar that broke out every so often. Ali took advantage of one such instance to ask Ana: "You don't . . . ?" and he mimicked clapping with his hands because the words eluded him.

"I didn't understand what he said," the girl answered. "I couldn't hear a thing. What did he say?"

The Turkish boy looked embarrassed and blushed, the ugly acne pustules distorting his features. "Me don't understand," he sheepishly avowed.

"Then why are you clapping your hands?" the girl sneered. She looked at him with bold impatience, trying to put him off.

"But . . . communism is good. Communism is very good," Ali spoke confidently, gazing at her with his dazzling green eyes. The audience had just broken out in another roar of approval and he instantly joined in, thumping his feet and shouting rapturously as many around him did. The boy seemed completely changed, and Ana scornfully turned her back on him.

At that time, a stocky little Albanian man lived in the camp with his numerous progeny. The story went that back in his mother country he had once had an even bigger family, some twenty-eight in all, it was said. They were part of an almost insignificant Roman Catholic minority, an oddity in mostly Muslim Albania.

One day, a busybody from their village, in order to find favor in the eyes of the local government, informed the authorities about the family's Sunday prayer gatherings. It happened to be during one of the fiercest among several campaigns to promote atheism organized by the ruling Albanian Marxist-Leninist Party. Therefore the political police, in an endeavor to eradicate religion, raided their houses; and everyone at home, including the eighty-nine-year-old great-grandmother and a baby of five months, was arrested. All except the baby, who was stabbed to death with a screwdriver, were shot after lengthy torture and a summary trial.

The rest of the family went into hiding and attempted to escape into Greece. Five more were killed while crossing the border, but at last, seven of them made it to the camp. They were a wild-looking bunch, shy and withdrawn. In the camp, the family members seldom left their room, and when talked to would sink into a gloomy silence, too numbed by fright to say or do anything.

The Albanian man was also present in the hall and slowly made his way toward the front row. There were several empty chairs, and the man took one right across from the speaker, whom he considered for a while with a sullen expression on his face; but he soon became conspicuously restless. He fretted and shifted as if the chair on which he sat was too hot for comfort. Over a few minutes, the man become increasingly uneasy and could no longer hide his difficulty in listening quietly.

. "Liar!" he unexpectedly shouted, jumping to his feet. Quickly, he perched on his chair. "*Malakas*," he shouted again using a rude Greek word. "You damn fool, moron," he addressed to the speaker, who—in his astonishment—could not say a word. "You say that communism is good? Communism is hell. Communists are killers."

The cheering had stopped as if by magic. An embarrassed silence fell, in sharp contrast to the enthusiasm that had prevailed so happily until then.

The little fire-eyed Albanian dominated the crowd, defiantly looking at the people surrounding him. "You are all bloody fools," he told the bewildered audience. "These idiots have no idea what they are talking about," he uttered, pointing an accusatory finger at the group of three activists huddled around the table. "Ask me if you want to know what communism is. Ask me, not them."

The man, overwhelmed by strong feelings, could not continue for a moment. "Down with communism!" he finally shouted, panting slightly. Then he climbed down from the chair and, ignoring the stammering speaker who wanted to say something, made his way out, impatiently pushing those around him.

Everyone in the camp was shocked because nobody had thought him so articulate. They couldn't believe his vocabulary was that rich.

YULETIDE

The night before Christmas Eve was stormy and rained one of those fast, surprisingly heavy downpours common around the Mediterranean during the winter. It came with spectacular flashes of lightning accompanied by loud thunder; and in the morning, it was still cloudy, dark, and unusually cold. At daybreak, following the sharp drop in temperature, several wide pools of rainwater that had formed overnight in the camp's courtyard were covered with a transparent skin of ice, making walking difficult. Although one of the cooks had thrown thick planks across some of those slippery spots in order to improve the traffic between kitchen and dormitories, his good intention was to very little avail.

The morning's bad start notwithstanding, after breakfast, a light wind began blowing in earnest, scattering and thinning the black clouds; and soon, rags of dazzling Tiepolo blue showed up in the sky. By ten o'clock, only a few puffy cumuli remained, the sun coolly shining among them and mirroring itself onto a multitude of delicate ice shards emerging haphazardly from the dirty water as the rainy pools visibly decreased in size and depth.

The previous evening, when they had finished work and all agreed to take a break over Christmas, Theodoros invited Stefan to come over the next day and pick up a Christmas tree. In a corner of his widespread lands, he had a grove where firs were growing wild, he had said. Thus Stefan and Val drove in their Trabant to the Greek's farm immediately after noon when it was already warmer and the roads were free of black ice. They took Carina with them in the hope that somewhere on the way, she would get a good run in the fields.

When the Romanians arrived at the farm, Stefan parked the car behind the house and then—strolling with Carina on leash—found Theodoros, his wife, and the two children gathered out in the sun. They made a colorful and animated group in the open area on the other side of the olive orchard where Stefan and Val had helped the farmer set up a large corral surrounded by a narrow dirt track. The children had their bicycles with them, and the farmer's three horses and his dogs were there too. They had almost finished the daily exercise the family performed conscientiously, rain or shine. It was a cavalcade in which all had their place as they circled the corral repeatedly. The young wife came first on the black stallion, then the children on their tiny bicycles, followed by the dogs jumping madly and chasing one another or the colt, and—closing the ranks—Theodoros riding the old mare. In spite of its lack of pretence, the routine was fun to watch. But the sudden appearance of a strange spaniel stirred the resident dogs into a frenzy of loud barking and mock attacks. Soon, their agitation got out of hand, and the orderly event broke up in a messy hubbub.

It took a lot of shouting from the men to calm the canines, and then the children surrounded Carina. They quickly forgot their bicycles, competing now for temporary possession of the cocker. The poor dog, threatened by her own kind, boisterously petted by the girl and roughly dragged by the little boy, appeared totally aghast at the outpouring of so many emotional expressions and so much noise and excitement. She looked with anxious eyes at Stefan, begging for help. He was still holding the leash but didn't want to stand up against her tormentors, afraid of offending his hosts. As many times before in similar situations, he had to let her down and as always felt guilty afterward for his behavior, a mixture of human cowardice and outright treachery. That the fact was more or less socially justified didn't ever ease his remorse.

An approximate order was presently established, and Stefan agreed to leave Val and Carina behind so the children could play with the spaniel under supervision. In the meantime, it was decided, he and Theodoros would fetch the Christmas trees.

Theodoros's Fiat pickup truck was already loaded with the necessary tools, and the farmer drove it up in the direction of the hills, a kilometer or perhaps two across the open fields where there was no road, just fallow land. After a scrubby expanse whose desertlike loneliness was broken only by scattered, rare pistachio trees and the odd carob, the ground subsided into a shallow ravine directed north. Both slopes of the ravine were tightly overgrown with majestic silver and Cephallonian firs, Aleppo and black pines, and splendid tall cypresses. The tiny island of evergreens, which had grown unchecked in many sizes and shapes, emerging suddenly from a sea of ocher dirt and dusty yellow grass, was an amazing sight.

"Is all this land yours?" asked Stefan, making a sweeping gesture with his stretched arm. There were probably several hundred hectares rolling gently from the hills down to the road.

"Most of it. Why?"

"There is plenty of room to expand your olive tree orchard here, Theodoros."

"I don't intend to."

"Why not? In ten years, they will be well-established. In another ten there will be a healthy olive grove here. Something worthwhile to leave to your heirs. And if you think that olive trees live hundreds of years . . ."

"No, Stefan. I won't do it. I won't do anything like that for my heirs. They will, of course, inherit everything I have. But what I am doing now is for my own pleasure only. This is not because I am a selfish man. No. Not at all. Dealing in real estate, you see, I learned a lesson. All this land here I have acquired from people who in some way or another had inherited it. The owners never had second thoughts about selling their inheritance because they needed money to pay gambling debts or make up what they lost at races on bad horses or spent on loose women or, even worse, on booze. Nobody cared to keep what their ancestors had painfully built or saved for them. See those tall silver firs there at the mouth of the ravine? In the past, there was for some centuries a monastery on that spot. There is nothing left of it. After the occasional heavy rain, I would find shards of splintered bones and pieces of broken pottery, nothing of much value. Even God's property is scattered in the end by fools, and you want me to believe that my work will last longer than the one done in his name?" the Greek said and chuckled. "Let's cut our trees. It is getting late."

Theodoros eyed two fine trees, and they cut the first for him. When they approached the second, Stefan declined it. "It is too big for us. We don't have room for it," he said and, after some searching, settled for a much smaller one—a young pyramidal spruce.

They loaded the trees into the truck and had a smoke, sitting side by side on the back bumper. The afternoon was clear and without clouds, a splash of pale golden red on the western sky accompanying the sunset. There was a sudden chill in the air after the wintry sun had disappeared behind the mountains, sending only an anemic, frigid glimmer through the rising opal haze.

"Do you know, Stefan, what I was thinking?" There was a hint of uneasiness in Theodoros's voice. He spoke in a low, confidential tone. "Have you noticed how much my children like your dog? If you would agree, er . . . if you would accept, er . . . The fact is I would like to buy Carina. Do not be afraid—I will give you a fair price."

Taken aback, Stefan didn't know what to answer. He felt a rush of adrenaline and the tumultuous tidalwave of bad temper. The thought of selling Carina was abomination to him. He managed to control himself though; and the unpleasant, bad feeling was quickly repelled. To gain more time, he took several puffs at his cigarette, deeply inhaled the acrid smoke, and then released it in long exhalations before answering. The farmer was a good man, and he certainly meant well, he thought. "Please don't get me wrong, Theodoros. You perhaps are not aware of the extra risks we took, bringing the dog with us . . ."

"I realize that it was quite difficult."

"I am sorry, Theodoros, but you cannot know. How could you? You have never lived under communists. Even at home, our life would have been much easier without a dog. We could have left the spaniel with my parents, which of course would have meant extra burden on their shoulders."

"I understand that."

"Perhaps," Stefan agreed, "but what you should know is that she is a member of my family. And I personally feel responsible for her in the same way I feel for my children. There is no sale price for my children and neither for Carina. And my children, indeed all of us, also love her . . . Sorry, Theodoros, the answer is no. Although I don't want to hurt your feelings, she is not for sale."

"Well," said Theodoros, "I thought you might need money. With three dependents, it won't be easy to start in Canada, especially without relatives, connections, or money. I really meant to help you."

"You are a generous man, Theodoros, and I am grateful for all the good things you have done for us. It is hard to find enough words to thank you. I hope you see my point. And let me tell you something else: Fortunately, we saved enough to pay for the dog's flight to Canada. Otherwise, I was ready to stay behind and work until I would have been able to take Carina with me," Stefan said. "I just wish you believe me."

"Okay, then. I believe you, and let's forget about it," Theodoros said. His tone was conciliatory. He didn't look upset. "It is time to go back."

They drove down and across the empty fields—now, after the early sunset, more frigid and unfriendly-looking—to Theodoros's house.

The little boy and the girl were still outside with the spaniel. Val was leaning on the corral's tall wooden fence, starring absentmindedly at the children's play. He was visibly bored, and when he saw the truck approaching, his face lit up. He immediately left the fence and hurried to help Theodoros unload his tree, which they carried inside the house. The children dropped the dog and followed the two men with shouts of joy.

Left alone, Carina, with the leash trailing along, came slowly to Stefan, who was busy tying his spruce on the Trabant's roof rack.

The dog was exhausted, and when he let her into the car, she curled up immediately on the backseat, closed her eyes, and sank into a sort of indifferent torpor.

The farmer returned with a wide grin on his face. "My wife has made some mulled wine. Come, Stefan. Come, have a hot drink!"

It was warm in the kitchen, and the fragrant smell of wine mixed with cinnamon and other spices Stefan couldn't identify filled the air. They were seated around the table in the dining area and treated with red mulled wine in fat black mugs adorned with Greek mythological scenes etched in gold. The wine was hot, and with each gulp, its warmth spread throughout one's body. Soon, a relaxed wellbeing and the pleasant feeling of close companionship engulfed them.

A low wall separated the dining area from the large living room; and while the men chatted lazily, they watched Theodoros's wife and children decorating the Christmas tree, which already stood tall in its sturdy support. Numerous open boxes were spread around, and the svelte woman hung shiny globes and multicolored figurines unpacked by the children. A lot of pushing and elbowing went on with the job; and on more than one occasion, a globe too roughly handled broke with a pop, followed by the children's distress. Their whining and whimpering lasted several minutes—being seated each on a separate chair without permission to move was the imposed punishment—until their mother would release them with a stern warning. The episode was soon forgotten, and the laughter and cheer escalated again until the next skirmish and subsequent damage to the decorations introduced another sad note. The animated scene was a heartwarming display of domestic bliss in spite of so many moody ups and downs. Softened by the warm atmosphere, Stefan had to make a real effort to tear himself away as he had things to do at home.

"Wait a moment," said Theodoros, "I have something for you." Without more ado, he vanished through the back door of the kitchen, only to reappear shortly afterward with a sizeable white plastic box. "This is a cage for pets, made to the airlines' specifications. It can be easily taken apart and reassembled," he told Stefan.

Theodoros knelt on the kitchen floor and quickly unscrewed several butterfly nuts. The box separated into two halves and a door made of narrow metal bars. "See, Stefan? It is much easier to carry it to the airport dismantled like this. I never used it. You will need it for Carina. This is my Christmas present to you."

Stefan tried to thank him, but the Greek didn't want to hear anything. He just busied himself with helping the Romanians carry the cage's sections to the car. When it was secured inside the trunk and they were saying their good-byes, Theodoros puzzled them with an unexpected question. "Do you have any decorations for the tree?"

"Not really. We will make some from colored paper," Stefan nonchalantly said.

"Ah, man. Colored paper? You must be kidding. Don't go . . ." Theodoros said, and made a disgusted face before running into the house. He returned in a hurry, his arms full of boxes. His face was lit by a big smile. "Here, you have lights, decorations, garlands, you name it. Take them . . . and don't ever mention colored paper."

Stefan stammered, struggling with his emotion. His English vocabulary was too limited and the use of the language still unfamiliar; and when deep feelings prevailed, as now, he couldn't react fast enough except in his native Romanian which, of course, didn't help.

"No, no. You don't have to thank me. This is my wife's present. We have too many decorations. We cannot keep all the stuff anyway. It would be a waste. The children are breaking them by the dozen . . . Honestly, this is nothing."

Theodoros's voice was almost apologetic. "Merry Christmas to you and all the family . . . Go now . . . Kala Hristougenna . . . Merry . . . Merry Christmas." He mixed Greek with English and was visibly uncomfortable with the outpouring of the Romanian's gratefulness.

Back at the camp, Stefan stopped the car in front of the gate and, with Val's help, unloaded the presents and carried them upstairs. Lia was especially pleased with the spruce as she felt it wasn't a real Christmas without a proper tree. An impatient Ana hastily opened

Theodoros's boxes, accompanying everyone with excited cries and showing her mother the glittering new decorations. Only when Stefan presented the girls with the last surprise, the doggy cage, they remembered Carina asleep in the car. He resolved to go park the Trabant and pick her up.

"When you come back, I'll show our surprise," Lia said.

"Your surprise? What are you talking about?"

"Dana is flying to Canada tomorrow," Ana couldn't resist spilling the beans.

"Dana called in to say good-bye and gave us two pots, two pans, several plates, some silver, and a Czechoslovak-made electric sewing machine. In Canada, she was told, the voltage is different and one cannot use European-made equipment," Lia explained. "She also wanted to speak with you."

Dana and her husband were a young Romanian couple, both nurses by profession, whom Stefan's family had found in the camp upon their arrival. The self-conceited and arrogant husband spent most of the time traveling around Greece, leaving Dana alone for long periods of time. Lia and Ana became acquainted with her through Carina. The young woman was a fanatic dog lover and liked to borrow the spaniel, which she spoiled, for long solitary walks along the sea.

"Maybe she will come again . . . I can't wait now. It is getting dark, and I must move the car and bring the dog in." Stefan's mind was clearly elsewhere, and he didn't grasp the urgency behind Dana's generosity.

"Maybe she will . . . Who knows? They must spend the night in Athens. They are in a hurry to leave . . ." Lia tried unsuccessfully to make him aware of their camp mate's imminent departure.

Ten minutes later, Stefan reentered the building with Carina on a leash. In the ground floor hall, he met Dana, who looked as if she was waiting for them.

Dana had black eyes, long dark hair, and was well tanned like a Greek. She wasn't what one could call a beauty—there were several more beautiful women in the camp, especially a couple of Polish girls—but with a curvaceous, well-proportioned body, sporty and young, she was quite attractive. Stefan, in a peculiar way, had known her for a long time.

Three decades ago, Dana's family had lived in Bucharest a few houses down the street from Stefan's parents. She was almost seventeen years his junior, and he could only vaguely remember her as a toddler. When she was born, he was a teenager, struggling with his early manhood, discovering love, experimenting with sex, and learning to court women—usually older than he was. He had no time for baby girls; and later on, when he left the capital to finish his studies at a university in the north, she was still a girlish gnome in kindergarten. When he and Lia got married and returned to Bucharest, they settled down in a completely different area of the city. He therefore saw Dana in her teens only occasionally, from a distance, when visiting his parents. They had never spoken except when exchanging courteous greetings until, to their surprise, they found themselves so many years later in the same refugee camp in Greece. Under the circumstances, they had become better acquainted, yet not enough for Stefan to consider her a friend. First, there was the age difference; and second, there was a sort of polite detachment she never relinquished. This Stefan didn't mind as she certainly wasn't his type of woman.

"Merry Christmas," he said.

"Merry Christmas to you. Unfortunately, mine is not that merry . . . I am on my way out. My luggage is already on the police bus. I looked for you upstairs . . . to say good-bye. Some people declined to fly to Canada during Christmas, and we have accepted their seats. Tomorrow, we will leave for Montreal . . . You went to fetch my lovely friend Carina, so Lia told me." Dana knelt beside the cocker. "Aren't you lovely, Carina?" She began to stroke the dog's golden red fur delicately.

"That's great news, Dana. Congratulations," Stefan said. "I am really glad for you."

Dana stood up brusquely. "I am not," she replied. "I would rather not go."

"Would you prefer to stay in Greece?"

"No, I hate Greece."

"Why?"

"The worst things happened to me in Greece."

"Come on, don't exaggerate, Dana. How can you say that? Surely, you don't mean it. You got your freedom in Greece, and while waiting here, Canada has granted you landed immigrant status."

"That's not the point . . . I am terribly afraid to go."

"What are you afraid of?" Stefan asked, wondering if there was a polite way to stop this rigmarole.

"I am so lonely," she said and looked straight at him with wet, reddened eyes.

It was only then that he noticed how dreadfully downcast she looked. It seemed as if she had cried before and was ready to start again.

"You are not alone. You have your husband, and the two of you will begin a new life in Canada together." Stefan tried to encourage her.

"We are divorcing, Stefan. We kept it secret until now. We didn't want to get into trouble with the immigration people." She let a couple of tearless sobs be heard. "I am so afraid . . . Oh, Stefan, how stupid I was . . . There is nothing I can do, only go and face my horrible destiny . . ." She stood in front of him with her head down and shoulders hanging low, as if crushed by an unbearable weight.

Stefan felt pity for the girl, so young and so unhappy. Knowing her from early childhood gave him a sort of fatherly complex, completely unjustified. For the moment, however, he felt an irresistible desire to cheer her up, to soothe her somehow. "You still have your friends."

"Friends? What friends?"

"You must have some friends and perhaps we and others. Soon, you know, we are coming to Canada too. Everything will be just fine, I am sure."

"Oh, yes, friends," Dana said, bursting into tears, "how can you be so blind?" She stretched on the tip of her toes, took a deep breath, and with both hands violently grabbed Stefan's head. Her fingers pulled his curled hair back while she kissed him hard on the mouth. It was a good-bye kiss all right, but not a friend's kiss. It was the burning hot kiss of a lover.

"Good-bye, my love," she whispered. "I have always loved you since I was fifteen," Dana said and rushed out of the building, knocking down a young Turkish refugee who happened to come in at that very moment.

"This woman is mad, mad like hell," the short fat man cried, making a significant gesture with a forefinger, as if thrusting an imaginary screw into his temple. His strident voice momentarily produced an awful racket inside the stairwell. "She should be put down like a mad dog," the youth mumbled furiously under his breath while limping up the stairs after collecting himself from the concrete floor.

Stefan stood in the middle of the hall unable to move, his face wet with Dana's tears. What had happened was so unexpected. Was it real? Did the young woman really mean what she said? *That is preposterous,* he thought, *I am too old, and she is too young . . . How on earth had she got this strange idea?* He definitely didn't feel guilty in any way. "I would never take advantage of someone's foolishness, or despair, or whatever . . ." he murmured to himself. Yet unlike the Turk, he knew she wasn't a fool. She was always considerate, dignified and well-balanced, except in her exaggerated love for dogs. He had never seen Dana lose her quiet composure until now. She was perhaps too quiet. The quietest waters are the deepest, they said at home. Who knows? Perhaps she told the truth. She must have been deeply disturbed to behave like that. Who could say what was going on between her and her wandering spouse? Strange things happen in many families behind closed doors. She definitely wasn't happy. A mangled soul, that was what she was. A mangled soul, for sure.

He calmed down, his face dried. That's how things happen, always when one doesn't expect them. Often one gets what he is not asking for and almost never what or when one would really like to get a particular thing. Every refugee in the camp would have been delighted to leave the camp ahead of the scheduled time, especially to go to Canada. That would have been the best Christmas present any of them could have dreamed of. Not Dana. Undoubtedly, there is a tragic irony in the fate of humans.

And what about me, he thought. *Look how stupid I am. Instead of being happy that a young woman can still fancy an old-timer like me, I am fretting like an idiot. I should know better. Destiny plays funny games with us, in which we are the losers, as the ancient Greek playwrights were so well aware. There was nothing to be done. I hope she recovers soon,* he wishfully thought as a wave of melancholy took hold of him. *Luckily, she is young; and once in Canada the novelty of her fresh experience will quickly sweep away all this stuff. Thank God they are leaving now. What a mess their lives and ours might become if they weren't . . .*

He climbed the stairs in a thoughtful state of mind, the dog jumping the stairs side by side with him; and when Stefan entered their room, his preoccupied face gave him away.

"What's the matter with you?" Lia asked.

"I met Dana downstairs."

"I see," Lia said, looking at him with inquisitive eyes. "She came here again a while ago, asking for you."

"Yes, she told me . . . They are divorcing, did you know that?"

"She hinted something, vaguely."

"Dana is quite disturbed . . . Those two always looked so close together . . ." As soon as he said that, he realized how untrue it was. "In fact, only God knows how their life was . . . She is a bleeding soul . . ."

"I think she is in search of a shoulder to cry on, if you know what I mean," Lia said. "Although she might be in the middle of a crisis, it is good they are leaving now."

"Probably it is best," Stefan agreed. He still felt the burn of Dana's kiss. "I cannot but feel sorry for my little neighbor of bygone years."

"She is not that little, and thank God she will not be our neighbor either," Lia said with dry finality. After a short pause, she continued as if nothing had been discussed, "Let's prepare dinner, dear. Our friends will be coming soon."

In fact, the use of the plural wasn't accurate. Luca was for the time their only friend in the camp since Abdur had immigrated to the United States two weeks earlier. As it happened, with the exception of the Turks, numerous refugees had taken advantage of the holiday to visit the country; and Váci, László and Stanislaw were spending Christmas with some Poles who had gotten temporary gardening jobs near Marathon. Even the Romanian engineer was away in Athens with his daughter's family. In their absence, Stefan and Lia planned to ask Luca to spend dinner together, as was the tradition, on the night when the shepherds had been told 'the news of great joy, a joy to be shared by all people.' In order to invite him, Stefan had gone to Luca's dormitory in the morning, before the trip to Theodoros's farm, and found that their intended guest wasn't alone as expected. Two new Romanian refugees had been billeted the day before with his friend.

When Stefan entered the room, Luca and the newcomers were drinking coffee. The elder one, who introduced himself as Mişu, was a mature, charming, and voluble man of pale brownish complexion, with gray hair over gray eyes and an aquiline nose. He didn't disclose anything about his person, choosing instead to introduce his mate, a gloomy character in his late thirties. His name was Ionel, a blond and fair-skinned factory maintenance electrician. In view of his imminent immigration to Canada, the electrician preferred to be called Johnny. "To get used to the English equivalent of his name," he said.

Luca offered Stefan coffee, and they all sat together chatting amiably. Although pleasant, the socializing interfered with Stefan's plans as he unsuccessfully waited for an occasion to talk privately with his friend. When pressed to leave for his meeting with Theodoros, he had on a sudden impulse extended the dinner invitation to these new folks as well. Lia had enough food, and he knew that two more guests would not be a burden for her.

Johnny anticipated the dinner with pleasure and effusively promised to come, unlike Mişu whom the invitation appeared to make strangely uncomfortable. "I am not a Christian," he said after a long hesitation.

"Doesn't matter," said Stefan. "We are not inviting you to a church service. It will be just a traditional dinner."

"I understood that. The truth is that I am not sure if you can call me a traditional Romanian either . . . I am a Jew," Mişu somewhat reluctantly confessed.

"Look, Mişu, I won't haggle about this . . . You have been invited, and you are free to do what suits you. A dinner is a dinner even if it is meant to remember the birth of Christ. After all, the newborn we celebrate today was a Jew himself, wasn't he?" Stefan asked, good-humoredly winking at his new acquaintance.

"All right, I will come then. You convinced me," Mişu said and smiled. "I don't want to upset you. It is just . . . oh. That's my problem. Thanks . . . I will come."

The guests arrived at the convened time, bringing presents although they had been told not to bother. Stefan held the door for them, unsuccessfully trying to stop Carina from getting under everyone's feet.

Luca was carrying cookies on a plate and a baby demijohn encased in yellow wickerwork. The cookies, which looked more like breadcrumbs buried in icing sugar, he had made himself; the heavy dark red wine was from a local producer, he discreetly whispered into Stefan's ear.

Johnny brought a huge freshly baked loaf of crusty bread, which he gave to Lia with two oranges and a handful of dried figs. "For the ladies," he said, blushing to the tips of his ears.

Mişu, who entered last, took Stefan aside and presented him with a big French Camembert cheese in a round metallic box. There was more than a kilogram in the box. "This is for dessert," he said.

Stefan didn't want to take the big box. "It is too much. You shouldn't do that," he said, overwhelmed by his guest's generosity.

"It is nothing, really," Mişu whispered. "My brother from the States keeps sending me more dollars than I can spend. He doesn't want to understand that I don't need so much money. Here, I have free shelter, enough free food, and wine is cheap."

"No, no. Please. You should keep at least part of it for you."

"No," Mişu said. "I don't even know exactly how it tastes. I thought this could be a good opportunity to find out as I never tried Camembert. You invited me to dinner, and this is my present. Okay? If you don't accept it, I'll return to my room right now." He made an about-turn as if he was going to leave.

"All right, all right," Stefan said, retaining him by the hand. "Don't go, please."

"Only if you accept my present . . ."

"I do, because you insist. I still loathe thinking that you felt obliged to pay for the dinner."

"I didn't feel obliged. This is not a payment. It was my pleasure to bring you something, and at such a short notice, I couldn't find anything better. That's all." Mişu, seemingly appeased, turned toward the rest of the company and said more loudly: "Merry Christmas, everybody."

The others, abruptly reminded of Mişu's presence, answered his greeting with various degrees of amused surprise. The interruption, however, silenced them as it was followed by a sort of playful expectancy.

"Look, Lia. Here, guys, look what we have for dessert." Stefan showed them the Camembert.

"Wow," Lia said. "That is some dessert. Thank you, Mr. Mişu. You shouldn't be so prodigal with your money."

"This is my Christmas present, madam," Mişu replied, conspicuously uncomfortable with so many eyes focused on him. "It is not worth too much. We have already settled this issue with your husband. Don't mention it anymore, please."

"All right, then. Let's start dinner," Lia said.

The table was already laid with an eclectic collection of unimpressive odd pieces from dispersed sets. Yet in spite of the poor inventory, the room had a festive atmosphere. On the Christmas tree, the new decorations glittered and shimmered; and from a cassette player Nat King Cole's unmistakable baritone could be heard softly singing "An Old-fashioned Christmas." The spruce's fine scent, the fresh food aromas, and the music made up for the lack of elegance and luxury.

The guests followed Lia's invitation. Standing around the table, Luca and Johnny, already in celebratory mood, began cracking walnuts by squeezing them in the palms of their hands, laughing and joking. Val and Mişu, engrossed in eating pistachios, didn't pay attention to what was happening around them. Val greedily picked up only the big open nuts he could easily empty with his fingers while Mişu patiently extracted even the most stubborn ones from the hardest shells with the blade of his pocketknife. All four kept working diligently with their hands and mouths, except when they paused for a drink from the glasses Luca kept refilling.

Crowded in the corner of the room where they had improvised a kitchen, Lia and Ana were hastily putting the finishing touches on the first course while Stefan carved the roasted ham.

"Hey, Stefan. If you and the ladies don't come to the table soon, you will only have water to satisfy your thirst," Luca warned his friend.

"We are coming. Don't you dare drink all the wine without us," Lia said as she and Ana started serving hot sausages with mashed potatoes and pickled green tomatoes. Stefan finished cutting the ham and placed a loaded dish in the middle of the table.

"Oh, God!" Johnny cried after chewing a slice of cooked ham. "Where did you find this? I haven't tasted something this good in years."

"We bought it here in town. There are several well provided butcher shops in the neighborhood," Lia replied.

"There are several butcher shops in my hometown, too," said Johnny, "all empty because everything is exported for dollars."

"I wouldn't be surprised if this meat was imported from Romania. Pigs are not one of Greece's riches," Mişu said. "By the way, have you heard the latest anecdote about the food shortage in Bucharest?" he asked.

"No, we haven't. Tell us. Tell us, please. I am always glad to hear a new one," Luca urged him excitedly.

"A Westerner is visiting Bucharest accompanied by a guide from the official tourist organization. The sheer emptiness of food stores shocks the foreigner. He is especially amazed by butcher shops as clean as a whistle, where not only is the meat absent, even the faintest smell of it is lacking. Overwhelmed, he cannot prevent himself from making a guarded comment. 'Your country seems to lag behind as far as domestic commerce is concerned, I am afraid,' he tells the guide.

"'What makes you say that?' the guide asks belligerently.

"'Take your butcheries, for example. In my country, they are packed tight with all kinds of meats and meat specialties from poultry to beef and from pork to the finest venison. Here all your meat stores appear to be empty.'

"'Oh,' the well-schooled guide replies, 'What you are telling me happened here a long time ago during primitive bourgeois-capitalistic eras. Eons ago, these stores were privately owned and teeming with meat products of unimaginable variety as you mentioned. Since the victory of the proletariat, however, we have made a big leap forward. Currently, we are building socialism—a more advanced form of society—and the stores belong to the entire people. Isn't it beautiful how clean the stores are? For us, the political aspect is paramount, not your much-worshiped affluence. I apologize for having to say it, but your country lags behind, not ours.'"

Johnny didn't enjoy the anecdote. "I don't understand this stupid propaganda. As I told you, there is no meat in my town's butcheries. We were systematically famished for the benefit of what they call 'the future generations.' This is the truth, I swear," he said.

"Don't get excited, Johnny," Mişu said, "Keep eating. I will explain it to you tomorrow."

The family only had four chairs, and the table had to be moved near one of the beds to accommodate three more people. Stefan, Val, and Luca had volunteered for those unenviable seats. During the dinner, the metallic bed frame, incompletely covered by the thin mattress, restricted the blood circulation in the legs of those seated, giving them cramps. Often, they had to stand up and massage their limbs. But the good food and merriment made them pay little attention to such a minor inconvenience.

The Romanian specialty *sarmale*, a mixture of ground pork and rice wrapped in sauerkraut, well-seasoned and generously basted with crème fraîche, came next, greeted with pleasant surprise. Mişu—after hearing how Lia had made the pickles and the sauerkraut right there in their small room, using a couple of glass jars, green tomatoes, cabbage, dill, salt and water—proposed a toast to the cook.

"I cannot believe it!" Mişu said, perhaps a little too loudly as he let himself get carried away by enthusiasm. "Did you prepare all these goodies here, cooking everything on that tiny electric hot plate?"

"My mother always said that when you have what you need, it is not too difficult to make a good meal."

"Maybe it is so, but to me, it still looks like an impressive performance. Not to mention your marvelous sauerkraut. You are a brilliant cook. Another glass to your health."

"I must confess that without Theodoros, bless his soul, nothing could have been made."

"Theodoros? Who is this Theodoros?"

"A Greek friend of ours, a farmer. We work for him," Luca said.

"At the beginning of December, we dug his vegetable garden to make room for the new seedlings," Stefan explained. "Incredible as it might sound, last summer's tomatoes and cabbages were still thriving. Before composting what we pulled out, he let us take anything we wanted, and there was plenty. Theodoros is a generous chap."

"That must be unusual for a Greek, I should say," Mişu mused. "'Beware of the Greeks even when they bring presents' is the saying, isn't it?"

"Contrary to the common belief, we found many Greeks to be quite goodhearted, generous, and caring," Stefan said.

"I am not sure now who was the author of that saying, Ovid or Virgil. He surely didn't spare the Greeks, and his depiction of them as treacherous had lasting influence. I am too new in Greece to judge for myself, but I will keep an open mind."

"The percentage of good and bad people is the same in every country," Lia said. "If one looks behind the façade they put on display, one finds they are not too different from us."

———

311

At the proper time, Stefan opened a bottle of Samos, and Ana served desserts. There were two kinds of rolled sweetbread, one filled with sweetened ground poppy seeds and the other with walnuts, and a multitude of small cookies.

"Don't tell me that you baked cookies and sweetbreads here," Mişu said.

"Oh, no. We baked them next door at Kosta's," Lia answered, "but Val kneaded the dough here. We had a lot of fun with him. Wasn't it fun, Val?"

"Yeah! I never did something like that before, and the dough didn't want to stay in the bowl."

"He punched it so forcefully that the dough flew all over. Fortunately, my son is a fast learner. In the end, he did an excellent job," Lia said.

"Only my poor knuckles can tell at what price. They still hurt," the boy complained.

"Don't worry, dear. By the time you have eaten the last cookies, you will be all right," Lia assured him.

"There is no learning without pain, young man," Mişu said and lifted his glass. "Good job! To your health, Val."

Each of them found new reasons for another toast, and nobody kept track of the glasses had so far. The wine brought the expected loosening of tongues, and when it was time for the Camembert, everyone was talking without paying much attention to what the others said.

"Only my Aunt Sânziana made such good sweetbread," Johnny reminisced. "This one is also very good . . . No, that is not what I wanted to say . . . Yes, it is what I wanted to say. It is excellent . . . Hers, however, was without match. I remember being a child and watching my aunt kneading and baking." He put another piece in his mouth. "Even now I can feel the smell of hot cake fresh from her oven. She is dead, God rest her soul. You cannot imagine the suffering she went through before dying." Johnny furtively wiped his eyes. He looked as if the alcohol had suddenly induced in him a pervasive melancholy.

"I prepared the dinner, now it is your turn to treat me," Lia said loud enough for all to hear. "While Stefan makes coffee, you guys must sing carols." She hoped the singing would dispel Johnny's melancholy bout. "Otherwise, you won't get coffee. No carols, no coffee," she jokingly threatened her guests. "Come on, start singing, please. Go on, guys. Go on!"

"Buna dimineata la Moş Ajun. Good morning on Christmas Eve," Ana timidly began an old, beloved Romanian carol. She had a clear, though untrained, voice, perhaps a little weak now and tremulous due to nervousness. Then Luca, Val, Lia, and even Mişu joined in; and soon, all except Johnny were singing along with her. Then someone started another carol, the one about the hunters who went hunting deer and shot a bunny instead, to make from its fur a fine coat for the little Lord. The carol about the star that appeared mysteriously announcing to the world the birth of the Messiah followed, and so the singing went on and on. There was magic in the atmosphere. It seemed as if the present didn't exist anymore, and they were all home again, in their long-lost childhood, before public celebrations of Christmas were forbidden in Romania.

The singing stopped when Stefan brought coffee and brandy. "You have a good voice, Mişu, and you know all the scores quite well," he complimented his guest.

"My mother was a Christian," Mişu replied. He took a sip from the mug. "You are a master and a connoisseur, Stefan. Your coffee is excellent, not to mention the brandy—twelve years old. Oh, my. Oh, my. Where did you find all these goodies? I shouldn't ask. You better keep your secrets because too much knowledge might mean my financial ruin."

"It is not that bad. Surely, you can afford a bottle or two. Our friend Váci, your absent Hungarian roommate, drinks only this brandy. And he doesn't have a millionaire brother in the States," Stefan said teasingly.

"Oho," Luca laughed. "Váci and his crooked deals. His sources are too good to be legitimate. And he is so tight-lipped that no one knows how he does business."

"Luca, you shouldn't talk like that about our friends," Lia reproved him and, deliberately changing the subject, asked, "was your mother really a Christian, Mr. Mişu?"

"She was, and in my early childhood, we spent every Christmas at my mother's parents. Their family was big, with numerous children, grandchildren, aunts, uncles, and cousins. And singing along was the most enjoyable part of the celebration. My father was a non-practicing Jew. And although he didn't like Christmas as such, out of love for my mother, he grudgingly participated in those gatherings. That was in the beginning. After the death of my grandparents and, soon after, my mother's death, we never celebrated Christmas anymore. When my father later became a fervent admirer of Marx and a Communist Party member, caroling became anathema," he said.

"You lost your mother quite early in life, I presume," Lia said. "I am so sorry, Mr. Mişu."

"Call me Mişu, Madam," he replied. "Indeed, I lost both my parents while in high school. Mother died of cancer when I was ten . . . My father was killed six years after her death."

"Was your father the victim of an accident?" Stefan asked, with the bottle of brandy in hand, ready to refill Mişu's glass.

"No more, please," Mişu covered the glass with his hand. "I would prefer some of that Samos. Brandy is too strong for me. I will soon start behaving stupidly. Although I really love your brandy, it is too much."

"As you like," Stefan said, passing him the wine bottle.

"That is better, thanks." Mişu filled his glass with concentrated attention, gulped a mouthful, and then sighed. "No, Stefan, it wasn't an accident. My father was killed on the building site of the Danube-Black Sea Canal."

The Danube-Black Sea Canal was a project initiated by the Romanian communist government in the 1950s. It was exclusively carried out with the forced labor of political detainees who died by the thousands due to inhuman treatment, insufficient food, and lack of medical care. For several years, until the work was abandoned, the canal was the preferred extermination method for whomever the leadership considered undesirable.

"In one of the labor camps, by any chance?" Val asked.

"Yes, in a labor camp. After my mother's death, he tried to solace himself and took refuge in reading philosophy. He was a high school teacher," Mişu said, "and I don't know how it happened, but he fell in with dialectical materialism and shortly became a lecturer at one of the Party's political schools. To his misfortune, he got involved in one of the often-recurring ideological struggles among the leaders of the day and during the next purge was arrested as a deviationist from the Party line. After a summary trial, he was sent to Năvodari by the sea, one of the worst forced-labor camps, where the average life of a detainee was less than six months. There he came up with the unheard-of idea of organizing a 'Marxist' union among inmates. During the repression that followed, he was roughly handled and died during torture, refusing to acknowledge being a Zionist spy and an Anglo-American agent. His conviction forever marked me as the scion of a people's enemy."

"I am surprised they didn't put you in jail too," Lia said.

"That I owe to my mother's older sister. As I was still underage, she adopted me, changing my name. There were seven more children in my adoptive family, some already married and with children of their own. Whenever I had to present my autobiography, it made for a lot of writing, and the bureaucrats always asked me to make it shorter. They had no patience to read every minute detail about such a numerous family, so I never got to mention my adoption or my biological brother who had fled the country before my mother's death." Mişu paused. "Without a doubt, my aunt saved my life."

"My Aunt Sânziana also saved my life," Johnny said in a loud, aggressive voice. So far he had kept silent yet didn't neglect his glass, which he had lifted diligently to his mouth with the regularity of an automaton, emptying glass after glass. "But I couldn't save her life," he cried in a shrill voice, prey to what appeared to be a violent outburst of passion. "Nobody could save her! You guys hear me?

Nobody!" He looked deeply disturbed, and from swollen eyes, big tears began flowing down his ruddy face.

They surrounded him with soothing words, but their efforts were in vain. He was shaking and continued to shed torrents of tears. There was a strange manifestation of sudden hysteria about him.

"Let's give him another glass," Luca suggested, moved by his roommate's distress.

"You must be kidding," Mişu said. "This man doesn't need more alcohol. Water would be better, I think."

"Coffee would help. Stefan, make a strong coffee for Johnny, please," Lia said. "It is a pity we don't have some sodium bromide."

"There is still coffee left in the pot. I will add some Ness and warm it up."

"I don't need anything," Johnny shouted between sobs, still in an agitated state.

"What about if we all start to sing another carol?" Ana said. She wanted to look smart and confident in a crisis.

"Yes, let's sing. Let's be merry," said Val, for once in unison with his sister. In fact, Johnny's behavior scared him.

"I don't need anything. I don't want to hear carols again. I can't stand them. It breaks my heart. Leave me alone, please, guys," Johnny said imploringly, blowing his nose and wiping his reddened eyes with a big, vividly colored handkerchief he pulled out of his pocket.

"Here, drink this. I made a good coffee for you." Stefan gave him a hot mug. "You don't have to drink it all if you don't want to. Even a little will make you feel better. Come on, take a sip, man."

Johnny, somewhat calmed, took the mug with a trembling hand and after a few gulps stopped weeping, grimacing at the bitterness of Stefan's concoction. He looked obviously impressed with the concern shown by the people gathered around him. "Sorry for that, folks," he said. "It happens every Christmas. I cannot prevent it."

They relaxed and did their best to assure Johnny that everything was all right.

"The carols are making me ill. The emotion is stronger than me," he apologetically said. "My Aunt Sânziana died on a Christmas

Eve, you see, and her tragedy also began on another Christmas Eve many years ago . . . You must think I am drunk or crazy. I am not. Perhaps I drank a little more that usual, but my mind is still clear. My heart is paining. If you can bear with me and listen, you will understand."

"Go ahead. We still have plenty of wine, and Stefan has good brandy. Every one is eager to listen to you," Luca said.

"By all means, go ahead if that makes you feel better," Stefan agreed.

"I was born at the end of the war, in a village in northern Transylvania," Johnny began. "What I know about the postwar years comes mostly from stories later told to me by Aunt Sânziana, who for a long time I thought was my mother. In reality, she was my father's youngest sister. She was beautiful. Of eleven children, she was the only one with milky skin and fine auburn hair, the color of old gold. She was tall, slim as a reed, and also had big, clear blue eyes. Villagers who remembered my aunt in her prime told me what an unforgettable appearance she made at their dances. When she married, shortly before the beginning of the last war, she must have been in her late twenties or early thirties.

"Aunt Sânziana's was a marriage of love. Uncle Ion, her good-looking husband, was the single child of a widow. His family, impoverished following the untimely death of Ion's father in the First World War, was descended from good stock. For that reason, both families strongly opposed their marriage. You probably know how villagers think about matrimony, always sizing up the dowry. His mother wanted Ion to take a richer wife in order to buy back their lost lands. My people pressed Sânziana to choose a well-off husband, which would have increased her wealth. Nothing could, however, prevent Ion and Aunt Sânziana from getting married. And after a long, bitter feud among the two families, they got their way.

"Uncle Ion had no land to speak of. He inherited, though, a little house and a small butcher's business, which produced modest but steady earnings. After marrying Sânziana, he began rearing sheep on the side and soon became quite successful at that. The new venture produced enough money for the young family to live well, and their first years of married life were blissful. Many things changed after the Hungarians, supported by Nazi Germany, occupied several Transylvanian counties, including ours. The occupants confiscated Ion's flock, and the butchery business declined under drastically enforced restrictions on meat consumption.

"The situation became worse the next year when the Germans attacked the Soviet Union. Luckily, Romanians from the occupied counties didn't get drafted into the Hungarian army and stayed at home for the entire duration of the hostilities. Despite their alien status, several villagers—especially the better-off ones who had good horses or oxen—were commandeered with their teams of animals for transportation deep into the battlefields, and some never came back. Ion wasn't among them, and he survived the war.

"Our village was liberated by the Romanian and Russian armies after more than four years of occupation. The freedom and the promised peace were welcomed with boundless joy, which soon proved to be unfounded. Life didn't return to normal as expected. On the contrary, new privations were added to those imposed during the war, while people were slowly torn apart by the internal conflicts the ascension of communism brought upon them.

"Numerous Red Army units were stationed in Romania after the war, and Uncle Ion somehow managed to do business with the Russians. He sold them horses and cattle collected from the neighboring villages, activities that required him to make frequent trips to the nearby town where the closest railway station and a Red Army's shipping point were located.

"On Christmas Eve 1945, he had just concluded one of his best deals ever and was loaded with money. Ion bought a few items they lacked in the village and a present for his wife and, before returning home, had a drink with a couple of friends. The talk of the town was the massive deportation of Germans carried out by the Soviets. Train after train, overloaded with civilians from the areas of Germany under Russian occupation, passed day and night nonstop through the town's station. They were destined for slave labor in the Soviet Union, it was rumored. Uncle Ion would not have believed such nonsense unless he had seen it with his own eyes, he told the company. He personally knew several Russians with whom he did business. They were good men, not slave drivers. He was ready to bet a fair sum of money that the whole story was a lie.

"The group of friends drank a little more, perhaps too much for their own good. Warmed by liquor and in an argumentative mood, they decided to walk to the railway station together to watch the trains. There were other locals as well hanging about in the station.

"Uncle Ion was still debating with his friends when a long train pulled in and stopped at the platform. There were many boxcars, the type used for shipping cattle, coupled together with a railway coach for passengers and pulled by a shabby locomotive. Russian military men got off the coach and went along the train, here and there opening the heavy sliding doors. The boxcars were filled with people in various stages of exhaustion, a ragged and miserable-looking crowd. The soldiers, working in pairs, extracted about two dozen lifeless, naked bodies, which they dragged roughly and dropped into the field bordering the railway tracks. Those appeared to be dead. The survivors began crying for water.

"Some of the onlookers, including my uncle, hurried to fetch pails of water for the wretched. But the Russian soldiers stood in their way, blocking access to the train, and threatened to shoot them. Everyone was arguing heatedly when an officer, who was watching from a window of the coach, barked a short order, which instantly stirred his men into action. In a swift move, the Russians rounded up a bunch of Romanians—Ion among them—and, before anyone could realize what was happening, pushed them into a couple of boxcars and locked the sliding doors. Immediately after that the soldiers boarded the coach, the locomotive whistled and the train drew out.

"That was the last anyone saw or heard of Uncle Ion for many years. My aunt tried to find out where he was taken, but nobody could say anything either regarding the destination of the transport or the whereabouts of the people on that ill-fated train. In fact, wherever Sânziana made inquiries, both Russian and Romanian officials derided her. They said that such shipments existed only in her imagination, although similar trains still ran for some time. She continued nagging the authorities without any result. Even Uncle Ion's Red Army connections couldn't help although they did some research of their own. After seven or eight years, if I remember well, Aunt Sânziana began, as is the custom in our village when someone dear dies, to wear only black and to pay masses at the church for the repose of Uncle Ion's soul. Even after her lands were taken to the kolkhoz, a time when she became poor, my aunt continued to give alms on his behalf to the poorer people of the village.

"I was four or five years old when the communists launched their campaign for the collectivization of agriculture. None of the farm owners wanted to join in the proposed kolkhoz because that meant losing their lands and animals, being forced to hand them over to the care of an imposed administration of Party bureaucrats. When indoctrination and threats didn't work, the securitate was brought in and through heavy beatings managed to 'convince' several weaklings to sign on.

"The very stubborn, including my father, were exiled together with their families to the badlands in the heart of Bărăgan, the southern prairies. The army was brought in the middle of the night. The soldiers kicked and smashed the door, and my people had half an hour to pack up before being marched under heavy guard to the train station. I was asleep, and in the confusion that followed, everyone had forgotten about me. That was my luck. In the morning, I woke up in my Aunt Sânziana's house. And from that day on, she was the one who took care of me. With the passing of time, the memory of my true mother faded, her waning image replaced by that of my aunt, who was a permanent, loving presence. Twenty or more years later, some of the exiled people were allowed to come back. By then I already knew the truth about my parents and awaited their return in vain. Apparently, they had never reached the badlands. The rumor had it that they were in a group of so-called saboteurs, whom the soldiers were ordered to shoot when passing through a forest and who were buried somewhere in a common, unmarked grave.

"Uncle Ion returned when I was thirteen, although nobody except Aunt Sânziana believed that would ever happen. Deep in her heart, she never lost hope of seeing him again. Ion was awfully changed and looked like a ghost to the people who had known him before, like someone risen from among the dead. He was a shadow of himself. The handsome, athletic, and energetic man of his young adulthood was gone. Now, at forty, he was worn out, weak, and sick, with white hair and yellow skin, in much worse shape than many old village men in their late seventies.

"Uncle Ion's miraculous return made him an object of local interest. Relatives and neighbors would gather to listen to his stories of suffering and survival. Some believed him, some thought he had made those stories up. The Party's men branded him a reactionary who dared to discredit the great Soviet motherland. My aunt couldn't stop crying every time she heard him storytelling and always continued crying long after he finished. Sometimes, she even got up during the night and cried quietly until morning. I know that because as a boy, those tales scared the pants off me. And quite often, my sleep was troubled by bad dreams. My aunt was always awake, ready to soothe me when I woke up from a nightmare. Even now the memory of some of the horrors he went through makes my skin crawl.

"My uncle's sufferings had started as soon as his mind, faced with the terrible reality of being abducted, emerged from the alcohol's vapors. He found himself in a cattle car in which about forty-two people of both sexes and all ages were crammed together like sardines. At the beginning, there wasn't even enough space for everyone to sit on the floor, let alone sleep. During the trip, however, people died frequently, making room for those who remained. For days in a row, they were given virtually no food—and then a few small salted fish and dry moldy bread would be thrown on the floor. To make life even more miserable, water was given only sparingly. There was a hole in the bottom of the car to be used by everyone as a toilet. It was a slow train that would stop quite often to wait for the passing of faster transports and passenger trains, and they traveled for about two months without being allowed to leave the boxcars.

"What scared my uncle the most was how easily people died. There was another man from our village with him named Traian.

He was what we call a *baci*, a respected senior shepherd, one who would manage big flocks, some of his own and some entrusted to him by other villagers. Traian was in his fifties, a strong character and quite physically fit. He spent most of his time in the high mountains, managing the flocks, making various kinds of fine cheese or other milk derivatives, and directing the many shepherds working under him. The man was a free spirit, used to breathing clean air, eating fresh food, and enjoying the vast horizons one can find only in alpine pastures. Forced confinement in the boxcar and its claustrophobic atmosphere maddened Traian. And at the first opportunity, when the soldiers came to take out the dead, he forced an escape.

"The Russians easily caught and subsequently beat Traian to a pulp with rifle butts before throwing him back in the car. There was a doctor among the Germans who did what he could and revived him. After he regained consciousness, the *baci* refused to eat or drink and spent his remaining days staring blankly at the empty wooden wall. He didn't want to talk to anyone and rapidly lost all his strength. In less than ten days, he was gone. In my uncle's words, 'he melted away like a burning candle.'

"Hans, an older German who spoke Romanian, soon befriended my uncle. The two stayed together and when food was distributed shared whatever they could put their hands on. Being stronger and younger, Uncle Ion always managed to grab more than his new friend yet never kept more than an equal share for himself. Hans liked Ion for his selflessness and in return taught him many useful things. The German had been a mountain climber and hunter and knew countless little techniques for survival in hostile environments, which in the years to come saved Ion's life repeatedly. Unfortunately, the old man had diabetes. And without medication, his health quickly deteriorated. One night while talking to my uncle, he closed his eyes and, without any word of warning, died. 'Just like that,' said my uncle, snapping his fingers, 'one moment he was with me, and the next was gone. That easy.'

"It was a harsh winter, and unknown to my uncle and his fellow prisoners, the transport was destined for the Komi Autonomous Soviet Socialist Republic in Russia's far north. It was freezing during most of the trip, and old people and small children got sick and died. Sometimes, the dead would be taken out by the soldiers and left on the side of the train tracks. Other times when it was too cold, the soldiers didn't bother to inspect the train, and the prisoners just stacked the frozen bodies in a corner of the boxcar. When that happened, there was always an awful fight among the prisoners to get the clothes of the dead. The car was miserably filthy, and the hole in floor froze solid, so they had to open new holes with their bare hands in order to get rid of their waste. At one point, they were transferred onto barges and taken along several rivers partially covered with ice. The last hundred kilometers were completed on foot, the convoy being escorted at gunpoint through blinding blizzards. The entire trip lasted almost three months, and less than half of the people in that transport survived to the end.

"The convoy's final destination was the coal mines of Vorkuta, about two hundred kilometers north of the Arctic Circle, a desolate forced labor camp isolated from the rest of the world by vast stretches of tundra and unbridged, big rivers emptying into the Arctic Ocean. The nearest significant city, Arkhangelsk, was about a thousand kilometers southwest. But my uncle wasn't a learned man, and he had never heard about either place.

"From the twenty-five Romanians initially rounded up, only seven arrived at the assignment center. They tried in vain to explain to the commanding officer that their presence was a mistake, claiming to be Romanians, not Germans. The only result they obtained was the services of an interpreter. This was a fellow countryman from Basarabia, a province of Romania occupied by the Soviets in 1939 soon after they and Nazi Germany divided Poland. Since then entire Romanian villages had been forcibly relocated to the Soviet Arctic while Russians settled in their homes according to Stalin's plan to denationalize the occupied province. The translator advised the newcomers to avoid the work in the taiga, the swampy coniferous forest where chances of survival were almost nil, and to volunteer for the mines instead. Although mining wasn't a bonanza either, at least it was windless and warm underground regardless of the season. Ion went for it.

"The work in the mines was exhausting, dangerous, and without reward. My uncle was teamed with a German and made to cut coal with pickaxes in galleries where the ceiling was so low that they had to crawl on their elbows and knees and so narrow that they couldn't turn around. The ventilation was insufficient, there were no safety measures or adequate equipment, and they routinely worked stark naked. Luckily, his mate was a university educated mining engineer whose specialty was coal mining. He taught John how to protect himself and trained him to work efficiently. Yet no amount of training could replace proper food, good clothing, and the basic amenities they never received.

"Vorkuta is a place where the winter lasts nine months or more. During the cold season, the temperature oscillates around minus forty degrees Celsius, though occasionally falls much lower. For several weeks, the sun is hidden under the horizon. A pitch-dark night replaces the day, and harsh winds never stop blowing. Having been captured in the summer, the prisoners, except the Romanians, had no proper winter clothes. Their boots were in bad shape and full of holes. They were forced to work fourteen-hour shifts or longer in the forest or underground and were fed starvation rations consisting of crushed salted fish and a small frozen potato. At night, they slept without mattresses on the floor of their barracks, covered with their own jackets. To avoid having their boots stolen by other prisoners, they used their boots in place of the pillows they didn't have.

"At the mines, prisoners died every day of illnesses, hunger, and cold, shot by guards, or killed underground in work-related accidents. In the winter, the corpses were piled up in deep snow. When summer came, the permafrost thawed, and a bulldozer covered what remained of the bodies with mud.

"In time, my uncle gradually lost all his teeth from lack of vitamins, and his body was covered with ulcers that never healed. He lost his last three molars when a drunken Soviet soldier repeatedly punched him in the face during a national holiday. The military got generous rations of vodka on such occasions, and in order to shake their boredom, they used prisoners as punching bags or as unwitting sparring partners in mock boxing matches. He didn't mind that soldier's brutality, Ion used to say when telling the story, because his molars were rotten anyway, eaten by cavities and infected, and there were no dentists in the camp to care for the prisoners' teeth. Not long after, probably toward the end of his detention, though Ion didn't remember which year it happened, he got sick. It started as a benign flu, got worse by the hour, and eventually he passed out while working in the mine. When he had temporarily regained consciousness after several days, he couldn't speak, suffered from an atrocious headache, and his left side was paralyzed. Ion knew he was really in bad shape because, as was common knowledge in Vorkuta, only dying people were given a rough mattress filled with wood shavings and he found himself lying on one of those rare items.

"The camp's physician, a Russian woman doctor, and the German doctor were called to attend to my uncle. While the woman had a soft spot for Romanians, she hated the German's guts, a feeling duly reciprocated. The Russian and the German agreed on one thing, however, when they diagnosed Ion's illness as encephalitis and declared him a goner. An epidemic had raged for some time through the camp—there were no drugs, and the infirmary was just a poorly heated, overcrowded wooden hut, which the Russians called *izba*. Thus they left Ion on his mattress in the main gallery of the mine in the hope he would soon die. There was nothing they could have done for him anyway. Eventually he lapsed into a coma.

"There was a Polish Jesuit priest in the camp, a prisoner of faith, who also worked in the mine. Occasionally, he would stealthily celebrate a mass for those who he knew were still secretly practicing their Christian faith. Ion, a churchgoer in his normal life, was, like all the people in my village, a Catholic of the Byzantine rite. He was acquainted with the Jesuit and used to frequent the forbidden religious gatherings the Pole organized. Uncle Ion couldn't remember but was later told how the priest came after shifts to attend to him. Every day, the priest brought him some soup or tea and water to drink and spent several nights in a row tirelessly wetting his forehead and limbs with a humid cloth, in an attempt to control Ion's temperature. When he got tired, he just sat beside the mattress and prayed.

"What my uncle seemed to remember most clearly from that difficult period was a singular hallucination. He dreamed of Sânziana crying in our village church. He watched her praying fervently for some time as if unaware of his presence. Then she turned, looked hard at her husband, and said, 'Don't die on me, Ion, for God has promised to bring you back home.' My uncle was then surrounded by an overpowering bright light, which hurt his eyes. He closed and opened his eyes several times to avoid the pain. And there was his friend, the priest, smiling at him. 'Your fever is gone,' he told Ion.

"Ion's recovery took a long time. He was exceedingly weak, pestered by recurrent headaches and harrowing memory lapses. His understanding was slow, his speech was impaired, and he couldn't walk as before. My uncle dragged his left foot and was left with a crippling limp ever after. There was no special diet or rehabilitation treatment for convalescents in Vorkuta, but the good Russian doctor moved Ion to the infirmary and after two weeks, when he would have had to go back to work, kept him as an orderly. The following summer, however, when the camp commander ordered the discharge of the sick regardless of their medical condition, he was sent back to the mine.

"If working in the mine had been difficult for Ion before, now it became a most wearisome task. His disabilities prevented him from fulfilling the daily norm no matter how hard he tried and made him prone to accidents and illness. The following spring, coming out hot and sweaty from the mine during one of the unexpected equinox blizzards, my uncle contracted a chill that affected his lungs. He developed a lasting fever and a persistent hack, which didn't let him sleep overnight. Everyone was convinced his death was only days away.

"It was then that, under high orders, all the surviving Romanians were transferred from Vorkuta to a sort of medical center in Syktyvkar, the capital city of Komi. There they were intensively fed, medicated with pills and injections, dressed in cheap civilian clothes, and allowed to grow a normal hairstyle. Initially, they were a bunch of gaunt and sickly men. After the treatment, their looks changed enormously. They became not fat or stronger, but puffed out. My uncle felt bloated and swore the Russians had injected him with air. In fact, nobody knew what kind of drugs they were given. Yet for the time being, his cough subsided and he felt better.

"After three weeks, they were herded to the train station, rushed into boarding a railway coach, and sent under light guard to an unknown destination. At several stations on the way, they were joined by other small groups of countrymen, prisoners like themselves. A rumor about their imminent liberation, which began circulating back and forth along the train, was mostly received with cautious disbelief as the guards neither confirmed nor denied it. The prisoners were encouraged though by being fed the same rations as the soldiers and considered this to be a good omen. The landscape they saw through the windows became more tamed and temperate every day. After a few more days, the train arrived at a station built high on a riverbank. The accompanying Soviet soldiers quickly regrouped on the station's platform, and the train drew out unguarded, rolling slowly across a truss bridge. On the opposite bank, they saw, for the first time in many years, the Romanian flag fluttering in the wind. Many of those hardened men, including himself, couldn't stop their tears, my uncle said.

"The day after Uncle Ion's return, my aunt began feeding and caring for him with selfless generosity and patience. She seemed oblivious to his decrepit state, and in her opinion, only the best was good enough for him. During the years of my childhood, she had a spinning wheel and used to spin yarns and threads for villagers during the long winter nights. From spring to fall, she also worked on a small vegetable garden from which she sold produce in town. Now Aunt Sânziana doubled her output in order to feed three of us. 'God has answered my prayers. It is my turn to show that I deserve such a gift,' she used to say. And from the first light of the day until late into the night, she went tirelessly about her chores.

"Sânziana also took her husband to a doctor in town for a thorough medical examination. Sadly, the list of Ion's illnesses was quite a long one. On top of the usual consequences of encephalitis, he suffered from advanced pulmonary tuberculosis, rheumatic fever, arthritis, uremia, and a host of other minor disorders I can't remember. Painful boils in various stages of infection ulcerated his skin. His knees and elbows were covered in thick calluses that would often crack, bleeding and suppurating. Ion would be dead in less than six months, the doctor told my aunt after two weeks of tests. Although Ion was in such bad shape and there wasn't too much hope, the doctor suggested having him hospitalized in a sanatorium.

"To be sent to a sanatorium, one needed the recommendation of the Party's local organization, which was denied to Ion. Too smart to waste her time fighting hostile bureaucracy, my aunt made arrangements for him to spend the summer with the shepherds instead. She paid them to give him only the best food and twice a week climbed into the mountains where the shepherds pastured their flocks in order to check if her husband was well cared for in their camp. In the fall, my uncle climbed down to the village in much better health as some of his minor ailments were gone. Undeterred by the doctor's prognosis, Sânziana tenderly nursed John, administering daily the prescribed medication and feeding him well. In September that year, when I went to Timisoara to study at a professional school, both of them looked younger and happier, almost like two newlyweds.

"I was away at school for the next three years, with the exception of the summer holidays. In the meantime, Ion didn't die, got better, and even began to earn a little money as a casual butcher. Working in the fields was out of the question for him, and so was the permanent practice of his old profession. Although his occasional wages didn't count toward much, they managed to live modestly with my aunt's earnings and even to send me some money as a supplement to my meager bursary. Once in a while, however, he would slaughter the odd animal illegally and then sell it in town on the black market, venture that always brought a hefty profit. Yet he couldn't do it too often and had to be very careful as informers watched him closely.

"I was in the fourth and final year of my professional training when Uncle Ion died. Only a couple of weeks earlier, I had received a letter and money from him. The tone of the letter was cheerful and optimistic, assuring me that he and my aunt were doing well.

He had, of course, his bad days as one would expect of someone in his condition. He didn't work too much and sometimes spent a week or so just hanging around the house, resting. But we were used to those bouts of weakness and his awful migraines, and nothing had pointed toward such a fast end. I rushed home for the funeral and found my aunt in deep mourning. Her life and world had been Ion, and now all that had crumbled. She cried and lamented all day long until exhaustion got the better of her. Then she collapsed on a chair, silenced, unable to do anything for a long while, the tears still running down her face.

"My uncle's death happened like this. One evening, he walked to the village store to buy lamp oil and matches. Earlier in the day, they had brought in a load of alcoholic beverages, and several people were already in various stages of advanced drunkenness. A couple of Party toughs from among those revellers followed Ion when he left the store, caught up with him in a dark lane, and started a fight. He struggled to escape but was no match for two young, strong, and healthy men. He cried for help, and more people got involved. It was a moonless night, and there was confusion. And by the time the militia arrived, he was lying on the ground unconscious. Ion had been stabbed repeatedly and was bleeding profusely. Both the resident doctor and nurse were at a meeting in town, so there was no qualified medical help at hand. The neighbors carried him home where he died during the night from multiple internal hemorrhages. I was not utterly surprised about this outcome as sooner or later, that would have been his fate anyhow. Ion was too outspoken, and his very existence was a continuous embarrassment to those in power. Eventually, there was an inquiry and a trial which, under pressure from higher authority, ended with the acquittal of the two rogues who had killed him. It was my uncle's fault, the judge decided, disregarding the depositions of numerous witnesses.

"After we buried Ion, I had to go back to school. It was the end of April, and in the summer of that year, we had our final examinations. Graduation was pretty close, and there were busy times ahead waiting for me. My aunt was sick with grieving, so I had to leave her in the care of some relatives. Although well looked after, Sânziana didn't recover as expected. She was in bed, taken ill, my relatives wrote me late in June. And so far, the village doctor couldn't pinpoint what was ailing her.

"With her illness in mind, I didn't lose too much time in the big city. As soon as the school year finished and we got our diplomas, I returned without delay to the village. Instead of the aunt I knew so well, Sânziana was now a strange-looking, emaciated old woman. She was utterly depressed, ate almost nothing, and confessed to me her longing to die. In her mind, only in death could she be reunited with her beloved husband. It broke my heart to see her so despondent.

"Together with my relatives, we decided that something urgently had to be done. While in school, I had done a few odd jobs for a physician from Timisoara, the cousin of a cousin, a big shot in the Party. With his help, we managed to put Aunt Sânziana in a special hospital. They kept her under treatment for almost three months. It was a good hospital. And after first feeding her intravenously and then treating her with an intensive cure of vitamins, anti-depressants, and what not, she began to recover.

"I forgot to tell you that with our diplomas, all of us were appointed and sent to work in the industry. I was assigned as a shift maintenance electrician in one of Timisoara's factories and for the time being lived in a worker's dormitory, noisy and crowded. Luckily, the dormitory was close to the hospital. As a beginner, my shifts were often longer than normal, but I spent all my free time with Sânziana. It was a late, mild fall. And weather permitting, I always took her for an easy walk in the hospital garden. If she got tired, we would sit on a bench and talk. She enjoyed my visits, and staying closely in touch seemed to help her get better.

"It was toward the end of her hospitalization when the last misfortune hit us. A debate about the need for new stables for horses had never died in our village since the beginning of the kolkhoz, the issue resurfacing ever so often with new intensity. Usually, it would make a storm in a teacup and then soon be gone without any practical consequence. When this time it happened again, the mayor and the Party organization decided to immediately start the work. The chosen building site included several villagers' properties, including Aunt Sânziana's house and garden. Rezoning of land was no problem, getting rid of the habitations was. After five constitutional changes, the ownership of land was assumed in its entirety by the state, but houses in the rural areas still belonged to their private, pre-socialist era owners. Despite the ownership drawback, the administration called in a specialized team, and the dwellings were demolished in no time. The houses were more than a century old, and their value was estimated based on a high rate of depreciation, the result being ridiculously low. As a consequence, the cost of the demolition work, the cleaning and removing of debris totaled and charged to the ex-owners couldn't be covered by the amount paid to them for their dwellings. In the end, the wretched owners, my aunt included, were left without homes and indebted to the state.

"I did my best to keep Aunt Sânziana in the dark about that matter, but it was to no avail. The authorities wanted to maintain an appearance of legality, and a clerk was sent to the hospital to get her signature on a heap of official papers. His intrusion stirred my aunt into a frenzy, and subsequently, her situation worsened. She was seized with a cerebral fever, which left her, after a week or so, exhausted and suffering from recurrent fits of mild insanity. Generally, my aunt was the same reasonable and kind person as before. Occasionally though, with a sudden switch of subject, she would withdraw into an imaginary world, oblivious for hours to what was going on around her in real life. That nowhere-world was populated with the dead people she loved, including Uncle Ion. And no effort could bring her back until the crisis passed by itself. When they discharged her from the hospital, the doctor said this was a transient episode and would eventually go away in time. Sadly, it didn't.

"Because she was homeless, I arranged temporary lodging for both of us with a widow of our acquaintance. The woman had two extra rooms into which we moved, I in a sort of small vestibule and my aunt into the bedroom connected to it. As Aunt Sânziana needed attention around the clock, living together was for the time being a dire necessity. For the same reason, I left Timisoara, taking a job in the little town near our village although that meant commuting everyday by bus.

"That year, the mild autumn was followed by an even milder winter, and the month of December was unusually wet. There were several days when, returning home, I found my aunt wandering the empty grounds where her house used to be, drenched with rain and talking into the wind to the shadows haunting her sick mind. The people building the stables knew Sânziana well and were kind to her. She was harmless and didn't interfere with their work, so they didn't mind her walking about. Sometimes, they brought her home, concerned about her getting lost. I repeatedly asked the widow to keep a closer eye on my aunt, but it was impossible to stop her going out when such a crisis hit. Days before Christmas, when a sudden cold spell swept through our area, she was caught in the ensuing storm and, beaten by the sleeting drizzle, couldn't find her way home. With our host, the widow, and a couple of relatives, we searched for hours in the frigid night before finding my aunt shaking and shivering, entangled in the bushy marsh by the creek that ran behind what was once her garden. We brought her home with a high fever and wheezing.

"That night, Sânziana developed a rasping cough and repeatedly expectorated blood. In the morning, she was unconscious, and the village doctor who saw her diagnosed pneumonia. Three days later, after another outburst of severe bloody expectoration, the doctor changed his initial diagnosis to galloping consumption. My aunt apparently had had tuberculosis even before since she contracted it from her husband. Now the sickness had aggravated, and she had only a few days to live—I was told—and there was nothing the medicine could do for her.

"I took unpaid leave to be at her side, hoping in my ignorance to prove the doctor wrong. She was everything to me, and no sacrifice was too big. I nursed her day and night. And during her rare conscious moments, we would talk about our beloved, so violently gone. That was how I learned precious things about my parents and acquired a deeper understanding of her special relationship with Uncle Ion. Alas, too often, her hallucinations and spells of absentmindedness shadowed those special moments.

"It was amazing how fast she wasted away. Sânziana had lost so much weight that on Christmas Eve I could lift her only with one hand. Since Uncle Ion's death, my aunt had never eaten enough and in her last days lived mostly on fluids. That afternoon, although gasping for breath, she insisted upon being seated and dressed. I called the widow to help her change into one of those traditional folk costumes she loved consisting of a heavily embroidered blouse; a white, richly pleated skirt; and colorful woolen aprons. She also tied a flowered head kerchief over her neatly combed hair, now almost white. With all her exhaustion and illnesses, she still had, even in that advanced state of decline, a certain dignified beauty.

"The carol singers came after dark, as is the custom, and Sânziana asked me to let them in. After the choir finished its repertoire, she prompted me to present the singers with gifts prepared in advance. There were a few children, a couple of teenagers, and an adult in that group. And they were so pleased with our presents that they decided to sing a few more songs outside under the window. It was beautiful. They didn't stop singing 'Wake Up Brothers, Do Not Sleep' even as they walked to the next door neighbor's house. My aunt was feverish and tired, so I suggested she lie down. 'No,' she said, visibly moved by the lyrics, 'I want to hear this last one up to the end.'

"When the singing stopped, Aunt Sânziana became suddenly agitated and tried to leave the bed. I don't understand how she did it, but somehow, she managed to stand as if magically animated by the soft tune. 'Mother, mother, don't go!' she imploringly cried, her blue eyes shinning wildly. 'Ion, my dear, wait for me, I am coming. Don't leave me alone again. Please wait, wait . . .' Her face was transfigured, displaying a mixture of heartbreaking sadness and hopeful happiness. I can swear that she really saw those people. For me, it was the most harrowing experience in my entire life. Then in a trice, she lost her balance, as if whatever power had brought her up had suddenly vanished. I rushed to keep her from falling. Unfortunately, everything happened too fast, and she collapsed lifeless on the bed. Before I could catch her . . . My aunt stopped breathing and was dead . . ."

With teary eyes, Johnny ended his story on a note of despair. He was crying again, though more subdued than before.

"Don't cry, my friend," Stefan said. "You did more for your aunt than anyone would have expected. Life is like that. We all are born to die." He felt pity and concern for his countryman. Deep inside, he was convinced that something was wrong with Johnny. He was either suffering from depression, or perhaps the circumstances of his life had made him overly hypersensitive to the point of sickness. Stefan couldn't say what was the trouble, but he hadn't ever seen such a sorrowful individual.

The man didn't answer, attempting to control his feelings. The others, touched by his suffering, preferred to remain silent. There was a momentary lull outside the door in the usually noisy camp. Only Johnny's discreet nose-blowing, his restrained sighs, and the dry scratching of a match as Luca lit a cigarette disturbed the quiet. Carina came out from her corner where she was sleeping on the blanket and stopped beside Stefan, her ears pricked up. She touched his hand with her moist nose and looked into his eyes.

"Carina, sit down!" Stefan commanded in a subdued voice. She didn't do what she was told, so he held the spaniel by the collar, gently forcing her to lie down. Out of the blue, there was a knock at the door that startled the entire company. The dog contracted, ready to jump.

"Who can it be so late?" Lia whispered.

"I don't know. It is not late, really. It is not even ten o'clock," Stefan said. "Who's there?" he shouted. "Come in!"

The door cautiously opened, and three young Bulgarian sailors—Sasha, Dimitar, and Georgi—walked in solemnly, singing a strange and melodious song. They had pleasant voices and sang with feeling in what appeared to be their language. Sasha was carrying a platter loaded with slices of cake, figs, apples, and oranges and topped by a small green branch of fir adorned with red ribbons. The Romanians had briefly met the young men in the English class.

Having recently jumped ship in a Greek port, they had been brought to the camp only weeks before Christmas.

"We saw the Christmas tree and heard the carols. It is our custom to visit friends and bring presents on Christmas Eve. We also sing carols and enjoy company—we hope you don't mind," Sasha said after they finished the song. He ceremoniously offered the platter to Stefan, while Dimitar and Georgi stood in the middle of the room smiling.

"Merry Christmas, brothers in faith, and God bless you all," Sasha said and bowed.

Mişu offered Sasha his chair, and the other two guests were seated on the bed. As there were no more glasses, Lia hurriedly washed three coffee mugs, and Stefan poured wine for everyone. Ana brought cookies, sweetbread, and cake. The newcomers sang another Bulgarian carol with the same solemnity, and then relaxed, tasting the wine and the sweets.

"Shall we sing a Romanian carol for them?" Val asked his mother.

"For God's sake, no! We've had enough sobs this evening. Play a tape instead. Nat King Cole will do," Lia said. She loved Cole's carols and didn't mind hearing them again and again.

"We already ran that tape five times. It is boring, Mama."

"All right, then, play whatever you like. Why are you asking me if you have already made up your mind?"

"Oh, Mama. I love you so much. You know that." He gave her a mock offended look. "By the way. May I have one more piece of cake?"

Lia turned a deaf ear to his cheekiness, convinced that he would do the opposite of what she had suggested. As if answering her thoughts, Kenny Rogers's distinctly intimate tone boomed into the room with the maximum power that the little tape recorder was able to deliver, making the windows rattle slightly.

"Val, turn that thing down, please," his mother cried, her face screwed up by pain. The music died instantly.

"We like that song," Sasha said, "is it American?"

"It is American, and we like it too," Stefan answered. "Not so loud though . . . Can you set it at a more bearable volume, Val? We are not deaf."

The music could be heard again, this time as a whisper. "Is this low enough?" Val asked, giving his father a big mischievous smile.

"You can make it a bit louder, if your father agrees," Luca suggested.

"Of course I do. My boy knows very well what is proper. Only sometimes, he likes to play stupid."

They drank another round and listened spellbound while Kenny Rogers sang with those subtle inflections he uses like no one else to get across his sensible reflections on life and his simple healthy wisdom. He sounded believable and moving, reaching straight into their hearts. The lyrics of his songs were evocative of that beloved America they had learned about from books and movies. An America that, without their knowing, was fast disappearing,

"Ah," Dimitar exclaimed when the tape ended and the tape recorder was shut off, "America is great. I love America."

"That is where you are going?" Lia asked.

"Yes, I am going to America," the young man said.

"What do you want to do in America, Dimitar?" Mişu asked.

"I will buy a big farm and grow vegetables."

"I am going to America too," Georgi said. "I will buy a ranch. I want to be a cowboy. Farming is too hard work for me. I want a ranch because cowboys have a lot of fun." He mimed drawing a pistol out of its holster and shooting an imaginary target. "Bang, bang."

"I would like to be a cowboy too," Ana said.

"You guys must be rich. Do you already have enough money to buy land in America?" Luca asked.

"Nooo," Sasha said, a huge smile splitting his face. "They don't have money. None of us has any money."

"We will work hard for two, three years and buy land," Dimitar said. He seemed quite confident.

"Yes," Georgi said, "two, three years, maybe four, enough to save money for ranch."

"From what I was told, land is not that cheap in the States," Mişu said.

"Where you go?" Dimitar asked.

"Canada."

"Canada? Land more cheap in Canada than in America."

"I don't think so, and—as I also heard—well-paid jobs are hard to find nowadays," Mişu said.

"What you want do in Canada?" Sasha asked.

"I used to be a teacher of physics in Romania. I would like to find a job in that line, if possible. Who knows if I could . . ."

"Mişu, don't you have a brother in the States? Why are you going to Canada, then?" Luca asked.

"It is my French. My English is not good. I speak French fluently, and for a teaching job, knowledge of the language is paramount. Canada is bilingual—they speak both French and English there."

"Our English not good," Sasha said, "we will learn."

"Yeah," Mişu said, "you are much younger, and people your age learn easier than old boys like me."

"You're right," Stefan agreed, "we are in the same boat."

"You sailors? You on the same boat?" Dimitar asked.

"No, my young friend," Mişu smiled condescendingly. "C'est une façon de parler—it is a way of saying that both of us are going to Canada for the same reason."

"Oh, I think you sailors and . . ."

"I won't buy land in Canada," Johnny said, inadvertently interrupting Dimitar, "because someone told me one cannot own land in Canada. One buys only the right to use it. The land always belongs to the government as it does now in communist Romania."

"No way. I cannot believe that," Luca said.

"It is true. They say that the land is the property of the crown, which means the government," Johnny said.

"Perhaps it belongs to the queen," Val said.

"Which queen?" Georgi asked.

"The queen of England."

"This is rubbish," Stefan said. "The private ownership of land is basic in any modern democracy. I don't believe that in the Free World, there is any country where the land belongs to the royalty or, as a matter of fact, to the government, except small portions assigned to military bases, railways, or highways."

"To own a big ranch in Canada is the dream of my life," Luca said. "The only thing that can stop me from buying one is the lack of money."

"Money is not a problem in Canada, the ownership of land is. I don't want to own just the right to use the land in a country where the government can take it from me at any time. Remember what happened to my aunt," Johnny raised his voice. Land ownership was obviously an issue that irritated him.

"Come on, Johnny. Don't get upset again. We don't know anything for sure. Wait until we are in Canada," Mişu said.

"Would you buy land in Canada?" Johnny asked.

"Well, it is not that simple," Mişu answered. "Right now, I don't have money. And I don't believe that in the years left to me until retirement, I will possibly save enough for such a venture. Even if that happens, it will be too late. Lastly, although becoming a farmer excited me once, now I hate even the thought of it."

"Why is that?" Johnny asked.

"Several years ago when I was younger, married, and more adventurous, my wife and I made plans to immigrate to Israel and work in a kibbutz. Then fate intervened, and I got so disgusted with the whole idea that my blood pressure goes up every time something reminds me those events," Mişu said.

"Excuse a woman's curiosity. Now that you have already remembered and your blood pressure is perhaps already up, would it be too much to ask what happened?" Lia said, "only, of course, if it is not too private a story to be told."

"You have been such a marvelous host that I cannot resist your request," Mişu said. "I only need a good shot from that old brandy your husband so generously shared with us before beginning my little story."

Mişu took the glass and emptied it with a swift jerk of his arm. "Ouf! This brandy is worth a million. It sets your blood pressure back," he said, putting the glass on the table with extreme care and looking around at his audience. "I will try to be short. When we got married, my wife had some relatives in Israel, and we decided to emigrate. To make things easier, I took her name before we began the usual paperwork. Although the State of Israel extended a generous hand to the people of Jewish descent willing to emigrate, even paying a per capita price for them to the Romanian government, getting visas was never an easy job. There were so many official steps to go through that required repeated visits to a special police office in charge of passports that it wasn't unusual for the entire process to take at least a couple of years or more. This is quite a long time, and without my knowledge—the husband is always the last to find out—my wife got involved with one of the officers We had almost gotten the passports approved when she divorced me. Afterward, she married that man, and they left Romania. The guy messed up my dossier before quitting his job, subsequently making my emigration impossible. I won't bore you with the details. The fact is I am here, fed up with dreams of a bucolic life style, and ready to go to Canada . . . May I have another shot of brandy, please?"

"Of course you may," Stefan said.

But there was only a little brandy left in the bottle, and Stefan divided it equally between his and Mişu's glass.

"Let's drink to the future and forget the past," Stefan said, "may all the good gather together, and all the bad be washed away." He felt mildly tipsy.

"Do you also want to buy a ranch in Canada, Stefan?" Mişu asked.

"He must," Ana said. "He had promised me a ranch and riding horses. Right, Dad?"

Faintly, they could hear in the distance the Ayia Praxedes's bells broadcasting to the world the birth of Jesus. It was midnight.

"Yes. I will buy a ranch, no doubt about that . . . First, I must work a couple of years to make enough money like each of you. Then I want to buy a small yacht and sail it around the world . . . I'll buy the ranch on my return before my early retirement."

Stefan had retained a childish streak in his mature years, which only manifested itself rarely when his defenses were weakened. It had been a long day; he was tired and had forgotten his recently celebrated birthday anniversary.

"I see . . ." Mişu murmured. "The Italians say life starts at forty. Nobody, however, has ever mentioned fifty . . ."

DISCIPLES OF HIPPOCRATES

It was now the end of January. The nights were still cool, but during the day, it was warm and pleasant. On the sunny empty fields leading to the nearby sheltered coves, which began to repopulate little by little with afternoon bathers, and on the wind-beaten escarpments bordering the never-tiring sea, solitary wild hyacinths and cyclamens had timidly bloomed overnight. Their refreshing vernal presence added intense splashes of pure color on the barren, dull ocher grounds ravaged by the winter's storms.

Responding to some secret impulses of nature, the fruits of the ornamental trees growing along the promenade had became fine golden oranges, inviting yet treacherous. Their enticing look notwithstanding, they tasted so bad that whoever was foolish enough to take a bite once would never try again. As nobody picked them, many of those oranges ended in the fermenting, smelly mash sprawled on the concrete slabs underneath, transforming every leisurely walk into a daring adventure.

Out in the country on the road to Marcopulos, in some of the better-sheltered gardens, beautifully colored early clematises occasionally put in almost unreal, astonishing appearances.

Springtime was everywhere in the air, and the news that Canadian authorities had granted Stefan's family landed immigrant status certainly made the promises of the season even more real.

Suddenly, the Romanians became busier with formalities and preparations, having to go to Athens sometimes to meet various officials or to buy—as their modest means permitted—things necessary for their future life. They enjoyed those trips enormously although there were more needs than money. The long-awaited opportunity was becoming a reality, albeit slowly, but its materialization gave them an exhilarating feeling that was difficult to explain in words. Every day was filled with excitement and, dazzled by the fast pace of the events, all four of them lived in a sort of dream too beautiful to be true.

On one of those unforgettable days, Stefan returned quite late from Voula, a small town on the road to Athens. To enter Canada, the spaniel needed a veterinary health certificate, and Theodoros had made arrangements with a veterinarian of his acquaintance to issue such a document. Thus after work, Stefan, instead of having dinner, drove Carina to the doctor's office for her appointment.

The days were still short, and it was already dark when he parked his Trabant in the usual spot under the locust tree and put the dog on leash. After all the fuss they had gone through, she deserved a walk to relax for the night.

It didn't take long to make Carina happy; but Stefan, who also felt the need to stretch his legs, gave her a complete tour of the main square as a bonus. The town was quiet and almost deserted at that hour, being too late for the moviegoers and too early for the taverns' patrons. He walked slowly, enjoying the peaceful atmosphere, the dog trotting at his side.

When they came back and entered the street between the school and the camp, he bumped against another man walking briskly in the opposite direction. After the first moment of confusion, they recognized each other and exchanged the excuses and greetings usual in such circumstances. The man was Boris Bernov, a Bulgarian physician and a fellow refugee. He was athletic with a sturdy build and wore his black hair rather short like a boxer. The doctor was, as always, dressed in an elegant dark suit.

"Mr. Stefan," he began after a short thoughtful silence, "I am really happy about this unexpected meeting because for some time, I have wanted to talk to you. Yesterday, you were away the whole day.

—

And earlier this afternoon, when I looked for you at the dormitory, your missis told me you would be late." A comely smile brightened the man's intelligent face, contrasting with his routinely cold, formal demeanor. "It seems that you, sir, never stay at home."

"Well," Stefan answered, "you have probably heard that Canada granted us landed immigrant visa. There are so many formalities to . . ."

"I know, I know. I already heard the good news," the doctor confirmed. "Congratulations. You must be quite busy, I imagine." He paused, carefully looked around to make sure nobody was listening, and continued in a more subdued voice. "That is actually what I wanted to talk about with you, sir."

They were under the street lamp, at the corner where the main building of the camp joined the courtyard's high concrete fence. Stefan stopped and looked inquisitively at Bernov. "When do you want to meet? Do you want to talk now?" he asked.

The dog absentmindedly continued her course, stretching the leash to the limit. "Sit down, Carina. Sit!" he ordered and pulled her back. The spaniel obediently sat on the sidewalk, stirring a minute cloud of dust and emitting a muffled sigh of canine protest.

"Yes, now, if that is okay with you. I would prefer, however, to have the chat in my room, not here. It would be much quieter. My wife and daughter went to a movie. There will be just the two of us, if you don't mind," the doctor explained.

"I don't mind," Stefan said without hesitation. "You must excuse me a few minutes though, because I must take the dog to our room first." In the excitement of the moment, he had forgotten his dinner. Bernov was an intriguing character and from the beginning of their acquaintance had puzzled Stefan. The doctor had previously worked for a number of years in Egypt or Sudan—on a government mission, it was rumored—and had defected at Athens airport when his superiors recalled him back to Bulgaria. In the camp, he and his family had kept themselves aloof. They always kept a reserved distance from the rest of refugee community and didn't even frequent the free English courses. Stefan couldn't remember speaking at length with any of them more than twice in six months, although they always exchanged cool, polite greetings. It could be interesting, even important, to hear what the doctor had to say.

The dog suddenly stood up without any apparent reason, attentively pricking up her ears, and began fretting and pulling on the leash. "See," Stefan pointed to the spaniel, "she is growing impatient."

"You can take the dog with you."

"No, no. It would be better to take her home," Stefan said as they began walking again along the high wall.

"Whatever suits you, sir. I will be waiting for you in the courtyard, then," Bernov agreed, apparently ready to accommodate Stefan's suggestion.

They walked slowly toward the camp's gate; but just before getting to it, the little narrow metallic door for pedestrians opened with a squeak, and Ana and Val came out, peering into the street. The spaniel, probably aware of their coming, hopped happily and enthusiastically pulled in their direction.

So that was what she was fretting about, Stefan thought. Although he had had her for over seven years since she was three months old, Carina always perplexed him with her never-failing mysterious ways of getting ahead-of-time, elusive warnings inaccessible to humans.

"Oh, Dad! Mama was concerned about you being so late," Ana said somewhat reproachfully.

Val held the door open until Bernov and their father had entered the courtyard while the dog jumped from one to another in a show of happiness.

"Good you are back. Mama was getting concerned," Val unobtrusively told his father. He sounded relieved to see Stefan. "Aren't you coming to the room?" the boy asked more loudly.

"No," Stefan answered, "Dr. Bernov has invited me for a chat. You take the dog with you—she's had her walk. Tell Mother that I will come home later."

The boy took the leash, yet Carina didn't want to leave without Stefan and looked at him with excited expectation. "Go with Val," he told her, "don't wait for me. Go, Carina!" The spaniel began moving slowly, turning every so often to look at Stefan and pulling on the leash.

"Don't stay too long, Dad," Ana shouted and playfully ran after her brother, laughing as she went. She bent down, took Carina in her arms, and continued running toward the main building, dragging Val with them as the boy didn't let the leash go.

"You have charming children," Bernov remarked when Stefan joined him under the skimpy mulberry trees.

"Thank you. Your daughter, I noticed, is a beautiful young woman," Stefan reciprocated the compliment while they crossed the courtyard, walking toward the older group of unpretentious, functional buildings where the Bernov family's room was located.

"Yes," Bernov proudly agreed, "but beauty and worries go hand in hand, they say."

"For one reason or another, one would always worry, even in the absence of beauty," Stefan said.

"You have that right, sir. Take you and me for example, we came here hoping to find instant happiness, and we have so much to worry about." Bernov finished the comment, halted to search for the key, and unlocked the door. He switched the light on. "Please enter, sir," he murmured, making an inviting gesture with his arm, "and feel welcomed in our modest abode."

The Bulgarians occupied one of the several tiny ground-floor rooms in the wing that also contained the camp's kitchen, the cold room, and the warehouse. It was one of the oldest buildings, built when the camp had initially opened long ago. Stefan knew the place well because it was next door to the room into which Váci had recently moved with his new girlfriend—a stunning, very attractive Polish beauty—and with his inseparable friend, Lászlo.

The room was crowded, a good section of it being taken up by a neatly stacked pile of high-quality, rather new-looking leather suitcases reaching to the ceiling. The Bulgarian family, it appeared, had fared much better than the average refugees who usually travelled light, considering themselves lucky enough to have arrived unharmed—only body and soul, so to speak—on the sunny side of the Iron Curtain. The beds were covered with colorful Greek woolen blankets called *flokatis*, not with the standard dull-gray camp variety, and the round table in the middle had an elegant embroidered tablecloth on it. A vague, rich smell of French perfume drifted in the air.

Women's shoes and clothes were carelessly spread around, and Bernov emptied a chair for Stefan by throwing the expensive cashmere shawl resting on it to the nearest bed. He then produced a bottle of Mavrodaphne of Patras, two glasses, and two bowls—one filled with roasted walnuts and the other with pistachios.

The doctor carefully poured the liqueur wine into glasses and then gave one to his guest, keeping the second for himself. He raised his glass ceremoniously—the wine was of a deep ruby red color.

"Good health, and good luck to you," he toasted Stefan.

Stefan sniffed the delicate aroma in rapture, and they drank in complete silence. He liked the syrupy wine almost as well as his preferred Samos. It was sweet, with a rich bouquet, and heavy. "Excellent wine," he said appreciatively.

"Try it with nuts," Bernov encouraged him. "It tastes even better. You might not find something like that in Canada."

"I doubt it. They must have everything there." Stefan nibbled some walnuts and the wine tasted even better, exactly as his host had told him, the mixed flavors of the roasted nuts enhancing its fruitiness.

"How are you so sure? Do you or your wife have a job?" Bernov asked.

"No. We don't. It won't be a problem to find jobs, we hope."

"How is it possible to be so casual about something so vital, Mr. Stefan? Surely you are aware of Canada's momentary economic mess. Right now, they are passing through their worst years since the war. The country is in what they euphemistically call a recession, in fact a full-on depression. Unemployment is rampant, over twelve percent of the working population being out of work. Every day, the newspapers tell about workers losing their jobs by the thousands, many of the unemployed ending up on welfare. Have you thought about that?" The man's voice sounded genuinely worried. Bernov, his complexion shadowed by concern, paused and looked inquisitively at his guest.

"Not really," answered the Romanian, "as a matter of fact, I don't believe everything the newspapers say. Thirty-seven years of Marxist rule have taught me better. The figure you mentioned might be just some hostile propaganda. Who can be sure nowadays of what is true in the media and what is not?"

"Well, sir, I believe it. I will show you something, if you don't mind." The doctor left his chair with a swift, almost fluid movement, unusual for someone so stocky. He knelt in front of one of the beds and pulled out a small attaché case. Bernov put his case on the table, opened it, and produced a piece of paper, which he handed to Stefan. "Read this, please."

It was a Xerox copy of an article, three weeks old, published by one of the leading dailies in Western Canada. The reporter wrote that many immigrants with higher education and extensive professional experience—among them numerous physicians—could not find positions in Canada, instead being forced to survive on unqualified menial jobs. She gave several examples, one being a Romanian doctor who, in more than eleven years of living in Canada, had been unable to get an adequate position in the health care system although there were shortages of qualified physicians across the country. Even more modest jobs were refused him although he was willing to work at anything anywhere. The local Laundromat, among others, had rejected his application, finding him overqualified; and a pharmaceutical sales firm said the Romanian doctor wasn't quite what the company needed. He was currently combing the highway's ditches for discarded bottles and cans to make a few bucks. A group of his frustrated colleagues, emigrants from various countries in similar situations, had decided to launch hunger strikes in order to attract the attention of government officials, stated the report. The doctor was quoted as saying that he was considering joining them, although in his opinion, the hunger strike was a desperate form of suicide.

"What do you say about that?" Bernov asked when he thought Stefan had finished reading.

"If this is true, it is very sad," Stefan said with a deep sigh. He returned the paper, putting it on the table and pushing it towards Bernov.

"Of course it is true. My friend spoke with the man before mailing the clipping." The doctor stood up, overcome by a sudden restlessness. He came around the table to get closer and confided to his guest, "You know what, Mr. Stefan? We have withdrawn our application for Canada and reapplied to immigrate to the States. That's what we have done, but please keep it to yourself. The reason I am telling this only to you is because I thought you might be interested in seeing this piece of information and maybe also changing your mind about immigrating to Canada. You have two children and ought to think about their future. After all, that unfortunate physician is one of your countrymen."

"I am grateful to you for showing me the article. But you see, Dr. Bernov, I am hard to convince. First is the authenticity of those facts. How could we check them?"

"I can't believe you distrust what I have already told you. The case is real," Bernov cried. "The Romanian doctor is a real person, and the situation is even worse than the newspaper said, believe me. My good friend from the States phoned and spoke to him personally. The man is on the verge of committing suicide, with hunger strike or without."

"Perhaps it is so. Don't get me wrong, please. I know and you know that foreign physicians have always had a very hard time getting licensed in Canada—it is a fact. It could be that now, times being as they are, not only doctors face difficulties resettling. Other professionals might have to share the same fate. I presume this is also why the Canadian consul asked my wife and I to sign off any claim to a professional status."

"Don't you think that their request is preposterous? I categorically refused to accept that," Bernov heatedly said and greedily gulped the wine from his glass.

"It is. Yet we have children, as you said, and have to consider their future. What choice do people like us have anyway? On the other hand, I am a good professional, a pioneer in my field, and feel confident that my peers will acknowledge my expertise. 'If you are a good professional, people who need your skills will cut a trail to your door through the thickest forest,' my father used to say."

"I am also a good professional," the doctor declared, "professional dedication is my motto. As a matter of fact, while in Africa, I gathered the most unique material of a pathological nature and a wealth of medical observations. Right now, that continent is at the epicenter of a new, mysterious epidemic, a deadly sexually transmitted disease nobody has described yet. People are dying like flies. The epidemic is just in its incipient stages, but it is spreading fast. And soon, it will be more destructive than an atomic explosion. So far, I am the only one to have firsthand observation as well as field data on it. And when this thing hits the Western world, my stuff will be more valuable than gold. In the meantime, I don't want to waste my time picking up discarded cans from Canada's highway ditches. I am not young enough for that kind of adventure—my time is too short, and in addition, I have my own theory regarding that new disease. The friend mentioned before has already found a medical job for me at a research institution in San Diego. That position is waiting for me."

Stefan sipped the rest of the wine from his glass and nibbled a handful of nuts. Definitely, it was excellent wine. "Congratulations, sir," he said. "I wish you good luck."

"Thank you." The Bulgarian poured some more wine in the glasses. "What about you? What do you intend to do?"

"Me? What do I intend to do? We will go to Canada. I am a loyal person, and the Canadians welcomed us in a moving, heartwarming way. It is only fair to offer my skills in exchange. Theirs is a beautiful huge country with exceptional outdoor opportunities, and all of us love the outdoors. More importantly, Canada is bilingual, and I am proficient in French. My French is much better than my English. And last but not least, we trust God will help us somehow in our search for jobs."

"May I ask, sir, what you mean by that?"

"What I mean by what? I can't really grasp your question, I am sorry."

"What is God?" Bernov smiled mischievously.

"Oh. God, you mean?" The unexpected question had taken Stefan completely aback. "God. Don't you know? The Creator, the Almighty, the Providence . . . the god of our ancestors." Stefan stopped short, at a loss for an immediate, more elaborate explanation.

Bernov was now laughing with an open mouth, his face contorted by amusement. "You are not by any chance one of the believers in that Christian nonsense good only for old peasant women? It would be presumptuous of me to ask if you ever met God because I know the answer. As a physician, I saw people being born, many dying, and some being cured in my presence or with my help but never with the intervention of this so-called God. You astonish me by expressing trust in something we all agree doesn't exist. I didn't expect to hear something like that from an intellectual raised in communist Romania, who grew up in an atheistic environment. You must certainly have been joking. I have to confess that in my practice of twenty-odd years on three continents, I have never, ever encountered God. God doesn't exist, period. Don't you agree?"

"I am sorry, Dr. Bernov," Stefan spoke very slowly, carefully choosing his words, "I will probably astonish you once more." He took a mouthful of wine. "This wine of yours is really good. To come back to the matter, yes, I am one of those backward people you describe. I believe in God. I even believe we are here because God, not humans, helped us. I personally see God everywhere and in everything. However, if you don't know where to look for him, it would be impossible to solve the problem of his existence here over a glass of wine. If you really desired with all your heart to meet God, it would be enough to look with attention in a mirror, sir. We are made in his likeness and his breath is in us. Might sound stupid, but that is what I believe."

"I did. Of course, I did look, and I always saw an aging communist physician," Bernov laughed deprecatingly. "If there is a God somewhere in the universe and he is so great, why is he not making his presence known? I asked him many times to show up, to prove his existence. He never answered my challenge."

"This is a very old debate. And to me, the question is superfluous, sir. Have you ever read any of Saint-Exupéry's books?

The doctor vigorously shook his head. "No. Never heard the name. Why? Who is he?"

"It is a pity you haven't. He was a French writer and a first-class pilot who disappeared at the end of World War II in one of the very last war missions of his fighter aircraft's unit. Most likely shot down by the Germans over a yet unidentified area of France. At the time of his death, Saint-Exupéry was writing an intriguing book, which remained unfinished, entitled "Citadelle." Among other things, in it he tells the story of a prince who felt lonely due to the servility of his subjects. Fed up with them endlessly parroting his words, he decided to go and seek God. God, the prince thought, should be someone to talk to as equal, not as lord to slave, the latter always presenting a reflection of the former's opinions and desires. For loneliness born of disappointment in our fellow humans always draws one to God. After a strenuous climb, the prince found God under the guise of a massive, solid basaltic block perched on top of an almost inaccessible mountain. When he challenged God to talk to him, the prince got no answer. Then he acknowledged the greatness of the Creator as a reason for his divine silence but nevertheless asked again for a sign, something small, comparable let's say to a wink or even less. A sign, no matter how insignificant, would prove that he, the prince, was not alone in the world apart from his own images as reflected by his subjects. But the Almighty continued to keep silent. After some thinking, the prince agreed with God, ignoring him. If God had lowered himself and answered his princely orders, he would have behaved like just another of his serfs. Would that be a true almighty and everlasting god, who would hurriedly answer any of our whims like a servant, sir? What do you think?"

Bernov distractedly poured wine in the two glasses and spent a long minute deep in thought. Then he looked at his guest. "Never thought that way," he confessed. "Strange. I should have thought about that. Your Saint-Exupéry makes a valid point, I must admit."

"Never mind, sir. You will have plenty of time to think while waiting for your visa." Stefan smiled at Bernov, gulped wine from his glass, and took another handful of nuts, crunching them with relish. "I am not sure if I understood you well, Dr. Bernov. Did I hear you say you are a communist? Perhaps what you meant was you were one in the past?"

The Bulgarian laughed good-humoredly. "Both are true. I was and still am a communist."

"Now it is your turn to astonish me. How come?"

"It is a long story. My parents were communists too. I absorbed materialistic philosophy with my mother's milk, I might say. Son and daughter of poor factory workers, they chose to go to school at any cost instead of becoming industrial laborers. Finishing high school among the top of their generation, both managed against all odds to be sent to Germany to study medicine. They independently arrived there in the mid-1920s and soon got involved with the communist movement. Later on, they met at a political rally, fell in love, and shortly got married in Berlin. For the occasion, Georgi Dimitroff was my father's best man. They brought me up according to their beliefs."

"Dimitroff of the Reichstag fire fame? The one killed by the Soviets in the fifties when he was already the dictator of their satellite Bulgaria?" Stefan asked. He couldn't believe his ears.

"Yes, that one. They remained friends up to the very end. Both my father and Dimitroff died the same year at a very short interval. In fact, we don't know for sure what caused Dimitroff's demise, except what the medical death certificate stated. It is true that he was our people's dictator, albeit a benevolent one, and he definitely believed in an independent Bulgaria. We worshiped him. The popular rumor had him assassinated by the Russians while visiting Moscow. Although at the time, I worked for the Ministry of the Interior, I wasn't aware of our intelligence getting any proof of foul play. My father, who was a high-ranking official in the Ministry of Health, died of pneumonia soon after. Before dying, he confessed to me in confidence that in his opinion, the KGB killed Dimitroff. However, he had no proof either."

"I gather you were a person of some importance in Bulgaria," Stefan mused, careful not to reveal his true feelings. He knew the role played by the most feared workers of the Ministry of the Interior in all countries of the Soviet bloc. They were the so-called 'organs,' the enforcers of terror, the professionals of oppression on which the whole communist system rested.

"Yes and no," Bernov replied. "As long as Dimitroff and my father were alive, yes, life was a beautiful dream. Our family didn't want for anything in those first years of revolutionary upheaval. And jobs, promotions, and political success came without asking. After their deaths, however, everything changed. Not very much, at least in the beginning, as we were still part of the new elite, but enough to give us a taste of insecurity. My father was a man of principles and honesty. I only once saw him doing something dishonest, an exception he made for the benefit of the cause. He helped doctor the first postwar elections so the Communist Party could snatch power from the despised bourgeoisie."

Bernov stopped, poured a full glass for himself, and drank it in a long gulp. "Although only a teenager, I, too, was involved in that campaign. It was children's play and a lot of fun to fool the foreign observers who couldn't believe a childish-looking teen could be so astute and efficient. The revolution demanded such actions, and I was trained for them. To my father's credit, he never before or after did another dishonest thing, and he bitterly regretted even that one. Unfortunately, the next generation of leaders—it soon became obvious—were greedy and rotten to the bone, condoning denunciation and corruption . . ."

"But, sir, denunciation and corruption were there from the very beginning. They went hand in hand with the dictatorship of the proletariat, and they were rooted in fear. Doctoring the ballots just cracked open the door," Stefan cried.

"I don't know. I don't remember seeing things that way in my youth. Certainly, I become more aware in my adulthood. Luckily, I managed in time to secure a good job abroad. When I was a child, we lived in Germany and Soviet Russia, and my knowledge of foreign languages was an asset as were some influential old friends of my father's. In my heart, I am and always will be a communist. The present leaders will one day be replaced with better people, dedicated to the revolution, not to their well-being only."

Bernov paused and, noticing Stefan's empty glass, refilled it. He again looked genuinely worried and resentful. The matter had obviously disturbed his composure.

Stefan watched Bernov with a thoughtful look. "May I ask you a question, sir? Pardon me, but I can't prevent being blunt. Why are you here? Personally, I have never been a communist, except in my youth, and only to the extent needed to be able to continue my studies and get a professional degree. Not a convinced one and never a member of the Party. On the contrary, right now, I am proud to be called an anticommunist, a dissident. And down into the depth of my soul, I am a true one. But you? A believer in that bogus philosophy, if I may call it so? What on earth are you looking for here in a refugee camp among your enemies? After all, your place should be side by side with your comrades, fighting for the final victory of your beloved cause. Shouldn't it? Is it because your job required things contrary to your professional code of ethics and that was your way out of a moral dilemma?"

"What are you talking about? What kind of moral dilemma? I don't really understand you." Bernov looked puzzled. He seemed not to have noticed the 'bogus' adjective or perhaps had nothing to say about it.

Stefan had already drunk too much of the sweet wine, and although still clear-headed, his defenses were rather weakened by a warm feeling of human solidarity totally out of place in that particular case.

"Ah, of course you know. The medical conditioning of political prisoners, scientific torture, psychological interrogation. Not to mention the internment of important political opponents in mental institutions. Those were the duties performed by the medical staff of the Ministry of the Interior. Weren't they?"

"Not always. Only sometimes. So what? Doctors must be ready to respond to the needs of their community. When the State must isolate some unruly citizens or change their minds, doctors have to accommodate. Opposition to measures deemed to better the life of an entire nation is pernicious to society at large and ought to be treated as any contagious illness. The existence of an isolated individual has no value when higher ideals are at stake. However, opposition was weaker in Bulgaria. And we didn't have to resort so often to punitive measures, not to the extent your Communist Party had to," Bernov stated with conspicuous conviction. "In fact, I wasn't involved in the sort of activity you mention because my job was in a different field. My appointment abroad had nothing to do with medicine either. As a matter of fact, moral or ethical aspects of my profession never bothered me."

"I always thought that society is made up of a multitude of individualities connected together—no man is an island, someone said. Even if you ignore such a conceptual approach, what about your Hippocratic oath, sir?" Stefan asked.

"Hippocratic oath? You must be kidding. Who complies with that piece of mythological nonsense nowadays? A bunch of Greek lies nobody ever took seriously. 'I will neither give a deadly drug to anybody nor will make a suggestion to this effect,' it pledges. Yet history proves that cases of poisoning by physicians were quite frequent even in classical times, not to mention the Middle Ages or modern times."

"I have to disagree with you, sir. I have personally met doctors, our contemporaries, who have been and still are faithful to their oath even when threatened with dire consequences. But this is a different story. You, sir, didn't answer my question yet. Why are you here and not on the barricades, so to speak?" Stefan asked with mischievous insistence. "If you don't want to answer, that is all right with me. Just tell me so, and we will forget about it."

"I would be very interested in hearing about those obsolete Hippocratic disciples. Maybe you will tell me more about them. The answer to your question is much simpler. While stationed in Africa, I did some medical practice aside from my official duties. In spite of prevailing poverty and backwardness, there were many incredibly rich people among my private patients, ready to spend fortunes on themselves or for the well-being of their loved ones. Every successful cure brought me not only substantial monetary advantages but also more of that rich clientele than I could possibly treat. When the government recalled me to Bulgaria, I was asked to hand in all the money made through my medical practice. They knew exactly how much money there was and where it was deposited. Ten lifetimes wouldn't have been enough to save so much in Bulgaria, not to mention that there is nothing on which to spend what amounted to a fortune in that country. Why not enjoy life in the capitalistic world if we have the means, I thought. The money was the result of my hard work, after all."

Bernov took a sip of wine, looked at the glass in his hand, and showed it to his guest. The glowing purplish red wine shimmered in the light like melted, liquid rubies. "Simple, relatively cheap things accessible here to the poorest Greek peasant, such as this wine, can't be even dreamed of in Bulgaria." Bernov laughed shyly, giving Stefan a coy wink.

"So much for the proletarian revolution," Stefan murmured pensively and smiled back at his host. "You wisely decided to withhold what legally belongs to your country. Good for you. As a fellow dissident, I full-heartedly congratulate you. However, it is hard for me to understand how your actions can be reconciled with your principles."

"But, Mr. Stefan, my friend, that is my money," Bernov cried, "the result of my hard work, based on my skills and professional expertise! Legally, it might belong to the state of Bulgaria. But rightfully, it is mine. This is an outrageous abuse. The law is against nature, and it hurts me, an innocent. Don't you agree?"

"Of course I do. That is why I am here. What surprises me, however, is that you have so quickly and completely forgotten the confiscation of private property, of businesses and financial investments, the real estate expropriations, and the so-called nationalization of mobile and immobile means of production, all of which were part of your revolution. Similarly abusive laws hurt, in every country where the Soviets exported their political system, a vast number of individual people who lost everything of what many had acquired, like yourself, through their skills and professional expertise."

"This is nonsense. That situation was totally different. Those people were representatives of the bourgeoisie, through-and-through reactionaries. I am a proletarian, a working man, sir, and proud of it," the doctor heatedly said.

"I am sorry to have to contradict you once more. You certainly know better than me how it works in your Party. If your father is a worker, then you are the son of a proletarian, but not one yourself except if you, in turn, eventually become a manual worker. Your father was the son of a proletarian. When he became a physician and a high-ranking functionary of the government, because it was a communist one, he automatically moved out of the proletariat. You also worked with your brains, not with your hands, which makes you a petty bourgeois or at least one of the despised intellectuals. You have never been a member of the worker's class as defined by any of the communist parties in the world. This is not the point, because for professional revolutionaries like you, they probably made an exception and allowed you to join the Party. After all, neither Marx nor Lenin nor Stalin, as a matter of fact, were genuine proletarians. The point is that when applied to you, the same law, which you considered fair for most Bulgarians, suddenly became an anathema. What is more, contrary to what you just said a few minutes ago, the existence of an isolated individual—you—took priority and had gained in your mind more importance than some illusory higher ideal. Do you see my point now, Dr. Bernov?"

The doctor had a short laugh. It was a quizzical, slightly embarrassed laugh, though friendly. He peered at Stefan with appreciative eyes as if seeing him for the first time. Bernov silently refilled the glasses and then looked straight at his guest.

"Let's drink another glass to your health, sir. I cannot deny that there is a kernel of truth in what you're saying. Yet in my soul, I like to believe that my allegiance to the communist ideals remains basically unchanged."

"All the same, Dr. Bernov, your disobedience, like my defection, is undoubtedly seen by your leadership as a crime against the state, an outright act of treason. I guess you are aware that none of those self-styled tribunals of the people so diligent at sending unregimented citizens to jail would ever agree with you. For your own good, it would be wise to stay out of their reach. As far as those ideals you mentioned are concerned, if one doesn't accept the state ownership of everyone and everything as you did, if one rejects the dictatorship and the brainwashing as I did, and when people abhor the spoliation and corruption associated with communist regimes as we both do, what is left?" Stefan asked.

"Ah, don't talk like that," the Bulgarian cried, "what about democracy, equality, freedom, equal sharing of resources, enjoyment of common wealth, and the abolition of human bondage and exploitation? All the beautiful things so many generations dreamed of and the best people of every epoch died for." Bernov stood up, fired by his own words, instinctively resting both hands on the table, and bending forward as speakers do at the rostrum of a popular rally. "You don't know, my friend, how much I long for an era of true human fellowship, when all of us are brothers, not enemies." He was so moved that when he finished, his voice almost broke down and the man nearly burst into sobs.

Bernov had turned his back to Stefan so that the Romanian couldn't see his face and made a few steps around the room, obviously prey to strong emotional turmoil. Shortly, though, he regained complete control of his emotions and returned to the table. "I am sorry," he said, "these are things very close to my heart."

"That is all right. These ideals are close to my heart, too. Unfortunately, when terror and hatred accompany them, they lose any meaning and become empty words, the most abject and noxious demagogy. The problem with the fathers of communism, you see, is that they hated their fellow humans. None of them were lovers of humanity. They were small people with huge egos, hungry for power and control. And their hunger was rooted in hate and envy. If you would set political goals aside, you would find that the gentle Jesus preached long before on similar themes driven, however, by love, charity, and compassion. It is easier, of course, for one to kill and torture than selflessly strive to change people's hearts or try to elevate one's soul. Christ demonstrated that through his own terrible experience."

"This is a subject quite unknown to me, I must confess," Bernov stated bluntly. "Religion was always something foreign to me, something bordering on superstition and reactionary thinking."

Stefan checked his watch. "I won't venture over that border with you tonight. It is late, and I had better go home now," he said and smiled conciliatorily at Bernov. "We may try another time, although I am not a preacher and don't have charisma. Perhaps it would be better if you crossed that boundary one day and made the exploration by yourself."

The doctor made a dismissive move with his hand. He seemed to posses a sort of peculiar listening selectiveness, enabling him to ignore things he didn't want to hear. "Don't worry about time. There are more than two hours before my girls come home. They went to a double bill movie. I am very keen to hear about your Hippocratic friends. You might soon leave for Canada, and who knows if we will have another opportunity like this one. Please, tell me about them," the doctor insisted. He knelt in front of a low cupboard hidden by the beds and produced another bottle of Mavrodaphne. He showed it to Stefan. "See, we are well provided with the appropriate stimulant."

"No, thank you. It is late. I should go home," Stefan said, standing up.

"Please don't go. Opportunities for such interesting and sincere discussions are rare indeed. You have made me extremely curious. Please sit down," he said and offered another glass to Stefan, whose earlier resolution was faltering under the man's insistent hospitality.

"All right, you are such a generous host, you oblige me. Still I will tell you only about one of my friends. If you don't like the story, it is your fault. You asked for it," Stefan said.

"I won't complain, be assured." Bernov smiled encouragingly and settled down comfortably in his chair with his glass handy.

"I met my friend the doctor, let's call him Damian," Stefan began, "in the 1950s. At the time, I was a student, and my right buttock muscles got infected from a hypodermic injection given to me at the high school. After two weeks, a bulging inflammation had developed in the place where the medicine had been introduced, and I was in atrocious pain. Soon, walking or sitting became first difficult, then almost impossible, and I was seized with a fever. Several doctors called in by my parents couldn't do much for my relief, offering only scant hope. One suggested having exploratory surgery done, followed perhaps by amputation if in the meantime, he said, septicemia hadn't set in. Things were looking really bad, and I was terrified at the prospect of losing my leg."

Stefan took a sip of wine. "When my mother was in despair, prayers were her last recourse. She went to one of our few churches still open, the Roman Catholic cathedral, and paid a mass for my recovery. Leaving the sanctuary after the religious service, Mother met one of her university colleagues that she hadn't seen for years. The man was a lawyer, recently out of prison, where he had spent several years for sheltering a group of monks banished by the power of the day. Their discussion passed from one subject to another, focusing on my illness and the medical profession's lack of success in dealing with it, which was my mother's main worry.

"Moved, the lawyer told my mother about a young doctor he had befriended during his captivity, also released not long before, and whom he held in very high esteem. The doctor, currently employed in a junior capacity at a first aid station on a major building site, had a wife and two small children and could hardly make ends meet. It was one of those unenvied medical workplaces that included long hours and little money, where the government sent people branded as reactionaries to do slave work and be 'reeducated' in the process. At least, that was the official slogan at the time. His political past didn't recommend the young doctor for safer or better-paid jobs. According to my mother's colleague, in the insalubrious and primitive conditions of the prison, that doctor had performed miracles, saving many lives—including the storyteller's—just by using simple remedies and a lot of personal care. In the end, the lawyer strongly recommended calling his ex-inmate for a consultation.

"The doctor came to see me late one evening after work. He was tired as anyone would be at the end of sixteen hours on a busy and messy building site where accidents happened quite often. He was a young man, about fourteen years my senior, well mannered, and—in spite of the long day he had already had—quite cheerful. He looked undernourished and thin, certainly the result of his years of imprisonment and more recently due to hard work, irregular eating, and countless privations. His consultation took over an hour, for he made a thorough examination. When he finished, Dr. Damian prescribed what he called a penicillin barrage.

"Penicillin was new at the time and something not every physician would have had the daring to use—its effects were little known in Romania. What he really meant was daily series of repeated hypodermic injections with hydrated penicillin surrounding the infected area. The treatment, which he personally administered, lasted about ten days. And he finished it by injecting deep into the muscle a suspension of penicillin in some special oily concoction to insure slow release, he said. The next day, following the first series of injections, I already felt better and the fever had decreased. When he decided to stop the treatment, I could walk again, the swelling had subsided, and my temperature had dropped to within normal values. No limping or other visible signs of my affliction remained. A faint tenderness of the muscle persisted for many months, indeed years, but slowly vanished with the passage of time. Everyone saw that as a miracle, and in truth, Dr. Damian had saved my leg.

"When it came to the payment for his treatment, Damian didn't even want to hear about money. He was paid in his capacity as a physician by the government, he declared, and my treatment was a duty as prescribed by his professional code. He was adamant about that, and my family's insistence conspicuously upset him. Only with great reluctance and after the intercession of our common friend, the lawyer, did he accept a present of honey, cheese, and ham my folks had procured from relatives living in the countryside. That, he made it clear, was accepted only because of his little children."

"This is nothing so special," said Bernov, who in the last minutes had appeared increasingly impatient. He sounded a trifle bored. "Many of us would have done the same thing. Perhaps he was afraid to lose his job. Private medical practice is forbidden in the entire communist bloc. As far as the treatment is concerned, that wasn't a miracle. It was the expected action of a powerful new drug—in your case, penicillin—on unaccustomed bacilli. This is a well-known phenomenon." The Bulgarian conspicuously suppressed a yawn.

"But Dr. Bernov, I haven't finished my story. This was just to introduce my friend to you. If you don't want to hear the rest of it, I can go home right now," Stefan said, indicating an intention to stand up, his movements slowed by stiffness and the mellowing effect of the wine. He didn't want to stay that long anyway, and Bernov's interruption mildly indisposed him.

"I am sorry. I thought you had finished. No, don't go, please. Please tell me the rest of the story." Dr. Bernov turned to Stefan and softly pushed him back into the chair. It seemed that the man genuinely regretted his interruption and felt uneasy about the reaction his interruption had triggered. "I mean it. Please, sir, don't go. I am anxious to hear the whole story. Please continue . . . Let's have another glass of wine," he said, refilling Stefan's glass.

"Don't pour another glass, please. I have had enough. Thank you very much. Your wine is excellent. After a day's work and an extra trip to Voula, I don't feel like drinking anymore," Stefan said, putting the full glass aside. "Oh, well! Let's go back to my friend . . . Dr. Damian usually came in the evening for my shots. Relying on the irregular common transport, which was never on schedule, he was often late. After the treatment, he enjoyed a relaxing chat with me before going home. During those short episodes, I had the opportunity to get to know him a little better. He appeared to possess a bright mind, his versatile knowledge extending to various domains much further afield than required by the practice of medicine. His readings were eclectic, covering history, philosophy, literature, and the arts. A discussion with him was always an intellectual feast, especially for a teenager like me, hungry for fresh ideas and fed up with the stalled atmosphere of political correctness and slogan-ridden culture characteristic of the early years of 'revolutionary' headway.

"Those initial contacts with Damian enticed me to look for opportunities to see him privately, and because we had common friends in the ensuing decade, we often came across each other.

Eventually, we became friends—such good friends, in fact—that at my wedding, he was my best man and then became the godfather of my children.

"Damian was someone who didn't like to talk too much about himself. Yet from what little he told me and with bits and pieces gathered during almost thirty years of our friendship from other people who had known him since his youth, I could easily reconstruct his life story and the events that led to his imprisonment.

"Like many Romanian intellectuals, Damian's father was descended from free peasant stock. Not rich but hardworking and intelligent, he showed great talent and promise, even from his early school years. Sent to university, he graduated with flying colors and in his adulthood became one of our country's leading scholars. When Damian was a teenager, his father was already a well-known and respected linguist, an academician, as well as the principal of a famous college in the capital, the oldest of its kind. Originally from Transylvania and raised under the oppressive Austro-Hungarian empire's domination, he was also a passionate Romanian patriot.

"Damian grew up in an atmosphere of almost mystical love for the country. In his childhood, he had already developed an early taste for the arts and literature. His intellect was above average, and later in high school, his knowledge of the ancients was exceptional. Yet when it came to making a career choice, he turned to medicine, being gifted with an analytic mind and an innate talent for natural sciences. That happened when he graduated at the age of sixteen after completing the last four grades in only two school years.

"In the mid-thirties, Damian was admitted to the University of Bucharest in the School of Medicine and afterward successfully completed the first two years. Then after his eighteenth birthday—the official coming of age—he took a year's leave of absence from the school and enrolled as a volunteer in the military academy. As many volunteers, he was trained to become an artillery officer. In retrospect, it was a fateful decision."

Stefan paused. "You might find all these details boring. They are important if one wants to understand the man's philosophy, but you can stop me any time."

"Please, don't stop. By all means continue. It is an intriguing story. I am really keen to hear every detail of it," Bernov said.

"All right, I will continue if that is what you wish," Stefan said. "After he had finished his military training, Damian returned to the medical school. It was just months before the war started, a particularly bad time for neutral Romania. The misrule of the reigning king, who only two years before had assumed dictatorial powers, ended in a catastrophic dismemberment of the country under the pressure of foreign powers he couldn't oppose, fight, or prevent. First came the occupation by the Soviet Union of both Bessarabia and a part of Bucovina, and soon after, the loss of half of Transylvania—imposed by the Germans through the Dictate of Vienna. Overnight, millions of families had been brutally separated by a blatant violation of international law. I know this tragedy well because my own family shared their fate, and some close relatives were killed on the refugee road or just disappeared without trace in the ensuing confusion. Faced with the complete failure of his political scheming and in order to avoid any responsibility for his regime's bankruptcy, the king abdicated in favor of his son Michael and fled to Portugal. It was the fourth time he had done so in less than twenty-five years."

"Wasn't that the time when Bulgaria also annexed some Romanian lands?" Bernov asked.

"Yes, but that wasn't so bad as Bulgaria got only two small counties and we exchanged the entire population," Stefan answered.

"I am not familiar with those events. We were in Soviet Union at the time. What happened to your country after the king abdicated?"

"By abdicating, the king had transferred his absolute powers into the hands of Ion Antonescu, a general, who became a dictator himself. The man's position wasn't one to be envied. The country was weak, bled by human and territorial losses, its army poorly equipped with outdated arms, without tanks or strong aviation. Being the fourth major oil producer in the prewar world, Romania was also the envy of Hitler, who needed that commodity for his war machine. Without support from our traditional allies, engaged in the battle of France, and with the prospects of Britain's collapse, the Romanian dictator had only two alternatives when the Germans launched their Barbarossa plan and invaded Soviet Russia. One was occupation, as Hitler had already threatened him on several occasions, with the complete annihilation of Romania. The other was participation in their war. The general was between a rock and a hard place."

"He chose the war, didn't he?" Bernov said.

"Yes. War was the only choice after the army was reequipped with German help. In the beginning, at least, many Romanians gladly went to war. It was a liberation war—they believed—as long as it was fought on what had been until recently Romanian territory. Some were even so naive as to think that Hitler, in recognition of Romanian sacrifices, would also return the Transylvanian lands to their rightful owners. In the existing circumstances, this was unrealistic, a sheer impossibility.

"It would have been quite easy for Damian to be declared a noncombatant when the war started. Medical school students, especially those like him in their last years of studies, were kept behind the lines or, if mobilized, commissioned to work in hospitals. The army needed doctors even more than artillery officers. To everyone's surprise, Damian volunteered for the front, refused any medical assignments, and was therefore sent with his battery to the first line of battle for the entire duration of the war.

"On the Russian front, he fought as far as the Caucasus, was wounded twice and, each time, went back into the fighting after short convalescence. Only on very rare occasions would he mention episodes from that period, allowing me a glimpse into what his life was like on the eastern front. He told me about days and nights of marches across the immensity of the Russian steppes. Damian's unit traveled mostly on horseback. And in many instances, men and horses alike were half asleep, trotting along unconsciously. He recalled, in particular, one attack against a pocket of Russian resistance, which ended in massacre. That day, he was directing the artillery fire from the top of a tree while Russian snipers, positioned not far away, aimed at him, killing his aides one by one, and decimating the battery's personnel. Once, he described how the people from a place his unit was sent to for recovery brought out from hiding an old priest. Under Damian's orders, his soldiers repaired the local church. And the villagers' great joy when the first mass was celebrated with the assistance of the Romanian military priest had made a lasting impression on my friend. The memory of those villagers brought tears to his eyes when, late one night over a glass of wine, he told me about the desperation left behind the day the Romanians had to withdraw.

"Following the major military fiascos incurred by Hitler's war machine, the eastern front collapsed and the battle front moved into Romania, which was forced to conclude a humiliating armistice with the Soviets. Its immediate effect was that Germans became the enemy. And Damian, like the entire Romanian army, was transferred to the new western front. During the battle for Budapest, he was wounded for the third time. Nevertheless, the capitulation of Germany found him with the rank of major, still fighting somewhere in the neighborhood of Prague.

"In the fall of the year, the war ended. Damian returned to university. He was now an experienced and mature man, a decorated hero, and the romantic dream of every would-be bride. No wonder that the next year he got married. The last two years in medical school were the happiest in his life, he confessed repeatedly, and everything happened very fast. So fast, in fact, that when he graduated, his wife was already nursing a baby boy.

"Whenever my friend mentioned his graduation, he always remembered how moving it was when the new doctors pledged allegiance to the Hippocratic oath. 'It was like we suddenly became different, a sort of chosen priesthood, apostles of an old and generous code of professionalism and honor, dedicating our entire lives to the highest ideals of humanity. For what can be more sublime than fighting death and illness?' he would rhetorically ask.

"Immediately after graduation, my friend was hired as a country physician and sent to an area in the western mountains where settlements were scarce, with houses sprawled at great distances. For centuries, people from that district had been shepherds, cattlemen, and high-altitude orchard owners. The boundaries of his jurisdiction were far apart. It wasn't unusual for Damian to ride fifty kilometers over high hills and scraggy woodlands just to visit a patient or to assist with a birth. His medical visits weren't always devoid of perils. He would sometimes have to take big detours in the summer to avoid angry female bears with cubs or packs of hungry wolves roaming in search of food in the winter. It was an adventurous and hard life, healthy though, and—when as young as Damian was—rewarding.

"In the postwar years, the rest of the world began to enjoy the pleasures of peace and freedom, while Romania, together with the other Eastern European countries quickly sank into Soviet slavery. The puppet government, which in Romania ascended to power through fixed elections controlled by the Russians, quickly implemented Draconian measures in order to cripple the opposition and physically eliminate any potential leaders. By the fall of 1947, in the wake of massive arrests of opposition activists, points of armed resistance sprang into existence in remote mountainous areas. Soon, several organized groups of anticommunist partisans began fighting in earnest. Their activities escalated during the next year, after the king's forced abdication, occasionally flaring up during the brutal collectivization of agriculture.

"The early successes of the partisan movements triggered huge repressive operations from the governmental forces in cooperation with the Red Army. Everything happened quietly, however, and neither the existence of the former nor the progress of the latter were broadcast either internally or abroad. In fact it was considered a crime against the new republican state to talk about the partisans.

"In spite of the terror unleashed by the government, the success of the repression was hindered from the start by the overwhelming sympathy the partisans enjoyed among the population. To that, the government responded with a new wave of arrests among civilians and the partisans by stepping up their attacks. All these developments couldn't escape Damian's attention, especially when an epidemic of 'hunting accidents' became rampant in his district. It is true that after the war, almost everyone in the country had at least one firearm of some kind, even though the new rulers banned their possession. But hunting fever couldn't account for the sheer frequency and gravity of such 'accidents.' He kept quiet though, doing his job as a doctor for the benefit of his patients, recording only those events supported by legal evidence.

"One night, in the dead of winter, Damian was awakened by two 'shepherds' bringing a heavily wounded 'hunter.' They carried the unconscious man in a blanket suspended between their horses. A cursory glance was enough for Damian to first recognize what had caused the wounds and secondly to identify his patient. It was common knowledge among locals that high up in the mountains, at a place called—in Romanian—Pietrele Albe, meaning the White Rocks, superior governmental forces kept a strong group of partisans under siege. He also knew that a fierce battle had raged day and night around the White Rocks during the last few weeks. The leader of that resistance group was rumored to be an ex-paratroop colonel whom Damian had befriended while in the military academy; this was the wounded man who had been brought to his door. He had been machine-gunned and was bleeding copiously from multiple bullet wounds.

"Damian immediately performed the surgical procedures required by the gravity of his patient's situation, repaired the broken bones, and stitched up incisions and gashing wounds. He worked intensely for a good part of the night because he also had to carry out a transfusion from one of the 'shepherds' who by chance had the same blood group as the patient. Then the men helped him to hide their comrade in the attic and vanished in the morning with the rising sun.

"Four nights later, they returned and took the wounded man, now conscious and on the mend, away with them. Although the colonel recognized his benefactor during the dressing sessions, he didn't say anything to his comrades, who remained oblivious to his friendship with Damian up to the end.

"Months later, in early summer, under the concentrated attack of an army division reinforced with specially trained commandos formed from mountain climbers and following heavy bombardments by aviation, the partisans' position was taken by assault. After a fierce battle, the guerillas were finally defeated. Two thirds of them, including the colonel, died in combat.

"During the inquiry that followed, the prosecutors reached the conclusion that the group leader had, at some point in recent time, been cared for by a skilled surgeon. The fact was confirmed during interrogations by one of the 'shepherds' who—before succumbing to torture, when asked who performed the surgery on their leader—mumbled with his last breath: 'That doctor.' The survivors were shot at the end of a mock trial, but the question of who that member of the medical profession was remained unsolved.

"The White Rocks were located at a point where the borders of several medical districts met. And the secret police, to be sure of catching their man, arrested all the doctors from the area, over a dozen in total. Damian was among their number. Every doctor at one point or another had—knowingly or not—helped the partisans, and many of them acknowledged such 'crimes.' Each confession produced new arrests. Some, especially aged professionals, couldn't stand the rough interrogations and died. Yet the identity of the doctor who had treated the guerilla commander eluded the investigators until the very end.

"During a so-called instruction stage, the preferred questioning method was torture. Two strong tormentors immobilized the victim, roping his arms and legs at his back in a complete circle. Then a bar was inserted inside the circle formed by the man's body and supported on two chairs weighted down with sandbags. This arrangement allowed the body to rotate around the bar, leaving the bare soles of his feet exposed in a face-up position. The interrogator asked a question, and if the answer was slow to come or didn't satisfy him, he prompted the torturers to action. Armed with rubber cudgels, they applied heavy blows to the victim's soles, skillfully directed not only to induce as much pain as possible but also to put his body in a rotating movement. The dizziness associated with the pain soon became unbearable, and usually, the blows initially given methodically ended being applied randomly wherever it pleased the sadist executioner: to the victim's head, to his face, to his stomach, and so on. They would stop only if the victim was ready to confess or lost consciousness and, even then, not always immediately. The frequency of the interrogation sessions was at the discretion of the person who conducted the 'instruction.' In between meetings with the 'instructor,' the victim was left for days on end to starve in dirty and insalubrious quarters, sometimes alone or at other times crowded with as many as could stand together in a small cell. Without medical assistance for the inmates, recovery was quite difficult and survival uncertain.

"Damian decided from the very beginning that he would rather die than disclose private information. Confessions, which could have hurt his patients, would have been against his principles. He learned early in his interrogations that if he managed to hold his breath just before the beatings started and hold it long enough, he would easily pass out. That made his 'instruction' sessions shorter and the effects of the beating less severe. It was a dangerous proposition, carrying with it the potential for sudden death through a heart arrest or suffocation—all hazards—which at the time were of little concern to him.

"Several months latter, when nothing of substance was found against him, Damian's interrogations became rare and far between. It took him a long time to recover from his last meeting with an 'instruction team.' When that finally happened, he unobtrusively began to practice medicine among the detainees.

"At the end of a year, still without having been sent to court, he was moved to a prison where many of the potential opposition were detained before being transferred to labor camps. He continued practicing medicine, risking reprisals from the jailers who had no qualms about treating the detainees worse than animals. Once, he spent three weeks in confinement because he had revived a colleague barbarously tortured after an attempted escape. During that time, he was locked up, sometimes alone but more often with two or three other political detainees in a tiny, blackout cell that had neither windows nor light. Over the entire period, his diet consisted of water and a piece of stale bread twice a day. There was an open hole in the floor instead of toilet but no beds or blankets in that room, and he never could lie down his entire length. In absence of proper ventilation, the noxious emanations of the toilet nauseated the prisoners. Sleeping and sitting on the concrete floor was uncomfortable and a health hazard. In spite of all this, my friend considered himself lucky to be punished in the fall, which happened to be mild that year. As the prisoners knew too well, during the cold of the winter, nobody had ever survived that harsh environment more than a week or so.

"Damian came out of confinement a shadow of himself, with abnormally swollen legs, sick, and in a state of extreme weakness. His only desire was to die but, helped by his cellmates, among them my mother's lawyer friend who shared with him part of their meager portions, he eventually regained some strength.

"It was during his second year of detention that one night, Damian was roughly dragged out from the cell. Taken to a prison office, he was asked to dress up in his own clothes, initially confiscated, which appeared from God knows where, and forced to climb into a small curtained car. He traveled for several hours with two taciturn civilian guards and a driver until they entered a big city. After many detours—he had the impression they were purposely multiplying their detours to confuse him—they stopped, opened the door, and ordered him to get out. Because he didn't move fast enough, one of the guards kicked him in the back, and he fell headlong onto the sidewalk, hurting his elbows and knees. Instantly, the car backed up, turned around, and vanished into the dark. But he had time to notice that the vehicle had no license plates.

"He was gaunt and weak, almost to the point of breakdown. The night was cold, and his clothes were fluttering in the strong wind around his skeletal body. It took some time until, shivering and giddy, he finally recognized the place. He was in Bucharest, not far from his father's house.

"Although he had never been taken to court, never been sentenced, and never been condemned, Damian remained forever labeled an enemy of the people. His career was stalled and his life made miserable every time he tried to improve his situation. He was a war hero, remember? A skilled, dedicated professional and, even more, a charitable man of great honesty."

Stefan finished and, without realizing what he was doing, drank the wine from his glass to the last drops. He put the empty glass down and stood up. "That was the story of my friend, and now I must go. Thanks for all."

"Hmm," Bernov mumbled, clearing his throat, "where is your friend now?"

"He died five years ago at age fifty-six of cancer of the spleen. Those beatings must have definitely done some damage to his body," Stefan answered. "In his later life, he worked at the Central Emergency Hospital in Bucharest. The man who saved several thousand lives in his career couldn't be saved himself."

"Perhaps your friend could have avoided all those tribulations if he had informed the authorities about his nocturnal visitors," Bernov coolly said.

"No doubt about that. In the few, very rare cases when that happened, the informants were promoted and decorated. Damian wasn't ready to sell his conscience for personal advantage. I thought you would have already realized that," Stefan answered. "I am sorry, but it is really late, and my wife is surely waiting for me. I must go." He didn't want to start another discussion.

"Well, you told me quite an intriguing story. Thank you." Bernov stood up, seemingly unable to find a more appropriate comment. He again looked cold and distant as he had before their meeting.

"Thanks for all. That wine of yours is something special," Stefan said and stretched out his hand. "Good night."

"Good night." Bernov clasped Damian's hand. "So you won't come to the States?"

"No, I already told you."

They were in front of the open door, Bernov affably holding it so that Stefan could step out. "Tell me, please, why don't you like the Americans?" Bernov asked, his face wrinkled by a waggish smile. "You can be sincere with me because I won't tell anyone. I promise."

"That's not true. I like the Americans very much. As a matter of fact, I see them as the defenders of our freedom. The reason is my knowledge of French, which we hope will make our start easier in Canada, as I already told you. That and our love for the outdoors. I don't have anything against them. On the contrary," Stefan said. He was already in the yard facing his host, whose stocky stature was profiled in the doorframe, lit from behind and looking very much aloof. The playfulness was gone as fast as it came. "Good night, and good luck," Stefan said before turning around.

Outside in the crisp night, it was chilly; but Stefan, warmed by the wine and still excited by his discussion with Bernov, wasn't immediately aware of the drop in temperature, which as usual followed the springtime nightfall. Walking across the yard, deep in his thoughts and oblivious to what was going on around him, he didn't notice a pair coming in from the street. Yet when they waved and called him, Stefan waved back, and it didn't take him long to recognize Váci and his Polish girlfriend. Presently, they met him under the mulberry trees. Váci gave him a hug, and the girl kissed Stefan on both cheeks.

For once, Váci was sober. "We haven't seen you for almost a week. Where have you been?" he said. "I was afraid you had left without saying good-bye."

The girl smiled seraphically, her perfect white teeth glistening in the sparse lighting. Her lovely face, like fine glazed porcelain, enlivened by clear blue eyes reminded Stefan of one of Botticelli's paintings. "We have missed you so much lately," she said in a sweet soprano voice.

"How could you even think something so bad about me? I would never leave Greece without telling you, my friends," Stefan answered. "We missed you guys too."

"You will excuse me. Unfortunately, I can't stay any longer. I have to run but hope to see you soon, Stefan." The girl continued to smile angelically as she hurriedly left after blowing a kiss to the men from the tips of her fingers. Her gracious silhouette vanished, swallowed by the darkness between the buildings.

"She had to answer an urgent call of nature. The movie, you see, was quite emotionally stressful. Women, you know . . ." Váci laughed. "By the way, talking about stressful events, I heard you lent some money to Lászlo."

"Yes, I did," Stefan cautiously acknowledged.

"Big mistake, my dear Stefan. You should have asked me first. One should never lend money to Lászlo because the man never gives it back."

"I learned that the hard way, but I don't resent it."

"I would like to return that money to you. How much was it?" Váci inquired.

"You don't have to."

"Don't be silly. How much?"

"A hundred dollars."

"My God. You must have been crazy to give him so much," a revolted Váci exclaimed aloud, afterward continuing in a lower voice, in Hungarian, "how could you do such a foolish thing, *Pista, my dear?*" *Pista* is a diminutive word of affection for *István*, which in Hungarian means Stefan.

"We saved money to pay for the dog's flight. As you know, the Canadians won't lend money for her ticket. But we had enough even without the money Lászlo borrowed. He is a fellow refugee, a brother of ours. If we don't help each other, who will? It was sheer luck for us to find jobs and earn that money. Working outdoors instead of languishing in the camp made for a pleasant change."

"That wasn't help, really. Lászlo didn't need help. He is an inveterate drunkard and certainly spent your money on booze." Váci sounded disgusted. He fumbled in his leather jacket's inner pocket. "Look, I have here my last money, fifty dollars. This is my personal reserve in case of emergencies." He held out the money to Stefan. "I am sorry, that is all. There is no more."

Stefan smiled at hearing the harsh adjective bestowed on Lászlo yet abstained from commenting on what makes one a drunkard. He didn't want to hurt his friend's feelings but didn't want his money either. "You owe me nothing, my friend. Why do you want to pay Lászlo's debts? Are you his father, or what?"

"I feel this idiotic responsibility for him. *Noblesse oblige*—don't you know the old French adage? The stupid Middle Age paternalist complex of the master's superiority, the inherited responsibility for his serf's behavior and welfare," Váci said with a faint smile, his wry face barely discernable in the poor light coming from the distant lamps.

"No. Better spend them with Ewa and have fun. I won't take your money. This is final. You understand?" Stefan resolutely said and pushed away Váci's hand holding the money. He began feeling the chill of the night penetrating his bones.

"Okay," Váci reluctantly agreed and slowly put the money back in his pocket. "I wish I had something else to give you. Something precious so you would remember me . . . I know," he happily exclaimed after a pause. "I found my present to you. You are my friend. You take Ewa. You can have her. She is very attractive and good in bed."

"You can't be serious, Váci."

"Of course I am. She is all yours as I said."

"Don't be crazy, my friend. It is no good to joke about such things. You might regret it one day," Stefan said. He shivered and would have preferred to go home but realized that it was now impossible to leave his friend just like that.

"Why not? I don't care. She likes you. She told me many times she really likes you. You are her type of man. We have great sex, but there is no true love between us. These Polish girls are crazy about what they call their manly type."

"What about you?" Stefan asked.

"I am only a temporary playmate, unfortunately, not her type of lover." Váci shrugged his shoulders. "Life is sometimes like that," he concluded, "what else can I say?"

"No, Váci dear. In all fairness, I am too old for amorous adventures, and I love Lia very much. It wouldn't be fair either to her, to Ewa, or to you. If I were twenty years younger and uncommitted, maybe I would have challenged you for her love. You are younger than I am, and Ewa is almost my daughter's age. Not for me this jackpot, my friend. She is beautiful, and if you really love her, you should fight to change her mind and prove to be her type. Nevertheless, your generosity and friendship moved me deeply. I shall treasure this moment forever—as long as my memory lasts." He couldn't continue, overcome by emotion, and was glad the other man couldn't see his face.

Unexpectedly, Váci violently grabbed the Romanian in his arms, hugged, and noisily kissed him. Stefan felt his friend's hard cold cheek, almost hurting; and short of breath in the clasp of that bear hug, he could say nothing. His cheeks were cold too, a sort of chilly numbness having taken him over completely.

"I will remember too," Váci murmured. Then as brusquely as he had started, he released Stefan from his embrace and ran in the direction of his room. The whole thing had lasted only a few seconds. Váci was close to the opposite building when he turned and paused for a short moment at the border between light and shadow. "This matter is not finished yet!" he shouted. "We will talk about it tomorrow. I will eventually find something for you. Don't worry."

"I won't," Stefan shouted back. "Why should I worry, for God's sake?"

FAREWELL

The night before flying to Canada, Stefan and his family stayed in Athens, in a cozy little hotel on Chalkokondyli Street, only minutes from the National Archaeological Museum. The Catholic organization that cared for refugees, in cooperation with the Canadian Consulate, helped them with the necessary travel arrangements, charging all expenses against the personal loan the Canadian government had granted to Stefan in order to make the Romanians' trip possible. The Canadian consul himself talked the hotel owners into allowing the dog to sleep for a night with the family in one of their rooms.

Since the tourist season hadn't started yet, the hotel was virtually unoccupied. One of the owners, a wary looking man, personally showed them around; and they could freely choose whatever rooms suited their taste. In spite of his host's persuasive manners and tempting offers, Stefan frugally decided to share accommodation with his son, and Lia and Ana took a second separate room.

After half a year in the refugee camp, with no traffic running under their windows, the unending swish-swash noises of the Athenian bustle and scuffle kept Stefan awake the entire night. Greek nights are not particularly warm in February, and local hotel owners are not overly generous in heating vacant premises; yet for some unknown reason, he felt hot, almost feverish. He spent most of the night sweating profusely between the light blankets as one does in the middle of summer. There was nothing wrong with the bed. It was himself and his lack of sleep that chafed Stefan. It may have been a mixture of too much happiness and melancholy or, as he came to believe afterward, that he was too much of a worrier to handle coolly contradictory feelings—in this case, hope and apprehension. God only knew what it was, but the whole situation gnawed at him.

As soon as he noticed the first glimmer of daylight, Stefan quit the bed and went to the bathroom, had a shave, and took a long hot shower. Around half past five, he emerged somewhat refreshed, finding Val still soundly asleep. It was, of course, too early to wake him. Only the spaniel welcomed her master by stretching lazily, but with an appeasing gesture, he quieted her. She retired on her blanket and curled up snugly, deciding to sleep longer.

Stefan tiptoed out of the room and down the stairs into the dusty lounge to have a smoke. Soon it occurred to him that he wasn't alone in the dimly lit room. At first, in the subdued light of the early morning, he couldn't discern who the person huddled in one of the big armchairs was. The curtained windows sifted only a trifle of gray into the lounge; and the stranger, perhaps purposely, had withdrawn to the darkest corner. The woman, because it was a woman, smoked and drank coffee, oblivious to his arrival. He could smell coffee even at that distance. Then he recognized the thermos made in Czechoslovakia—their thermos—and Lia.

"What are you doing here, dear?" he said, pleasantly surprised. "Why are you not in bed?"

"I couldn't sleep any longer."

"You too?"

"Yes." Lia poured some coffee in the second plastic cup of the thermos set and offered it to Stefan together with a tiny cookie from her bag. Now—as always—she had prepared a few goodies of her own for the trip. "Do you want some more?"

He shook his head and took the treat. "Very good. That's enough, thanks. I badly needed it," Stefan acknowledged, sipping his coffee.

"What about you? You're up quite early, aren't you?" Lia said.

"It was too hot. I couldn't close my eyes more than a few minutes. I fretted the whole night long."

"Poor Stefan, I am sorry for you. We have such a long flight ahead of us. You will probably be completely smashed at the end of it. Nineteen hours they said, didn't they?"

"Nineteen, at least. Could be longer, though, with formalities and unscheduled stops . . . Don't worry, I will manage. How are you feeling?"

"Not so bad. I was able to sleep a few hours. I am certainly feeling better than you."

"Oh, yes," he stared at her and laughed, "much better, I should say."

"No, no, seriously, I am all right. The only thing I would like is some fresh air."

"Then let's go for a walk before anyone gets up," Stefan said and stood up. "I need some fresh air too. Perhaps Carina will also be happy to take a walk before the long flight. Come on. It will be fun. Our last walk in Athens."

After an animated night, the city was surprisingly quiet, indeed appeared dead. Around the hotel, the streets were utterly deserted as far as the pair could see. There was not a single soul in sight. Somewhere backstage, the sun struggled to climb over the horizon; and the dawn's avant-garde had already dispelled the night's shadows, giving way to a luminous shade of pale cerulean green lavishly splashed across the southern sky.

Stefan and Lia sauntered aimlessly arm in arm through the maze of unfamiliar downtown streets bearing resonant Greek names, deeply breathing the crisp morning air. They walked silently, the dog leading as usual with that preoccupied air of someone going on serious business. It looked as if Carina was taking them for a walk, not the other way around.

Stefan felt better now in Lia's presence. They still were very much in love—of course, not that first, crazy love of their youth. It was something more subtle, deeper, which wasn't apparent from the outside. Stefan especially always avoided showing his most private feelings in public. Lia was a part of him. He felt that in many ways, not only physically. It was a sort of intimacy that went beyond bodies, minds, and words; and sometimes, he truly believed it was the closest thing to a communion of souls, which had very little to do with the material world. In such moments, they didn't need to speak, each other's presence being enough. Naturally, he kept that special feeling for Lia hidden even from his children. It was his most secret and treasured good, at the same time strong and vulnerable, so precious that Stefan didn't dare to think about it too often, afraid of somehow damaging it.

Lia was much less talkative than Stefan, and her feelings surfaced only in those rare moments when she felt really safe from any outside intrusion. That morning wasn't one of those circumstances, and she didn't feel inclined to demonstrations.

Defying their optimism, the ghost of the unknown, the uncertain future so dangerously attractive and at the same time scary, was oppressively present in the pair's minds during that good-bye walk. The troubling song of the sirens, enticing and simultaneously repellant, which has played havoc with humans since pre-Homeric eras, troubled their souls in a mysterious way. And in spite of the rousing early spring's sweet scent that drifted in the air, they didn't feel like talking about love or anything else.

Unpremeditatedly, they came to the tourist-haunted Omonia, strangely silent at that hour. So quiet in fact that the scratching noise of Carina's nails touching the pavement generated echoes. As they strolled around the square, the numerous little cafés that proliferated in the area had just started opening their doors, somnolent staffers leisurely rearranging chairs and tables on the sidewalks. In the corner of Patision Avenue, a grinning waiter glanced hopefully at them; and the friendly, smiling man standing in the open door, probably the owner, shouted a greeting: "Kali mera kirios. Ena kafes?" Good morning, mister. A coffee?

"Efkharisto poli kirios. Ohi! Thank you very much, mister. No!" Stefan shouted back.

Stefan laughed good-humoredly and turned to Lia: "This is what I like about Greeks. They are always polite."

"Yes," answered Lia, "and ready to make a buck."

"What's wrong with that? I have met many people doing exactly the same without good manners."

"True."

"We will miss them, the Greeks I mean. I have learned to like them. Maybe you won't agree with me, but I will definitely miss Greece, its soul-healing environment and its people," Stefan said dreamily, "and our friends . . . We have made so many good friends here who perhaps we will never see again."

An inexplicable sadness descended upon him like a wave of overpowering surf. "The boy, Abdur," he said. "Thanasis, Theodoros, Luca, Dana, Váci . . ." He suddenly felt an immense emptiness inside and around him.

"Oh, Dana again," Lia said, "poor, dear little Dana."

"Yes," he said, "poor little Dana and Abdur and the others." Dana's crying image and her burning kiss still haunted him; and Stefan, who perceived his wife's implied reproach, preferred to change the subject. He didn't want to hurt her.

"See there," he pointed to a massive neoclassical building complex dwarfed by perspective. "That is the National Archaeological Museum, dear. I wish we could have visited it." He put a loving arm around her shoulders. "You know what's in there? Schliemann's famous discoveries at Mycenae, the largest collection of Hellenic art in the world, the Minoan finds made at Akrotiri on the island of Santorini, and many more."

"It sounds fascinating," Lia said, "but now we don't have time for them."

"Yes! We never had enough money to visit it, and now when we do and are so close to it, there is no time. It always happens to us." There was disappointment in Stefan's voice.

"We might come back one day to visit all the famous places. The Greek islands, the ancient sites, the old marvels of the classical world. One day, we will be rich and have enough money for everything, my dear."

"One day, always another day . . ."

"Cheer up, Stefan. After all, you always boasted that we fled Romania because you wanted freedom. We got our freedom, didn't we? And where are we going now? There is no better country in the world, they say, than Canada. There we will have our freedom and much more. Am I right?"

"Maybe. Who knows?"

"What do you mean, maybe? What about our ranch, what about your sailing boat or Ana's horses? You dreamed so many times about them and made us share in your dreams."

"Yeah. That was before my little chat with Bernov, remember?"

"Come on, now. You used to be more enthusiastic, more optimistic. What happened to you, Stefan?"

"I don't know. Perhaps it is the lack of sleep. The night at the hotel . . . By the way, speaking of the hotel, it is time to go back," Stefan said, checking his wristwatch, eager to change the topic for the second time that morning. Obviously, there wasn't a right moment for remembering daydreams and unsubstantiated promises.

Thanasis and Vassilakis, the policemen, were already waiting for them at the reception desk. They made an intriguing picture, those two, much alike in their well-pressed uniforms though strikingly different in physique. The Cypriot was dark-haired, tall, and slim. The junior, the fair Vassilakis, a native of Zakynthos, was chubby and cheerful, his easygoing manners contrasting with Thanasis's gentlemanly demeanor. But freshly shaven and dressed up in their finest for the occasion, they both looked dauntingly official.

They had come to take the family to the airport and eventually smooth things over for a safe departure, Thanasis told Stefan, who expected that. He had already discussed the matter with the police chief when the last flight details had been clarified. He had no documents or pocket money, except for some small change, leftovers from his last week's wages from Theodoros. Everything else was supposed to be handed to him at the airport, only a short time before takeoff. Stefan wasn't too impressed with the much-talked-of official anxiety for their safety. Biased by his past experiences with governments, he maliciously held the view that the authorities wanted to make sure the Romanians left for good and wouldn't sneak back into the country, using the new documents and grant money to perpetrate who knows what evils against Elliniki

Dimokratia, the Greek Republic. That heretic opinion he had wisely chosen to keep to himself. What else could he have done anyway?

The policemen, who went to fetch a taxicab, returned with two vehicles instead. No Athenian taxi would take more than four passengers, it appeared—the dog being also considered anathema by many honest cabmen—and there were six of them, not counting the undesirable animal.

The taxicabs' arrival gave the signal for a flurry of final packing. Pajamas and toilet kits were collected, suitcases were locked, and then everyone stormed up and down the stairs, carrying the luggage out of the rooms into the street.

The hotel's owner watched the last-minute rush with apprehension. He fidgeted in the middle of the reception hall, trying to keep a close eye on those untrustworthy foreigners. Such were the moments when, as had happened several times in the past, some of his property was stolen, he unhappily grumbled. The presence of the policemen had not been proven to be a guarantee in similar circumstances, which he knew too well. He breathed with relief only after the baggage was loaded and his guests set off, together with their 'chaperons.'

On the way to the Ellinikon International Airport, Ana and her father were seated in the back of the leading taxicab. Thanasis, who had come with them, took the front seat beside the driver. Nobody said anything for a while, trying to recover from the last effort. Traffic was just picking up, forcing the driver to slow down; and exhaust fumes leaked inside the car, making them sneeze and cough.

In the vicinity of the university, unruly passers-by jammed the sidewalks, and jaywalking students brought the traffic almost to a stop. Enraged drivers cursed and shouted insults at the crossing crowds, which laughingly shouted back. But as everybody knows, shouting has never produced any positive effect on the movement of vehicles.

Noticing the verbal duel's inefficiency, Thanasis whispered something to the cabby, who mumbled a sort of halfhearted agreement. After a moment of hesitation, the man nervously backed his car a short distance and skillfully made a sharp turn into a narrow lane. The maneuver was followed by several other quick direction changes as he weaved his way through the spiderweb of old Placa, wisely avoiding Sintagma Square. A final jerky turn, and they emerged into Leoforos Amalias Boulevard, right across Hadrian's Arch. Most of those alleys and backstreets were one-way only, and he drove through almost all of them the wrong way. As if that wasn't enough, the other cab also followed him like a shadow.

The policeman sighed with relief when they stopped at the traffic light and looked over his shoulder at Stefan. "The cabby would have never done this if I hadn't ordered him to do so. It is late, and we wouldn't have made it to the airport on time. I hope he doesn't do that too often," he said sheepishly, a mischievous smile on his handsome face.

"Maybe," Stefan half-heartedly agreed. In fact, he was mentally far away. Half of his mind followed Thanasis's explanation while the other half was busy imagining their departure, the flight, the landing in Montreal, the immediate future in Canada. There were too many unsolved problems whose threatening spectra buzzed in his head like a swarm of angry wasps.

The young Greek was unaware of the older man's worries. "I have some good news," he said, "I was admitted to the law school."

"Oh, Thanasis, that is excellent. Congratulations," exclaimed Stefan, suddenly brought into the present, genuinely happy for his friend. He knew about Thanasis's admission examinations and his anxious wait for the results but, caught in the agitation of their departure, had forgotten everything else. "I wish you good luck. When are you starting?"

"In the fall, in September."

"Where is the school?" asked Ana.

"Here in Athens."

"Wow. You'll soon become one of these smart and presumptuous Athenians. That will be very exciting. You have to move here and find a new home, perhaps a new girlfriend as well," Ana teased him.

"Right now, I don't have a girlfriend. I have been too busy lately to court ladies." Thanasis, embarrassed, smiled back at Ana in his most polite manner. "But I have a house in Athens, Miss Ana."

"Good God, you have already bought a house? You are really fast, Thanasis. When did you buy it?" Stefan wondered.

"I inherited it when one of my uncles died a few years ago. It is currently rented to a Greek-American family from the States, but I kept a room with annexes for my personal use," he said. There was pride in his voice.

"Very smart of you! Then you are already set, ready to start. Aren't you, my friend?"

"Oh, yes. I can barely wait . . ."

"Too bad we can't celebrate. Such news deserves a big party," Stefan sighed and smiled at his friend.

"A big party with a lot of dancing and singing," Ana said. Her eyes shone with delight at the thought of those colorful Greek dances. "I love sirtaki," she added.

"We will. We definitely will when you return to visit Greece. The sooner the better. We will have a big party, and I will cook baby lamb on charcoals in the pit for you," Thanasis said. "It would taste better than anything you have ever eaten. I promise." He was fumbling with the flap covering one of his breast pockets, from which he pulled out a neatly folded piece of paper. He handed the paper to Stefan. "Here is my address. Whenever you come to Athens, feel welcome to stay with me. I would be most honored."

Stefan took the address and, although deeply touched by his friend's largesse, was prevented from expressing his gratitude as the taxicab had just arrived at the airport terminal. They all got out in a hurry, and everybody was overcome by departure fever. There was no time to think of anything else as the numerous bureaucratic formalities absorbed all their attention. So it happened that Lia found Thanasis's note only two weeks later in Ottawa, in their newly-rented apartment, where she unpacked the luggage and put the family's coats into storage until next spring, for they were much too light for the rigors of the Canadian winter.

Kirios Papadopulos, the organization's man, was also at the airport, impatiently waiting and welcoming them with a wide, oily smile on his round, rubicund face. He had brought a big official yellow envelope from which he produced passports, landed immigrant visas, airplane tickets—everything but money. Money, he assured Stefan, who was unpleasantly surprised and objected bitterly, would be provided upon their arrival in Ottawa.

"You didn't bring even money for a coffee, not to mention a full meal," Stefan protested. "My understanding was that you would give us some pocket money in case we need it for food and drinks or for an emergency."

"You will get plenty of food and drink on the plane. You don't need money for that," Papadopulos assured him.

"What about an emergency?" Stefan asked. "After all, the money is mine. I am the one who took the loan, and I will have to pay it back."

"You borrowed from the Canadians. They will give you money in Canada. We don't have money here for you. If anything happens on the way, the local authorities will surely provide for. You people have stateless, one-way only passports, which are your protection. There are international agreements that protect refugees. Sorry, I can't do anything to change this. I did what I was told to do," the man said apologetically, shrugging his shoulders and looking at Stefan with round liquid eyes, his face crimson with offense.

"Which state protects a stateless?" Stefan rhetorically asked. Then it came to him that Papadopulos was only a small cog in a huge machine, and it was useless to argue with a merely casual employee. "Well, if things are like that," he said, "forget about it. I am not happy. You should tell this to your superiors. Now let's go. I don't want to be late."

Except for the absence of money, everything went smoothly, and Papadopulos proved to be efficient and helpful. His experience in dealing with the airline's staff at the luggage check-in and at the ticket counter was obvious.

When Stefan and Val had assembled the dog's cage—whose shipping the Romanians had paid for in advance from their savings—Papadopulos was the one who cleared the matter with the air carrier's clerks. Somehow, he pulled the strings so masterfully that Carina could travel in the same airplane as the family did. Stefan, being a complete novice in such affairs, had to acknowledge the man's skill.

Once the check-in formalities finished, Kirios Papadopulos bade them farewell, invoking some obscure pressing business at the headquarters, and withdrew his presence in a hurry. That left the family with the two policemen who, friendly as they were, didn't show any sign of releasing them from official 'protection.'

They walked together to the security checkpoint and waited outside until Thanasis spoke with the policeman sitting at a small desk by the door and to whom Stefan had to present the passports. The man carefully studied the documents and appeared to be satisfied. He made a vague invitation to proceed with a large sweep of his hand, turned his back, and from that moment on didn't pay any attention to them.

Swarms of passengers passed by and quickly disappeared through the door, swallowed by the security checkpoint.

"Everything is okay," Thanasis said. "We must stay here. You should go now!"

"We cannot go with you. Just enter that door, pass through the metal detector, and follow the corridor to the gate," Vassilakis explained. "You won't have any problem."

"Well, then, we should say good-bye to you." Stefan stretched out his hand for a last handshake. "Thank you for your help and friendship. We will always remember you."

For a moment, Thanasis hesitatingly considered the outstretched hand, then ignored it and, opening his arms wide, gave the Romanian a vigorous hug. The two men embraced in a tight grasp. "Come back soon. God bless you," the policeman murmured in Stefan's ear. He was obviously deeply moved after embracing Val and noisily kissing the women on both cheeks.

Stefan didn't have time to answer because it was Vassilakis' turn to give him a big hug. The young man's eyes were wet, and when he finished with the whole family and drew himself away from them, tears ran down his face.

At the door, they all turned once more, waving to the policemen, two sad-looking youths lost in the middle of the characteristic airport hubbub. The martial brashness was gone, replaced by a genuine display of human feeling.

"Have a good trip. Come back soon," Thanasis shouted, waving both arms energetically while Vassilakis wiped his chubby face with a white handkerchief, "and please bring Miss Ana with you!"

The Romanians, also with wet eyes, saw them slowly vanish in the tear-blurred distance.

As the airplane rolled down the takeoff runway, a stewardess came along to check the safety belts and, squatting beside her seat, said something to Ana. The girl fumbled with a miniature red appurtenance, hiding it in her purse.

"What was that?" her father asked. Lia was seated between them, and he couldn't hear what the stewardess had said.

"It is forbidden to use any electronic equipment—in my case, a radio—during takeoff," Ana said.

"I didn't know you bought a radio."

"I didn't buy it, Dad."

"So how come you have one?"

"It is a present," Lia said in a conciliatory tone.

"A present? From whom?"

"From Ali," Ana said and blushed, oblivious to Lia's warning frown.

"I told you not to encourage that boy," Stefan said severely, upset that Ana hadn't followed his advice. He would be happy only when a whole ocean separated those two.

"Actually, I didn't. He popped up for a minute yesterday, before we left the camp. This is a good-bye present." His daughter looked at Stefan with innocent eyes.

"How come? What for?"

"It is an old custom in that part of Turkey where he comes from, Ali told me. Brings good luck." Ana smiled angelically.

"So is buying their wives," Stefan said. "One of these days, I might succumb to the wishes of the highest bidder, Ana. Do you want to end up with that would-be-revolutionary-rough-boy as a husband?"

"You cannot be serious, Dad. You know I don't want him. I was only afraid that he would have done something foolish if I hadn't accepted his present. The poor boy appeared to be grief-stricken. He threatened suicide."

"And you believed him?"

"Just a little bit," Ana said. She laughed lightheartedly and turned to Lia, "do you think Thanasis had a crush on me, Mama?"

EPILOGUE

Stefan and his family settled down in Canada. Only occasionally did they comb highway ditches for discarded bottles and cans to make a few bucks—and only in the beginning. They saw such a pastime as a sport for sedentary people, and they were an active kind, too busy struggling to foster their careers. They never made enough money, though, to buy the dreamed-of ranch. Perhaps this is another story, which should be told at another time.

Regarding Katyn, none of the adults present at Stefan's eleventh birthday party lived long enough to find out who was right. They had all, except Uncle Alexandru, died of more or less natural causes by the time the last ruler of Soviet Union, Gorbachev, publicly admitted Stalin's guilt in the Katyn genocide. The Soviet leader solemnly apologized to the Polish people for the barbarous slaughter of more than twenty-five thousand of their countrymen. It was a grand gesture that mostly profited the international media.

Uncle Alexandru was arrested after the communist takeover of Romania sometime in early 1948. He survived the severe beatings and maltreatment for quite a long time due to his robust constitution and fit physique. The torturers wanted to know what documents and issues he had handled in his previous work as a decipherer with the Ministry of Foreign Affairs and with the army. They spared no method of inflicting pain they knew of to get every secret out of him. Up to this day, the circumstances of Uncle Alexandru's death have never been clear. Taken unconscious from the overcrowded and dirty underground cell he shared with twenty other inmates,

Alexandru never returned from his last interrogation, vanishing like a puff of smoke into thin air. Even his place of burial is unknown. The jailers buried their victims in unmarked graves along the banks of the nearby river. In the spring of 1971, Romania went through a season of catastrophic floods; and afterward, the riverbed changed beyond recognition. Subsequently, no traces of a cemetery could ever have been found, and skeptical historians in the future would eventually be able to easily discard such things as inventions.

As history is only seldom included in contemporary schools' curricula, very few people will probably learn anything from what was arguably the biggest human tragedy to date. The seasons will come and go, years will come and go, many generations will come and go, and soon, nobody will remember the millions of wasted lives; thus in another century, the same mistakes might happen again.